KT-221-702

"You came," he whispered. "I worried that you would not care to meet me."

"Curiosity was my downfall," she said with a smile. "Why e you whispering?"

"Shh, listen to the night, my fair. It has its own song, and ly he who is quiet can hear it.'

She listened to the silence, noting the peace that seemed to tretch out far beyond the limits of the Earth, contained only in the distant dome of transparent darkness that was the sky. "It's lovely," she whispered back. "The stars are looking at us."

"Without condemning us, I'm sure." He stood and squeezed her hand, and she looked into his face, disconcerted by the sk and her inability to see his features clearly. The Midnight ndit, a shadow figure.

"The world would not be so generous. Am I very scandalous meeting you like this?"

He nodded, his smile like a beacon. "Yes, very wicked."

"Would you mind removing your mask so that I can see r face?" She touched the soft leather, but he captured her hand quickly and pulled it away.

" nd recognize the identity of the Midnight Bandit? No. If could identify me, you might be the person to one day send me to the gallows. I'm sorry, but I cannot risk that."

She touched his face again, pulling a fingertip along his jaw. would never denounce you."

Dear Readers,

Last month, we launched the Ballad line with four new series, and each month we'll present both new and continuing stories set everywhere from medieval England to the American West—the kind of passionate, romantic stories you love best, written by the most gifted authors. At the back of each book, we'll tell you when you can find subsequent books in the series that have captured your heart.

Veteran author Jo Ann Ferguson explores the shattering results of the French Revolution in the first *Shadow of the Bastille* book, **A Daughter's Destiny.** In this sweeping series, a mysterious thunderbolt crest will reunite siblings separated by the Terror—and whose destinies have been forever changed by love. Next, newcomer Shelley Bradley takes us back to medieval England with **His Lady Bride,** the first in a series called *Brothers in Arms* which introduces three daring knights fostered together as boys who have become men of strength, honor—and breathtaking passion.

Experience the extravagance and splendor of Georgian England with Maria Greene's *Midnight Mask* series, beginning with **A Bandit's Kiss,** which introduces us to the secrets of a notorious highwayman—and the hearts he has stolen. Finally, Sylvia McDaniel presents **The Rancher Takes A Wife,** the first in *The Burnett Brides* series set in rough-and-tumble 1870s Texas, where one matchmaking woman is determined that her three stubborn, handsome sons will marry the right women—even if she has to find them herself! Enjoy!

Kate Duffy
Editorial Director

Chapter 1

Charles Boynton, the Earl of Mortimer, watched with amusement as fairy-tale creatures surrounded him. Romans, knights in armor, ancient deities, and a dour-looking Henry VIII wearing a red velvet beret formed a carnival in the street. Fauns and wood nymphs laughed and beckoned to Charles to join them. Right behind the false king with his many gold chains danced a group of goddesses, and Charles smiled as his gaze was irresistibly drawn to Flora, the goddess of spring. She wore a diaphanous toga of white muslin, and flowers peeked out of every fold of the material as she moved. Her reddish gold hair rippled and curled to her waist, and a thick wreath of primroses circled her head. She embraced a hundred yellow daffodils that she threw, one after the other, to the crowd. Her teeth flashed in a warm smile, and Charles found himself holding his breath as a sad memory tugged at his heart.

The glittering, capricious April sunlight glanced off her white half-mask and her hair, the richest copper color he'd ever seen.

It reminded him of someone, a lady he hadn't met for years, a lady who had jilted him most cruelly . . .

No, it couldn't be! Yet his heart spoke differently, reminding him of the stark pain that he'd managed to confine to a dark corner for six years. The memories surfaced only when he was lonely, dead tired, or dead drunk, and today he was only slightly inebriated due to the festivities.

Gripped by painful memories, he followed the goddesses as they chatted and laughed, danced and skipped like young girls. But girls they were not; they were women with rounded curves and slender waists. Longing to touch that rippling copper mane so tantalizingly close, Charles studied the back of the one who commanded his particular interest.

As she capered, he caught the glimmer of jewels on a satin slipper and the flash of a slim ankle. Her sheer toga did little to conceal the length and shapeliness of her legs. Her hips swelled beautifully below the golden girdle that held the toga in place at her waist. Beneath the curling mane he could see the shape of her sleek back, and she waved arms that expressed strength and purpose as she shared the bounty of her flowers.

"By God, she's magnificent," Charles murmured to himself as he followed her toward the four Doric columns that were the entrance to the Ranelagh rotunda and pleasure gardens. Over the cheer of the people, he could hear her sparkling laughter, as intoxicating as the clear, cold water of a brook on a hot day.

As they entered the rotunda, trumpets blared in triumph, and the crowd clapped and stomped their feet. The War of the Austrian Succession had been over for some time, and the peace treaty had been signed at Aix-la-Chapelle the previous year. This was the belated celebration that King George II was giving his subjects, a dizzying week-long extravaganza.

"I'm thirsty. Let's find some punch," one of the goddesses said to the others.

Charles watched as his goddess flung the rest of her daffodils to a group of staid city gentlemen in powdered wigs and somber coats. Startled, they stared at her, first with suspicion, then delight. "Yes ... yes, let's," she said and whirled around. She came face-to-face with Charles, and her eyes glittered mischievously behind the mask as she noticed him standing so close.

"Oh," she said, and clapped her hand to her mouth in surprise. "Pardon me; I didn't know you were standing there, sir." She gave him a smile that rivaled the April sunlight outside.

He inhaled sharply, catching her floral scent. Her expression filled his heart with sweetness, a warmth that settled and spread in his chest. His thoughts floundered in a morass of memories. "My lady," he said, and executed a sweeping bow, cocked hat in hand. "I could not but admire your lovely appearance."

"You're too kind, sir."

She didn't recognize him behind his mask. A highborn lady, he thought; she was a guest at the jubilee festivities at the rotunda. George had invited two thousand members of fashionable society to help him celebrate, and celebrate they did—at the gaming tables and on the dance floor.

The music filled the structure with thrilling tunes. Shopkeepers sold knickknacks and sweets in the stalls lining the walls, but Charles had eyes only for the lady whose smile beckoned him to rush forward and crush her in his arms. The urge overpowered him, made him dizzy with desire.

She laughed, and in a whirling motion, disappeared like a wisp of fog in the crowd. As if drugged, he followed her, elbowing his way among spectators who stood admiring a gondola decorated with flags and streamers. Pipe and horn players dotted the grounds outside, making their own cacophony of sound.

With gazellelike fleetness of foot, she ran into the gardens and down a path lined with shrubs. He hurried after her. His heartbeat thundered in his chest, in his ears. It truly was her.

"Wait! Don't be afraid; I want only to introduce myself," he called after her, but she responded with a teasing laugh.

"Vixen," he muttered under his breath as she slipped around a thick stand of oak saplings. He arrived at the spot where she'd disappeared, but saw no sign of her. You're acting like a lovesick fool, he told himself. A single smile from her had reduced him to an idiot and robbed him of his customary levelheaded reason.

Cursing silently, he glanced in all directions. Where the deuce had she gone? Everywhere he looked, masked guests in colorful costumes mingled, but no one he recognized. In his fevered desire to study the goddess more closely, he'd left his party behind in the street, his old friends Carey and Francesca McLendon.

He looked down and saw a trail of yellow flowers on the path. The primroses in her hair! With a laugh, he followed the trail before the brisk breeze could whisk the blooms under the shrubs.

She was standing on another path admiring a group of jugglers. Evidently she had not yet discovered that her wreath was falling apart. He grinned as he stepped up behind her.

"You cannot shake me off that easily, goddess," he said softly in her ear, and chuckled as her mouth formed an "O" of surprise. She bolted down the lane, but her laugh gave her delight away.

He followed, more intrigued than he had been in a long time—and more frightened. He would have to remove her mask to make sure, but he had no doubt who hid behind it.

He found her hiding under a tree, partly concealed by the sun-dappled leaves.

"Milady, you have to try harder than that." He stepped to her side, and, as she was leaning against the tree trunk, he braced his hands on each side of her head and gazed at her downturned face. He noticed a handful of tiny golden specks across her cheeks and forehead, the freckles bright against her pale complexion.

When she raised her gaze to his, he stared straight into her, and she into him. He lost his breath yet again, wholly entranced.

Her eyes were the color of old amber, with a luminous golden depth, and framed with a thick sweep of copper lashes.

His heartbeat ran a mad race. He inhaled deeply and dug his fingers into the bark. The truth of her identity sank in, bringing back a familiar wave of pain.

She was Marguerite, Lady Lennox, the woman who had occupied most of his waking thoughts for six years and tinged them with bitterness. His hands clenched, but he did not move. He had to remain close to her; no force could pull him away.

She acted like a trapped doe, wary and alert, yet soft and infinitely graceful. She made an effort to dart under his arm, but he captured her shoulders, and she gave a small whimper that could as easily have been a giggle.

"Who are you?" she whispered. "Take off your mask so that I can see your face."

Charles shook his head, glad that he was wearing a face mask and a powdered bagwig over his own hair. She didn't recognize him, and he would have the chance to steal a taste of her lips, something he'd longed to do ever since he'd become a man. Knowing that she was as unattainable as the moon while married to another man, he had forced himself to stay away from her for the last six years.

However, times had changed dramatically, but had she? It seemed hardly likely.

"Marguerite," he whispered, folding his arms around her and pressing her close. He was aware of her generous curves molding against him, the tang of the primroses in her hair, the feminine allure of her skin. In the distance, a horn blared, and a group of people cheered, but he did not care. Why should he, while he held this precious goddess in his arms?

He tilted up her chin with his thumb and gazed deeply into her eyes.

"You know me? Who are you?" she repeated, some of the light fading from her eyes. "You have no right—"

"You don't want to know my identity," he said, "but don't be afraid. I won't harm you." He gathered her luscious form tighter and claimed her mouth with his. The sweet curve of her lips fitted to his perfectly, just as he knew it would, and the honeyed taste of her made him dizzy as his tongue fought through her resistance. She struggled against him, but he delved deeply into the velvet softness of her mouth, drugging himself with the feel and scent of her.

As pliable, yet as strong as a yew branch, she finally broke away from his embrace. Before she could escape, he captured her face between his hands, and touched his lips softly to hers once more.

"But—"

"Sssh," he whispered, as further protest gathered on her tongue. "Be quiet and savor the moment. It might not come again."

"You're taking shameless liberties with me," she said, yet her eyes had darkened with desire, and her cheeks—or what he could see of them under her mask—had warmed into a blush. A pulse beat rapidly under the translucent skin of her throat, and he touched her there, dragging his finger to memorize the texture of her skin. Because surely he would never have the chance to touch her again if she discovered his identity.

Her breath caught, and her eyelashes fluttered as if disturbed by an inner breeze. He dropped his hands to his sides, and she bolted to safety, like an animal that had been freed from a trap.

He watched her run, yellow flowers trailing down her back, then the wreath falling altogether to the ground. Her copper hair blew like a bright banner behind her, and that was the last thing he saw of her. He longed to stroll alone through the orderly garden and ponder upon the fate that had brought her path across his once more, but he'd pondered too much over the years, and had no inclination to dig into the memories.

Instead he bent and retrieved a handful of primroses and held them to his face. For a moment he relived the kiss, recalling the intoxicating softness of her, the jolt of pleasure that had been his—a glorious moment in time, so sweet, so perfect.

After putting the wilting flowers in his pocket, he walked

briskly back to the rotunda. Without hearing, he listened to the band playing a popular song. Without looking right or left in search of his goddess, he returned to the spot in the street where he'd left Carey and Francesca.

"There you are," Carey said as they ran into each other. "We were looking for you." His gray eyes gleamed suggestively. "Francesca said you were lured away by a pack of goddesses."

Charles laughed derisively and studied his tall, dark friend. Carey looked happy, happier than Charles could remember ever seeing him. Married life suited him. "I acted like a hound on a fox trail, old fellow. One of the goddesses held irresistible allure."

Carey raised his eyebrows. "By thunder! Anyone I know?"

"The Poison Widow, Lady Lennox." Charles made his voice flat, but the words hurt nevertheless. "Since we grew up, she has had nothing but scorn for me."

Carey whistled between his teeth. "Lennox? Begad, that ill-starred lady. Not that I believe the rumors that Marguerite, Lady Lennox poisoned her husband. She could never be a murderess." He plucked at the gold braiding on the wide cuffs of his green brocade coat. "Are you still in love with her after all these years?"

Charles shook his head vigorously. "Love? Lord, no! I don't ever want to feel the pain of unrequited love again." He studied Carey's handsome face, knowing he would see no mockery in those sharp gray eyes.

"I was a fool, but I won't be a fool a second time. That fair lady stepped on my heart once, but never again." Charles knew he was lying. He hadn't forgotten Marguerite and never would. He'd learned that when his heart was attached, he remained loyal forever, be it to a friend, or in this case, to the woman he loved.

Carey tapped his lips with one finger as if deep in thought. "You are right, of course, but I have yet to see another lady make such a deep impression on you." He gave Charles a quick glance. "Anyhow, she must be out of mourning. One year has passed since her husband died."

"The world is unfair to give her such a vile name," Charles muttered to himself. He brightened as Francesca wound her arm through Carey's. The dark-haired beauty smiled up at her husband, and affection stirred in Charles's heart. Up till now he'd been content watching his best friends' love deepen and prosper, but now he wondered if he would ever have the chance to find such a love himself. He doubted it, but it wouldn't help to brood over what could have been.

He heaved a deep sigh and struggled to push aside the stirring memory of copper hair and a teasing, most alluring smile. *Damn all goddesses to hell!*

He slapped Carey's shoulder and winked at Francesca. "By God, McLendon, look at you! The very picture of a country squire." He viewed his best friend's immaculate coat, and flicked the lace ends of the cravat at his throat. "Is that a spot of provincial mud on your linen, old fellow?"

Grimacing, Carey shoved him in the chest. "One more joke from you about my new life as a man of property, and you will have your backside browned with London mud, mark my words."

Charles grinned. "Well, I can't risk that. What do you say, a picnic in the gardens? My servants have already arranged it. I've invited others to join us, Nick and Ormond and their friends."

With a mischievous smile, Francesca wound her arm through Charles's and, walking between her two escorts, headed toward the Ranelagh gardens. "I wouldn't miss your cook's jellied pigs' ears, calf's brain, and fried oxtail for anything."

Charles smiled ruefully. "Don't rob me of my appetite, Francesca. Serves you right if I offered those dishes, but you have naught to worry about. My cook has put in strawberry tarts and dainty sugar cakes especially for you, and an excellent bottle of claret for Carey."

Before long they were seated at a table topped with a white

damask cloth under the spreading boughs of an elm. Due to the special festivities, there were picnics under every tree, and the rotunda itself was packed with people. As darkness crept in, lanterns were lighted, casting a soft glow on the assembly. A bower of fir trees hung with flowers had been erected in the middle of the rotunda, and below the firs were tubs of orange trees. The meat of the oranges had been scooped out, and now a candle glowed in every fruit "bowl." The night had an air of gaiety and romance, but Charles could not quite shake off his feeling of loneliness.

If it hadn't been for Carey and Francesca, he might have left the festivities early. Damned bad luck that he'd run into the one person who had the power to break his heart. Again. He waved to the lackeys to put out the food.

His friends must have sensed his subdued mood, because Francesca put a soft hand over his. "I'm happy you're with us tonight. It wouldn't be right without you."

"I miss you here in London. The town is dull without your presence," Charles replied. "But I know you're happy at Burgess Hill, and that gladdens my heart."

"You would be closer to us if you stayed at the Meadow more," she said. "You're barely ever down in Sussex anymore."

That was because his ancestral home was too close to *hers,* Charles thought, remembering the teasing light in Marguerite's eyes and the sweet curve of her lips. *Stop it!* "I lost interest. The heap is falling down around my ears anyway, and I don't have any funds for repairs."

"The East India cargo should bring in a nice profit in spices for us. I'm grateful you persuaded me to invest. The ship should dock at The Pool in a month," Carey said, scooping up brown sauce with a piece of bread. He dried his greasy fingertips on a crisp napkin. "This ragout is delicious. I'll buy your cook from you. How much is he worth?"

"A new roof for the Meadow?"

Carey moaned as if in pain.

"Not for sale, Carey." Cheered by the prospect of gaining dividends from the gambling profits he'd invested in the East Indiaman, Charles laughed and bit into a crusty roll. "Even if King George gave me an offer for Monsieur Goulot, I would not be tempted to get rid of him. My only asset in gold." He cut a wedge of cheese and joined it to the bread.

"You know how to drive a hard bargain."

"If I didn't, my ancestral home would now be in total ruins—which it isn't. Have you ever tried bargaining with the local craftsmen?"

"Constantly," Carey said with a frown. "The new stables are taking much longer to build than I thought."

"You've made the decision to go into the horse-breeding business then?" Charles shook aside the froth of lace at his wrists and reached for a plate of sweets, which he offered to Francesca.

"Yes. It's a gamble, but my cattle herd bores me. I have to try something different." He gave Charles a keen glance in the encroaching darkness. "Morty, I'd say you're the true horseman in this assembly."

Charles felt a rush of envy as he gazed at the man who'd had very little to call his own when he met Francesca Kane, but now was a rich man. But the envy dissolved instantly as he remembered the McLendons' constant kindness to him. "However much I care for my stallion, Thunder, horses are convenient creatures for traveling and hunting, no more, no less."

"What a flippant remark!" Francesca said. "Some write odes to their horses. Take the Midnight Bandit of the road, for instance. I've heard he writes poems to his mount, Pegasus."

Charles snorted. "Mark my words, that cheeky highwayman will hang one day—from the highest tree along the Sussex road."

Francesca clapped her hand to her heart and uttered an audible sigh. "I can't help but feel that it would be a pity. He's so romantic. Sometimes I wish I could catch a glimpse of him. He recites poems to his victims, and kisses the ladies' hands.''

"Pshaw!'' Carey laughed derisively. "If he so much as looked at you, I'd have his head on a platter. I don't understand how a lady like you, who usually has a level head, is completely taken in by this scoundrel of the roads. Why, he's a common thief! Nothing romantic about that, surely.''

"He has quite a reputation. All the ladies are besotted with that bounder,'' Charles said. "They talk of nothing else at the balls and gaming parties.''

Francesca sighed. "He has the silkiest of tongues. He recites the most romantic poems to his victims—''

"Who are mostly ladies traveling alone or with their maid-servants,'' Carey filled in with a disgusted snort. "The knave is not man enough to face the wrath of husbands and brothers, no doubt. A coward.''

"Those are the robberies we hear about. The ladies talk about them, but the gentlemen might be too mortified to confess to being robbed by a highwayman.''

Charles and Carey did not reply.

"What do you two know of poetry anyway?'' Francesca scoffed, her dark eyes flashing. "I haven't heard any odes of beauty on your lips lately.''

"Mayhap you haven't inspired any,'' Charles said with a wink. He could have created a verse for her right then and there, but he kept silent, not wanting to divulge that one of his secret pleasures was writing romantic poetry. He had always felt that his delight in the written word would be scorned by his sportsman cronies, and he was reluctant to face any banter concerning his secret diversion.

Carey only muttered something as a boisterous group of people came running toward their table.

"Ah! There they are,'' Charles said. A tall and powerfully built man, Charles's old crony and neighbor Nicholas Thurston, came first. Flanking him were the redheaded Stephen, Lord Ormond, and three of the goddesses Charles had followed. The new arrivals chatted animatedly among themselves. A goddess hummed a tune to prove some point, and another laughed.

Charles stiffened as he recognized that trilling laugh. Flora was part of the group, and he glimpsed her red-gold hair behind Nick.

"I'll be damned," he murmured.

Nick swept a handsome bow to Francesca and clapped his tattered hat back onto his head. He wore the costume of a blacksmith—gaiters, clogs, and a leather apron over a grimy shirt—and his arms and face were blackened with soot. His eyes glinted drunkenly, and he flashed a roguish smile. "I say, Morty, where's a bottle of wine for my parched throat?"

"You've had enough, Thurston," Carey said before Charles could respond. "You're unsteady on your pins as it is."

Carey nudged Charles's elbow. Charles shot a look at his friend. Carey looked tense as he watched Flora emerge from behind Nick. "She's here, Morty. Do you want me to send them away?"

Jealousy curled through Charles as he watched Nick sling his arm possessively around Marguerite's slender shoulders. Nick was a good fellow, but in his cups, he turned overly amorous, and Charles didn't want him to romance Marguerite. Still, before he could reply, she had slid away from Nick's embrace and folded her graceful form onto the grass in front of the table. The other revelers followed suit. Charles noted the flash of bitterness that crossed Nick's face, but Nick threw around impertinent remarks as if her rejection hadn't touched him.

Charles looked at Marguerite, but she avoided his eyes.

Francesca chatted with the newcomers and handed Marguerite a glass of wine. Charles remembered his manners, and snapped his fingers at the two lackeys standing motionless under the tree. "Wine for all the guests, and hand around the platters of food."

"Thank you. Making merry is thirsty work," Nick Thurston said as Charles gave him a bottle of claret. He took a swig straight from the bottle, then winked at Charles. " 'Tis my lucky night, I think. I gathered a handful of lovely flowers." He indicated the goddesses with the bottle. "A feast for my eyes, and music to my ears . . ."

"Luck has always been on your side, Nick," Charles said.

"Poetry to my nose," Nick continued.

Francesca laughed. "You're in possession of a silver tongue tonight, Nick. We were discussing just such a glib person when you arrived. The Midnight Bandit."

Nick's blue eyes widened in surprise. "You would compare me with that blackguard? Fie, my fair!"

Francesca said to the guests, "Nick always possessed a slippery tongue, just like Charles when he's inebriated."

Charles drank from his glass and savored the tart taste of the red wine. "Begad, don't compare me to Nick, Francesca. I'm a staid fellow by comparison."

Carey said, "Never loath to throw yourself into an adventure, though. I'll never forget that mad ride through Sussex in forty-seven. Danger suits you, Morty."

Charles noticed from the corner of his eye that Marguerite had lifted her gaze to him as his nickname was mentioned. He could feel her sharp scrutiny, and he was grateful for the darkness shielding his embarrassed flush. If she remembered him, how harshly would she judge his kiss earlier in the day? He was sure that she held nothing but contempt in her heart for him. . . .

Marguerite heard the names Charles and Morty, and knew that the man who had kissed her in the afternoon was her childhood playmate and neighbor in Sussex, Charles Boynton, the Earl of Mortimer. Even though he'd worn a silk face mask, there had been something so familiar about him. It had been years since she last laid eyes on him, and she had not dwelled on him in her thoughts. Now his presence startled her.

Did he remember that time when he'd proposed and she'd

turned him down? It was so long ago. Surely he wasn't still holding a grudge against her for breaking her promise that they would always be together. They had made that promise when they were children, even cut their fingertips and mingled their blood. Charles had been a good friend then, and she wished he still were. But his feelings had developed into love for her, and destroyed their amiable association.

Friendship was all she'd ever wanted from him. She could have used his support over the years. Perhaps she should have wed him to escape the horrors of her forced marriage to Lennox, but it would've been just another loveless union.

She studied the man Charles had become. He'd been twenty-one at the time of their bitter parting, and now he must be twenty-seven to her twenty-four. Charles had always been tall and lean, but with the years he'd acquired a powerful physique, with broad shoulders and slim hips. His tight breeches displayed muscled thighs, and the white silk stockings emphasized well-rounded calves. She remembered the unyielding strength of him as he'd enveloped her in his embrace earlier. She knew from memory that his hair was chestnut brown and curly under the powdered wig, and his eyes were the silver blue of ice in a winter shadow. Yet usually there was nothing cold about his eyes, and he was quick to laughter, as he laughed now at one of Nick's jokes.

She recalled that Charles had a mercurial mind that was forever concocting schemes to keep his ancestral ship afloat. Besides the congenial side he presented to his friends, she knew he had a deeper side to his personality that always questioned, always evaluated the world around him with sharp accuracy. He seldom showed that face, but all the while, his mind was constantly at work. She suspected he harbored secrets he didn't reveal to anyone.

Would she have found greater happiness in Charles's arms than in those of Viscount Lennox? No, love could not be forced. Besides, Charles had pushed her away when she told him she would marry another. Lennox, a deeply jealous man, would never have condoned her friendship with Charles.

Marguerite studied Charles's decisive jaw and cleft chin, which were not covered by the mask. His graceful hands gestured as he spoke, but she wasn't listening. It would have felt good to lean her head on his strong shoulder and close her eyes to rest. She wished they were friends again, because nobody knew one as deeply as the people who had grown up beside one.

A raucous cheer rose to the sky from a group nearby. A cacophony of music filled the night, and she longed to get up and dance around and around on the soft grass, feel the wind under her arms, feel her freedom, feel her life again after six years of quiet, desperate, iron restraint.

If she'd been alone, she would have tossed herself flat on the grass and dug her fingers into the soil and pressed her face against it to smell its freshness. She would have rolled the way she used to roll down a slope at her childhood home, every time exhilarated when narrowly skirting the riverbed and its soggy mud. If she'd come home with a muddy dress, her mother would have thrashed her for her wild ways. She never got muddy, and Marguerite had reveled in that secret game—a game she'd shared with Charles.

Lithgow Pierson, Viscount Lennox, had not beaten her, but his religious fervor had quelled any gaiety left in her. She'd been a rattling autumn leaf, an empty box, a shell, for six long years.

No more. The mourning period was over. Now she was free; even if they called her the Poison Widow, she was free from all shackles that would pin her spirit down like a dead butterfly on a display board.

She probed the cool thatch of the grass with her fingertips, and dug her heels into the verdant mat under her. The scents of moist soil, grass, wine, hair powder, and perfume wafted past her nostrils, and, intoxicated by life, she inhaled deeply. She would like to run barefoot in a meadow, wearing only the thinnest shift, feeling the cool wind against her heated flesh. . . . She would laugh and laugh. . . . Lithgow was no longer there to frown.

She would invite love; she would find it for real this time. Love would fill her emptiness. She would find someone to care for, someone who would understand the wild feelings roiling inside her. She would give everything to the right gentleman— if she could find him. He would be everything to her, she thought with a sigh of longing. They would roll down the slopes entwined, avoiding the muddy spots.

"What do you think, Marguerite?" Francesca asked, her voice so close.

With difficulty, Marguerite pulled herself away from her sensual reverie of a virile body entwined with hers. "Think of what?"

"She hasn't listened to a single word," Nick chided, his thigh leaning into hers. "Who were you dreaming of? Me?"

"I'm sorry. I was woolgathering, but not about you. So many things to contemplate. It has been a full day, a very—"

"We were wondering what you think of the Midnight Bandit," Charles interrupted her sharply. "All the ladies gathered here tonight yearn for a glance from his wicked eyes."

"Surely there is no need to be sarcastic, Charles. And don't scowl." She thought about the stories she'd heard about the Midnight Bandit, and found them amusing. She smiled. "I think the Midnight Bandit knows how to approach a lady's heart. He knows how to intrigue and cast romantic spells— which most gentlemen don't."

Carey slapped the table in outrage. "I don't believe what I'm hearing! The man is a scoundrel, a thief, and a conniver. How can you praise such a man?"

Marguerite wound a long curl around her finger. "Why, you gentlemen have to learn the way to a lady's heart. Very few do. Mayhap you could take lessons." She winked at Charles and grabbed her fan, which hung by a cord around her wrist.

She flipped it open and fanned her face vigorously even though a breeze cooled the air.

Charles's lips flattened in outrage. He glowered, and his gaze burned straight into her soul. She could not help but laugh at the tickling sensation.

"You shall pay for that observation, mark my words," he said.

Francesca gave a teasing chuckle. "Marguerite, your eloquent words touched Charles on the raw."

Carey snorted and gave Francesca an irate glance. "What more do you ladies want besides our love and support, our very souls?"

"Even though he's a rogue and a robber, the highwayman understands a women's need for romance," Marguerite replied. "Married gentlemen often feel there's no need for romance in the wedded state."

"I take it you speak from experience," Charles said pointedly. His gaze seared her anew with its intensity.

Marguerite didn't answer, but she remembered the long, lonely days of her marriage to a man who understood the Bible better than he understood the needs of a woman. She didn't want to think about it, lest her desperation for life and happiness burst forth and she make a fool of herself.

She watched as Carey braided his fingers with Francesca's under the table, and wished she could have found someone like him to love. He had strength, courage, honesty, and beauty. Emotions ran deep in him, and it was clear that he loved Francesca beyond reason. A love like that came only to some people.

Marguerite sensed keenly the love and passion flowing between the couple, and wished that—if only once in her life— she could plunge into that special sea of happiness. If only she were that lucky, she could finally demolish this barren, constricted shell that she'd lived in for the last six years and find her own way.

Nick interrupted her thoughts. "I think all this talk about

romance is wildly exaggerated. That villainous highwayman will find his head on a pike one day. Then no more poetry will flow over his maggot-ridden lips.''

Francesca made a sound of disgust, and Marguerite rose from the damp grass. The music was pulling at her, but before she could convince her friends to move toward the rotunda, Charles had risen as well.

''Let's take ourselves to Pall Mall and view the fireworks. The royal family will be there, and so will the rest of London.''

Everybody cheered, but it was Marguerite's eyes Charles sought, as if it mattered to him that she came along. She saw that the desire for her company fought with animosity inside him, and she vowed not to be alone with him again.

Chapter 2

In East Sussex, the month of May arrived with unseasonable warmth. The sun shone benignly on Charles's crumbling estate, on the thick stone walls, the diamond-paned windows, the slate roof with its many missing and cracked tiles, on the thick mat of ivy that covered the entire south wall. Even if the mansion was in disrepair, the grounds had the immaculate look created by a dedicated gardener. The lawns rolled like a lush green carpet toward the pond, where ducks squabbled. Clipped privet hedges and weeded flower borders gave dignity and color to the old estate with its stately chimney pots and somnolent atmosphere.

Within, Charles was lounging in a chair in the morning room, which was decorated with light blue damask wall panels, two armchairs and a settee a hundred years old, and a faded Turkish carpet. He chatted with his cherished maiden aunt, Emilia Wetherby, who had lived at Mortimer's Meadow since the time of his parents' wedding. The younger sister of his mother, she had been there to comfort him when his parents died, first his mother during childbirth, then, ten years later, his father in a riding accident. Her rotund form and kindly face shook with mirth as her fat pet pug, George, tried to steal a sugarplum from the crystal bowl at her elbow.

"Look at Georgie," she said. "Such antics for an old dog." Sitting on the settee, she shoved the pug aside with the book in her hand. The canine gave her a baritone growl and fought his way onto her lap, where he finally settled.

"If he eats another sweetmeat he'll get sick," Charles warned, and looked askance at the spoiled animal. The dog returned his glance slyly. "What are you reading, Emmy?"

She waved one pudgy hand in dismissal, and peered at him over the gold rims of her spectacles. "Nothing that interests *you*, Charles. You would call it romantic drivel, and I'm in no mood to be teased this morning."

Charles held out his hand to take the book from her, but she shook her head. Stray wisps of white hair danced around her powdered face, and the many satin ribbons attached to her lace-edged cap fluttered.

"Come now, Emmy, let me see." They fought over the book until, with a wail, she had to relinquish her hold on the leather-bound copy. Charles clucked his tongue and read the title. *"Journey of Love, Poems for Lovers,* by B. C. Rose. Really, Emmy, I thought you were not interested in such romantic nonsense."

"Give it back, Charles!" She reached over the side of the settee and snatched the book from his hands and glared at him. "You mean I'm too old for romantic twaddle? Fiddlesticks! You're never too old for something that touches your heart. These poems certainly do. The poet's voice is literally dripping with longing and pain." With evident agitation, she flipped through the pages and stopped at a place where she'd placed a red silk ribbon. She pressed a handkerchief to the corner of her eye. "Listen to this: 'Years came, years went / But my heart knelt to you / To love / That burned / Consumed me with its fire.

" 'Years came, years went / And you were lost, my love / Forever / Leaving my heart in the ashes of your betrayal.' "

She glanced at Charles. "And that's just the beginning; there's so much more."

Charles held his breath, and he could feel heat rising in his face. Emmy's blue gaze glowed bright with tears.

"Have *you* ever experienced such strong emotion, dear?"

Charles let his breath trickle out of his nostrils. Tumultuous feelings clogged his chest, tilted his world, and he found that he couldn't speak. He cleared his throat, "That's a very probing question. Have you, Emmy?"

Her hands fluttered to the lace on her cap, then smoothed the gray taffeta of her hooped gown. Two red spots glowed on her cheekbones. "I have loved, Charles," she said in a voice quite unlike her usual bright twitter. "But my beloved was unattainable." She leaned forward and placed her plump hand over his. "It pains me to see you so lonely."

He pulled his hand away. "I'm not—"

"Charles, I know you have many friends, but isn't there a lady, someone special to whom you could give your love? To whom you could recite love poetry at night?"

The memory of Marguerite seared him, her rapturous face upturned to the multicolored explosions of the fireworks in Pall Mall on the night of the festivities. Rockets had shot up and pinwheels had spun in the night, as they had in his heart when he'd witnessed her delight. They had stood apart, their friends separating them, but his heart had reached out to embrace her. That had been a week ago, and every waking moment since then he'd suffered the agonies of old memories.

She lived only five miles away, but was as unattainable as the stars. Somehow he had to get her out of his thoughts, but how? His heart was forever branded by her, like the marks burned into the hides of his cattle. His unrequited love felt like a sickness inside him, and he detested his weakness, his helplessness—his inability to wipe her from his memory.

He clamped down his emotions. "Don't worry your head

about the line of the family, Emmy. There will be Mortimers to inherit the title someday.''

Her smooth brow furrowed. ''I'm not thinking about the family line,'' she said sharply. ''I'm thinking about you, agonizing over you, in fact. I can see that something is very wrong.''

''Don't . . .'' Charles slowly released his hands, which were gripping the armrests too tightly. He was relieved when Bottomly, the butler, knocked on the door.

''A visitor, Lord Mortimer. Mr. Nicholas Thurston.''

With a sigh of relief, Charles rose. ''Thank you, Bottomly. He's come about the calves he wanted to see.'' Charles bowed to his aunt and whispered in her ear, ''Do put away that book, Emmy. I don't like to see you so maudlin.''

She slapped his arm. ''Rubbish! I shall learn every poem by heart. I wish I knew the real identity of B. C. Rose so that I could convey my admiration.''

''Don't . . .'' Seeing the mutiny in her eyes, he turned on his heel abruptly.

She recited as he walked out of the room, '' 'Love came to me but once / Like a comet / Unfettered / Radiant / Celestial / Trailing sparks of ecstasy and pain.' ''

Charles closed his ears to her voice and adjusted his features as he stepped downstairs. *Damn and blast!* Why did emotions always rub him raw?

Nick displayed a fine figure in buckskin breeches, boots, and a dove gray riding coat that lacked embellishment except for a series of brass buttons. His starched cravat had been arranged with flair, and his long black hair was tied back with a ribbon.

''Ah! There you are, Morty. Let's take a ride, or have you already been out this morning?''

Charles said ruefully, ''No, I was reined in by my aunt and forced to swallow a spoonful of verse. The romantic soul was feeding Georgie sugarplums and reading love poetry.'' He took his three-cornered hat, gloves, and crop from the lackey by the door and followed his friend outside.

"Poetry, you say?"

"Yes, evidently B. C. Rose is very popular. Emmy was reading *Journey of Love*. Shameless hussy," he added fondly.

"The ladies in my household speak of nothing else," Nick said with a snort. He gave Charles an embarrassed grin as he took the reins from the stable boy in the yard and heaved himself into the saddle. His horse danced and fretted. "Not that I'm wholly against romantic nonsense. Only a poet can express what really is in a man's heart."

Charles swallowed hard as he listened, and he could not dispel the painful lump in his chest. "He's a poet only if he listens to his heart," he muttered under his breath. He whistled, and his black stallion, Thunder, galloped up from the stables, reins hanging loose over the animal's neck.

"Does he always come when you whistle?" Nick asked with awe in his voice.

"I've trained him thus. But he only obeys my whistle, no one else's." Charles swung himself up into the saddle and patted the shiny black coat of the horse. "Let's ride down to the farm first and look at the calves. None better in all of England," he bragged with a laugh.

The morning smelled of fresh milk, manure, and wet grass as they stepped away from the field where the calves were penned in.

"Ah, what a glorious morning," Nick said, and slapped his gloves against the palm of his hand. "I'm happy when I'm in the fields and unfettered by the restraints of polite society." He gave Charles a keen glance. "Listen, I'll send my bailiff for the calves, and you shall have a draft on my bank."

"No hurry, old friend. You've no more funds than I do, so pay me when you can. The calves are yours." Charles punched Nick's shoulder, sensing that Nick had slipped into one of his brooding moods. Being of humble birth, the adopted son of Sir James Leverton, Nick sometimes complained that he didn't fit

in with Charles and his friends. Charles always told him it was
nonsense, but anger sometimes seethed deeply in Nick's eyes.
Charles often wondered what kind of horrors Nick had lived
through before he met Sir James. Nick seldom spoke of the
past, and Charles didn't push. He walked up the path toward
the farmhouse and enjoyed the glittering spring morning.
"Come on! Cheer up, old fellow."

Nick clapped a hand onto Charles shoulder. "Thank you
for the calves, Morty, and for always being such a good
friend." His heavy grip slowed Charles down. "What do
you say we go to see Marguerite? It's a good ride through
the forest."

Charles flinched as if slapped. He stiffened. "I have no desire
to see her. Since the time of her marriage we have not been
close. Better not stir the cauldron of old memories."

"She needs the support of her friends now more than ever.
Her mourning is in the past, and she's brimming over with lust
for life. I have watched her struggle since Lennox died. We
must see to it that no one takes advantage of her."

Charles gave his friend a hard glance. "And how are you
going to aid her, by offering her your protection?"

"Don't bite me, Morty. I truly care for the lady." He pulled
on his gloves. "Let's visit her. You can't spend all day riding
through your own spinney."

Charles knew he should say no, but the temptation to see
Marguerite again was too strong. He breathed deeply of the
fresh air and climbed into the saddle. Mayhap he would find
a way to forget her if he saw her in her former husband's house.

Marguerite shook the dust from the white apron she'd borrowed from one of the maids and glanced with satisfaction at
the pieces of furniture she had instructed the lackeys to carry
out of the house. The wagons were coming today to take the
lot to the auctioneers. She was going to sell the overlarge and
somber Dutch pieces, and refurnish her house with air and

light. In fact, she would have the heavy curtains pulled down. The servants could make dresses of the gloomy brown velvet. The only problem was, did she have enough funds for her plans?

"Oh, Pru, this is a step in the right direction!" she said to her companion, Prunella Trent.

"Yes . . . we can finally *breathe*. There were far too many pieces in these small rooms." Pru, a lady of comfortably rotund proportions, wore a brown hooped gown and a large mobcap with lappets. Wisps of gray hair curled around her homely round face. Pru was Marguerite's father's cousin, a poor relation who had brought up many children over the years, and fetched and carried for bored ladies who did not suffer poverty and who rather liked giving orders to lesser people. Pru had found a haven with Marguerite, and respect. Here she would stay.

Marguerite shook the dust off her voluminous frilled cap, then pulled it once again over the tight chignon on the top of her head. Standing on the gravel of the curving drive, she stared up at the tall, narrow house that had been Lithgow's castle. The house reminded her of her husband's spare and parsimonious frame. The only adornment on the brick walls was the ivy and the climbing clematis, which would show blue flowers later in the summer. The garden had been planted haphazardly. Shrubs and flowers mingled, and a tall brick wall kept out any visitors.

When she'd met Lithgow he'd been more carefree—and wealthy. In exchange for her hand, he had promised to pay her parents' debts. They had not hesitated to sell her then and there, and the memory of their betrayal still stung.

Hers had been a strained marriage, but she had learned to adapt, to conceal her true feelings. Lithgow had sensed her uneasiness, and as the tension mounted, he'd been unable to handle the problems. He'd turned more and more into himself. Soon he'd managed to bar her altogether from his life and turned toward religion. She'd discovered that he'd secretly been a fanatic Catholic in a Protestant country. She wondered if some madness had seized Lithgow to light such a zealous fire in him.

She still had difficulty shaking off the heavy feeling that had filled the house for years, and which had remained during her year of mourning.

Over, over! She kept singing the word silently. Her heart danced at the thought, and she made a sudden twirl as she went toward the house. She laughed and hooked her arm through Pru's.

"It delights me to see you happy again, Marguerite."

"Yes! I will guard my happiness—and yours."

Pru chuckled and patted Marguerite's hand. "Thank you, dear."

The sound of hoofbeats on gravel reached Marguerite's ears, and she shaded her eyes to see if the rented wagons had arrived already. Two riders approached through the gate, and she instantly recognized Thunder, Charles's beautiful horse, which was something of a legend in the area.

Her heart skipped a beat. Was Charles here to make new demands on her, demands she could not meet? She wouldn't have any of that! Relieved, she saw that he was accompanied by Nick Thurston.

"I'm going upstairs, Marguerite, to rest. You must entertain your friends on your own."

Marguerite gave Pru a quick hug. "Thank you for your help. Have a good, long nap."

"Good day to you, Marguerite," Nick called out, and waved his cocked hat.

She waved back, happy to see his grinning face. Nick had remained a good friend since her marriage, contrary to Charles. There was something wild and dark about Nick, deeply hidden fires—perhaps of anger—that made her slightly uneasy. But she knew he had a good heart, and always gave a helping hand.

"A fine day it is." She smiled at Charles, noticing the tension in his lean face and the dangerous glitter in his ice blue eyes. He bowed stiffly, then jumped off his horse. He walked toward her, handsome in buckskins and a superbly tailored coat of blue cloth simply adorned with gold braid. His features had lost all the softness of youth and now held strength and purpose. He was virile, and dangerous to a woman's heart, she thought, surprising herself as her heart beat faster. A chestnut brown curl fell over his forehead as he bowed low over her hand. He glanced up at her as his lips touched her fingers, his gaze probing hers until heat rose in her cheeks.

She jerked her hand away. "May I serve you gentlemen refreshments in the garden? We ought not stray indoors on a lovely day like this."

They followed her, and Marguerite was conscious of her apron and simple hooped gown of gray serge, a white kerchief wrapped around her shoulders and filling the deep décolletage. She knew she looked like a chambermaid, but that was just as well. Since she was hard at work, her friends would have to accept her careless appearance.

"Are you moving out, Marguerite?" Nick asked as he waited for her to take a seat on a wooden lawn chair.

She remained standing. "No, only selling part of the furniture. I shall order some new things in London from that fellow Matthias Lock. I admire his airy designs."

Wondering what she would discover in his eyes, she gave Charles a cautious glance. He smiled enigmatically, and she drew in a sharp breath. She hoped he had returned to her with an offer of friendship—nothing more.

"What would you like to drink?" she asked, noticing the slight tremble in her voice.

"Ale for me," Nick said, and Charles nodded in agreement.

" 'Tis a hot day for cleaning house," Charles added. "Do you need any help?"

"No . . . the servants are just about finished, but you could carry one of the tables out onto the terrace. If you don't mind."

Nick rose, and both men followed her into the house. She could feel their eyes on her back, and, flustered, she bit her bottom lip. Both men's admiration was palpable, but she wasn't sure she had any desire to parry flirtatious remarks. She wasn't ready for that, even if they were.

She explained which table to move, then went through the house to the kitchen at the back.

Charles cleared off a stack of newspapers from the table, and Nick whistled as he held aloft a book. "Look at this! Another copy of B. C. Rose's *Journey of Love*. The ladies are completely taken in by this drivel."

Charles gave him a narrowed glance. "You said you had nothing against romantic poetry earlier. Have you read it?"

Nick hemmed and hawed. "I've glanced through some of the pages. Definitely a silver tongue at work there."

"Male or female?"

Nick studied the cover leaf with its curlicue lettering. "Hard to tell. But someone who knows a woman's heart so well must be a woman, don't you think?"

Charles laughed. "Maybe it's the Midnight Bandit, writing under his real name."

Nick let out a long whistle. "A startling thought. A distinct possibility. I suppose we should take lessons from the fellow if we're ever going to turn the heads of the ladies." He pushed aside an armchair. On it rested a lute swept in white linen. He unfolded the material and pulled out the instrument. "The Academy of Romantic Fools. Headmaster, B. C. Rose, alias the Midnight Bandit." He cocked an eyebrow. "Would you like to enroll?"

Charles snorted. "Certainly not. You must have lost your wits, Nick."

The other man laughed and tested the untuned strings of the lute. He made adjustments, then started to hum a ditty taken straight from the gin shops in London. The full-throated sound of the lute filled the gloomy room, and Charles somehow felt that the house had lacked music for many years. The walls seemed to absorb the sound.

Nick capered around with the instrument in his arms, strummed, and sang. " 'She was a willing wench, tra-la, tra-la, and he was a willing jack, tra-la, tra-la, with the cocked pistol in his hand, tra-la. . . .' ' "

Charles stomped the rhythm and joined in at the refrain: " 'Tra-la-la, with a pistol in his hand, tra-la-la . . . He tumbled her in the hay and squeezed the trigger! Yes, he tumbled—' ' "

Footsteps drummed on the hallway floor. Marguerite entered, her face red with mortification. "How dare you sing a lewd ditty in my house! I'll be the laughingstock of my servants."

Nick stopped abruptly, made a pirouette, and returned the lute to the armchair. His eyes gleamed with mischief, but he apologized. "*Mea culpa.* I'm sorry. I'm sure I'm the most thoughtless fellow ever born."

Charles could not suppress a laugh. He roared, holding his stomach, and Marguerite glared at him. Slowly the tension in the room evaporated, and she chuckled ruefully, then laughed out loud. "You two are incorrigible. I swear you never reached manhood." She gestured toward the table. "You were supposed to carry this onto the terrace."

Nick swept the fabric around the instrument. "I remember that you played the lute with flair, Marguerite. Do you still?"

She shook her head. "I just brought it down from the attic, where it has stayed since my wedding day."

Silence hung in the room as her words suggested hidden sorrow. Charles sighed, noticing the color rising in her cheeks. Wanting to change the subject, he lifted the copy of *Journey of Love.* He waved it under Marguerite's nose. "Your favorite reading material has been discovered."

She snatched the book from his hand. "Who says it's mine?"

Charles enjoyed viewing her flashing eyes. "It could be the stable groom's, I suppose," he drawled, "but I have my suspicions."

"It's none of your business what I read, or don't read."

"Tsk, tsk," Nick said. "We thought that the Midnight Bandit might be the author of these poems, since the ladies are so taken with them. What's your opinion?" He leaned over Marguerite and looked deeply into her eyes.

Corroding jealousy washed through Charles. Nick was after the woman he loved, and surely any lady with a heart would fall in love with the handsome scoundrel. Charles suspected that Nick would have been married a long time ago had he possessed material wealth to offer a bride. Charles stepped closer, hemming Marguerite in.

"My opinion?" Her amber eyes narrowed with suspicion. "What do you want me to say? Whatever my answer is, you'll only tease me."

Nick's face held a question mark. "Come now, fair Marguerite. You cannot be much different from my sister, or Charles's aunt. They read the volume from morning to night. Tell us the truth. You're a great admirer of B. C. Rose."

She flung the book onto a chair. "Very well. If you must know, I find the poetry touching to the point of tears. The author feels love very deeply, but painfully."

"Male or female?" Nick went on relentlessly, and picked up the book.

"Does it matter? Love is love." Marguerite went outside, and Nick winked at Charles.

When they had moved the table, a maidservant carried out a tray with a pitcher of ale and two glasses. Marguerite poured and addressed Charles. "The book belongs to my husband's sister, Miss Pierson. She's staying here." Marguerite threw a resentful glance toward a window on the second floor. "She's here to make sure I won't do anything to sully my husband's memory. As if I would."

Charles noticed the surge of yearning in her voice, and some of the angry fire had died in her eyes. He wished he knew the source of her longing. He drank deeply of the cellar-cold ale and contemplated kissing her distress away.

"Surely you will travel up to London now that your mourning is over," Nick said. "You will soon have a trail of admirers after you, myself included."

Charles stiffened and exchanged a glance with his old friend. Were they to become rivals over Marguerite? Nick's eyes said as much, and Charles felt that old tightening in his chest—disquiet, worry, the knowledge that Marguerite would never choose him to love.

She was looking at him now as if reading every thought going through his mind. He glanced away, refusing to let her see the pain in his heart. She sat so close he could smell the lavender scent of her clothes and the sweet femininity of her skin. "I'll be the first to congratulate you, Nick," he said stiffly.

"Glad to hear it," Nick said.

Marguerite rose with a flurry of petticoats, and Charles and Nick followed suit. "You're talking as if my future is already decided. Let me tell you now—and remember this—I will not marry again. Besides, with my reputation as a woman who poisoned her husband, no suitors will be beating down my door."

"Oh, I'm sure a few could overlook your murderous tendencies," Nick said with a laugh. "You're a *wealthy* widow, after all."

She slapped her hand on the table. "Is that what you're after, Nicholas? My money?"

He shook his head. " 'Tis not my primary concern. I had other things in mind . . . though wealth—"

"Ooh, you! I want you both to leave and not come back until you've learned some manners."

Charles said, "Don't glare at me! I do not endorse Nick's uncouth manners, but at least he's frank." He dared a glance into her molten amber eyes and almost lost his voice with desire. He'd love to tame the angry line of her mouth and watch the anger in her eyes turn into passion. He reined in his dream with difficulty. "By the way, I don't understand how you received the unsavory nickname of the Poison Widow."

"Her acerbic tongue, of course," Nick said with a display of extravagant surprise. "It's poisonous in the extreme."

"No, really," Charles said seriously. "What happened?"

She seemed deflated as anger seeped out of her. She sank

down on the chair and stared unseeing into the garden, as if looking into some painful corner of her mind.

"I . . . I don't know what happened that day. Lithgow had dinner as usual. I had gone down to the village, brought some broth to a sick cottager. When I got back, Lithgow was dead. They said I had poisoned his food, but could not prove it. Ugly rumors started. His sister, Sophie, accused me of wanting my husband dead." Her voice faded, trembling, and she tilted her head down.

Charles looked at her slim, vulnerable neck and fought an urge to press a kiss to her pale skin. A wayward curl had crept out of her cap, and it aptly reflected her character: Marguerite was a woman of calm respectability and integrity, but a tumultuous side of her, as wayward as that copper curl, fought to emerge from the strictures of her life.

"I never wished his death. I've waited for the rumors to die down before stepping back into society."

"Have they died?" Charles asked, knowing that such a nickname as hers would follow her till the end of her life.

"I don't care anymore," she said almost inaudibly, and crushed the fabric of her apron with her hands. "It's enough for me to know that I didn't commit the crime. Some think I did, but that's neither here nor there."

"How do you think Lithgow died?" Nick asked softly He'd placed an arm around her shoulders, and held her close.

She tilted up her head, her chin jutting aggressively. " 'Tis my belief that he died of a weak heart. He'd been complaining about chest pains for about a year. The doctor shared my view, and spoke for me at the inquest."

Nick leaned back and took one of her hands in his "If you marry again, the ugly rumors will die—that is, if you refrain from poisoning your next husband."

Marguerite slapped his hand lightly. "Nick! Can't you be serious for one moment?"

" 'Tis difficult, but I believe that you're innocent."

She glanced up at Charles with a question. "And you, do you suspect me of murder?"

Charles shook his head. "No."

His heart almost stopped as a dazzling smile appeared on her face. "Thank you. I see that I can call you friend again."

Charles wanted so much more, but he knew she didn't. "If you wish. But I might not visit you as often as this bounder here." He bowed formally to her, concealing the longing in his eyes. "But if you need help of any kind, don't hesitate to summon me, or call at the Meadow."

There was a rustle of skirts at the door, and Charles glanced up. A tall, slender woman with a washed-out complexion and an unadorned cap stood on the threshold. Her dark eyes were flat pebbles of dislike, and the black fabric of her mourning gown emphasized the severity of her expression.

Marguerite rose and greeted the newcomer. "This is Miss Pierson. She's my companion now that Lithgow is gone."

Charles sensed the tension between the two women, and knew that Marguerite's lively personality would clash catastrophically with the rigidity of Sophie Pierson.

"A pleasure," he murmured, and bowed.

"It was my husband's wish that Sophie stay with me in the event of his demise. Lithgow always took care of his family with a most generous hand."

Hat in hand, Nick came to stand next to Charles. "That hatchet-face will create discord in Marguerite's life. We must rescue her," he said from the side of his mouth. He pulled Charles with him, but Charles was loath to leave now that he'd made the trip to see Marguerite. It had been long overdue.

"We shall come again," he said, and bowed once more to the ladies.

"It's not seemly that Marguerite should see gentlemen callers unchaperoned. Tongues will wag," he added.

"They already do," Nick said smoothly as they went around the house to the front. "I will not see Marguerite with that gorgon hovering over us."

Charles said, "I sensed that there's something furtive, something hidden in that house. Did you get the same impression?"

"It's the mourning. Marguerite will change all that now. At our next visit, the gloom will be gone."

"I doubt it, what with Miss Pierson in residence." Charles swung himself into the saddle and tossed a coin to the stable lad who'd cared for the horses.

Nick got onto his mount and gathered the reins. He said, "I shall sweep Marguerite away from all this. There's no gloom at my estate."

Charles forced all asperity from his tongue and all jealousy from his heart. "So you intend to make her your wife?"

"If she'll have me. There's no guarantee." Nick shot a long glance at Charles. "What about you? Are you going to be resentful?"

Charles wanted to tell the truth of his love for Marguerite, but he couldn't bare his heart lest he see scorn in Nick's eyes. In his current mood he could not bear any ridicule. "Resentful? Why? I have no claim on Marguerite. Besides, I doubt that she would ever consider me as a matrimonial prize. I do not have your flair."

Nick slowed his horse and gripped Charles's reins. "Listen, old friend, are we going to be rivals? I don't want to step on your toes, but neither am I willing to give her up."

Charles pondered the situation, then laughed. "This conversation is ridiculous! You don't love Marguerite."

Nick's voice was soft as he answered. "I do care deeply, and I mean to make her mine."

Charles could see his beloved slipping even farther away, but he must try at least once to declare his love to her. Then he would abide by her choice. "Nick, you're like a brother to me, and I don't want to hurt you." He took a deep breath. "I don't deny that I'd like to make Marguerite my wife someday."

Nick sat very still in the saddle; then he dropped Charles's reins. "I don't want us to fight over her, but let the best man win." He kicked his heels into his horse and took off in a cloud of dust. The events of the afternoon had drained Charles, and he suspected that he'd lost his best friend. But he had to try to win Marguerite one more time.

Chapter 3

By evening, a stiff breeze blew in from the sea and whipped the tulips in Marguerite's garden. She watched in dismay as yellow and red petals flew across the flagstone terrace, and wished she could protect the tender blooms. She glanced at a posy of violets on the desk in the library that had been Lithgow's but now was hers. The purple-blue color of the flowers glowed as if lit by an inner light, and she wished she had her sketchpad and watercolors at hand.

She heaved a sigh of resignation. A mountain of bills demanded her attention, and she cast about for ways to pay off all of Lithgow's debts, but saw no light at the end of the tunnel. Mayhap she would have to sell everything. She had thought she was a wealthy woman, but Lithgow had squandered his fortune on something that made her shiver with fear every time she thought about it. The memory of Lithgow's clandestine activities hung like a pall over the house.

She had thought she was the only one who knew about his support of the Jacobite cause that would one day put Prince Charles Edward Stuart on the throne of England and Scotland.

Stuart had raised an army with the help of loyal Highlanders and French weapons, and fought the English in several battles. He had finally been beaten at Culloden Moor in 1746, and, in September the same year, he'd returned to France, barely managing to evade capture. After the peace treaty of Aix-la-Chapelle, Stuart was no longer allowed refuge in France, but he was working to amass weapons and funds in other parts of Europe to raise another rebellion. There were still many influential supporters of the Stuart cause in England—and many Jacobite spies.

The vicious persecution of the Scottish rebels had gone on for a year after the Battle of Culloden, and Lithgow had helped many escape to France. The house was ideally suited to harbor refugees, as it was located close to the Channel.

Stuart's spies still approached her, but she'd been adamant about stopping all support that otherwise one day might lead her to the gibbet for treason. Another shiver of dread went through her at that thought, and she flung open the window to feel the fresh air against her skin.

She so yearned to fill the dead corners of the house with fresh air that would blow away the old secrets. Her family had been staunch Protestants, and her brother, Jerry Langston, who now was the head of the family, would be shocked if he ever discovered that she'd helped the Stuart Catholics against the law of the English Crown and the fundament of her upbringing.

This branch of Scottish Lennoxes had converted to the Protestant faith when they moved to England, but Marguerite knew that her husband had been a Catholic at heart, and had practiced the religion in secret. She had discovered the truth after her wedding; there were many things she'd found out, crimes that forever had taken away her childish trust, her belief that all people were basically good. She had never thought there could be so many sides to a person as there had been to Lithgow.

He had been capable of killing another human being.

She moaned and dragged a hand over her eyes at the distressing memory, as if to wipe it away.

A gust of wind knocked over the vase of violets, sending it to the floor. As the glass shattered, water seeped into the cracks of the wooden floor. Startled, Marguerite looked at the ruined vase and wondered if it was a bad omen. She had tried to let a new wind blow through the house since Lithgow's death, but it seemed impossible to remove the stain of guilt stamped on the very walls of her home.

Marguerite's legs weakened as if under a heavy burden, and she had to sit down at the desk. As if paralyzed, she could not make herself gather the pieces of the shattered vase, and could only watch as the rest of the water sought its way into the Oriental carpet.

A knock on the door forced her to collect herself. "Enter," she called.

Betsy, the chambermaid, stepped inside, her mouselike features wearing a question mark. She curtsied. "Milady, there's a gent t' see ya."

"Is it another dunner?"

"No, milady. 'Tis Mr. Renny."

Marguerite flinched as if bitten by a snake. Montagu Renny was one of her husband's old cronies. "Tell him I'm away from home, Betsy, and that you don't know when I'm coming back. Tell him to leave immediately."

Heavy footsteps sounded in the hallway. "No need to lie to me, Marguerite, my dear. You never were any good at it."

Marguerite said to Betsy, "Very well, I guess there's no need for you to deliver the message after all. I can do it myself."

The slender, wiry man halted the maid by gripping her arm as she walked by. "Bring me a glass of ale, and don't dawdle."

Betsy threw a frightened glance at Marguerite, who nodded. She grimaced as he slammed the door behind the maid and advanced across the floor, his black cloak fluttering.

Despite his thinness, Montagu Renny had the strength of a much larger man. Narrow of face, and wearing a mocking expression, he gave her a bloodless smile. His extremely pale skin held lines of dissipation; he might have been called handsome if not for his cold demeanor. His blond hair flopped in angelical curls around his ears, but there was nothing divine about him. Quite the contrary. Eyes, green and icy, pinned her with a stare that made her cringe with loathing and apprehension.

His pale, spiderlike fingers worked at the hat in his hand, then swept back the curls from his forehead. Marguerite noticed the grime under his fingernails and felt slightly queasy. The first time she'd ever laid eyes on him, she had silently called him the devil's henchman. She still did.

"What do you want, Mr. Renny? I told you not to bother me again after the last time."

"It matters not what you say, dearest Marguerite. I'm sure Lithgow would have been more than generous under the circumstances. He would not refuse my wish." He sat down in Lithgow's old leather chair at the desk and cast a keen glance at the bills strewn across the surface. She hated to be close to him, but she spread a ledger over the bills, then moved away from him.

"I doubt you would've pressed him for funds in this rude manner, Mr. Renny. Supposedly you were his friend, but I've seen precious little support from you since he died. Rather the opposite."

Marguerite yearned to clear up the matters of the past so that she could get a fresh start, but Renny kept ruining her plans.

He chuckled, a threatening sound that ended in a long cough. "You know I'm always there should you need me." His cold gaze traveled the length of her body, and Marguerite wished she were still wearing her gray serge gown instead of a form-fitting silk bodice and hooped skirt. Thank goodness a lacy scarf covered her décolletage, and a cap her hair. She knew he had great fondness for her fiery tresses.

"I hope to one day make you my bride, Marguerite; that's the truth."

"Never!" Marguerite clenched her hands in the folds of her

skirt until her fingernails dug into her palms. "That is completely out of the question."

He pursed his thin, bloodless lips and pulled his hands slowly through his hair, which kept falling forward. "I am a patient man. If you need more time—"

"Why have you come to torment me again?"

"Torment?" He laughed and lifted his pale eyebrows in mockery. "Why so suspicious, my dear? I'm visiting the bereaved widow of a good friend. Anything less would be unacceptable."

"I'd rather you not visit me at all."

Betsy returned with a pitcher of ale and a glass, which she reluctantly set before the visitor. Marguerite wished she could ask the maid to stay, but she could never trust what Montagu would say next. As if standing on needles, she moved agitatedly to the window. She inhaled the fresh scent of grass and new leaves, and wondered if she would ever manage to put the past behind her.

Betsy left, closing the door softly behind her. Montagu drank with audible swallows, as if he'd spent the day in the desert. He slammed the glass down on top of the ledger, and Marguerite jumped. "Now then, since you're not in an amorous mood, let's get down to business."

She stiffened, her blood running cold. "I already paid all I'm going to pay you."

Silence stretched between them, filled with menace.

"I would think your secret is worth a great deal more," he purred.

She steadied herself against the windowsill, breathing turning into an ordeal as air seemed to evade her nostrils.

He continued, "I want another thousand pounds, and you have two weeks to collect the sum."

She struggled to find her voice. "I don't have any more money to give you. It's all gone. I can barely settle the household bills as it is." She faced him. "That's the truth."

He sneered. "You got rid of Lithgow's favorite pieces of

furniture. There's lots more to sell, including artwork and knick-knacks.''

"It's none of your business what I do with this house. It was left to me, and all its contents.''

He spread out his arms. "Well, there you are! All you have to do is sell off the surplus.'' He rose, the chair creaking as his weight lifted. He came to stand behind her, and she moved aside just as he murmured in her ear, "One thousand pounds.'' He gripped her arm hard, and she fought back a scream.

"Let go of me! You have no right to touch me.''

When he started pulling her toward him, she twisted herself free and jumped aside. As he took a step forward, she bent down and quickly retrieved a piece of broken glass from the floor. "Don't come any closer, or I will cut you.'' She waved the glass at him, and the lecherous smile died from his face.

Silence descended once more as she sensed his mind evaluating the situation. He shrugged at last, his eyes glittering coldly as he viewed the piece of pointed glass. "As I said, I am a patient man.'' He went abruptly toward the door. "I'll be back in two weeks to collect the money.''

"Blackmail is a crime,'' she said, feeling trapped in a shell of fury and hopelessness. The glass had cut her hand, and a rivulet of blood blazed a hot trail down her wrist.

"Blackmail?'' He clucked his tongue. "Surely I can expect payment for assisting your late husband in, let's say, an extremely delicate matter.''

Her voice lowered to a trembling whisper. "You're as guilty of murder as he was. In fact, you probably did the foul deed yourself. Lithgow might have been a weak and befuddled man at the end, but he was not a murderer.''

He gave a snort. "Your story might convince the magistrates, but I doubt it—''

"*I* had no part in your foul deed,'' she said, already knowing his answer.

"You concealed Jacobite spies, and that is treason, my dear.'' He laughed, a sound that rasped along her nerves. "I would hate to see your lovely head broken, but I would not hesitate to step forward with the information."

Still clutching the shard of glass, Marguerite advanced on him. "If I'm to pay you one thousand pounds, I want to know where you buried that young sergeant."

He gave her a long look full of merriment. "We shall see. Maybe one day I will divulge the secret. It all depends on how you treat me. Your future is in your own hands, dearest Marguerite, and you'd better use your superior sense."

"Go!" Her composure shattered, she could not remain standing any longer. Sinking down onto a chair, she dropped her weapon. A long smear of blood marred the mint green silk skirt. "You're a cruel man, Mr. Renny."

He left without another word, but Marguerite noticed the bounce in his steps. He would return, and there was nothing she could do to stop him. She lifted the wilting violets from the floor and touched the soft petals.

She felt that, just like the blooms, her life had a limited time of glory before it faded. Maybe her life was like that of a star as it blazed fire across the sky for a brief moment before dissolving into a trail of ashes.

She would be old and faded before she could reclaim her freedom. Someone had always told her what to do, and if Montagu Renny had his way, she would have to become his chattel as she'd been Lithgow's.

Something inside her shouted loudly in protest, and she had to knock her fist against her chest hard to stop the tumult of her feelings. Somehow she would have to find the strength to fight Montagu Renny, and others who wanted to rule her life.

Never again. Freedom had been hard to come by, and she would not easily give it up.

Chapter 4

Charles sat at his desk staring out the window. Not that he could see anything in the inky blackness beyond the latticed glass, only a weak reflection of himself cast by the oil lamp on the desk, but he wasn't looking for anything outside of himself.

Ever since he'd met Marguerite at Ranelagh, his mind had been on her—in utter turmoil. Not to mention his emotions, which had come alive after years of lying fallow. Every second reminded him of his pain, of his failure to win her love.

Restless and aching, he plucked at the goose quill and stared at the splotched paper before him. Ink stains, but not a single word would come to describe what had happened in the last week. There was too much to write about, not just about the changes in his life, but about a suppressed love that had lain folded and tidy in the darkest corner of his heart. It had broken loose, flapping this way and that in the storm of his emotions. All he could feel was disgust—for himself, for his weakness.

With a suppressed snarl, he dipped the quill into the inkstand and poised his hand over the spotted sheet of paper. Another drop of ink joined the rest. His publisher was pressing him to deliver new material for another volume of poetry by B. C. Rose. Charles had promised a date of delivery, and it was now past.

Marguerite ... Marguerite ... Marguerite ... he wrote, remembering only her amber eyes and brilliant smile. A thought came, an expression as vivid as if she stood right before him. Charles read aloud as he wrote,

> *Your smile lit my heart with a thousand candles*
> *A velvet glance*
> *Knowing eyes*
> *You, your beautiful, compassionate smile, swept away*
> *The cobwebs and dust in my frozen palace.*

Charles recognized the frustration, the fever of creation coming over him. It had happened so many times, and would probably happen as long as he lived. Poetry was both a blessing and a curse.

> *Images racing, paper-thin*
> *Words as hollow as bones bleached by time*
> *... something ... temple*
> *Mine ... yours*
> *Holy to me*
> *Untouchable, unattain—*

''Damn it all to hell!'' Charles tossed the quill onto the desk without finishing the verse. It wasn't working. Ink spattered his verses, making a worse mess than when he started writing. Whatever came was twaddle, a victim's sorrow. But he was damned if he was going to be a victim all of his life when the opportunity had come to fulfill his longing for her. He had longed for her from the moment he had attained maturity. His verses would continue to reverberate with maudlin self-pity if he didn't see to rejuvenating himself, his life, if he didn't grab the chance and make something of it.

With an impatient growl, he pushed aside the sheaf of poems he was working on, hoping that perhaps the fourth volume of poems by B. C. Rose that Berber and Sons would publish would show new vigor, true inspiration, and not the tragic despair for which his earlier work was famous. The truth was, however, that the ladies of England liked tragic despair. Reveled in it. They felt poetry *should* bring a tear to the corner of the eye, or else it wasn't real poetry.

Verse that reflected happiness ought to be as popular as the more depressing kind, he thought. Many times he felt that his fever to express himself with words was a heavy yoke to bear rather than a pleasure, but he couldn't stop—not now. Perhaps never.

Besides, he needed the funds the popular B. C. Rose brought to his accounts. Without them, Mortimer's Meadow would have been a ruin by now, and at present it received improvements such as his funds allowed. He kept the estate afloat, and his farms produced well, bringing in revenue to keep Emmy in style and Georgie in sugarplums.

Charles got up and stretched, rolling his neck to ease the stiffness. His gaze fell on the letter he'd received from Joel Berber, the senior partner in Berber and Sons. Charles had memorized the words.

We are concerned at the delay in publishing your next volume. We are forced to stress the importance of your submitting your work at your very earliest convenience, or we shall be forced to annul the contract. . . .

Charles hadn't had problems with the schedule before, but this time none of his poems rang true. He couldn't send Berber something that was not up to his usual standard, but what would his publisher say if the tone of the poetry changed from defeat to hope? Charles shrugged. Berber would have to accept that life changed, and with it, poetic expression.

The clock on the mantelpiece emitted ten fragile chimes. Time to have a glass of brandy and relax with the London news sheets his solicitor had mailed him.

But first a breath of fresh air. He went through the open French door to the dark terrace and strolled across the uneven flagstones. An owl hooted in the distance, and a warm breeze rustled the leaves of a nearby elm tree.

With deep pleasure, Charles inhaled the scent of damp earth and newly scythed grass. There surely could not exist a place more deeply steeped in peace than the Meadow.

He stiffened as he heard the sound of quick footsteps on the sandy paths weaving through the garden. Jenkins, the gardener, wouldn't work this late at night. Intruders? The steps held urgency and purpose, and Charles drew a sigh of relief when he recognized Nick's broad shoulders and dark hair just below the terrace.

"Nick, old fellow, why are you sneaking around my house in the dark? Is this some new sort of lark, a treasure hunt perhaps?"

Nick laughed as he bounded up the steps and shook Charles's hand. "No, but your suggestion gives me a novel idea for my next house party—a treasure hunt. I rode up and decided to go around back so as not to rouse any of the servants. Bottomly is such a dour stick that I'm loath to encounter him any time of day." He glanced toward the study. "I knew you would be buried in papers, as usual. Estate business so late at night?"

Charles looked at his desk, wondering if he'd have time to hide the poetry before Nick laid eyes on his work. Charles did not like the idea of revealing the secret of his alter ego. If the truth seeped out, B. C. Rose would not remain the romantic enigma that made the ladies swoon, and Nick would probably be cruel in his teasing. Not that it mattered much, but Charles had no desire to become a laughingstock to his friends, as writing and reading love poetry weren't exactly the favored pastimes of his cronies. Betting, hunting, and gambling were.

Charles headed inside and gathered the papers into an untidy stack that he pushed into the desk drawer. "Care for a game of two-handed whist, Nick? I feel lucky tonight, so watch your purse carefully, or you might find it empty by midnight."

Nick laughed. "Damned arrogance, if you ask me. *I* will turn your purse upside down. Ten pounds a rubber."

They sat down by a table covered with green baize in front of the fireplace, and as Charles shuffled a deck of cards, he observed his friend. Nick's jaw looked tight, and his mouth was thin. He wore his dark hair in the usual careless queue, and there was no fault to be found with his gray riding coat, but he wore an air of restrained anger and restlessness.

"What's eating you, Nick? Has the fair Marguerite stated that she does not want to see your ugly face?"

Nick threw him a quick glance out of dark, thunderous eyes. "Don't you dare chide me! She has not shown you any preference, so we stand equal at this point." He scooped up the thirteen cards and watched as Charles removed part of the deck to make guessing the opponent's hand impossible. Charles did not take his eyes off Nick's face.

"Then why the storm clouds hanging around you?"

Since most of his cards were below ten, Charles decided to play nullo, which meant he had to take fewer than seven tricks to win. Nick agreed.

Nick put the six of diamonds on the table. "If you must know, I worry a great deal about Marguerite. She's vulnerable in that gloomy old house with only that hatchet-face, Miss Pierson, and old Prunella Trent for company. Marguerite's brother ought to take a hand in running her affairs."

Charles leaned back after placing the five of diamonds onto Nick's card. It was Nick's trick. "I'm not sure Marguerite would accept interference from her brother. Jerry Langston is a cold, calculating man, and no friend to Marguerite. Jerry would pocket her jointure, sell her belongings, and enhance

Langston Hall with the proceeds.'' Thinking of Marguerite, Charles stared at Nick. ''Lennox *did* give a jointure to her, did he not?''

Nick put down another card after collecting three unwanted tricks with a frown. ''As far as I know, Marguerite does not suffer financially, but she's very closemouthed about her business dealings, so I don't know for sure. I wish I could help her.''

''She would not thank us for interfering, any more than she would thank Jerry. She's determined to lead her own life, to take only her own counsel, it seems.'' Charles tapped the edge of his cards against the table. ''You should have taken a chance to play grand with cards like those. You won't be able to discard your court cards,'' he drawled teasingly.

''You're too damned good at this game, Morty.'' After gathering seven tricks, Nick threw down the remainder of his hand. ''Damn it all! I suspect you play with a marked deck.''

''That is a disrespectful observation.'' Charles lazily pulled the cards into a heap. ''I don't see a need to worry about Marguerite. She's strong willed and independent, and won't take advice from the likes of us. She wants to keep us—and everyone else—at arm's length.''

Nick pulled a finger thoughtfully along the sharp ridge of his nose. ''I don't like it. That Montagu Renny, whom we know nothing about other than that he's an old friend of Lennox's, skulks about her place, and she agrees to see him. I have seen him on several occasions.''

Charles stared in surprise, a sinking feeling in his stomach. ''I hadn't noticed. Could mean that he plans to propose, or that he feels obliged to make sure she's safe. Three ladies on their own need protection.''

''Protection? She needs protection against him! Anyhow, she would never accept that devil's proposal. He's cold as ice and shifty-eyed. I hope Marguerite won't be taken in by the likes of him. He has nothing to offer her but debts; he's an inveterate gambler.''

Charles caressed the soft surface of the baize cloth thought-fully. "Hmm, you're right on that score. From now on, we'd better keep a closer eye on the goings-on at Lennox House."

Nick's eyes glittered with something that Charles couldn't read. His friend pounded a fist into the table. "I would like to keep a *very* close eye on the fair Marguerite—the closer the better."

"You owe me ten pounds, Nick, old fellow." Nick's restless-ness rubbed off on Charles. A diffuse danger, a dark current, swept through the room. "I still don't understand, Nick. Your worry seems strangely inflated."

Nick shrugged. "Call it intuition; call it experience. I just know that Renny has entry to a house where he should be barred, and I don't like it. Marguerite is too stubborn for her own good if she refuses the protection of her family and friends."

As a cold fist closed around his heart, Charles watched Nick deal another hand. "We'll watch over her without her knowl-edge. I don't like the thought of her alone in that secretive old house."

Two weeks later

Marguerite woke up in the morning to the sound of rain stabbing the windows. Wind howled in the trees, hurrying the raindrops to meet their end against the panes. Fighting sleep, she raised herself on her elbows and stared at the sullen skies. Thunder crashed in the distance.

"Oh, dash it all! I had so looked forward to the picnic at the Hollows with Nick," she said to the empty room. Anything that would make the days go faster attracted her, especially entertainment out-of-doors. Inside this house she often felt that she couldn't breathe, or that she would be smothered by the walls as she closed her eyes and put her head on her pillow every night.

She glanced toward the door. It was closed, and locked as well. She always protected herself—against *what* she wasn't sure—by locking the door. Mayhap to safeguard herself against Montagu Renny.

The longer she lived at Lennox House, the more she felt the need to get out, but it was her home. Jerry had reluctantly offered her room and board at the Langston estate, but that would be exchanging one prison for another.

If it weren't for Sophie's predicament, Marguerite would have sold Lennox House directly after her husband's death. Sophie had nowhere to go, and no funds to pay the rent at a boardinghouse for genteel ladies. Sophie would be as poor as a church mouse if their roads parted, and Marguerite could not with a clear conscience throw out Lennox's sister, no matter how much she disliked the woman. Still, the debts were mounting; Lennox's old creditors were renewing their demands for immediate payment for old services rendered.

With a sigh as gloomy as the day outside, Marguerite eased herself out of bed. The hem of her muslin nightgown trailed on the floor as she walked to the window and stared at the wind-tossed garden. She lifted her heavy hair from her neck and scalp, ruffling it, but the gesture did not improve her spirits, or make the dazed feeling go away. She looked at the rain-streaked meadow beyond the stables, yearning for *something*— adventure, happiness, romance deep, deep in her heart. She did not know exactly what.

The ache, the longing, never quite went away, no matter how she filled her life with a whirl of gaiety. Basically she was alone only at night. During the day she frantically sought the sounds of voices and laughter so as not to remember the hollow feeling inside. Her strategy had succeeded. Almost.

But at night there was no barrier of friends to protect her, and the walls seemed to shrink, closing her into an ever smaller room. The property was all she owned besides the furniture and a few odds and ends. She could have sworn the house was working against her, like a living entity. Then there was always the worry about money, and she spent many sleepless nights thinking about how to fund her future.

Her life would not improve as long as she remained at Lennox House. She would have to come up with a solution for Sophie, Pru, and herself.

The wind increased to a howling torment outside, and thunder boomed, coming closer every minute. A timid knock sounded, and as Marguerite unlocked the door, Betsy entered with a cup of tea.

"Good morning, milady. I'm 'ere if ye need me." The young maid gave Marguerite a cheerful smile, the only ray of sunlight in the dark room.

Lennox had not accepted the extravagance of a large staff, especially not a lady's maid, and Marguerite had made do with Betsy, who every day gained more knowledge of dressing hair and mending ripped lace with dainty stitches.

"I'll wear the yellow muslin sack gown, Betsy. I want to look bright even if the day isn't." Marguerite sipped the hot tea and studied the dresses in her wardrobe. They were old, and no amount of alterations would make them more fashionable. She'd removed every black and gray gown except one, and thrown away her black fans and ribbons. She had planned to refurbish her entire wardrobe until Montagu Renny came with his sordid blackmail demands. Now she would have only enough money to order two ball gowns and a new *robe d'Anglaise*. It was better than nothing.

Betsy laid out the quilted green silk petticoat—with the hem that had been mended countless times—stockings, and garters.

"Ask the stable boys to bring up the hip bath and cans of hot water. I'm not ready to face the world without a warm ablution this morning."

Betsy nodded and disappeared into the gloomy, damp hallway. Marguerite brushed her hair and wound it into a thick braid. She waited in the adjoining dressing room while the boys brought in her copper tub, then dismissed everyone so she could alone enjoy the soothing sensation of hot water against her skin. It closed around her like a caress as she slowly lowered herself into the bath after tossing her nightgown across the room.

She shut her eyes and leaned her head against the metal rim. She listened to the violence of the storm outside, but wasn't frightened. Thunder and lightning cleared the air magnificently.

Sinking down as far as she could, she reveled in the relaxing softness and the scent of rose oil rising with the steam. Water lapped around her hips, and she pictured a strong male hand soothing her skin, rather than the slippery water. Firm and hot, it would travel over every valley and mound of her yearning body, and . . . and bring joy to every pore of her skin, bring *something,* peace . . . wonderful satisfaction to her restless mind. Satisfaction as deep as the marrow of her bones. And happiness. Caring and love. Someone would whisper sweet nothings in her ear and hold her close.

She knew she was dreaming—lonely, vapid dreams, wishful thinking. Sighing, she took the soap from its porcelain dish beside the tub and worked up a lather that she applied to her torso and her breasts, which felt tender and heavy with longing.

She soaped her arms, following the firm whiteness of her skin all the way to her fingertips. How much more fun it would be to have a lover do it for her.

A door slammed downstairs, and a wild gust of wind moaned down the chimney. A loud crack of wood splintering sounded right outside her window. Marguerite jumped with fright. She dropped the soap and craned her neck, but couldn't see what had shattered outside.

Voices and stomping feet echoed in the hallway below. Marguerite glanced at the clock on the mantelpiece and hurriedly washed the rest of her body. Guests? Surely no one was abroad at this time except the servants? Voices floated up the stairs, and Betsy sounded her usual buoyant self, exclamations liberally interspersing her speech.

Who was with her? Jona, the neighbor's stable boy, perhaps. He sometimes brought over fruit and berries in season, or a roasted chicken or hare from his employer, retired Admiral

Hancock, who didn't hesitate to court Marguerite even though he had long since passed the age of eighty.

The voices came closer. The door to her bedchamber creaked, slammed back against the wall. Marguerite automatically pulled her knees to her chin, shielding herself; she stared aghast at the intruder. Betsy tried to stop him, but he strode across the threshold with singular purpose.

"Charles! What in the world are you doing here? How dare you barge into my bedchamber without so much as a knock to announce your presence!"

His gaze raked over her naked body, and her skin grew hot with embarrassment. He seemed fixated, unable to find either his voice or his composure. His hands fell slowly to his sides as he stared at her in blazing admiration. Betsy was tugging at his sleeve.

"My lord, ye must leave!" She addressed Marguerite. "I kept telling him, milady."

Marguerite thought she would faint with mortification. "Get out, Charles!"

"Sorry," he mumbled. "Truly, I didn't realize you sleep here and not in the master suite. There's an enormous tree branch ready to crash through this window. One more heavy gust, and you will bathe in shattered glass." He pointed toward the window next to the fireplace. "You'd better get dressed and leave the room while we work to bring the branch down."

She nodded, placing her forehead on her soapy knees to conceal her embarrassment.

Charles left without another word, but she could still feel the lingering heat, the pounding heat of his gaze upon her body. Had he known that she abhorred the master suite with its heavy bed and its memories? Had he lied, and barged in to get a glimpse of her? She didn't think so.

She hastened to dry herself and slipped her silk chemise over her head. As Marguerite fastened white silk stockings with garters above her knees, Betsy entered to help her tie the padded panniers and petticoat at the waist. The fabric rustled as Marguerite moved.

"I'm sorry, milady," the maid said with downcast eyes. "I didn't know Lord Mortimer would burst in 'ere without as much as a by-your-leave. Said 'e was going to push the branch away from the window."

"Very well, but you'll have to be more vigilant in the future." Marguerite pulled on the formfitting yellow bodice and arranged the chemise's ruffled lace around the deep neckline. Betsy tightened the lacings in the front over the plain stomacher, and tied the overskirt back to reveal the becoming quilting stitch of the petticoat in the front. She helped Marguerite wind her hair into a chignon and topped the whole with a lace cap with streaming ribbons. Marguerite slipped into her dainty satin slippers, gripped a fan, and straightened her back to face the trials of the day.

"It 'as stopped rainin', milady," said Betsy in subdued tones. "The storm left as fast as it came."

Marguerite noticed that the dour clouds had let up, revealing bursts of golden sunlight. She cautiously looked out the window. The tree branch hung drunkenly against the wall, close to the glass. Charles stood below, gesticulating and talking to the stable boy, who was halfway up the tree.

"How dangerous!" Marguerite hurried downstairs and out into the steaming garden, where puddles gleamed and the sun glittered in a million raindrops. "Be careful! Peter might fall down," she shouted as she came around the corner of the house.

"Nonsense," Charles said with a lazy grin, his gaze traveling suggestively over her body. "He volunteered. Climbs better than an ape. All the branch needs is a good shove and it'll drop to the ground." He turned his gaze toward the boy, giving occasional encouragement and advice. "Excellent, Peter; just another step and you'll be able to kick it loose. Hold on to the top branch."

Prunella, dressed in a gray gown and voluminous cap, came running around the house as fast as her short legs could carry her. "I almost had an apoplexy when I saw the boy in the tree," she said breathlessly. Putting her hands to her round bosom, she stared worriedly at the agile stable boy.

"Charles says everything is under control."

Marguerite scrutinized her old friend and admirer in the unforgiving sunshine, but she could find no fault with his attractive form. The black cocked hat pulled low over his eyes gave him a secretive look, but his mouth formed a smile, and she was acutely aware of the wide, sensuous lips and the hard jaw, the pugnacious cleft chin Appreciation of his strength, purpose, virility—oh, such heady virility—throbbed within her, but she must not let her secret longings sweep her away on a wave of futile admiration.

She tore her gaze away from his handsome face and penetrating ice blue eyes that so easily stripped away her defenses, baring her yearning soul.

He wore a well-cut blue camlet coat with wide cuffs and brass buttons along the front and on the pocket flaps. Lace foamed over his wrists. Rain had dampened the cloth on the wide shoulders and the brim of the hat. As always, he wore his elegance with casual negligence, an air only someone comfortable with himself could accomplish.

"You are abroad early, Charles," she said warily, every moment sensing his magnetism, his stalking of her, even if his gestures and his demeanor seemed disinterested and nonchalant enough.

"I could not sleep. Went out for a ride at six, before the storm. I came through the spinney at the back of your stables just as the gusts battered your property. Just in time, it seems."

"Yes . . . I'm grateful." Marguerite spread her painted vellum fan and fanned her face. She studied him over the rim. "You are far away from home so early in the morning."

"Nothing like a long ride to clear one's head," Charles said, the corners of his mouth lifting in a suggestive smile. "I can't think of a more attractive spot for a ride than your property. You won't ban me, will you?"

Marguerite averted her gaze, turning her shoulder toward him and staring at Peter, who had aimed a well-placed kick at the branch. "No, surely I have no reason to ban my friends. You're welcome to ride on my property anytime, Charles."

"You are a generous woman, Marguerite. I expect I shall meet your many admirers on lonely rides about your acres."

Marguerite snapped her fan shut. "Don't be foolish. Your words suggest that I'm so lovesick I attract gentlemen like bees to nectar."

He didn't respond, but his silence was response enough. The thought, the realization that her admirers flocked to her, annoyed her more than she could express. Did her longing for romance show so clearly?

The branch crashed to the ground along with her pride, crushing some saplings at the tree's base.

"Good work, Peter," Charles shouted. He and another stable hand went to inspect the branch, then carried it away.

Charles was not afraid to take part in the labor, and the fact endeared him to her even though she seethed in a haze of anger and hurt pride.

She stalked toward the lilac hedge and the terrace that stretched the length of the house at the back. Who was he to hint at her loneliness, at her longing for love? Yet she realized that she was mostly angry at herself, not at him. Evidently she bore her loneliness like a blemish or bruise for all to see. Musing over her own weakness, she didn't hear him join her on the wide terrace steps. She started as he said, "I wouldn't say no to breakfast if you care to invite me." He pushed his hat back and stared down at her with his inscrutable eyes. "Then again, mayhap you find my presence intruding upon your peace?"

"No . . . of course not. 'Tis the least I can do to repay you for your help." She hurried through the open terrace door and, temporarily blinded by the contrast between the sunlight and the gloomy interior, rang for Betsy. She ordered a tray to be brought outside. As she went to join Charles, she noticed Sophie standing in the deep shadow cast by the drab velvet curtains that still hung in the windows.

"Marguerite, I see it as my duty to warn you that you'll be the talk of the neighborhood if you entertain gentlemen callers at this time of day," Sophie said in her crisp voice. Her bloodless face looked like a frozen mask, her dark, unyielding eyes staring at Marguerite with disapproval. Her black dress hung too loosely, its hem dragging on the floor. Her hair had been raked back into a careless knot under an off-center white cap, giving her a slightly crazed appearance.

Marguerite knew that Sophie was far from crazed; she was cool and calculating, always using the same measuring stick as had Lennox to judge situations, more often censorious then approving.

"You startled me, Sophie. You may say what is on your mind, but I will follow my own judgment in all matters concerning my personal life. I have no intention of scolding you for your actions. Besides, you can join me, or Pru shall."

"You should know better than to flaunt your body to gentlemen," Sophie said curtly, snatching a fold of her skirt and sweeping across the room.

"Pray halt your hasty retreat, Sophie. I have no patience with your ill temper. I work every day to make life tolerable for all of us, and I resent your constant strictures and sermons. If you cannot accept this new life without your brother, I suggest you seek a way to live according to what he would have wished. Perhaps a nunnery would have a place for you."

Her body rigid with disapproval, Sophie turned and faced Marguerite. "Lithgow's last wish was that I look after you and this house. All this was *his*. Please don't forget that. You brought very little with you, but never hesitated to live off my brother's bounty."

"Bounty? You exaggerate. Whatever is left, mostly debts, he left to me. And I have struggled to clear the Lennoxes with the merchants. Otherwise we would not have food and wine on our table. Don't you dare to forget that!" Marguerite turned on her heel and left the room, her heart pounding with agitation. Confrontations like these with Sophie would give her gray hairs before her time. The door slammed behind her. It was clear that Sophie lived in a state of deep agitation as well.

To Marguerite's surprise, others had joined Charles in the stableyard behind the house. Nick sat atop his large hunter, and his stepsister, Delicia Leverton, rode a smaller sorrel mare. To Marguerite's dismay, Montagu Renny had stepped down from his horse, holding the reins loosely as if waiting for Peter to take the mount away. Renny, his hand arrogantly propped upon his hip, stood as if he owned the ground beneath his boots.

Marguerite's back stiffened as she watched him, but she forced a welcoming smile to her lips as she crossed the terrace. "Well, I never thought I was this popular! My friends seek my company at all hours."

Nick swept off his three-cornered hat and gave a sweeping bow. "Your admirers fight to find some time alone with your fair self. I had hoped that I would catch a moment with you this morning, but I see that my hopeful calculation was too optimistic."

"Yes . . . well, no matter." Marguerite shot Renny a dark look. She knew why he had come: to demand the one thousand that she'd barely managed to scrape together from the sale of the furniture and some old paintings. She veered away from Nick and his sister to speak with Renny in private. She sensed Charles's gaze on her as she stepped around Renny's horse as if admiring its lines.

"I know why you're here, Mr. Renny," she said in an undertone, "but I suggest you return at a later hour for our business transaction. I do not wish to invite you to breakfast."

"I'm not leaving without the money," he muttered, his cold green gaze following her. Aloud he said, "I'm flattered. I gladly accept your invitation to breakfast, Lady Lennox. The ride has given me a keen appetite." He winked at Marguerite suggestively, and she drew a sharp breath, feeling like a cornered rabbit.

For once she wished she dared to confide her difficulties to Charles or to Nick, but would they believe her innocence concerning the death of the militia man? Why had she kept it a secret for so long? they would ask. And they were right. If she'd been able to, she would have revealed the secret sooner, but the sergeant's death concealed a darker secret that might cost her her life if she didn't take care.

An icy shiver rippled through her, and cold sweat broke out on her neck. Sometimes she thought she would break under the burden of the Lennox secrets.

"Ah! Another visitor," Charles said, and shielded his gaze from the sun.

Marguerite flinched as his voice sounded so very close to her ear. She hadn't noticed that he had shifted his position. How much had he heard of her conversation with Renny? How much of her inner turmoil did he sense? "Who?" she said in a croak.

"Captain Emerson. I see he left his small force by the gate." Charles went to shake hands with the officer, and as fear filled her, Marguerite thought she'd grown into a pillar of stone. She could not move.

Emerson was the name of the officer who had lost one of his men, the sergeant that Lennox and Renny had killed and buried somewhere on Lennox land.

It took all her concentration to walk forward with an outstretched hand as Charles introduced her. "Captain Emerson. Welcome to Lennox House. I hope you'll stay for breakfast with all the others. Simple fare, I'm sorry to say, ham and eggs, but you'll find that the company is congenial."

She studied the earnest man, straight, dark blond hair tied back, a rigid face, and a body of medium height, a ruthless mouth, but quite a kind gleam in his blue eyes.

"Lady Lennox," he said with a bow. "I didn't come here

to deplete your larder, only to speak of a matter that concerns a missing man.''

''La! You cannot talk about business on an empty stomach, Captain Emerson. I certainly cannot,'' she said evasively. To give herself time to think, she led the way to the terrace, where Betsy and two other maids were busy wiping the table dry and spreading a tablecloth.

The gentlemen brought extra chairs from inside while Marguerite chatted with Nick's sister, Delicia. All she could think about, however, was the dead sergeant and Renny's threatening presence beside her. He seemed unable to take his eyes off her. Even though the morning sun warmed her back, Marguerite shivered with unease. What lies should she feed the captain at breakfast?

Charles set down a chair, and his gaze locked with hers. His eyes narrowed with questions, and Marguerite averted her gaze in haste. She sensed that he could easily look through her forced smile. His attention burned into her across the table as she sat down next to Prunella, as if hoping the older woman could give her much-needed protection. Pru prattled brightly with the captain and Delicia Leverton.

Marguerite concentrated on Nick, who was discussing the weather with Captain Emerson. She wished she could tell them all to leave so that she could gather her wits. But outward appearances were important when one had secrets to hide.

Chapter 5

Montagu Renny took the chair beside Marguerite without so much as a by-your-leave. A polite hostess, she could not demand that he move to the other side of the table. She watched in silence as Betsy poured coffee and tea and served heaping plates of breakfast to the guests. Bacon strips sent out a mouthwatering aroma, and the eggs had been cooked to perfection. Marguerite could not enjoy the fare, not when her nerves were tied into knots.

Raindrops glittered on the windowpanes and on the flag-stones, but Marguerite rejected the beauty of the newly washed day. Her mind full of shadows, she could not relax enough to enjoy the season around her, or the company of her guests. Renny, crowding her with his presence, was too much of a threat, and Captain Emerson in his red uniform suggested another kind of danger, a larger, dizzying danger that might end with her neck in a noose.

She picked at her bacon and bit into a piece of buttered bread automatically. She smiled brightly—if falsely—at Captain Emerson as he started into his meal with vigor.

"This is the best time of day, don't you agree, Captain?" she said. "A new start after a cleansing storm, a surprise party when I least expected it. Never a dull moment."

Captain Emerson gave her a brisk smile. "It is entirely my pleasure to consume such excellent fare after a long, tiring night of searching for smugglers. A ghost would be easier to apprehend than the elusive 'gentlemen.' " He took a sip of coffee and looked at each face of the guests. "Have you heard or seen anything suspicious in the area? I'm convinced that some of the local people are involved in the nightly illegal activities."

"Smuggling? I highly doubt it." Charles glanced at the captain keenly, and Marguerite wondered what was going through her old friend's mind. She'd never realized how secure in himself Charles had grown over the years. Warm, yet aloof. Strong, yet sensitive. He was the total opposite of Lennox, who had lived in a fragile castle of his own making, an inner abode that had easily crumbled under the strain of his deception.

"Well . . . there might be other activities. It is a known fact that Stuart spies have fled across the Channel via smuggling vessels—in this very area. I would be grateful if you keep your eyes and ears open to unusual goings-on."

Stuart spies. Marguerite stiffened with unease as she heard Renny inhale sharply beside her. Could everyone read the truth on her face, that she had something to hide? She prayed no one sensed her terror, and smiled with more determination than sincerity.

"Most of us sleep at night when such deeds take place," she said, glad that her voice did not tremble or sound flat.

Captain Emerson let his sharp gaze travel over the assorted guests. "All I ask is that you keep an eye on your servants and business in general. By the way, we're also searching for an escaped prisoner, a spy. He's most likely traveling this way. Sussex and Kent are covered with militia men on the lookout. He was taken red-handed in London with secret instructions for Charles Edward Stuart. There are known Jacobite sympathizers in the Capital, but I daresay they are not flaunting their leanings any longer. Too dangerous. Stuart will not succeed with another rebellion. The authorities will tie off all routes of communication with the Pretender in Europe.''

Despite the bright sunshine, silence hung like a heavy fog among the guests, and Marguerite noticed the furtive glances thrown across the table. The only one unperturbed was Charles. A smile played across his firm mouth.

He said, ''I'm sure that no one can slip through your net, Emerson. You've the reputation of superb leadership. I doubt the spy can match your wile.''

Emerson smiled briefly. ''Well, at this time I'm more interested in local smugglers and their vessels hidden in coves along the coast. Very elusive, alas!''

''Like ghosts, you said?'' Marguerite asked to avert the captain from the dangerous topic of spies.

The captain drained his coffee, and Betsy went around refilling the cups. Steam curled lazily from the spout of the silver pot, and Marguerite stared at it as if it would transform into a genie that would be her support in an increasingly tilting world.

''Yes, like the most malevolent specter,'' the captain said tightly. ''I'm quite out of patience.''

''Talking about ghosts, Lennox House is haunted by a lady in a gray dress. She has no head . . . and there's blood . . . as if she'd been beheaded. My husband said she was a murderess in the time of Queen Elizabeth, a member of the Renny family from which he bought the house.''

A chill permeated the air. A coffee cup rattled against the saucer beside her, and she glanced at Renny. Sweat glistened on his forehead, and his skin had taken on a pale, bluish tone. Was he afraid of ghosts?

Relieved to have found a possible chink in his armor, Marguerite took a deep breath and continued. ''Are you familiar with your ancestors' connection with this house, Mr. Renny?''

Renny nodded, his mouth pulled into a hard line. He surreptitiously wiped his forehead with the linen napkin.

"Then perhaps you know the entire story," Marguerite suggested, but he shook his head.

"I don't know anything about it."

"Aren't you afraid to stay here with only women for company?" Delicia asked breathlessly. "I would not be able to sleep a wink at night knowing there is a ghost walking the halls."

"She is a gruesome sight, but she has done me no harm. She does not appear very often, but when she does, she gives off an air of unhappiness. I find living people are more threatening." Marguerite glanced pointedly at Renny, noticing his trembling hands on the table. "Don't you agree with me, Mr. Renny?"

"Excuse me," Renny said, and stood. His chair screeched against the flagstones. He gazed at Marguerite coldly. " 'Tis rude of me to leave so abruptly, but I just remembered that I have guests arriving at my house in fifteen minutes." He bowed formally. "Lady Lennox, you are generous as ever." He bent over her hand and whispered, "I will return this afternoon to conclude our discussion."

Marguerite inclined her head slightly. She wished she could tell him never to return, but she knew she wouldn't get rid of him that easily, not until he had the blackmail money in his hand. In a flash, she realized it was wrong to give in to Renny's demand, but what other choice had she?

Renny left, and she turned her attention to the table. She sensed that Charles studied her face. His gaze touched hers, a warm, tingling sensation, and she shifted her eyes away from his. A blush crept up her neck, and for a mad moment she wished she could place the burden of her precarious secrets onto his capable shoulders. No, such a coward she was not; she would have to deal with her difficulties on her own.

Fatigue made her limbs heavy, and her eyes felt hot and gritty, as if she were about to cry. Tension sat like iron bars across her shoulders, and she drew a sigh of relief as the captain put down his napkin beside his plate.

"I'm indebted to you, Lady Lennox," he said. "My strength is greatly restored after a trying night."

Marguerite rose, and the men stood politely. She held out her hand to Emerson. "I hope you find the smugglers and the escaped prisoner. I might not be afraid of ghosts, but I will not rest easy until the matter of the spy is cleared up."

The officer looked up at the tall facade of the mansion. "You ought to have the protection of male servants, Lady Lennox. These are uneasy times."

Marguerite followed his glance. "There are three stable boys and my elderly coachman."

The curtain twitched in Sophie's bedchamber. Miss Pierson had been spying, and Marguerite wondered uneasily what other secrets Sophie might be hiding. Walking on the tightrope of her uncertainty, Marguerite escorted the captain around the house to his horse.

"As I'm curious about the outcome of your mission, I expect to see you again, Captain Emerson. Please come to dinner one night soon."

He clamped his cocked hat on his head. His expression held a somber shadow. "I will be very busy, my lady, but I shall be honored to accept your invitation at some future date." He bowed at the waist, and Marguerite felt both frightened and comforted by his words. Unlike Renny, Captain Emerson was a true gentleman and would never do anything to embarrass her.

He kissed her hand and smiled. "Good morning, Lady Lennox. May the sun always shine over your house."

The cloud smothering Marguerite's spirits lifted for a moment. "Why, you're very kind, Captain."

She watched him leave, wondering if one day he would arrive with a warrant for her arrest. Shivering as if a cold shadow had touched her, she turned abruptly. Instantly she saw Charles leaning against the corner of the house, his arms folded over his chest and his hat tilted low over his eyes.

"You seemed extremely preoccupied just now," he said,

drinking in the view of her neat ankles under the swaying gown. Her feet looked impossibly small in the satin slippers, and Charles was filled with the urge to take one of them into his hands and caress the gentle arch and the slender ankle, perhaps let his fingertips stray upward to the explore the roundness of her calf . . . and farther. *Dreams, you idiot,* he thought. *Nothing but intoxicating dreams that will eventually drive you insane.*

"You're still here," she said, ignoring his statement. "I thought the gathering was breaking up."

She walked so close by him that he could smell the faint perfume of her soap—a sweet, seductive waft, rose blossom—and the dizzying scent of *her,* her skin looking so soft in the revealing neckline he wanted to bury his nose against her bosom and run his hands over its creamy smoothness.

"The gray lady, Marguerite?" he chided. "We invented her when we were children, and I don't think she ever walked on this earth."

Marguerite cursed herself. She should have known better. Of course Charles would remember that old invention. He evidently remembered everything that she had ever said or done.

"There *is* a gray lady ghost—" she began.

"And she creeps along the corridors in the dead of night," he filled in, his voice taunting her. "And I am Julius Caesar."

"Don't be ridiculous!" Marguerite snapped. She hurried away, but he fell into step with her on the path.

"Don't lie. It doesn't suit you," he said.

Marguerite moaned with frustration. "Very well! I wanted to see Mr. Renny's reaction."

Charles barred her progress. "Like we used to frighten the servants at Langston Hall with our hair-raising stories of ghosts."

She pushed his arm, but he did not budge. "Mr. Renny is not a servant. Now get out of my way." He stood so close she could smell the scent of his shaving soap and see the light in his blue eyes. So close he overpowered her senses, and her breathing grew ragged. She despised herself for her reaction to his nearness, but Charles seemed undisturbed. Could nothing rattle him?

He inhaled her fragrance and, like a person starved for beauty, savored every inch of her face, her throat, and her bosom. He was totally intoxicated; his senses reeled and his hands ached to pull her into his embrace.

"Step aside, Charles. I have guests waiting." She tried to move around him, but he parried her.

"Gentlemen ready to stare at your loveliness and pay you bold compliments."

"Like you, then," she said tartly. "Really, Charles, why are you preventing my progress?"

"I want to caution you to take care. Renny ogled you, and Emerson showed uncommon interest," he said, having difficulty stopping himself from crushing her to him. She would only become angry, angrier than she already was. "Renny is not someone whose acquaintance you should cultivate, and the captain—"

"Don't!" She gave him a haughty glance with those iridescent amber eyes he loved so much. "I do not tell you whose friendship to cultivate, Charles. I daresay I'm old enough to make my own decisions."

"Renny has a rotten reputation. He's a rake and a gamester."

"Like most gentlemen I know, then," she said with rising anger. "Renny was an old school friend of Lennox's. I can't very well throw him out of the house when he visits."

"I could do it for you," he drawled, studying her magnificent suppressed rage. Her thunderous expression did not bode well for him, but he didn't care as long as he could remain in such close proximity to her.

"I do not need a bodyguard, Charles. Thank you for not meddling in my affairs. I'm capable of looking after my own house." Her amber eyes shot golden fire. "I don't need another father, and as my friend, you have no right to order my life."

"A friend is not a friend if he's not truthful. I have your best interests at heart. I advise you—"

"If I need your advice, I will ask for it."

"Your manner is much too easy with the gentlemen."

"I suspect you're . . . jealous, Charles. At least you sound like it, peevish and censorious."

"Jealous? Me?" As the truth stung him, he pushed away from the path to let her pass. "That's infamous, Marguerite! Of all the ridiculous—"

"True, nevertheless. Don't meddle." Her hooped gown swept against him on the narrow path as she hurried onto the terrace.

Jealous. The word felt branded on his chest, and damn it all, she was right! He'd put his foot in his mouth again; he cared too bloody much. If only he could not worry so much about her. Something—he didn't quite know what, an indefinable threat, perhaps—hung over her, and her back had the rigid look of deep tension. Surely there was no reason for such strain if she didn't have problems.

He followed her. She wouldn't let him solve her problems—that much was clear—but he would keep an eye on her, and be available if she needed him. Now she was laughing at one of Nick's burlesque jokes as if nothing had happened.

A voice inside said, *Forget her, Charles; push her out of your mind, or you'll go mad with longing.* What other way was there to put an end to his hankering other than to put a bullet through his head? He certainly could not turn off the thoughts or the images of her that riddled his mind night and day.

Feeling old and heavy with disappointment, he joined the trio on the terrace. Delicia was a lovely young woman. Why didn't her beauty and wit speak to his heart? It was a mystery.

"You haven't forgotten the picnic this afternoon at my house, Marguerite?" Nick said, winking.

Disgusting, Charles thought. *Thank God she doesn't respond in kind.*

Nick looked at Charles. "I expect you to attend, too," he said pointedly.

"Thank you for remembering to include me," Charles said sarcastically. He glanced at Marguerite, knowing she would attend. She had thrown herself into the social whirl with gusto after the peace festivities in London. "I wouldn't miss a picnic by the river for anything," he said. He smiled coolly at Marguerite. "Do you want me to escort you, or would that be an imposition?"

She snapped her fan shut and glared at him. "Thank you, but I have made other arrangements."

So neatly cut off, Charles thought. He bowed stiffly. "I'll have to leave. It has been a most unusual morning." Knowing he was rude, he ignored her outstretched hand. Finally her rigid stance softened somewhat.

"Thank you for dealing with the broken branch, Charles. I'm sorry if I snapped at you earlier, but I have so many things on my mind at the moment." Her eyes gleamed, and Charles battled another wild urge to take her in his arms. He tore his gaze away from her lovely face.

He slapped Nick's back. "Keep a bottle of hock cold for me." With a smile and a bow toward Delicia, he left.

Unable to understand her unreasonable ire, Marguerite watched his broad back. He'd only offered to help her, so why couldn't she gratefully accept his kindness? Why did her hackles always rise in Charles's presence? Her personality was not usually that of a prickly hedgehog, rather the opposite. Sometimes she couldn't understand herself at all.

Right before she left for the picnic in the afternoon, Montagu Renny returned. She had expected him, as he must be eager to get his hands on the one thousand pounds she had raised. He walked into the study as if he already owned the house.

Marguerite clenched the goose quill in her hand until it bent and broke. She flung the ruined writing implement on the desk. "The vulture has arrived to pick the bones."

"A very unkind observation, my dear." Renny leaned his slender body across the desk. "I'm only here to collect what is rightfully mine. Call it payment for the work I did for your squeamish husband."

Marguerite pressed her hands against the wooden armrests of the chair. "Where did you hide the body of the sergeant?"

He folded his willowy frame into the well-worn chair opposite the desk. "There's no need for you to know that unsavory detail. Just give me the funds, and I'll take myself off the premises."

"Never to come back!" she said with suppressed rage. "You have to promise that."

A pale smile hovered around his thin lips, and Marguerite sensed his silent elation. He had power in his hands, and he reveled in it every minute. Frightened and powerless, she could only stare at his thin, devious face. His eyes glittered darkly, reminding her of a snake coiled to strike.

"You are a cruel woman, Marguerite. Why would you bar your husband's old friend from the house?"

"You're not my friend. I usually don't invite my enemies to join me for a cup of tea or to dine at my table."

"I would be careful if I were you, Marguerite. *I* don't consider myself your enemy, but if you make me into one, I could be a formidable opponent."

Marguerite stared at his cold face. Sensing that he was right, she subdued the desire to fling an insult at him. There was no need to antagonize him more. She pulled out the desk drawer and extracted a leather folder. In it was a draft on her bank in Lewes. Even though she was cringing inside, she shoved the piece of paper across the gleaming surface of the desk.

"Here. I should think this ought to keep your debtors away for some time, Mr. Renny. You really should find some honorable—*acceptable*—way to make ends meet, and stop harassing me."

As he took the draft and idly folded it, she said, "I would like to know where you buried the sergeant in return for the money."

He studied her for a long time from between his pale eyelashes, and a shiver snaked over her skin.

"Maybe one day, Marguerite, when I find that I can trust you. I have every confidence that one day there won't be any secrets between us."

Marguerite held her breath in frozen dislike as he strolled out of the room.

"I'll be back. Soon," he said, and closed the door softly behind him.

Chapter 6

Alighting from his stallion outside Nick's house, the Hollows, Charles watched as Marguerite arrived on her sorrel mare, the horse's white tail swishing to chase away the flies. Sounds of laughter came from the garden in the back. Nick, dressed only in his shirtsleeves and a chamois waistcoat, came running around the corner of the house carrying a wineglass.

"I've been waiting impatiently, Marguerite," he cried with one of his devilish smiles. Damn the man! Charles thought, but couldn't work up a real grudge.

"Don't I get a greeting, Nick? A kiss on the hand, perhaps?" Charles asked sarcastically.

"Charles, my friend," Nick said from the side of his mouth as he gripped the bridle of Marguerite's horse, "I can't very well greet my rival with the same effusion as I greet the lady of my heart. All is fair in love and war. I would hardly invite my worst rival, but you are my best friend. And I am a fool. I've noticed how Marguerite looks at you—as if she's rediscovering your sterling qualities." He heaved an exaggerated sigh. "I can only be the loser in this game."

Marguerite laughed as Nick helped her down and held her waist much too long, in Charles's opinion. "You two are utterly ridiculous!" she said. "Your rivalry is futile, I assure you."

"What did I say?" Nick addressed his question to Charles. "She admires you greatly."

Charles snorted. "Yes, you hear only what you want to hear, Nick. Truth is, my presence annoys her beyond understanding, and I haven't the faintest clue why."

"Don't speak about me as if I'm not here," she said, and flapped her fan seductively. Charles stifled an urge to crush the damned article that shielded her smiling face from him.

"You're lovely as the brightest cornflower," Nick said, and Charles gritted his teeth.

Marguerite gave an exclamation of pleasure and kissed Nick on the cheek. Charles thought she was indeed lovely in her *robe à la Francaise* of blue cambric, its tight bodice dotted with a row of velvet bows. The skirts dragged on the ground, and she lifted them deftly in her hands and moved forward to greet him. She made a charming picture, an achingly wonderful picture, and he had eyes only for the roundness of her breasts partly concealed by the filmy kerchief crossed over her chest. Her amber eyes glowed with mischief under the wide brim of her bergère straw hat tied under her chin with blue ribbons.

"Charles?"

He stared at her, unable to find his voice. He'd seen her this morning, but a lifetime had passed since then, a lifetime tortured with longing.

He cleared his throat. "You . . . your smile is star bright against the darkness of this world," he said, gripping her hand. If only she would kiss his cheek as she had Nick's, but her smile came no closer. It glittered, taunted him, robbing him of all coherent thought. He inhaled deeply, savoring her perfume. The skin of her hand was velvet soft against his, and he squeezed it.

"Goodness, I think Charles waxes poetic," she said, literally purring. She turned to Nick. "Quite the nicest line I've had composed in my honor."

Nick caught her other hand, his eyes darkening with jealousy. "Charles will always surprise you. A very deep fellow." He shook his fist in mock anger. "You won this round of battles, Charles, but don't believe for a second that you shall win the war."

Marguerite flapped her fan and looked from one gentleman to the other. A half smile lurked on her face. "I don't believe I am a *war.* Anyhow, I don't see that there's a need for battle, surely."

Charles murmured, "Innocent you are not, my dear. I doubt that you're ignorant of the undercurrents, but feigned innocence is endearing nevertheless." Charles pulled her arm through his, leaving Nick behind. "Let's investigate the picnic hampers. I'm starving."

The party had arrived to the picnic spot down by the Cuckmere River that bordered Nick's property. The water flowed beneath boughs of weeping willow and meandered around boulders and tussocks, reeds and clumps of alders. A capricious breeze danced in from the water, and the grass was a springy green carpet underfoot. Charles's stomach rumbled as he watched Nick's lackeys spread out blankets and arrange chairs for the ladies.

Heaps of crusty rolls of white bread surrounded plates of cheeses and spicy sausages. Attached to strings, wine bottles cooled in the river, baskets of cold chicken sent out a mouthwatering scent, and Charles couldn't wait to taste the salmon in aspic centered in his vision. Cakes soaked in rum and tarts filled with preserves and custard beckoned hungry guests.

Charles leaned back in the grass feeling content—if hungry—and closed his eyes. Marguerite was near, near enough so that he could hear the sweet cadence of her voice as she chatted with Delicia and Emmy. He could rest here all day as long as he was allowed to listen to the lilt of her voice, the same voice that sometimes came to him in his dreams.

Nick flung himself down beside Charles. "Here, a cold glass of hock, saved especially for you, my friend."

Charles pushed back his hat and cocked an eyebrow. "Not laced with poison, I hope."

Nick laughed. "Hmmm, you just put a great idea into my head. It would be one way to get rid of you."

Charles studied Nick's face, noticing the unquiet, the longing under the schooled facade of gaiety. Nick was a consummate actor, and sometimes Charles wondered what really went on behind that devilish smile. Whatever it was, Nick wanted to hide it at all costs. Charles touched his glass to Nick's. "Your health, old fellow. Are you hankering after the fair Marguerite, or what is that dark shadow in your eyes?"

Nick's features congealed in an all-concealing smile. "Nothing, Charles, except that I'm somewhat worried about Marguerite living alone without male protection. Besides the smuggling, there are spies and who knows what else. Violent death," he threw in as an afterthought.

Charles grimaced. "You're thinking of Sergeant Rule's sudden disappearance. That was about a year ago. He could have deserted and moved abroad, as far as we know."

"Emerson is convinced he didn't. Rule was not a coward, and he liked his work. He was a damned good soldier, and honorable to his fingertips."

They were interrupted as the ladies oohed and aahed over the feast set out before them, and Nick hurried to pile food on plates and send them via the footmen to the fair members of the company.

Charles helped himself, and had just lifted his glass when he noticed Marguerite's gaze resting on him. His heart jolted as if struck by a hard blow when she smiled. That smile had always been his undoing. . . .

Goddess of the sun, fair radiance,
Let me embrace you, my fire.
Light spilling against me, over, around,
But never through,
Never to fill me, my dear,
Until I can call you my own
Until you are me and
I am you.

The verse came to him, like water running and giggling over pebbles in the river, then was gone, leaving nothing but an aching longing behind. He couldn't return her smile. He averted his gaze and stared at the slowly moving river. Sometimes he wished he could cut out his heart and throw it away.

The food tasted delicious, and he drank too much wine. Nick smiled his devilish smile and flirted shamelessly. Charles clenched his fist, but somehow he could not see himself punching Nick's jaw. Angry at himself, Charles got up from the soft grass and moved away from the company.

"I'll get another bottle of wine," he shouted as an excuse, and slid down the slope to the river's edge. Here he could not hear her laugh or see her sparkling amber eyes, her radiance. But what did it matter? He was trapped in the silken, suffocating trap of unrequited love, and he'd been a fool to accept Nick's invitation to the picnic. Torture it was, and he deliberately put himself in the painful, squeezing grip of it. *Damn it all to hell!*

He found an old stick and saved a beetle that floundered in a puddle on a lily leaf. How had it gotten there in the first place? The brown insect scurried under a heap of rotten leaves at the base of a willow tree. Charles followed the natural path between the swaying tussocks. He watched a parcel of ducks squabbling and quacking as if their voices had to be heard and the river claimed as their own.

Slashing at the tall grass with his stick, he went to where the river curved around an island. He found a narrow strip of sand and a boulder to sit on. The sounds of the guests had faded. Here he could hear only the incessant rustling, chirps, and sighs of nature, and see the wind play in the reeds as it had for all eternity. He sank into the sounds and sought to cool his frustration. The water made lazy patterns, swirled and rolled over itself. He had no idea how long he lingered in the peaceful spot.

The hiss of fabric against grass, the crunch of boots on sand came to him. He was reluctant to turn around and learn who had arrived.

The scent of her rose perfume gave Marguerite away before he saw her. Emotion gripped his heart fiercely, and he stood. Throwing away the stick, he faced her, towered over her much shorter body.

"What do you want? To torment me, Marguerite?"

Her amber eyes were dark, unsmiling. "Torment you? Why would I want that?"

He crushed her to him, seeing the rapid lift and fall of her breasts, feeling, *absorbing* the softness of her, touching the pliant arch of her back. He leaned down and nuzzled her tense throat so vulnerably offered to him. "God, can't you see, Marguerite? Can't you feel my frustration?" He growled and pressed her so hard against himself that she must feel the aching tightness in his loins and the wild pounding of his heart.

He nipped her throat, forced hard kisses to her soft earlobe and throat even though she struggled and pounded against his chest. He gripped her fists in one of his hands and squeezed tight, wanting to show her that his patience had boundaries.

She gasped, her eyes widening in shock. "Charles!"

He grasped her neck with his other hand and kissed her hard, forcing his tongue through the barrier of her teeth, tasting the silken softness of her mouth. She whimpered under his onslaught, then went limp against him. He let go of her hands.

He could not stop himself from caressing the inviting round breasts so carefully concealed by bodice and kerchief. All he could think of was ripping the fabric apart and catching the warm flesh in his hand, caressing and savoring, but he didn't.

He mauled the honeyed sweetness of her mouth, and cared not if she responded. He could so easily toss her onto the grass and take his fill of her, perhaps slake his burning thirst for her body and her mind. One would cancel the other, and it would be over. He would be purged.

She gave him a hard, stinging slap to his face. It only incensed him further. She slapped him again. He slowly lifted his face and stared at her flushed cheeks and furious eyes. Her frivolous hat had fallen to her back, the blue ribbons clinging to her throat. Her hair hung in disarray, and her lips were swollen. His longing to kiss her again was so strong it took all his willpower to respect her rejection.

"Oh, God!" was all he could groan.

"What are you doing, Charles? Unhand me immediately!"

Charles took a deep, shaky breath and eased his convulsive grip on her shoulders. He dropped his hands to his sides at last, leaden weights that trembled.

She looked at him from beneath lowered lashes. "Really, Charles! This is an outrage." She righted her bodice and straightened the kerchief across her bosom. With an angry tug, she pushed the hat down on top of her head. "Aren't you going to apologize?"

He took a deep breath and folded his arms over his chest. Numb, yet wildly alive inside, he only stared at her, memorizing every expression. "No. I don't regret any of it. I've wanted to kiss you for a long time, and you must have been aware of my admiration."

She swished her wide, voluminous skirts around and turned her back to him. "You're wasting your time, and that is a fact with which you'll have to live."

"So wholly unmoved you are not, Marguerite." He expected her to leave in a huff, but she only glared at him over her shoulder. His loins throbbed with unfulfilled desire, and he felt an urge to shout his fury and throw something far into the river. Her, perhaps. Or himself. He eased his tense body back down onto the boulder, and she stood silently watching him.

"Do you remember, Marguerite? We used to play down by the river farther north. Always something new to discover with each season: red leaves floating toward the sea in the autumn, tadpoles in the spring, rustling dry reeds in the winter that could be braided into a wreath. Do you remember? You made one and tied bunches of holly to it for your mother at Christmas one year. We promised each other devotion, Marguerite. I can still smell the blood that we mingled. I didn't want the small wound to heal, as it reminded me of our sacred promise. I kept picking at the scab so that it would bleed again." He slanted a glance at her, and suffered the depth of his pain upon seeing her expression so cold. "You didn't, though, did you? Your wound healed and you forgot."

"I thought I was rather courageous to cut my finger with your knife," she said wryly. "But I was prepared to hurt myself for you."

"But it meant nothing to you, not really. You cared nothing for me. You married—"

"Charles! You knew my parents. My father had a volatile temper, and he accepted no one else's opinion. He never respected me, as he never respected my mother. He treated me as a burden of which to rid himself, and my mother as a burden with which he had to live. He barely tolerated her. He tried to control everything and everyone around him."

Her voice rose with suppressed anger. "I meant nothing, and when Lennox proposed, Father failed to ask if I wanted to marry the Scotsman. It was a good match, and therefore I had to accept. Mother was kind, and she had her own ideas, but Father ruled her with an iron will. I despised her for her weakness, but I later understood that she made the most of what she had. She made her own life in her prison. She accepted her obsequious position even though she loathed my father for his callousness."

"You were free and spirited, so happy, Marguerite. You were the strongest person I knew. You were always up to any lark, and when I didn't invent them, you did. Remember how we learned to swim in this river? You wore only your shift. If your father had seen you, he would have whipped us both."

Marguerite sat down in the sand beside him and pulled her knees to her chin. He caught a glimpse of her slender ankle. "Yes, Father considered you a bad influence on me, said you gave me ideas that were unsuitable for a young woman."

"Woman? Man? We weren't defined as such, even if we'd reached a certain maturity; we were more like spirits, one with nature and the beauty around us. Today I always struggle to find that again. Every day was golden sunshine and masses of flowers. I don't remember any rainy days, do you? Winter was a landscape that inspired awe and respect, but it was an icy kingdom of discovery and adventure. The snow was magic until it melted on the knees of my breeches and froze the fabric to ice."

Marguerite laughed, her cheeks tinted with pink at the excitement of finally remembering the good years of their childhood. Charles could not take his eyes off her delicate features, as if he had to memorize every curve, every nuance of her expression.

"There was one winter especially," she said, "when blizzards whined down chimneys and covered the ground with tall drifts of snow. When the storms ended, a white, blinding sea remained. The sun held little warmth, and the sky was robin's-egg blue. The wind had made a mountain, and we played on top of it, pushing each other down until our boots were filled with snow and our clothes soaked through. I hated wet feet and frozen fingers, but the game went on until someone fetched us inside. We could not stop." She sighed. "Now we complain if the wind nips a bit too hard, or if a single snowflake floats to the ground. Where did the excitement and the wonder go?"

"Familiarity breeds contempt," he said, and tore a piece of grass out of a tussock in the sand. He chewed on it thoughtfully. "I believe we have to work at our happiness. Nothing comes easily anymore. I look upon the Meadow with jaded, empty eyes. I don't look upon my home as a place of excitement and adventure. I see a dilapidated house that has to be saved from ruin. It costs a mint to keep it from falling down around my ears.''

"We never thought about such things when we were children. Everything would go on the same forever. There was no question of funds or repairs.''

He took her hand gently and braided his fingers with hers. She didn't resist. ''Do you long for your childhood home, Marguerite?''

"Jerry and his family live there now. It's not the same since Mother died. The house will never be what it was, the home that you describe. 'Tis no longer important, all behind me now. I'm a different person altogether. Besides, I rather like my freedom as a widow. I have no desire to place myself under my brother's despotic rule. He's quite as impossible as Father.''

"Do you look upon all gentlemen as potential rulers?''

"I am free only when I can decide my own fate, and I have no intention of wearing the shackle of a wedding band. Marriage stifles me—I'm forced to surrender to another's will, no matter if the will is brilliant or skewed or ignorant.''

Charles chewed on the grass. It tasted both sweet and bitter. ''I should hope love could rule a marriage, let it grow in all directions.''

"You're a romantic, dear Charles, always have been and always will be,'' she said matter-of-factly. ''When the romance is over, a lifelong tug-of-war begins.''

"You're so very cynical. Still young and so disillusioned. Clearly you have not experienced love in its depth and glory. If you had, you would be willing to work at maintaining that special tenderness.'' Charles traced the veins of her hand, her skin translucent and milky white. He yearned to kiss the softness, to cup her hand to his heart, but restrained his urge.

"Do you know what you are talking about, Charles?'' she said with a hint of irritation. ''You haven't shown any inclination to plunge into matrimony and put your idealistic words to the test. Reality is so very different from your romantic dreams.''

"I won't settle for less than fulfilling my highest goal, to make real my most sacred dream. I won't marry unless I can wed the lady my heart has chosen." He did not dare to look at her, but he could feel her searching glance.

"So you believe one loves only once?"

"Yes ... There are different kinds of love, but only one other half of oneself, one's true mate."

Her voice sounded thinner, almost tortured. "And what if you never meet that other half? Is one doomed to live alone?"

"Or settle for a lesser love, companionship, maybe friendship." Charles had the sensation that he was burning the bridges behind him as he bared his deepest thoughts to her. He didn't want to be her adviser, her friend; he wanted to be her lover, and savor all the intimacy that came with it. He stopped touching her hand and stood. Righting his waistcoat and adjusting the lace-edged cuffs of his white shirt, he looked down at her upturned face.

"I'm not the local vicar, or your confidante. If you need advice, find someone else. I have no patience with your cynical views on marriage."

He assisted her to rise, and she brushed off her skirts. "You started the whole conversation, or did you forget that fact?" she asked with some asperity.

"I didn't see myself as your adviser, but you sought me out. If you recall, I wasn't eager to talk, not at first."

Her eyes held a gleam of anger. "No ... you quickly tried to take advantage of me. Just like other gentlemen. Despite your claims that love means everything, you're no different from any man who pushes himself on me against my will."

He bowed stiffly. "I regret my rash action. I'm sorry if I offended you, but I wouldn't be so harsh in my judgment if I were you. My desire could be taken as a compliment if you cared to look a little past your righteous indignation."

She stared at him for a long moment, her eyes searching the depths of his soul. His heart pounded, but he felt dead and hollow under her hard scrutiny.

"Be that as it may," she said, "I had no desire for your ardent attention at the time. There is no hope for our union, Charles, and I want you to remember that."

He died some more inside and his heartbeat seemed to hover on the brink of stopping. It tottered once, as if hesitant, then slowed down to its regular rhythm. "I shall not forget."

They joined the party together, and Nick gave him a dark look. "I thought you would fetch another bottle of wine, old fellow."

"Yes . . . I forgot, but my lapse shall now be remedied." Charles went down to the river and pulled out another bottle of hock—cold, cold as Marguerite's heart. *Damn all women; damn them all to hell!* He was lucky not to have become ensnared in the wiles of any of them over the years. There had not been a lack of opportunity, but his heart had already been given away to Marguerite. *Fool!* He was such a damned fool for loving a woman he could not have. She was right; he was a witless romantic.

Chapter 7

Stephen, the good-natured Lord Ormond, had joined the party in her absence, as had Carey and Francesca McLendon. They were eating bread and drinking wine. Marguerite looked with envy at her friends' happy faces as they sat closely together, as if glued into one piece. "What are you talking about so animatedly? I could hear your laughter a mile away."

Nick smiled a roguish smile that made women's hearts jolt with pleasure—at least it did hers. "We're talking about smugglers, spies, and ghosts. And right now we're discussing the rise in crime over the last twelve months, what with the Midnight Bandit continuing his raids against wealthy travelers. Impudent scoundrel! Methinks he would have gathered a large enough fortune to retire from his lawless activities by now."

"His latest poem has come to my ears," Emilia Wetherby said, and flapped her fan coyly. "One of my cronies' cousins was robbed by the bandit and remembered the verse he delivered while aiming his pistols at the coach: 'Traveler alone, travelers of riches / Despair ye not / As the Midnight Bandit will stop the witches of greed / From boiling your hearts in their pot.' "

Nick rolled on the grass with laughter.

"Terrible," Delicia Leverton cried, and stared wide-eyed at her stepbrother, Nick. "Who in the world would have the insolence to assault travelers with such drivel? Do you know anyone with a penchant for bad poetry, Nicholas?"

Nick sat up and mopped his brow with his napkin. His measuring gaze wandered from face to face as his mirth died down, and Marguerite had the sensation that the Midnight Bandit might be any one of the male members of the party. No, she must be imagining things! Nick's gaze rested on Charles last, then moved away.

Marguerite suppressed an incredulous laugh. Charles would not voluntarily hold up coaches at night. He disliked fights, always had, even though he could handle a sword very well. Pistols for robbing coaches? *Hardly!* The thought was too preposterous to contemplate.

"The verse might be amateurish, but quite sweet, in my opinion," Marguerite said. "After all, the bandit gallantly rescues the wealthy from their own greed—a point in his favor, surely."

"A redeeming quality only if he saves his own heart from greed, which is hardly likely," Carey McLendon said. "He pockets the spoils."

With a smile, Marguerite looked at each of the curious faces around her. "Have we all met him and spoken with him at some time? As I haven't been out of mourning for very long, I have not danced with him. Have any of you ladies mayhap placed your hand trustingly in his during a country dance, or faced him in the minuet?"

"I note the chiding tone of your voice, Marguerite," Charles said, his eyes never leaving her face. "Do you think the highwayman's antics are no more than idle pranks, the pastime of a gentleman?"

Due to the intensity of his gaze, a seductive warmth washed over her skin, and her heart made a quick somersault. "No . . . it is clear that he is a thief and a scoundrel. I do not condone such crimes, even though he treats the ladies in a gentlemanly fashion.''

'' 'Tis revolting that you would find anything favorable at all to say about the villain,'' Charles said with a snort of disgust. ''I'm surprised you can mention his name without swooning with fear.''

''Not all females are the fainting type,'' Marguerite replied tartly.

''She's right,'' Nick said, ''but such ladies are a rarity.'' He leaned back on his elbows in the grass. ''Your sisters are rather the opposite, I find.''

''The cynic speaks,'' Marguerite chided. ''You have much too low an opinion of us poor ladies, Nick. Too high expectations that we cannot fulfill. You'll never find someone to marry if you keep judging women so harshly.''

''I have never judged *you* unfavorably,'' he said with one of his reckless smiles.

Flustered to be the recipient of so much male attention in one day, Marguerite looked away. Mayhap it wasn't too late to find a gentleman who would love her for herself and not treat her like a piece of old furniture. Perhaps she still had some attractiveness left, even though Lennox had done everything in his power to leech all animation out of her. To be honest, she yearned desperately for love and romance, but on her own terms, not those dictated by a husband or a possessive lover. *Possessive.*

She glanced at Charles from the corner of her eye. If she returned an ounce of his ardor, he would devour her. She abhorred the idea even though something about him touched her deeply. Curiously enough, they shared so much even now, after so many years. She'd found earlier that she could talk to him, and he understood her, but she didn't want to be burned by his fire.

''I daresay poetry is never wasted, even when delivered by the Midnight Bandit,'' Emilia Wetherby said, and twitched her

rose silk skirts to chase away a bee. ''You should not berate
Marguerite for appreciating poetry, Nick.''

Everyone laughed, and the strange tension left the air. Marguerite smiled at the older woman, and the day that had held
little promise was now filled with delight. She looked at each
of her friends to see if they shared her happiness, and noted
the warm speculation in Charles's eyes.

Charles had been struck with a brilliant idea. *Of course! How
simple.* She loved romance as much as the next lady, and she
adored poetry. He did not approve of her defense of the Midnight Bandit, but let the bandit help him open her heart, tear
down the brick wall she had raised against himself and other
gentlemen. He saw no other way to enter her heart than by
stealth.

Two weeks later a gentleman dressed in black, including the
black mask covering his face, rode a hired black horse out of
the woods north of Hayward's Heath. The voluminous cloak
billowed around him like the wings of a dark angel, a threat
to all travelers. A dark cocked hat shielded the slits of his eyes,
and the hooves of his stallion had been tied with rags so as to
silence the gallop. Attached to the saddle were two loaded
pistols. He wore his hallmark white gloves, the only bright spot
on his person.

The night had the color of pitch. It was moonless, starless;
rain clouds roiling over the treetops bore fierce gusts of wind
that frightened birds off their perches. The sounds of a coach,
leather squeaking, harness jingling, springs creaking, came to
his ears.

A coach was coming around the bend, the horse cantering
despite the darkness of the night and the badly rutted road. It
was as if the nag knew the foolishness of being out at night
courting danger, and wished itself off the road as soon as
possible. Horses often had a sixth sense for peril.

His white gloves tightened around the reins, and he nudged the stallion forward with the heels of his boots.

Marguerite wished she had waited for Nick to escort her home, but he'd been involved in a card game and she'd been reluctant to disturb him. Still, she'd lingered for half an hour, then sought him again, only to discover that he'd gone out, and would return in a moment.

She suffered from a fierce headache. A cold, damp cloth on her brows and a soft pillow would soothe her pain. She longed to be alone after a tiring if exhilarating night of dancing and chatting with her friends. Her feet ached, and her head pounded more with every breath.

There might be a storm brewing in the air. She had always been sensitive to changes in the atmosphere. Wind whipped even now, shaking and rattling the coach.

Nick would be furious when he discovered that she'd left without him. He had preached about the dangers on the road all the way to the ball. As if she were completely helpless. She grimaced. *How annoying!* A nursemaid was the last thing she needed, and Nick reminded her of one.

She thought she heard a crash, and the coachman on the box cried out.

Listening tensely, Marguerite was pushed forward, then tossed back against the squabs. The coach slowed, wobbled, then was still. The horse pawed the ground, neighing in agitation. "What in the world? We're so close to home." Swearing under her breath, she pulled down the window. The wind tugged at her hair, and she could feel the curls fall away from the pins. "What is going on?"

"I think we got stuck in a mud hole," the coachman shouted. "There's a dip in the road right here, and the ditch is overflowing after the last rain."

She looked down saw and nothing but a darker area under the coach. The coachman got down. He slogged through the mud and opened the door. "Milady, I think the wheel is mired in the ditch. I took too sharp a turn in the curve."

"Can we lift it back onto the road?" With the coachmen's help, Marguerite stepped to the ground, carefully keeping the hem of her gown away from the mud. Cold water seeped through her slippers, and she cursed silently. She didn't know if she could afford to buy a new pair.

The coachman held the carriage lantern aloft to spread some light. They studied the wheel from the grassy verge of the ditch.

"If we had a sturdy branch, we could use it as a lever to lift the wheel while the horse pulls," Marguerite said, and chewed on her bottom lip. Perhaps she should have waited for Nick after all. . . . Her thought was interrupted by the sound of a horse.

"Someone is coming," she said. "We must ask for assistance."

The coachman scratched his grizzled head in thought. "Depends who rides at this time of night." He set down the lantern and went in search of the loaded pistol Marguerite knew he had under his seat.

The rider came to a halt, a figure in black, except for the hands. White gloves gesticulated, sketching a bow, but the rider did not step down.

She gasped, spellbound by the gloves. "Oh, no! It's *you*. The Midnight Bandit." She closed her mouth with a snap as fear rolled through her body in a great wave. She had never anticipated that she would be the victim of the bandit. Never in her wildest dreams.

"What seems to be the problem?" he asked, his voice low and gravelly.

She gulped, her hands trembling. "An accident," she said breathlessly. "If you would be so kind, sir, as to help us get the wheel back on the road."

Silence fell over the area, a dense blanket of unasked questions. Marguerite tasted her fear, sour like bile. Her heart slammed against her ribs so hard she thought it might stop.

He jumped down from the horse. He was unarmed, she noticed. Every detail of his tall, lithe body etched itself on her memory. She quaked.

"Are you going to rob me now?" she asked.

"I wouldn't rob a lady in distress," he said. "Perhaps later, when I've helped you back onto the road."

"You're too kind." Marguerite wondered if the coachman would slam the bandit over the head with the pistol. He crept along the side of the coach, completely concealed in the shadows.

"Put your hands up where I can see them, sirrah," the old coachman growled. "Then lie down on the ground with your arms behind you." He addressed Marguerite. "Find something to tie his wrists with."

Then everything happened so fast that Marguerite could only stare with her mouth open. The bandit swung out his arm in a powerful arc, smashing the pistol out of the coachman's hand. It landed with a splash in the ditch.

"My intention was to help you, not lose my life," the bandit said with a snarl. He stared at the coachman, who cowered, his hands clasped to his head. "Find something to use as a lever, and be quick about it!"

The servant loped off toward the woods. Marguerite noticed the authority of the criminal's voice. A gentleman. There was no doubt about it.

He stepped toward her, and she flinched. His teeth gleamed in the light of the lantern. "Afraid, are you? No need for that, milady."

She breathed deeply to calm her fear. "You know who I am?"

He did not answer, only stared deeply into her eyes. His eyes were liquid onyx in the weak light. He wore an elegant powdered bagwig as if he, too, had attended a ball. "Do not be afraid."

She fingered the double strand of pearls that clasped her neck. He would ask for them next—the gift her grandmother had received on her wedding day, then passed on to Marguerite's mother. The pearls had been given to Marguerite after her nuptial ceremony.

She took a deep, trembling breath. "As you have discovered, I'm traveling . . . alone, but another party is right behind me with outriders," she lied.

"Alone?" he echoed, his teeth gleaming white in another smile. He smelled of leather and of hair powder as he towered over her. "That was very foolish of you," he purred.

"What I hear is that you're gallant to the ladies, not a ravisher of innocents," she blurted out defiantly. What if the rumors were untrue? What if he thought that she should be the exception? She had nothing, no one to protect her. The pistol lay useless in the ditch.

She unclasped her necklace. "Here. Take them."

He slowly took the pearls from her and held them up to the light. The cloak billowed around him. "You're the first person who has offered her valuables without being asked."

"I have nothing else to offer."

His gaze raked over her. "I think you're wrong on that score, milady. You will make some gentleman very happy."

He stepped forward, and she forced herself not to cringe as he lifted his gloved hands and clasped the necklace around her neck. "There. The pearls look lovely against your creamy skin, milady."

"You call me milady," she said, touching the pearls. "How do you know my title?"

"Simple. A lady is a lady. I will not call you other names." He smiled, and Marguerite's heart flipped over. Her fear slowly melted as he bent down to study the wheel. Clearly he had no intention of ravishing her or stealing her jewelry. She studied him. Handsome broad shoulders, a quick step, muscular arms, a roguish grin. He was romantic and bold, all that the previous victims had said—and more.

The coachman returned carrying a thick branch. He flung it

to the ground in front of the highwayman. Marguerite noticed the servant's frustration.

"Well," the bandit said in his gravelly voice. "Better get to work then. When I tell you to pull, make the horse move forward." He dug the end of the branch into the mud and under the steel-rimmed wheel. Jumping to the other side of the narrow ditch, he tested the strength of the branch by leaning on it. Marguerite pushed against the other wheel as hard as she could. Her hands were slippery with mud, but better that than spending the rest of the night in the company of the Midnight Bandit.

"Pull!" he shouted, and put all his weight onto the branch. A creak, a movement, then the wheel turned reluctantly, sliding over the branch. The horse struggled, finally pulling the wheel back onto the road. The bandit lifted the branch and flung it into the woods. "There, it did the trick." He sauntered to Marguerite's side. "Happy now?"

She held her muddy hands away from her gown. "Yes. I can't thank you enough, and now—"

Her words were torn from her abruptly as he gripped her hands and pulled her into his arms. She smelled a faint aroma of wine on his breath. His mouth covered hers for a sharp, breath-stealing moment—hard and soft all at once, punishing, yet wildly exhilarating. Warm and pliant, his tongue roamed over hers, titillated her senses and ignited her yearning for more intimate play. God, he tasted so good, and his body felt so strong against hers. He was a dangerous man. His hands were icy manacles around her wrists. She struggled to free herself. How could she enjoy herself in the arms of criminal?

A groan burst from him as he lessened his grip. He stared intently at her face, then lifted her as easily as if she were a feather. He moved to the coach and settled her inside. "Go home. If I meet you again, I don't know if I can act in a gentlemanly fashion. Next time I will ravish you."

He slammed the door shut, and the carriage rocked as the coachman leaped onto the box. The bandit laughed and sent a kiss on his fingertips through the open window. "I would offer a poem, but your kiss made me speechless.'' He held his hand to his heart and bowed from the waist.

Disgusted at her own sensuous reaction to his amorous assault, she wiped her mouth.

He laughed softly. ''Admit that you liked it. A secret tryst. No aphrodisiac is as potent as secrecy. Farewell, goddess of my dreams.''

Without another word, he jumped onto his black horse and disappeared into the woods.

''I did not like it!'' she cried after him, and kept wiping her mouth. But it didn't help much. His kiss had stirred her longing so easily, and she loathed herself for opening herself even in the smallest way to a highwayman. A criminal. Yet he was so charming, so virile.

''Did he hurt you, milady?'' the coachman cried through the hatch.

Marguerite sighed and pressed her hands to her pounding heart. ''No, he only gave me a scare. I thought he usually perpetrated his foul deeds closer to London.''

''No, milady, he appears on all the roads in the south counties. A rascal, and as slipp'ry as an eel.''

''Let's not tarry here. He might come back.'' She pulled up the window and closed the curtains.

The only other time she'd been this upset was when Lennox and Montagu Renny had killed the sergeant on her front steps. She also felt shame, as if somehow she attracted such sordid experiences. She was the first of her circle to actually encounter the Midnight Bandit, and somehow it didn't surprise her in the slightest. She lived with a rather large dosage of bad luck, or was her fate tied to violence and danger? As if she secretly thrived on it.

Nonsense! She vowed to herself that she would not speak about the Midnight Bandit to anyone. Shivering, she forced herself to think about other things, but she kept coming back to the searing heat of his kiss.

Chapter 8

One week later at the McLendons' ball at Burgess Hill, Charles wondered why Marguerite looked so sad and lost in thought. She was part of the small group of friends the McLendons had invited for dinner before the ball. She ate without appetite and spoke little. He wished he could bring the impish smile back to her eyes, but she looked at him as though she cared for none of his scintillating conversations.

Charles sensed her distress and could only speculate what had brought on her apathy. He watched her leave early, escorted by Nick.

Charles had thought about her a lot since their conversation by the river; tonight would be the night he put his devious plan into action.

Two hours later, he sneaked along the brick wall surrounding Lennox House and came upon the loose brick he'd discovered at an earlier visit. It was very close to the gate; he saw no difficulty for Marguerite to retrieve the letters. All she had to do was walk down the gravel drive and remove the brick.

He touched the sealed letter in his pocket. Rain dripped

from the brim of his hat, and the cloak hung sodden from his shoulders. The rain would soak him through; he'd better hurry. He remembered the letter word for word. The lines hadn't come easily. He'd struggled for the right tone. As he watched the shadows around the stables for any movement of servants, he saw his scribbles before his inner eye. He'd had to change his handwriting so that Marguerite wouldn't recognize it.

Dearest lady,

I know your name, and your beauty is admired in circles far greater than you can imagine. I have seen you; I have touched you. Now I yearn, crave, hunger for your caress. Your smile is a beacon in my life of darkness.

Another touch, a kiss—I would pay a fortune for them, but I know they cannot be bought. Those are yours to bestow on the fortunate gentleman who can capture your heart, angel of my dreams. Some will try to ensnare you; some have tried, and you shy away as if your wings have been singed by fire. I know. I have watched you. I am a humble man who would grovel at your feet, would you only send a smile in my direction. My love for you is stronger than the most sinuous rope across a bottomless chasm. If you cut it, I will fall, and forever be lost in darkness. Please respond. I want to hear your heart beat against my own, with no barrier to separate us.

The Midnight Bandit.

He put the letter in the dark hole and replaced the loose brick. The wall smelled of damp moss, and his boots trampled the soggy grass as he headed toward the front entrance of the dark house. How would she react? Would she believe that the bandit had written it? Was his letter too strongly worded? At least every expression was honest, and she would sense that.

The last thing he had to do was to insert the note of instructions between the door and the frame. He'd written it earlier, sealed it with wax, scrawled Marguerite's name across the front. He wished he could see her expression when she read the message. He could only pray that she would not fling it into the fire with a snarl of displeasure. She wouldn't. Not if she was as romantic as she claimed.

Marguerite got up early, and dressed. From the window in her study she watched the listless rain and the mist diffusing the lines of her garden. She'd been going over her mountain of bills until the wee hours of the morning, trying to come to grips with her imminent bankruptcy.

After she'd paid Montagu Renny, there hadn't been any funds left over for the bills. If she sold off everything except the house and the land, she might manage to clear her debts. It would be for the best.

She glanced at the shadowy corners of the study and the white ceiling with its grimy plaster moldings. She'd never liked the timeworn house with its brooding, dead air. If she sold the whole property and invested the proceeds wisely, she, Pru, and Sophie would be settled for life. There wouldn't be much to live on, but Marguerite had learned to turn every coin when Lennox showed the miserly side of his character. She needed so little. That thought didn't quite ring true, and she glanced at her royal blue sack gown that once had been the height of fashion. Now the jeweled blue had faded, and the fine lace at her bodice and at the elbow-length sleeves had a gray tinge, even though it had been laundered with the strongest lye soap. Soon it would hang in tatters if she wasn't careful. No, she could not bear the thought of wearing ragged gowns. It wasn't all vanity; it went against her grain to cut down on quality, be it her clothing or other items she considered important, like well-made pieces of furniture and fine carpets that would age gracefully. The rags on her floors would not fetch much, but it would be a relief to get rid of them. She would be happier away from all the dark memories.

And she would order some new gowns today.

A knock sounded on the door, and Betsy entered with a tray. She poured coffee from a silver pot and set down a plate filled with slices of bread that she'd roasted on the hearth in the kitchen and a pot of jam—last year's raspberries. She touched a slightly damp letter on the tray. "Milady, I found this stuck in the door this mornin'. 'Ave no idea who delivered it."

Marguerite stiffened as visions of Montagu's leering face went through her head. No, she'd already paid him! He couldn't demand more. He just couldn't. If he did, she didn't know what she would do.

"Thank you," Marguerite said with a shiver, but she did not touch the letter. First she drank some coffee to fortify herself against possible bad news. Betsy hovered, no doubt curious about the contents of the letter. When she'd left, Marguerite glanced at the handwriting on the front—not one she recognized. She slowly turned it over and studied the seal. The wax blob held no insignia. Hands trembling, she tore it open. If it was from Montagu Renny, she had her own blistering message for him!

She read aloud, "At the gate, loose brick on the left side, fourth brick from the bottom, two in. There's a letter waiting." Puzzled, she frowned.

Was this a new trick of Renny's, or who else was playing games with her? She wouldn't find out if she didn't go down to the gate and look behind the brick. Even though every fiber of her rebelled against the idea, her curiosity had been tickled.

She finished her breakfast in a hurry and went to fetch her old cloak. She pulled up the hood to protect her head from the rain and slunk out the door. Loath to reveal to the servants her errand at the gate, she was grateful for the mist that swallowed her as soon as she left the protection of the house.

The fog transformed the grounds into an alien landscape of vague shapes and floating tendrils of moisture. She easily found the loose brick; it should be mended posthaste. Extracting the letter, she tore one of her short nails, and she moaned at the pain. Sucking on the digit, she turned the letter over and read her name written in a forceful hand.

Her heart in her throat, she leaned against the wall and tore it open, reading the surprising lines. She blushed, realizing this was the first love letter she had ever received, and it was signed *The Midnight Bandit.*

The highwayman had taken a fancy to her after only one illicit kiss. Her cheeks burned with embarrassment. She went through the events of the last weeks—the balls, the bucolic picnics, the dinner parties—to remember if she'd seen anyone remotely like him. No one came to mind, but he'd been wearing a wig and a face mask.

He wrote that he'd watched her. Surely he hadn't been invited to the same events?

She sucked in a deep breath. Was it too farfetched to suspect that one of her friends was the infamous highwayman? She laughed out loud at the presumptuous idea. But if her suspicion had substance, who could it be?

Some of her gentleman friends were spirited enough—Nick and Charles, for instance—but the bandit could as easily be someone like Montagu Renny, who had said on more than one occasion that he harbored tender feelings toward her. *No!* She couldn't bear the thought of Renny in the guise of the romantic villain.

She read the letter again, and it touched her heart as nothing had for years. But why would the highwayman single her out? Perhaps he would reveal his identity to her in due course. She promised herself she would keep a close eye on her friends in the future.

This clandestine way of communication titillated her, fueled her desire for romance. She would respond, mayhap not in such flighty words of passion, but a reply explaining that her curiosity had been touched. She folded the letter and stuck it inside her bodice. To get out of the rain, she ran back to the house. She shook the water off her cloak and closeted herself in the study.

Sharpening the nib of a goose quill, she felt the edges of the letter rub her breast with every breath. The paper felt cool and slightly damp, belying the heat of the emotion written so eloquently.

As her heartbeat accelerated, her chest seemed to expand to make room for the wealth of feelings flowing through her. After all these years of a withered existence with Lennox, this message hinted of something new, a promise, even if it never came to more than a romance by letter. In fact, she doubted she would ever link her life to that of a criminal—even if he were a gentleman. But a flirtation by letter fired her senses.

She racked her brain for a suitable reply.

Bandit,

You have taken a shameless liberty in writing such a message, gallant villain of the roads, and I should berate you. I enjoy, however, your spirit of adventure. Your words of admiration brought a smile to my lips and dispelled my loneliness in this dreary time of rain and mist.

It is as if you can see into my heart and read all my longings. But, dear sir, I am in control of my own destiny, and no romantic verse of yours will make me succumb to your blandishments and imagine myself in love. You are forever the scoundrel and I'm one of your victims, and in no other guise shall we meet. If we do, I shall only turn a cold shoulder, as I cannot condone your robbing of innocent people.

Marguerite

When the ink had dried, she sealed the letter. As she was about to go back outside with her reply, Sophie entered the room. She looked pinch-faced, her eyes surrounded with dark shadows. Her hair had been raked back into a tight bun and covered with a plain mobcap.

"Good morning, Sophie," Marguerite said pleasantly. "You don't look like you slept very well."

"I think the ghost walked in the night. I heard her moaning and sobbing, dragging her feet."

"Oh, I didn't hear anything. I'm sorry you can't sleep. Nevertheless, I'm glad you're here. We need to have a discussion about the future, and it cannot wait, as we'll have to make decisions as soon as may be."

Unsmiling, Sophie viewed the letter in Marguerite's hand. Marguerite dropped it casually on the desk and pulled the stack of bills over it. "Please sit down, Sophie. I fear we have quite overdrawn our account, and to pay for these bills we'll have to sell off all the things in this house."

Sophie's breath hissed as she exhaled. "You can't do that! Lithgow brought many of these heirlooms from Scotland."

Marguerite had expected a fight, and the first flare of disapproval brought back the old fatigue she always felt in Sophie's presence.

"You can keep the most valued treasures, Sophie, but the majority of them will have to be sold right away." She laid out her plan for selling the property and starting over in a smaller abode. "After all, you've never liked it much here, and the thought of a ghost frightens you. Admit it, Sophie." Marguerite wasn't about to explain that the gray lady was a figment of her own imagination.

Sophie pulled her mouth into a hard line. "Yes . . . I admit as much, but I would want to leave my brother's legacy intact. *He* would not approve of your scheme."

"Lennox is no more. We must move forward. Do not be afraid of the changes; they will improve our lives. You shall see." Marguerite fingered the bills, but without really looking at them. "I promised Lithgow I would see to your comfort, Sophie, and I won't break that promise. As I well know that you don't have any relatives who would readily take you in, I consider it my duty to secure your future."

Silence hung heavy in the room, and Marguerite sensed her sister-in-law's antagonism. Sophie had no reason to dislike her, but Marguerite knew the dislike stemmed from Sophie's almost sick attachment to Lithgow in the past. Sophie would have to pull away from the stifling bonds and treat herself as a person, not merely as an appendage to her older brother.

"Lithgow would turn in his grave if he knew you were tearing his house to pieces." Sophie clenched her hands on the armrests, and Marguerite sensed that she was on the verge of exploding.

"I do not want to end up in Fleet Prison or some other unmentionable jail for failure to pay my debts. No, there is no other way out, and you'll have to get used to the idea."

Sophie stood, her shoulders rigid and her expression grim. "I see that no amount of persuasion will stop you from this folly."

Marguerite leaned her elbows on the desk and rested her chin in the palm of one hand. "Do you have any better ideas, then? As you well know, you're completely dependent on the fact that I intend to clear these debts and plan for the future. Alone you would be penniless, since Lennox left everything to me."

Sophie inhaled another hissing breath, then spoke. "He condemned his roots by marrying you! You're not a Scotswoman, nor do you care for our traditions or value our views."

"The fact remains that Lennox married me, and nothing can change that," Marguerite said matter-of-factly. She felt tension gather between her shoulder blades, and she wished she didn't have to argue with Sophie. A flare of guilt went through her as she wished that her path would not continue to march along with that of Sophie.

Marguerite sighed. She would have to be more patient, and hope that Sophie's venom would abate with time.

"You should not have taken his name! You never lived up to his dreams and wishes."

"He wished for something that is illegal in this country: the return of the Stuarts. I could never share his views or his fanaticism, and the less said about it, the better. I know the secrecy and the crimes broke him in the end."

Sophie smiled a thin smile. "No matter how much you reject his vision, you're as much a part of them as I am. You'll never get away from that."

Marguerite dropped her arms on the desk. "I might have to live with the taint of his secrets, but don't make it harder for me. Please. If the truth ever comes out, we'll both be thrown in prison to await a traitor's death."

"You could never elevate yourself above your own small concerns, Marguerite. You would never sacrifice yourself for a greater good."

"Don't be so sure about that! If I believed in the cause, I might—"

Sophie's lips curled with dislike. "Don't say another word! You were never worthy of him, and I think it's wrong that you should decide what's best for this house—for me."

Completely out of patience, Marguerite crossed her arms over her chest and stared hard at the other woman. "Make your own life, then, and don't crawl back to me when your larder is empty."

Sophie strode to the door and slammed it as she left.

"Idiot." Marguerite said between clenched teeth. She always hoped that she could make Sophie see reason, but Sophie's anger corroded everything. The situation was deteriorating more every day. "How do I make her stop living in the past?"

She stared out the window for half an hour, or mayhap it was longer. The clock on the mantelpiece chimed. Frozen into immobility, she mentally sorted her options, knowing she had very few. She noticed from the corner of her eye that Sophie had left the house and fetched a horse. It wasn't often Sophie chose to take exercise, but perhaps she was too agitated to remain in the house.

With a deep sigh, Marguerite sat down and pulled her writing material toward her again. This time she wrote a formal letter to the auctioneer in Lewes.

Chapter 9

Charles stuck his hand into the damp hole behind the brick, and his heart lurched with delight as his fingers closed around a folded piece of paper. She had replied.

He replaced the brick and slid into the shadows of the night. He went along the path to a clearing in the spinney behind the estate. Thunder, who had been tied to a tree, whinnied in greeting. After sliding the letter into his pocket, Charles rode back home.

In his study, he eagerly tore the seal and read the short message. He chuckled at Marguerite's censoring words, but her curiosity had been thoroughly piqued. If he played his cards right, she would be more than eager to keep up a romance by mail. After that it would be only a matter of time until he revealed who was the real author of the love epistles.

To give her time for her curiosity to expand, he would wait to deliver the next letter. Besides, it would take some time to compose an ode that would shock her senses and open up her heart. For a moment he recalled that Marguerite wasn't interested in him, and no matter how heated his love letters—penned by the Midnight Bandit—he would not gain her love.

Well, he would have to show her that, with him, she would lack for nothing. He had enough attention to shower upon her—a lifetime of love. Clenching his jaw with frustration, he pushed Marguerite's letter into a desk drawer. She might never forgive him when she discovered the truth. He stared into the snapping fire in the grate as if it had a solution to his dilemma. There wasn't one. He would deal with her anger when it happened.

He glanced at his muddy riding coat and realized he'd better get ready for the ball at Bentworth Court. He'd promised he would escort Emmy, who had her heart set on seeing the lovely estate that sat like a jewel in a hollow by the Downs. Tonight the mansion would be wearing its finest decor. The owner, Jack Newcomer, the Earl of Bentworth, was Carey McLendon's cousin, and thereby a friend of Charles's. Still, Charles hadn't seen Jack since he married Bryony Shaw, and he looked forward to furthering the friendship.

Two hours later the coach rolled through the gilded gates of the Bentworth estate, and Emmy exclaimed, "It's glowing like a star, just like I knew it would."

"Lit candles in every window. Look how it reflects in the swan pond."

"The swans look like the finest marble sculptures, don't they, Charles?" Emmy's eyes glowed as if also lit by inner candles. She was dressed as if bound for the royal court in her hooped blue brocade gown and her powdered wig adorned with strands of pearls and velvet bows. Diamonds sparkled around her neck and around her wrists.

"Hmmm, I think marble cannot do justice to nature's own creation, Emmy." He braced himself as the carriage came to a halt by the front steps. A surge of warm expectation went through him at the thought that Marguerite might be among the guests. According to Nick, he had promised to escort her, the lucky beggar!

Guests on the vast front porch with its massive double doors waited to greet their hosts. Charles glanced from face to face for Marguerite, but didn't see her. The ladies looked alike, with their powdered hair and costly gowns, but Charles was sure he could sense if Marguerite was anywhere near.

Fans fluttered, and more than one flirtatious female smile flashed in his direction as he recognized some of his friends and their escorts. He greeted them, grinning, while his thoughts still lingered on Marguerite.

At times he wished he could cut his love for her out of his heart and start afresh with someone new, but his heart was the one thing over which he had no control.

With Emmy in tow, he entered the enormous circular hallway with its gold-enhanced moldings and white silk panels. His gaze roamed for Marguerite. Emmy said she would leave him alone. "Enjoy yourself, Charles; flirt and be merry," she said, and went to speak with an old friend.

"Yes, Emmy," he said dutifully to her back.

Charles's breath came to an abrupt halt as he finally laid eyes on Marguerite. She was a fairy tale in cream silk, gold embroidery and lace dripping from her elbows and lining the deep neckline. He might have noticed all the details that made such an alluring picture, but he had eyes only for the creamy skin of her shoulders and the teasing smile at the edge of her spread fan. A black velvet patch, attached to the corner of her lips *à la coquette,* seemed to invite him to take part of that smile, and more.

He flourished a sweeping bow, one hand held over his heart. "You take my breath away, Marguerite. I am a starving man when my gaze is not feasting on your exquisite person."

"La! Charles displays silver-tongued tendencies this evening," she said, her voice laced with laughter. She turned to their hosts, Jack, dark and saturnine in a gold-embroidered black velvet coat, and Bryony, her dark beauty enhanced by red silk strewn with pearls.

"The ladies expect gallantries. It would be rude if I didn't arrive in the right mood for festivities," Charles said after kissing Bryony's hand.

"That would indeed be intolerable. I can't abide a sour face," Bryony said with a smile. She attached her hand to Jack's arm. He squeezed it affectionately. "Let's leave these two turtledoves alone, Jack. I'm certain they can entertain themselves. There's a line of guests waiting for us."

"Turtledoves?" Marguerite commented with raised eyebrows, but she readily placed her fingertips on Charles's arm and let him lead her toward the ballroom.

"The kind that coo plaintively," Charles said matter-of-factly.

"Plaintively? They are the symbols of lovers!"

"Really?" He knew that perfectly well, but he desired to hear her speak of love. "Pray tell me more about lovers."

She blushed and looked away. "I don't know why Bryony compared us to turtledoves. They are dirty, raucous—"

"What I hear is that Bryony always possessed a sharp eye. Mayhap she sensed something between us?"

"Bosh and nonsense!"

He glanced down at Marguerite's profile, wanting to run his finger along the straight, bold ridge of her nose and trace the soft skin over her cheekbones, to trace the contours of her jaw to the soft plumpness of her mouth. Begad, if only he could seize her right here and taste that inviting mouth, those lips that so easily turned upward at the corners with laughter or with scorn.

He studied her as she prattled, not listening very closely. Come to think of it, her lips had not smiled much lately, only held a stiff downward turn. What worried her so much?

"Does it shame you so to talk about love?" he said at last, knowing his comment was completely out of context.

Her amber eyes had darkened with distress, and a flare of

anger shot like gold through her pupils. "Why do you always want to raise the issue of love in my presence?"

He squeezed her hand and kissed her fingertips in the slow, seductive way of a lover. "Perhaps talking about it helps you overcome your bitterness. You're a disillusioned woman, Marguerite, but not all gentlemen are like Lennox. You should give yourself a chance to enjoy life again."

She tore her hand from his grip. "That's exactly what I'm doing! Don't you see? My pleasure lies in being free to enjoy my life any way I choose."

"But your freedom has also raised a wall that bars you from the sensual pleasures of love. Don't you want to feel closeness, shared intimacy with a gentleman? Find out what love truly can be when it is right?"

"You are shameless!" She held her head high, and he thought she would curse him to his face, but she only lowered her eyes and flapped her fan thoughtfully. "Mayhap I should, but not with you, Charles."

Charles's protest died on his lips as Nick strode across the checkered marble floor and joined them outside the ballroom. "There you are, Marguerite. I should have known that Charles would whisk you away as soon as I turned my back." He placed a glass of champagne in Marguerite's hand. "As you ordered, milady. Always at your service." He smiled that devilish grin of his.

"I ought to cut that smile off with a blunt knife for you, Nick. Won't hurt a bit," Charles grumbled.

Nick only shook his head in wonder. "Charles, old fellow, I didn't know you harbored such dark, dangerous plans for me." His grin widened. "I would not like to be lipless. Really, I don't know if I dare to stay in the same room with you. Why don't we take a stroll in the garden and inspect the sparsely placed lanterns, Marguerite? 'Tis a night for secret romance."

Marguerite tilted her head sideways and gave Charles a cool smile. "Dangerous deeds might happen in the dark, Nick, especially with Charles nearby."

Heat rose in Charles's face at the double meaning. Clearly she alluded to the kiss he'd stolen on the banks of the Cuckmere River—or did she suspect the secret letter was his? "I'm not carrying a knife tonight," he said, ignoring her insinuation. "So you're quite safe with me."

Unable to keep up his resentment toward his friend, he slapped Nick on the back. "I wish you more luck than I've had. Maybe you'll be better suited to tearing down Marguerite's defenses." He winked at her outraged face, bowed, and turned on his heel.

Again he'd been too eager; he'd been a fool for pushing himself on her. He wasn't even going to ask her to dance. It would only bring back the sense of futility in his heart. He watched them leave, Marguerite a regal queen with mercurial eyes, Nick a king in a blue satin coat with gold braid across the front and around the wide flaps of his pockets. His waistcoat was a masterpiece of gold brocade, and Charles noted the many female glances thrown in his friend's direction.

When Marguerite decided she was ready to fall in love, would Nick be the lucky recipient? Charles couldn't bear the thought of having to attend their wedding. Cursing himself for his vivid imagination, he hailed a waiter with a tray. He downed two glasses of champagne in rapid succession and went in search of the card room. He wouldn't force himself where he wasn't wanted.

Marguerite and Nick strolled along the path in the garden. The night was balmy, the sky clear and deep blue. The moon held court with the stars, brilliant points of light across eternity. Marguerite wished she could relax enough to enjoy the wondrous evening, but her shoulders ached with tension, and the joy of seeing her friends was conspicuous in its absence. Too many problems weighed on her mind.

"You know, Nick, you and Charles are like those stars," she said, and pointed to the distant glimmer above. "Glittering, you vie with each other for my attention. I should be flattered, but I am not.''

''I suspect I won't have any more luck than Charles in winning your favors.''

She nodded, unhappy that she couldn't find the exhilaration of romance with Nick, the heady seduction of a kiss in the sweet-smelling garden. ''I'm flattered by your attention, but you can't expect me to respond when I have nothing to give. Inside I'm as empty as a shell.''

Nick halted her progress along the path by putting his hand on her arm. He turned her toward him. ''Only in your imagination. Something, someone, will spark the tinder in your soul, and I wish I were the lucky gentleman.'' He lifted his shoulders in a shrug. ''Evidently I'm not, but I'm not ready to give up yet.''

''I don't know,'' she said forlornly, and as she said those words, she realized they were all too true. She liked Nick well enough, just as she liked Charles. Mayhap she would feel more for one of them in due time.

''Something is burdening your shoulders, Marguerite. If you wish, I can be your confidant. You don't have to suffer alone, you know.''

Marguerite immediately rejected the idea. There was no one she could talk to about Sophie Pierson and her financial difficulties, Montagu Renny and the dead sergeant. Or the highwayman. She would have to deal with her problems alone, lest the truth about the past get out.

An urge to cry came over her, but she resolutely pushed it aside—not an easy feat, not when tension seemed to drown her, to ooze out of her every pore.

''Nick, let's inspect Jack and Bryony's roses. I hear Jack is an expert in the field, and they cultivate new strains in the greenhouse. They won't flower until later in the year, but the smell of earth and fresh green things is overwhelmingly pleasant.''

''Your wish is my command, Marguerite.''

''Would you fetch two glasses of wine first? I'm thirsty. We could sit down and have a chat on one of the wrought-iron benches inside.''

''I don't like to leave you alone here. It's almost pitch black.''

''Pish, you'll be gone only a minute. Besides, I have the moon to accompany me, and I'm not afraid of the dark.''

''Very well. Wait here for me.'' He strode up the path to the terrace, and Marguerite mused that Nick's handsome figure ought to spark a flame in her heart. Perhaps time was all she needed, time to fully appreciate the sterling qualities of her admirer. She strolled slowly toward the greenhouse, where lighted lanterns beckoned, their golden glow complementing the moon's silver sheen. A walk for lovers, she thought.

Hurried steps crunched on the gravel behind her. A heavy breath on her neck. A muttered curse.

Her reverie tumbled in confusion as someone gripped her arm hard. She cried out and whirled to face the man leaning over her. A dark cloak concealed his body, and a hat shadowed his features, but she recognized Montagu Renny's thin, bloodless face. Those cold green eyes filled her nightmares—and sometimes her waking hours. She could never be sure what he would do next.

''I take it you're not invited to the ball,'' she said, and snatched her arm from his grip. ''The Bentworths do not make friends with the likes of you.''

''Be careful not to raise my ire,'' he said in a deadly soft voice. ''Your taunts might be the end of you. I'm known for my terrible temper.''

''Are you threatening me?'' she asked, casting surreptitious glances toward the brightly lit house. If only she'd listened to Nick's warning.

''No use looking for help from your beau. Nick Thurston is taking a nap in the shrubbery even as we speak.''

Marguerite shook with worry and anger. ''Have you hurt him?''

''I needed some time alone with you, and you're always surrounded by people at these dull gatherings that you attend.''

"The only time they would be dull would be when you attended. I have no desire to speak with you." She started running toward the house as fast as her wobbly satin slippers could carry her. She felt his presence like a cold wind as he followed her and barred her way.

"What you desire matters not, sweet Marguerite," he drawled. His hand closed cold and bony around her wrist, and he dragged her away from the house and down the darkest path.

"What do you want? I've given you all I'm ever going to give, Mr. Renny."

"I think not!" He pushed her down on a bench at the edge of a tall, dense shrub that swayed eerily in the breeze.

Her breath was knocked out of her for a moment, and she stared at him in fear. For the first time she felt that she didn't have the strength to deal with his threats, and her mind scurried around for possible ways to avoid this forced interview. Only fragments of ideas came to her, nothing useful, nothing creative. Fear stiffened her and congealed her thoughts until everything came to a halt. She could only concentrate on his menacing presence. A murderer.

"We should talk about treason. How much is your freedom worth to you, Marguerite?"

"I have already paid for my freedom," she said, her lips stiff. She could barely utter the words. "And I've paid enough."

"I need more, funds that Lennox would not have hesitated to give me. You're only his deputy. You're living on his bounty, and he wouldn't be pleased to know how quickly you've forgotten him."

Marguerite laughed incredulously. "I suppose you have contact with him in hell—to know his opinion on my new friendships. Anyway, for the sake of convention, I mourned him longer than most would. I owe him nothing."

"You'll have to share everything with me, or you'll find yourself in traitor's prison."

Marguerite stood, anger fueling her. "I'm never going to

pay you another groat! If you so much as threaten me again, I shall go to the authorities and confess the whole story. Clear as I'm standing here now, you'll be implicated in the sergeant's death and go to the noose at Tyburn Tree.''

He chuckled, a cool, enervating sound. "No use threatening me, Marguerite. I was not at Lennox House on the night the sergeant died. I have witnesses that say I spent the night in a gambling house in Lewes.''

"Be that as it may, you *were* at Lennox House that night. I saw you.''

" 'Tis your word against mine. Who will believe one woman—a traitor to England who harbored spies—against three witnesses who'll say I spent the night elsewhere?''

"You either paid them well to keep silent, or you made sure they drank themselves under the table before you slunk out.''

"The sergeant's death was not planned," he said, his voice hard as flint. "So you see, there's no use in your going the authorities. You'll only end up with a longer neck.''

Marguerite bit back a scathing reply. There was no use arguing with the scoundrel. "Mr. Renny, if you'd invested what I gave you wisely, you would never have to suffer financially again. But I can tell you wasted the bounty. What card game was it? Piquet, whist, vingt-et-un? I'm disgusted!''

"I don't put much store by your emotions, Marguerite. I want half of everything Lennox left you. That's fair. After all, I could leave you penniless.''

Marguerite wondered if he'd found out that she planned to sell Lennox House and the surrounding land. From whom? Betsy? One of the stable hands? From Sophie Pierson? She wouldn't put it past Sophie to raise the opposition, but this would hurt Sophie as well. "If I sell everything there won't be enough to live on if I have to halve the proceeds with you. I have others to consider.''

He sneered. "How commendable. . . . Well, there is the other solution. You could always marry me and—''

"Never! I'd rather starve to death than wear your ring upon my finger."

"Then you have no other choice but to pay for my silence. We should both live well, don't you think? Well enough to conceal the shocking secrets."

Marguerite sought frantically for a solution. "I'll go to the authorities. I swear I will."

"We've already discussed that. Anyway, someone with the epithet 'Poison Widow' would do well to stay away from suspicious lawmen. They would certainly wonder how you came by that suggestive name."

"You're wily," Marguerite cried in anger. She shoved him in the chest and started up the path. If she got a bit closer to the house she could cry for help. She ran, but the festive facade of the great house didn't seem to get any closer. She sensed his attack right before it happened. He threw himself forward, pushing her hard in the back so that she staggered, lost balance, and crashed onto the path. The gravel raked her skin like claws, and the hard impact jostled her shoulder. Tears filled her eyes at the pain shooting through her upper body. His tall, slender body trapped hers, the gravel digging into her with a thousand granite points of pain. She curled her fist and slammed it into his face repeatedly, but he only laughed at her futile efforts.

His thighs pinned her wide panniers to the ground, and she couldn't move her legs high enough to smash her knee against him. Her breath was giving out, and tears of rage and fear built painfully in her chest. His cold hands closed around her neck. He squeezed, hitting her head against the ground repeatedly. "You'll do as I say, Marguerite. You'll do as I say."

She knocked his hat off and tore at his long, lank hair. She tried to rip his ear from his skull, but without breath she didn't have much strength left.

Vaguely she heard footsteps pounding on the gravel, and for a second she thought she had died and left her body, because the painful weight lifted from her chest. She saw Renny's arms flail for balance. His cloak whirled crazily, and he gave a strangled groan as someone knocked him into the air. He fell down on his knees, but came up with fists flying as the other man attacked.

Bone crunched against bone. Groans and grunts filled the night as the men danced around each other, punching any unguarded parts. Dazed, Marguerite watched as Renny kicked out, catching the other man in the thigh.

He swore viciously as her rescuer gripped the leg and tilted Renny over. He fell upon Renny, grabbed him by the cravat, and slammed a fist into his face. Words came between hard breaths: "Damn . . . you, Montagu Renny. Damn you . . . to hell."

Renny crumpled on the grass beside her, a figure bereft of all stuffing.

Marguerite felt herself being lifted and cradled in a pair of strong arms. She recognized the lemony scent of Charles's shaving soap.

"Thank you, Charles," she whispered, and clung to him. He held her close, caressed her powdered hair, which had come free as pins and plumes fell off somewhere during her flight. He muttered endearments in her ear.

"I'm here. There, there, do not worry, my sweet. He will not hurt you again."

Her hysteria slowly abated. His arms held her; his chest felt broad and comforting, his breath soothing against her cheek. She breathed deeply to calm herself. As if they had lost all substance, her legs could barely support her. "I think I will fall," she whispered.

He lifted her up, found a bench nearby, and carefully deposited her on it. "Rest, Marguerite. I shall deal with that villain."

Renny rose slowly, as if not sure of his bearings. He gingerly touched his head as if to soothe a growing lump.

"What the hell do you think you're doing accosting a lady in the dark?" Charles roared. He gripped the other man's coat. "Answer me," he said, shaking Renny, who swore loudly.

"Take your hands off me, Mortimer," Renny said in a hiss.

He tore himself free, only to find himself knocked to the ground once more. He got to his feet and backed off the path. Charles followed, swearing, his hands bunched into fists.

"No!" Marguerite cried as she saw his determination to continue the combat. "Don't fight with him, Charles. For me . . ."

Charles slowly lowered his arms and glanced at her. His body retained a stiff, wary stance, and he kept his concentration on Renny.

"Renny's capable of . . . In the end, he'll . . ." Marguerite could not finish the sentence aloud: *kill you.* Renny was looking straight at her, as if daring her to denounce him. If she did, would the whole sordid truth come out?

Would Charles find himself bound to report her to the authorities? She didn't know if Charles would protect her or feel forced to honor justice at all costs. He was her friend, but she wasn't sure if he valued her friendship more than justice. How would he react if he discovered that she'd been married to a Stuart sympathizer, and that she'd helped others to escape to France?

Renny held out his hand toward her in question, and she knew she had no choice.

"Let him go," she said dully to Charles. "I will faint at the first hint of bloodshed."

Charles looked at her in outrage. "He molested you, Marguerite! If Renny can't show common decency toward a lady, he needs some manners knocked into him."

Marguerite took a deep breath. Her next words would taint her soul just as much as if she *were* a traitor to England. "He didn't molest me. He didn't."

Renny relaxed. His triumphant smile glowed white in the moonlight, and Marguerite stiffened with loathing.

Charles snorted. "Rubbish! I saw him maul you on the ground."

"He fell on top of me, and I couldn't get up."

Charles stared at her for a long moment, and she sensed his

deep suspicion. He didn't believe her. She'd felt his support and concern from the moment he'd saved her on the path, but now all comfort left the air, and a bleak loneliness filled her. She shivered with sudden cold.

"Marguerite! How can you say—"

She threw up her arms. "Let's leave the subject. I would like to go home, if you can find Nick. He—" She was about to say that he'd been knocked down, but that would make Charles challenge Renny once more.

Charles gave Montagu Renny a hard punch in the shoulder. "Get away from here. Leave! I should take you to face Lord Bentworth for trespassing, but I don't want to spoil their ball." He forced Renny toward the woods at the back of the property, and a final push sent him into the clipped box hedge.

"Mark my words, you'll regret your violence, Mortimer," Renny shouted as he made his way through the hedge and into the stygian darkness of the woods.

Charles turned to Marguerite as she tried to readjust her hair and straighten her clothes.

"Damn it, Marguerite. Why did you lie to me?"

"I didn't," she said, her face bent down as she struggled to fasten the hairpins at the back of her head. "As I said, he was running and stumbled on top of me." Which was true, she thought, if not the whole truth. "I don't know why he was in such a hurry." She winced as she lowered her arm. Her shoulder ached abominably. "Please go find Nick for me. Only minutes ago he went inside to fetch champagne. I don't know what is keeping him."

"Nick likes to talk," Charles said ruefully. He glanced at Marguerite, and then at the woods. "I don't like to leave you here alone."

"Don't worry about me. Nothing else will happen to me tonight."

"Nick shouldn't have left you here alone. Come along; we'll look for him together."

Marguerite knew it was useless to argue. Her hand clasped

in his, she followed him as far as the terrace, but when she saw how dirty and torn her gown—her one truly elegant gown—had become, she refused to go inside.

"If Bryony sees me like this, she'll insist that I spend the night here." She gave Charles a pleading glance. "I only want to go home."

He nodded. "I understand." He went into the glittering ballroom through the open French doors. Laughter and violin music reached her ears, and Marguerite wished she'd stayed inside the entire evening. It would have saved her a confrontation with Montagu Renny. Not that he wouldn't have found her another day, but at least the misery would have been postponed.

She waited, scanning the shadows under the bushes for Nick. There was no sign of him, and she prayed that he had recovered from the blow.

Charles returned carrying her cloak and his own. "Nick is resting in the library with a cold cloth on his head. Seems that he had some kind of misfortune." Charles glared at Marguerite. "Do you know what kind? Does it somehow involve your friend Renny?"

"No. Didn't Nick tell you?"

"Only that he'd stumbled on something in the darkness and hit his head on the edge of the fountain."

Relief washed through Marguerite. "It was rather dark on the path."

"Nick has cat eyes; he sees perfectly well in the dark." Silence lay dense between them, filled with unspoken words and suspicion. Charles sighed. "He asked me to escort you home."

Chapter 10

Charles kept silent most of the way to Marguerite's house, and she suffered in the uneasy atmosphere that had blossomed between them.

He finally spoke. "I know you're hiding something, Marguerite, but I also know it isn't my place to pry into your private affairs. I wish you would confide in me, since . . ." He sighed. "I'm your friend, am I not?"

Marguerite nodded convulsively. "Yes . . . I consider you my dear friend, Charles. That will never change."

He pondered her words in silence, and she sensed that he struggled not to press her into divulging her secrets. The fewer people that were privy to the Lennox secret, the better, she thought, but the burden of her problems weighed her down.

Her eyes were gritty, as if she hadn't slept for days, and her throat throbbed after Renny's harsh treatment. She drew a sigh of relief as the carriage reached her front door.

"I'm glad I could see you safely home," Charles said, and headed back toward the coach after escorting her to the door.

"If you care to, you're welcome inside. I would appreciate

your company for yet another while." She smiled. "I have some good brandy put away for special occasions."

He grinned, and she could tell he was very pleased with the invitation. "Is this a special occasion?"

"I think so," she said, and preceded him inside.

Carrying a branch of dripping candles, Betsy met them at the door. She yawned. "There's a fire in the front parlor, milady, and a tray with bread and cold cuts. Thought ye might be famished after a night o' dancin'." She peered more closely at Marguerite. "Didn't 'spect ye 'ome so soon, though. Cor lumme! Ye looked like ye've been pulled through an 'edge backwards. Whatever—"

"I had an accident. Nothing serious," Marguerite said in dismissive tones. "Go to bed, Betsy, and thank you for your thoughtfulness."

Betsy bobbed a curtsy and disappeared down the gloomy corridor to the kitchen stairs. Marguerite went inside the parlor, her mind filled with misgivings. She looked down at the torn gossamer silk of her skirts and cried out, "It's ruined! I don't see how this can ever be repaired." Her back rigid, she went to the round, gilt-framed mirror above the fireplace and stared at her reflection. Dark smudges marred her chin and cheeks, and her hair hung in a tangled dusty mess, a worse tangle than any fishwife ever pushed under a mobcap. "Oh, my goodness. I never realized—"

"The dust and powder will wash out. Most important, you weren't hurt. If you had been, I would be very worried." He came to stand beside her. "So you understand now why I know you were lying to me in the garden at Bentworth Court. If Renny had merely stumbled and knocked you to the ground, you would not be in such a state."

Marguerite averted her face from his intent ice blue gaze. Charles saw entirely too much.

"I thought Renny was a friend of your husband's. For what reason does he harass you? Is he pressuring you . . . er, romantically?"

Marguerite flinched as if slapped. "No! He is nothing to me, nothing. I don't consider him my friend, even if he and Lennox were close in the past."

"Then what does he want?"

Marguerite closed her eyes and gripped a fold of her skirts to do something with her fluttering hands. She molded the soft fabric around her fingers. "He visits here sometimes—for old times' sake. I've told you all I'm going to say."

"Let me guess. You have difficulties . . . mayhap financial problems, and somehow Renny is involved. Have you borrowed funds from him? Is he dunning you?"

She stared at him in disbelief. "No! That's a ludicrous suggestion." She patted her ruined hair, then went to a table and lifted a crystal bottle from a tray. "I promised you brandy." She poured two glasses and held out one toward him. The fire sent shadows over his face, adding a saturnine cast to his strong features. He looked dangerous, and strangely alluring, different in his powdered wig and his gold braid–encrusted coat. The sartorial elegance gave him power and virility, and she could only admire his tall, straight figure and his muscular legs encased in knee breeches and white silk stockings.

Her heartbeat fluttered at the predatory look in his eyes, and a blush flowered all over her body, making her cheeks burn.

He walked very slowly toward her, as if measuring every step and her reaction to his approach. His magnetism crowded her, surrounding her, and she wondered why she found it so hard to breathe all of a sudden. He did not accept the glass.

"You know what I find hardest to accept, Marguerite? That you call me friend, but won't trust me. Not one bit." The last words he said in a savage whisper, and Marguerite backed away, only to find her backside pressed against the table.

"There are things one cannot tell a friend. You'll have to accept that." When had her voice taken on that breathless quality? And why did her legs shake like jelly?

She pressed back hard against the table, but it wouldn't move.

Trapped by his hot gaze, she could only await his next words, his next gesture.

"I'm not certain I want to be your friend," he said. "It's so boring; not much better than being a brother, and *that* I am not, thank God." He leaned over her and captured her arms in his warm grip. She could not pull away, as she still held the brandy glasses. His fingertips moved tantalizingly and caressed the tender skin on the inside of her wrists. She gasped with the thick-as-syrup pleasure moving up her arm and traveling through her body.

She could barely keep her hands cupped around the brandy glasses. If he continued his sweet torture she would surely drop them and the crystal would shatter at their feet. Just as she would.

He dragged one sensitive finger along the outside of her hand, following the bones and sliding over the hollows between her knuckles. Such rich tenderness his hands evoked. She'd never known that the skin of her hands could be so sensitive to a man's caresses. If they were . . . what about the other parts of her body? Would they respond as readily to his slow, hot but tender touch? She slowly raised the glass to his lips.

"Here, drink this."

If he hadn't stilled her hand, she would have shoved the crystal hard against his teeth in her agitation. Her hand lay trapped in his, a small fragile bird that had to surrender to a superior strength. His power was tenderness, but if he unleashed his carefully controlled ardor, what—*who*—would emerge? A demanding lover or a raging beast?

He lifted the glass with her hand still wrapped around it and slowly sipped the amber liquid. "Excellent brandy, my sweet. Smooth and warm as sunshine, smooth as a lover's kiss, and as blazing."

She found a tremulous smile for him. "And evidently it frees a poetic tongue. I think you are a dreamer, Charles."

His lazy smile burned all the way to her soul. "I suppose the world harbors all sorts of creatures, some of them dreamers.'' He took another sip and planted a brandy-thick kiss on her fingertips, which still cradled the crystal. A tremor went through her hand. He pried each stiff finger from the glass and set it down on the table behind her.

His move trapped her, his arm pressing into her side and the gilt buttons of his velvet waistcoat digging into her chest. His thigh moved against hers, and she was well aware of the steely firmness of his leg. He could have felled her with a breath, and it was clear by the dangerous glitter in his eyes that he found the situation highly to his liking.

''You're crowding me, Charles,'' she said, staring at the white lace–edged cravat at his neck. A diamond pin winked at her as his chest rose and fell in a chuckle.

''You offered me a glass of brandy, and I accepted the invitation,'' he said, so close his breath tickled her ear. He blew away the errant curl, and his hand cupped her neck. His warmth traveled the length of her back and pooled in her loins. The longing that always nagged at the back of her mind blossomed forth, and she gasped at the tempest of her emotions.

Standing rigid, she dared not show her yearning or he might take it for granted that she'd fallen in love with him. She needed distance, needed to think . . . before she did something foolish. Charles never did anything by half measures, and she didn't want to invite him to . . . Oh, but his caresses felt so good!

His hands sought the pins in her hair.

''What are you doing?'' She stayed his movements, her arms being the only parts of her body that she could move.

''Your tresses are falling down, and I'm only helping them along.''

''No—''

''It won't look so untidy,'' he said as an excuse to continue his probing for pins.

Before long her heavy coils had rolled down her back and relieved some of the pressure on her head. It was liberating, she thought, and very wanton. With her hair down, she felt young and carefree.

"There. So much better, don't you think?" he purred in her ear. He pulled his fingers through her curls without snagging unduly, then wound them around his hands. He sighed deeply. "Your hair is soft as silk. I knew it would be."

A protest rose to her lips, but somehow she didn't have the strength, or the heart, to utter it. For once she wasn't alone; someone's arms cradled her love-starved body, someone's heart beat close to hers, someone took actual pleasure from touching her. She hadn't felt as cosseted since her nursemaid had rocked her in her plump arms.

"Would you like me to brush it for you?" he murmured.

"The brush is upstairs." She could barely speak for the tremors going through her body as he made small, circular caresses at the nape of her neck.

"There is one on the table behind you."

"Hmm, I guess Betsy must have left it there for some reason. Her housekeeping leaves a lot to be desired."

"Tonight that's to our advantage." He slowly released her, and with the pressure of his embrace gone, she felt bereft.

She sank down on the nearest chair without looking at him. He started pulling the brush through her hair in long, soothing strokes. She thought she was going to swoon with pleasure, or at least fall asleep as she gradually relaxed.

"Marguerite, you once talked about redecorating your house. You said it was too gloomy. I don't see any evidence of new furniture or fresh curtains. Have you changed your mind?"

His strokes lengthened, and she had the sensation that her whole body was turning inside out. "My plans are not . . . complete," she hedged. It wouldn't hurt to tell him the truth, not really. "Actually, I've been pondering the idea of selling this property and moving Sophie, Pru, and myself to a smaller abode. Much easier to manage, you must understand."

"And much less costly," he muttered.

"The farm is not producing the way it should," she explained lamely. "And the horses that Lennox kept . . . well, I have not the knowledge nor the aptitude for horse breeding. Anyway, they were sold off right after his demise, all except my mare, Sophie's, and the carriage horses.''

"He didn't leave much, did he?''

She inhaled deeply as she recalled the abyss of her monetary difficulties. "I do not wish to discuss my financial situation.''

"Hmm, let me only remind you that I'm at your service, Marguerite. I am not a wealthy man, but together we might discover a solution to your problems.''

She failed to answer. His wizardly wielding of the hairbrush smoothed away her misgivings, and she gave herself up to the simple pleasure. He massaged her skull and her temples, making her into a boneless beggar for more delights. He tilted her head forward, and nuzzled her neck with his lips. Fizzles like champagne ran over her skin.

He continued exploring every bump of her backbone until he came to the tight lacing of her bodice. Holding her breath, she waited . . . and waited. Though she had thought he would, he did not start to unlace her.

His hands came around the front and cupped her breasts. Tingles shot all over her skin, and a liquid pool of yearning filled her stomach. He gripped her firmly, and she could only lean back against him, savoring the warm, demanding touch.

Charles thought he would collapse then and there from the effort of keeping his raging desire at bay. He squeezed her breasts, firm like two oranges, but much more tantalizing, much sweeter than the fruit—forbidden fruit. He was amazed, startled that she let him touch her in this most intimate way.

He held his breath, waiting for the explosion that must come if he kept this up—his from desire, hers from outrage. He wished he could push the bodice down and touch her naked flesh, but the damned garment was too tight, and the neckline not low enough for such a coup. . . .

"God, you smell so good, Marguerite . . . jasmine and rose, yes, a whole summer meadow.'' A line to a verse welled up in him, and he spoke without thinking. " 'Barefoot she walked among the flowers crushing petals / Blooms worshiping her skin / Scent lingering forever.' "

"Oh, that was lovely," she said softly. "You revere women in a most uncommon way, Charles. So very flattering, and so attractive in you."

"I'm glad you see my fine qualities, my sweet," he whispered, and squeezed his eyes shut. God, the desire was killing him! He sat down on the floor, and pulled her off the chair and into his arms before she had a chance to protest.

She laughed as if she'd had too much champagne. "You're also mad, Charles."

"I know. Mad for a taste of your lips." He took her mouth, silencing her laugh abruptly. He explored the hot insides, mating with her tongue. Silk and brandy, slippery warmth that drugged him with its sweetness. He reveled in the nearness of her, a handful of slender limbs and inviting curves, layers and layers of frothy silk, skin as luminous as a pearl. He'd died, and this was heaven. Sinuous arms wound around his neck, a so very kissable mouth kissing him back.

His loins ached, his manhood almost burst with desire as she rubbed her padded hips against him. Oh, devil take it, he'd spread her on the floor and lift up her skirts to her waist. . . . As his hand boldly traveled up her silk-clad leg, she stiffened, her arms falling away, and her eager mouth closing, leaving him aching for more.

"Don't!" she croaked in fear. "Please . . . don't."

He glanced down at her upturned face, noting her flushed cheeks and glittering eyes. Moonlit amber, he thought. With a supreme effort, he stilled his movements, and remained motionless until he'd found some semblance of composure. It was extremely difficult under the circumstances; every ounce of him was filled with a desire that had a life of its own. He removed his hands from her while taking deep, steadying breaths. She remained silently staring at him, now a wooden doll in his lap. He needed fresh air, a cold, stinging northerly breeze, a hard gallop, a swim in the icy sea. *Damn it all!*

As she rolled from his lap to her feet, she jarred that most sensitive portion of his person, a move that almost set him on a course of no return. He could so easily take her, mayhap easily convince her that lovemaking was what she yearned for. She had, he knew, dreamed of it for a long time. But not with him.

Swearing under his breath, he got to his feet and arranged his clothing to hide the telltale bulge in his breeches.

She righted her tangled hair, her face averted from him. "You'd better leave now, Charles, before I do or say something I might regret later."

He turned toward her, barely able to look at her. The rejection in her gaze burned through him, making it difficult to breathe. "You enjoyed our closeness as much as I did, Marguerite. You can't deny that."

"You took me unaware. We have spoken of this matter before, and I haven't changed my opinion. My . . . friendship is still the same. Tonight I am in a vulnerable state, and you took advantage—"

"Desist!" He slammed his fist onto the table so that the tray rattled against the crystal. "Don't blame this on me. If you can't accept pleasure, then don't invite a gentleman to your parlor."

"I thought I could trust you to behave in a gentlemanly fashion, Charles," she said coolly.

He shouldered past her. "As far as I know, I didn't ravish you. Go to your lonely bed, Marguerite. You can't accept a compliment to your beauty, or give an inch of your precious freedom to an admirer—a *sincere* admirer. I'll wager that even the king himself would find no favors with you."

Her mouth, which had been so kissable only minutes ago, was set into a thin line of displeasure.

He clapped his hat onto his head and threw the cloak over his shoulders. "I think our friendship does not exist. You play your cards too close to your chest. In other words, you don't trust me as a friend would.''

Without another word he let himself out, and he heard her push the bolt on the other side. *Damn that woman!* Why had he ever lost his heart to such a coldhearted, secretive lady. She would never change her mind concerning him. Would he never learn?

He knew Marguerite would avoid him like the plague, and, despite his better judgment, he finally decided to continue his mission to woo her into loving him with letters from the Midnight Bandit. Perhaps that scoundrel could find a way to her heart, if no one else could. She would be furious, though, if—when—she discovered the truth. . . .

Marguerite leaned her forehead against the door for a long time before she could gather her exhausted limbs and drag herself upstairs to bed. God knew she had wanted to taste the full glory of Charles's lovemaking, but it was wrong. She had no right to lead on someone whose love she could not return. Not that she didn't feel something; how could any lady be immune to his virility?

But he wanted more than she could give him. The amorous activities had to stop before she would have to hurt him deeply with her rejection. It would be callous to give her body but not her love.

Frustrated by the desire singing in her blood, she went to bed—probably to face a sleepless night. She snuffed out the candle on the bedstand, and stared into the darkness.

Chapter 11

"I know she's hiding something," Charles said a week later to Nick as they sat on the terrace of the Meadow enjoying the warm night air. Between them, on a small three-legged table inlaid with ivory, stood a decanter of brandy, glasses, a plate of cold cuts, and pie, and on the flagstones lay Georgie, Emmy's pet pug, his rotund body stretched out like a sausage. He snored with a total lack of delicacy.

"Yes, I haven't made any progress with Marguerite at all. She pushes me away at every turn," Nick said with a sigh.

Charles chuckled. "That's a sweet tune to my ear. Tell me more!"

Nick smiled ruefully. "Marguerite seems to loathe men. She refuses to let anyone close. I wonder what that dried-up prune, Lennox, did to her. The name 'Poison Widow' seems more and more feasible. The more secretive she acts, the more I suspect that all is not out in the open concerning Lennox's death."

Charles's eyes widened in shock. "How can you suspect her of foul deeds? Marguerite is not a cold-blooded murderess."

"Then what the deuce is she hiding?" Nick refilled his goblet and scooped up a slice of meat pie. His expression brightened as he bit into the food. "Damned good, this! Monsieur Goulot has outdone himself, as usual."

"I could swear Marguerite has financial difficulties. But she won't confide in me. Has she hinted anything to you?"

Georgie lifted his flat snout, slobbered, and sniffed the air. He rolled to his feet with difficulty and ambled across to Nick. Shamelessly, he placed his front paws on Nick's leather riding breeches, and gave him a well-practiced begging look.

"I'd say you're too preoccupied with Marguerite Lennox, Morty. Can't be healthy to think about her all the time." He flung a piece of crust onto the terrace, and Georgie pounced clumsily.

Charles downed the dregs of his brandy. "Damn it, Nick, mind your own business. You think about her more than you like, yourself."

"Prickly, aren't you? It's clear I hit upon the truth. Anyway, I've kept my eyes on Montagu Renny since the Bentworth ball, and he's been gambling heavily at the clubs in London. He left London yesterday, and might be back in this area."

"Hmm." Charles rubbed the cool base of his glass against his jaw. "Mayhap we ought to interview him directly. Marguerite won't say a word against the man, even though we know he did more than stumble and fall on top of her. What I really want to know is why she's protecting that damned rat."

"We could always pay him a visit at his estate or at one of his haunts in Lewes—the gambling hells. I'm sure you wouldn't be against winning some funds. 'Twill also take your mind off a certain lady of our acquaintance. Let's get ready. We'll ride up to his place tonight."

On that same day, Marguerite had found another letter from the gallant highwayman hidden in the brick wall. She already knew the contents by heart, and she recited the words softly to herself as she stood in her study:

> *Dearest heart, Marguerite,*
> *Amber stones, eyes of fire,*
> *Gold and red, hair of silk.*
> *Tie a rope around my breath*
> *In sweet imprisonment.*
> *Smile, flash, and fickle fire*
> *Through morning mist and milk.*
> *Captive is my heart, my breath,*
> *In sweet imprisonment.*

Please, my goddess, say that you will meet me some night, in the meadow behind the spinney. Say yes, say yes to love, as I've hopelessly lost my heart to you.
> *The Midnight Bandit.*

Marguerite sighed and smiled. Excitement rushed through her body. This was like a verse by B. C. Rose, the same longing, the same melancholy, as if he could not hope to reach his beloved. It touched her heart. Was it true that the bandit was B. C. Rose, as some hinted?

How had he found out that her eyes were amber and her hair red-gold? It had been so dark the night she had met him in the road. The thought that he knew her so well exhilarated her, but also frightened her. Was the bandit spying on her, knowing her every move?

The thought made her heart pound with expectation. He might come to her door, apply the knocker, and ask to see her. Would she know him? She remembered only the black shape of him, the wide shoulders and the powerful physique as he helped the coachman to dislodge the wheel from the mud. He'd smiled, his teeth white, and he'd shone a lantern on her face, but hidden his own. He'd gently kissed her hand and savaged her mouth. To meet him clandestinely, to let him love her . . .

was it possible? No one would know and judge her too harshly. No one would know.

That evening, driven by an unexplainable excitement, she went to the window and looked outside. She could see only darkness, trees swaying against the weak moonlight, and silver-edged clouds sweeping across the sky.

She swallowed convulsively and wondered if right this moment he was staring at her. She surprised herself by waving at her own reflection in the glass, then swept the old curtains across the windows. The parlor took on the heavy, secretive air she remembered so clearly from Lennox's time. She could turn around and find him sitting in the chair by the fire. . . . Not his favorite chair, since she long since had sold it, but he would be in hers, bent over a much-thumbed prayer book.

She closed her eyes and moaned out loud. She would have to leave this house to get rid of the memories of suffocation and miserliness. Thank God the auctioneer was coming tomorrow to evaluate all her belongings.

She jumped with fright as a faint knock came on the window by which she was standing.

"We could always go by Marguerite's house on the way," Charles suggested, "find out if everything is in order. I don't like her to live alone in that dreadful old house." He nudged Thunder onto the road, heading north.

Nick chuckled and pulled his hat lower over his eyes as his stallion fell into step beside Thunder. "Yes . . . I wouldn't mind seeing her myself. After all, it might be *days* before we ride this way again. Especially since we don't have any legitimate reason to see Marguerite."

Charles shuddered. "You're right, alas."

They looked at each other and laughed. "Splendid idea," Charles said, "but I'm afraid I'm not dressed to impress a lady in riding breeches and top boots. I left my manservant in my bedchamber morosely powdering my wigs and sponging my coats. He always has high hopes that one day I will move in court circles and wear all his finery. He thinks he's solely responsible for my splendid wardrobe.'' Charles gave the last words a wry tone, and Nick chortled.

''According to Carey McLendon, that man of fashion, you're never dressed fit for even the pigsty on the farm.''

''No, beside Carey, one's star is always bound to dim. He likes to keep himself well turned out.''

The wind whipped through the trees, bringing a smell of rain from the sea. ''A storm is brewing. I'll race you to the spinney behind Lennox House,'' Nick cried, and pushed his heels into the sides of his stallion.

Thunder fell into an easy canter, finding firm footing on the road, but Charles feared for holes. The last thing he needed was a lame mount. Nick's cloak flowed out behind him as he leaned low over his stallion's crest. ''The loser is a coward.''

''Damn you, why do you always have to win?'' Charles said under his breath and urged Thunder to a longer stride. The big stallion ate up the distance, but Nick still held the lead, since he'd started earlier.

A rumble muttered in the sky, and a bank of stygian clouds rolled in from the coast, obscuring the moon. The night became a deep gray haze. Trees flew by as spidery shapes, and Charles recognized the wall surrounding the property of Admiral Hancock, Marguerite's neighbor. Thunder's eagerness affected him, and Charles was filled with elation at the thought of seeing Marguerite again, even if she wouldn't speak to him. Let Monsieur Glib—Nick—carry the conversation.

Petrified to a spot in the middle of the room, Marguerite stared at the window. The knock came again, this time harder, more impatient.

''Marguerite,'' someone called. A male voice.

Could it be the highwayman? If so, should she let him in?

The possibilities titillated her, but she had no desire to receive a thief in her house—no matter how charming and gentlemanly.

"Marguerite." The voice came again, this time louder. She recognized Montagu Renny's slightly nasal voice. She should have known! Angry now, she tore aside the curtain and unhooked the window. She discerned the contours of his three-cornered hat, and the pale length of his face. She opened the window a crack.

"What do you want, Mr. Renny? It's too late for a visit."

"Never too late," he drawled. "Let me in."

"If you've come to harass me, I won't speak with you."

"You cannot dismiss me in such a flippant manner. You know you have to talk with me sooner or later, and since I had an errand close by, I thought I'd pay you a visit."

She stared at him for a long moment, the cold glitter in his eyes unnerving her. He would execute his every threat if she didn't agree to his terms. She would have to find a way to outwit him. It was the only way he would leave her alone.

"Very well, go to the front door." She slammed the window in his face. Taking a deep breath, she went to receive him. She thought she heard the sound of soft steps on the landing upstairs. She glanced at the darkness above, the white posts of the railing the only brightness. A darker shadow moved, but she couldn't be certain if it was a real ghost or one of the servants. In fear of meeting the alleged gray lady, Sophie probably didn't dare leave her room.

"You took your time," Renny complained as she admitted him " 'Tis rather cold outside, and the rain is increasing to a veritable downpour."

"Are you afraid to get your toes wet?" she asked with as much condescension as she could muster.

"I don't take kindly to jokes at my expense," he said coldly.

She led the way into the parlor and faced him. She did not offer him a seat. "State your business; then leave, Mr. Renny."

His fingers clenched around the upturned brim of his hat as he pulled it off. Raindrops scattered on the worn carpet. "You know very well why I have come, Marguerite. We have unfinished business, and this time I won't leave until I have a promise from you."

"I informed you at the Bentworth ball that I've already paid you all you're going to get."

"I think not." He came closer, every step soundless, threatening.

She stood her ground even if his menacing presence shot urges to her mind to run away from him. If she promised now . . . mayhap he would go away. Later she might find a way to trick him. That was, if she hit upon a brilliant solution that she hadn't thought of in these endless weeks of turning over the problems in her mind. He stood so close she could smell his scent: wet horse and a cloyingly sweet aroma she couldn't identify.

"Very well. When I've sold the property, you shall have half of the proceeds. After that you'll have no reason to pester me. You can't want me to end up penniless." She flinched as he reached out and caught an errant curl that had escaped from her cap. He wound it around his finger and stared hard at her

"My financial demand could be voided if you but agree to marry me, Marguerite. You know I've always looked upon you with a fond eye."

It took all her willpower to remain standing in the spot where he could fondle her hair, and perhaps other parts of her if he took the idea into his head. She had to appear in control.

"I've told you repeatedly that I cannot marry you, Mr. Renny, but if the proceeds from the sale of this estate shall remain in my bank, then I might reconsider your offer. After all, we would both gain from that solution, and the secrets would always remain hidden."

He chuckled, showing all his teeth. His green eyes glittered avidly. "I always knew you were a lady of great circumspection and taste."

"Give me some time to think this over," she said, her back rigid with outrage as he dragged a finger along the side of her face and pinched her chin. She thought he was about to kiss her as he leaned forward, his gaze fixed on her mouth.

"I don't think it is wise to take liberties in advance of my decision," she said primly as his face came closer. If the devil had green eyes, he was staring right at her—cold as an arctic winter, avid, calculating. Waiting. A false move on her part . . .

"Mr. Renny, I expect you to behave in a gentlemanly fashion until I've thought about your offer in peace."

He opened his mouth to answer, but his next words were interrupted by the door knocker. Wind moaned in the badly fitted windows, and rain lashed against the house.

"Who in the world . . . ?" she said, letting out a trembling breath, relieved that she would no longer be alone with Montagu Renny. " 'Tis so late."

"Mayhap not too late for one of your admirers," he said, his voice an icy whiplash. "Get rid of him!"

Marguerite moved. Her legs shook with the strain of keeping her composure. She picked up the lit candle on the hallway table and cracked the front door open. "Who is it?" She recognized Captain Emerson instantly and opened the door fully. "Captain! Isn't it late to be abroad?" She'd never been more relieved to see a near stranger on her doorstep.

"Yes, Lady Lennox, but your neighbor reported seeing a prowler on his property. We found no one, but I thought of inquiring here. Have you noticed someone lurking about your house tonight?"

Marguerite wondered if the captain could see Montagu Renny in the parlor. She would like the soldier to see him. "No, but I have a guest. Mayhap he saw something on his way to my house."

She brought the captain to the parlor, and the two men stared at each other warily. "Mr. Renny," Emerson said. He clasped his hat under his arm while rivulets of rain rolled down the back of his heavy cloak. He turned to Marguerite.

"I'm afraid the smugglers might be out on a night like this.

They expect not to encounter any lawmen in inclement weather, and we haven't found any of the 'gentlemen.' Not yet.''

"I saw no one along the road," Renny said, and flung himself into a chair as if he already lived in the house.

Captain Emerson smiled coolly. "The smugglers don't usually travel along the road." He gave Marguerite a long stare, as if asking her what Renny was doing in her house so late. She felt a blush rising to her cheeks even though she was innocent of his silent accusation.

"I certainly hope you can catch those villains soon. Would you like a glass of brandy to warm your insides, and some bread and cold cuts?" She smiled. "I would like to think I could help to keep up your spirits."

He bowed. "Your smile has already lifted my spirits, Lady Lennox, but I wouldn't say no to a goblet of brandy. Since no prowler could be found, I'm officially off duty. My men have gone home."

"Have a seat, Captain, while I speak to my maid."

Marguerite ran into Pru in the hallway. "I thought I heard voices," Pru said, righting the brown knit shawl over her shoulders.

"Yes, Captain Emerson's and Mr. Renny's. You might entertain them while I find refreshments."

Pru grumbled but obediently entered the parlor. Pru would lend her moral support, Marguerite thought, relieved.

Just as she returned from the kitchen, someone pounded heavily on the door. "What now? I don't believe this!"

"You are a very popular person, Lady Lennox," Emerson said with a nod. He joined her in the hallway as she went to find out the identity of her next caller.

"Charles and Nick!" she cried. "Why, you look sodden. What's going on? Has something happened?"

Charles gave her a guarded smile. "No. Nick insisted on racing me along the road. We have business farther north, but got caught in the storm. May we come in?"

She held the door for them. "Certainly."

Charles pushed Nick lightly in the back. "I'll see to the horses."

Nick entered after shaking off his cloak and hat on the front steps. "Hard to believe summer is here. This rain is as cold as the autumn fog." He stared intently at the captain and at Montagu Renny, who was still slouched in the armchair in front of the dying embers in the fireplace. Renny evidently saw no reason to greet the newcomer. "Didn't know you were in the midst of a gathering of admirers."

"Well, now I am," she said, and hung his hat on a peg behind the door. "You and Charles will make the company complete."

"I shall return shortly. Must have a word with Charles," Nick said, and flung his cloak back on.

Charles wiped down the sweating horses with Tom, one of the stable boys. Eager to be finished with the chore, he hurried through it and then sprinted down to the brick wall. His excitement rose as he discovered another letter. She had responded to his latest, very daring, suggestion. Would she meet him in the meadow, or had she said a firm no?

Charles thought of reading the letter in the light thrown by the lanterns by the stables, but as he headed up the drive, Nick called to him.

"Marguerite has company—Captain E. and that scurvy fellow, Renny. We might not have to ride up to his place. We'll question him after he leaves the house." He clapped a hand to Charles's shoulder. "What do you think?"

"Marguerite might not be so keen on a night of male company."

"We'll keep her safe. Besides, Pru is present. The ladies can retire if they want, and we'll see to it that the others leave in an orderly fashion."

Nick's excitement touched Charles, and his spirits rose at the thought of spending the evening so close to his beloved.

He wished he'd had time to read her reply before entering the house, but it would have to wait.

"Let's take the opportunity that is presented to us. I'm sure Renny won't turn down an offer of a card game. Let's fleece him."

"Grand idea."

They returned to the house, and Charles gave Marguerite a cautious glance. After their latest meeting, a tension had risen between them that was hard to ignore. He was aware of her every move, every sensuous swing of her hips, every nuance of her smile as she graciously poured four goblets of brandy. Charles also noticed that she ignored Renny's gaze even though those icy green eyes seldom left her lovely form.

"What are you doing out so late, Nick?" she asked as she handed each man his glass.

"I visited a friend, met Charles, and we decided to look in on you and take shelter from the storm. A card game would nicely round off the evening. Would you mind if we play some cards? You can go up if you like. Charles and I will do the hosting duty."

She nodded and sat down on a chair by the window, close to Prunella, who had pulled out an embroidery frame to her to keep busy. "Very well, but I'll stay and chat for a few minutes." She darted a glance at Renny, and Charles observed the fear and the tension in that look.

Nick addressed the captain. "Will you stay and play a hand or two?"

"Cards would be more to my liking than gossiping with my men in the alehouse. Anyway, I would like to discuss the people in the area, and hear your thoughts on any strangers roaming the roads. We're still looking for a spy, and there's also that one dastardly thief whom I would like to get my hands on, the Midnight Bandit."

Marguerite gasped, and Charles noted the delicate blush tinting her cheeks. Surely she felt like a traitress to the law, he thought, and could barely suppress a laugh. "I hear he has amused himself again. Lord Elton-Fox was set upon as he traveled to London last week. The highwayman wore white gloves, his personal mark.''

"I'm sure he didn't recite a poem to that pompous old goat,'' Nick said with a snort. "Elton-Fox can afford to lose a purse or two.''

Emerson gave Nick a hard stare. His fingertip circled the base of the glass thoughtfully. "Hmm, a lawless act nevertheless. I don't think you ought to look upon it as a joke, Nick.''

Nick sat down and crossed one leg over the other. "You're right. But you have to admit he chooses his victims with care.''

"That he does. But after he hangs, I guarantee Saint Peter won't look upon him favorably as he approaches the heavenly gates. He'll be pointed in the other direction, surely.''

Nick laughed. "Was Robin Hood turned away from the heavenly gates, I wonder? After all, he was a folk hero, stole from the rich and gave to the poor.''

Emerson gave a dry chuckle. "You forget one detail, Nick: the Midnight Bandit is not likely to share his bounty. I'm certain he lines his own pockets before he gives away any alms.''

"You're probably right,'' Nick said with a shrug. He sipped his brandy and looked expectantly at Marguerite. "Where do you keep the cards? An unmarked pile would be proper, since we have an officer among us.'' He winked at Emerson, who shook his head at the joke.

"I'm sure there is a deck in the study.'' She got up, but Charles intercepted her by the door.

"I could fetch it. No need to wait upon us as if we're royalty.''

She lifted her eyebrows in mock surprise. "Aren't you? A lady was born to wait upon a gentleman, to serve his every whim. Don't you agree?''

Charles laughed and followed her out of the room. "I always thought the opposite. A gentleman is dirt under a lady's silk slippers.'' To prove his point, he held the door to the study with a deferential bow. "Hold doors and fling cloaks over mud puddles and slay dragons. Then there's the matter of courtship, with flowers and love epistles, fine gems, and the promise of an inexhaustible fortune.''

She sighed. ''I would not look askance upon a fortune,'' she said more to herself than to him. ''In fact, I would welcome it.''

Charles's heart hardened. ''That I cannot give you, but I can devise any number of flowery phrases for your lovely ears, and slay a dragon or two.'' He touched the sword at his side.

''I don't need that, as I can read B. C. Rose any time of the day, and dragons do not exist.'' She gave him a teasing smile as she pulled out the desk drawers to look for the playing cards. ''By the way, you have a true rival in B. C. Rose.''

'' 'Tis clear that my feeble attempts at gallantry are not well received.''

She blushed. ''Mayhap my stony heart will break at a flowery compliment, but I doubt 'twill come from your lips.''

He moved to her side of the desk and leaned over her. ''You give me no chance to show you what I'm willing to do for you.''

She heaved a deep sigh, and his gaze riveted to her bosom under the lacy kerchief crossed and fastened with a cameo brooch to her bodice. What wouldn't he do to unclasp the ornament and unveil her creamy skin underneath? What wouldn't he do to push her back against the desk, kiss away her protests, and lift her skirts to savor the treasures she so effectively concealed from him? Begad, his longing would burn him, shrivel him into a cinder. His blood pounded.

''Your persistence pushes me away,'' she said, cards in hand, and forced him to move aside so that she could pass.

''Call me a stubborn fellow.''

She turned to him, and the mischievous light in her amber eyes made his heart lurch with pleasure. ''I'd rather call you a foolish fellow who does not know when he'd be better off holding back.''

He crossed his arms over his chest and trapped her with his

eyes. "Oh? You like a mystery gentleman, do you? Would a stranger make more progress with your heart than I?"

"Perhaps," she said with an upward quirk of her lips. "If he captures my imagination." She tilted her head to the side, and Charles longed to seize her neck and press a kiss to those slightly mocking lips.

"You call me a foolish fellow, but *you* are the ill-advised person in this room, as you express that a stranger has more to offer than do I."

"A stranger might not pester me in this manner." She swished her skirts sideways, brushing his legs as she moved toward the door.

Two long strides took him to the door, and he barred her progress. "A stranger might not listen to your protests, to your pleas to uphold your chastity. He might ravish you on the spot and ask questions later."

"I suppose I'll have to take that risk if I am to make a stranger a friend. Would you please move out of my way now?" She made as if to turn the doorknob, but he caught her wrist.

"So that you can flirt shamelessly with Nick, or do you have your eyes set on Captain Emerson? He's a strong and reliable fellow, probably an accomplished lover."

Her voice lowered with anger. "At least they would behave like *gentlemen* toward me, and not trap me like this."

He held her hand to his lips and slowly caressed her fingertips. He had hoped that he could kiss her, taste the ambrosia of her mouth, but a dangerous light had come into her eyes. Before he could release his grip on her arm—not that he wanted to—she had slapped him with her other.

"Since words don't convince you," she said, her chest heaving with wrath.

With a shrug of defeat, he loosened his grip and she tore herself free.

"I can't very well throw you out, since I don't want to reveal my humiliation to the other guests, but I would dearly like to do so, since you probably won't leave on your own.'' She pushed him aside and tromped into the hallway.

Charles swore at his own clumsiness, but he found he could not have acted in any other way. His longing chewed at his patience endlessly, and he regretted having put himself in the temptation of her presence.

He sighed heavily and followed her. Nick was coming out of the door leading to the cellars, and Charles wondered at his friend's strange behavior.

"What are you doing, Nick?" Charles whispered as Marguerite entered the parlor.

"Marguerite has some excellent ale in a barrel down there, and I need something to drink that won't befuddle my brain like wine or brandy." He winked, holding up a pewter pitcher. "We're here on a mission, and I intend to see that it is accomplished successfully." He lowered his voice. "We'll fleece Renny of his last groat tonight."

"Yes . . . it shall be a pleasure." Charles gathered his composure and reined in his longing for the woman he could not have—at least not by any conventional means. He touched the stiff letter in his pocket and wondered what response she had given to his outrageous suggestion of a clandestine meeting.

"At least I doubt Marguerite has marked cards," Nick said under his breath as he followed her into the front parlor.

"Don't be so sure of that," Charles said in an undertone. Where Marguerite was concerned, he didn't know what to expect.

"I think I'll join you in a game or two," Marguerite said. "Pru, you will stay, won't you?"

"Yes," said the older woman with a disapproving look at the gentlemen, who were arranging chairs around a table.

Renny's icy gaze slunk from one face to another as the group sat down at the table, and Charles placed himself on the opposite side of the main opponent. Emerson sat to Renny's right, and Nick between Renny and Marguerite.

"What do you want to play, milady?" Captain Emerson said as he watched Marguerite shuffling the cards.

"How about Reverse?"

"Ah! I know that game. All the hearts taken in a trick are minus points." Charles glanced at her provocatively.

A pink blush rose in her cheeks. "Yes . . . exactly. We could play for penny points."

Everyone agreed, and Marguerite dealt the cards and upended a cup of numbered wooden counters she'd unearthed in the desk. She gave equal amounts to all players. "There! May you lose them all to me," she said with a mischievous grin.

Charles's breath stilled at the beauty of her expression, which reminded him of the day in London when he'd first caught sight of her again after six years. He'd thought he'd forgotten her. What a fool he'd been to live with such an illusion.

"You start, Charles," she said, pulling him out of his reverie.

They played in silence, and the heap of counters got avid or calculating stares as most of the tricks were taken. The person who had gotten no hearts would get the pot, or share it with another equally lucky player. Marguerite had soon amassed an astounding pile of counters.

"I daresay you should be a gaming hostess in London and make your fortune, Marguerite," Nick drawled as he pushed his last counters to the middle of the table.

"She lost her calling when she married Lennox," Renny said disdainfully. "I always thought her talent and beauty were wasted in this godforsaken corner of England."

"You sound jealous, Mr. Renny," Nick said coldly. "Do you criticize your old friend's judgment even though he's not here to defend himself?"

Renny tossed a card on the table carelessly. "I've known Lord Lennox all my life. I'd say he had great taste, but it was wrong to bury Marguerite here in the country. She should have been a shining star in London. They were sadly incompatible."

"I resent that you talk about me as if I'm not here," Marguerite said, her eyes flashing with anger. "And I resent your discussion about my deceased husband, may he rest in peace. Do not mention his name if you have only insults to deliver," she added, and looked hard at Montagu Renny.

"You are always quick to berate me," Renny drawled. "But I am a patient man. Lennox was a friend of mine, and anyone connected to him is also my friend."

Steps, slow and hesitant, sounded on the second floor. The chandelier swayed eerily.

Charles glanced at Marguerite as if to learn from her expression who walked upstairs, but she looked only vaguely amused.

Marguerite glanced toward the ceiling, suspecting that Sophie was suffering from another bout of insomnia. Sophie often did, especially if guests—gentleman guests—were present. She never approved of seeing men at home, not even with two chaperones. No wonder the sour girl had turned into a sour spinster. Marguerite had often wondered what kind of heavy-handed parental guidance Lithgow and Sophie had received. Lots of lectures and mayhap heavy beatings to cultivate the right fear of God.

Marguerite shivered. She hated the thought of such a mean-spirited and tightfisted God, which had followed everywhere Lithgow had walked, and had steeped the walls of this house for so long.

The steps retreated, and a beam creaked in a sinister fashion. "I think that the Gray Lady is present tonight. She walks with the heavy tread of sorrow," Marguerite said.

She glanced at Charles and gave him a wry smile as she remembered how the Gray Lady had been invented. He winked at her, and a veil—of anger and disdain—fell from her eyes. Charles, filled with tenderness and many other qualities, looked at her with such devotion that her heart melted for a moment, and left a lightness behind.

After that, she sat steeped in a molten glow that made the most commonplace comment sound either inspired or absurd. She laughed and amassed a fortune of wooden counters. If only they were gold coins . . .

Montagu Renny's snakelike green eyes followed her moves with close concentration, spikes that might nail her to a display board if she sat too close.

"You truly insist there is a ghost in the house?" Captain Emerson asked and turned down a trick. His gaze darted from corner to dark corner.

His skin held a slightly green cast, as did Renny's. The only sound in the room as the men's eyes turned to the ceiling was the rasp of Pru's needle through the canvas.

Marguerite glanced at Pru, and the widow rolled her eyes at Marguerite, who had difficulty suppressing a laugh. She held the audience captive as she stared in mock fear at the swaying chandelier. Heavy, muffled steps walked above.

"The Gray Lady is restless tonight. She senses evil in this house, perhaps. She walks in times of great upheaval." Marguerite let her gaze fall slowly on Montagu Renny and noted with satisfaction that his forehead was bathed in beads of perspiration. To her surprise, a candle in the candelabra on the table flickered wildly and died, casting the room into longer and darker shadows.

Charles's eyes had narrowed with suspicion as he stared at Marguerite. She only gave him an enigmatic smile. Let him wonder if there really was a ghost at Lennox House. And mayhap there was—another candle flame had just flickered and died.

"She starts as a thin gray wisp of smoke sometimes," Marguerite said dreamily, her gaze fastened on the curling gray plume rising from the extinguished flame.

Renny threw his cards down on the table and pushed back his chair with savage force. It fell back with a clatter. Silence stretched, then sank like a stone in the room as everyone followed his hurried movements.

"I completely forgot another appointment," he said thinly. "It flew my memory in your delightful company," he added with a quick bow in Marguerite's direction.

"Good night, Mr. Renny," Marguerite said firmly, and put

down her cards. "I don't think the Gray Lady will harm you as you walk out, but she has her likes and dislikes. I never know which of my guests will find her approval, or which will feel her wrath."

Charles snorted beside her.

"Your jest is not wholly in good taste, Marguerite. You're making me into an object of ridicule," Renny said, his lips stiff and colorless. He threw a harried glance toward the closed door as if measuring the distance.

"I would never jest in your company, Mr. Renny," Marguerite said. "I wouldn't *dare* to treat you so shabbily. At least Mrs. Trent and I have nothing to fear from the lady."

"Why not?" Renny wiped his forehead with a folded handkerchief. He righted his chair and seemed to gather his wits before his flight through the door.

"She never plays mischief on ladies. A gentleman betrayed her, and she has turned her hatred toward—"

"Marguerite, my dear," Nick said in a dry voice while his eyes twinkled recklessly. "Are you saying I should fear the Gray Lady's revenge?"

"It would be wise," she said, lifting her cards and spreading them in front of her face like a fan. "Very wise."

Nick shook his head as Renny fled to the door. He flung it open and braved the shadowy hallway. A cool draft wafted across the floor, soon filling the room.

The front door slammed shut behind Renny, and Marguerite drew a sigh of relief. The tension in the room had deflated at last, and she could breathe easier. The residue, a vicious headache, pounded at her temples.

Nick sighed, put down his cards, and leaned back in his chair. "I had planned to fleece that gentleman. Don't know why he always gets my hackles up, but there you are."

"I doubt he has anything to fleece," Marguerite scoffed.

"We could always fleece his hide," Charles said with a laugh.

"That lank hair won't fetch much at the wig makers," Nick said in dismissive tones. He rose and stretched his tall frame. "I think I've had enough of the Gray Lady and her grudge for one night." He turned to Charles. "What do you say, old fellow, a hard ride back to the Meadow and a glass of brandy?"

Charles nodded and stood. "Emerson, will you join us, or are you going to stay here and offer yourself on fair Marguerite's altar?"

Marguerite slapped his wrist, but Charles only smiled enigmatically. Captain Emerson blushed crimson and fumbled with the chair as he tried to push it back under the table.

Charles lingered over Marguerite's hand, and that delicious sensation of a golden glow enveloped her with renewed force. He gave her fingers a last squeeze and smiled, a smile that brought back worlds of memories from a time when life had been simpler.

"Good night, my fair," Nick said, also lingering over his farewell. He hovered on the threshold, his gaze traveling from Charles's face to hers. Then he grimaced and left with the captain.

Charles said not so many words, but he seemed reluctant to go. With a last smile, he closed the door after him and left a hollow silence behind.

"There! Good riddance, I say," Prunella said, and pushed away the embroidery frame. "They gawk at you as if they want to eat you alive. Shameless. *Shameless,* I say."

"Rather sweet, I should think," Marguerite said with a half smile. "Makes me feel younger every day."

Pru snorted. "Your behavior is very *youthful,* if that is your goal. Too precocious, if you ask me."

"Let's bring a glass of hot milk up to Sophie. By the sound of her heavy steps, I'd say she's spending another sleepless night."

"So would I, if I had devils for companions," Pru muttered. "So would I."

* * *

Charles and Nick fetched their mounts from the care of a sleepy boy in the stables. Thunder stood docile while Charles swung himself into the saddle. Nick's stallion trotted shortly behind. "An unexpected ending—a flat ending on a promising evening of cards. Can't recall—"

"Ladies were present. I'm convinced we could not have engaged in deep play with Renny with Marguerite and Pru there. Couldn't very well clutter up Marguerite's parlor all night."

"Yes, but nevertheless. Renny makes my teeth ache with frustration." Nick rubbed the back of his neck. "Something about him touches my more primitive instincts. I want to punch his nose."

Charles stared at the stars that sprinkled the sky after the storm. The wind had died down, the drops of water falling from the trees the only noise in the night. Thunder whinnied, and Charles inhaled the moist, woodsy air of the country lane. Shrouds of fog clad the shrubs lining the ditches.

"What galls me is that he makes himself at home in Marguerite's house on the pretext of an old friendship with Lennox. After what he said tonight, I doubt he held Lennox in high esteem. Rather the opposite."

"Yes, exactly my thought," Nick said in a growl. "He has his frigid eyes set on Marguerite; mark my words."

A lone figure moved into the middle of the lane. Charles, who had the lead, instinctively pulled in the reins. Thunder's great head bobbed, and he shied as the cloaked figure swung his arms. A cocked hat had been pulled down over invisible eyes.

"Whoa, who goes there? The Midnight Bandit?" Charles shouted, as Thunder danced around in fear.

"By God, let's catch the scoundrel and bring him to the magistrates," Nick cried. His stallion reared, and Nick had to concentrate on staying in the saddle.

"I'm not the Midnight Bandit, but I'd like to even the score. You almost broke my jaw at the Bentworth ball, Mortimer, and I want to break yours in return."

"Renny! By thunder, just the man I'm itching to fight," Nick said with delight.

"No bloodshed, Nick," Charles said as he brought Thunder to a standstill.

"I don't have a quarrel with you, Thurston, but with the cur you call your friend."

"Steady on. Charles might be a patient and levelheaded man, but when his ire is provoked, he's a dangerous fellow, and quite brilliant with the sword."

"At least we won't have females here to take his side," Renny said scathingly. "Actually, I've marked Marguerite for myself, and this is my way of settling with potential rivals. I saw how you stared at her, Mortimer, and I won't have my future bride ogled by yokels like you."

Nick laughed incredulously. "He called you a yokel, Charles. You want me to show him a lesson?"

Chapter 12

"I'm quite capable of delivering my own lessons," Charles said with a snarl, and slid from the saddle. "But you can cheer me on." He tied Thunder to a tree, and Nick followed suit with his own mount. Charles tossed off his hat and cloak. "Should take only a minute."

Sword blade sang against scabbard as Renny readied himself for the fight. Charles whipped out his blade and swung it in a circle twice. The air hummed. He took up the *en garde* position on the lane.

"Defend yourself, Renny. I don't take kindly to insults, nor do I like to hear Marguerite's name on your tongue, as it sullies her reputation. I don't know why she allows you over her threshold, but her kindness shows a certain naïveté."

Renny laughed coldly. "You're a fool, Mortimer. Marguerite would choose me before she chooses you. You're not man enough to admit it."

Charles lunged, and Renny parried. The blades ground together at the hilts, steel jarring. Before he jumped back to deliver a quick jab, Charles smelled the feral scent of battle on his opponent. "Cur," he spit, and sidestepped a lunge.

A series of feints and jabs had Renny dancing around as if the ground scorched the soles of his feet.

Renny whirled sideways and slashed down as if to sever Charles's hand from his wrist, but Charles evaded the move and managed to draw blood as the tip of his sword sliced into Renny's left upper arm.

Renny shouted and jumped back, his arm hanging lifelessly. He guarded his chest with a series of jabs that missed their target.

Charles advanced, avoiding tussocks and forcing his enemy back toward the edge of the ditch. He hooked the wide cuff of Renny's coat and slashed upward, ripping the fabric to the elbow.

Renny teetered for a moment, then shot forward, his sword raised under Charles's guard. Charles made a lightning-fast turn, and the deadly blade went by him with an inch to spare. He slammed the hilt down on Renny's wrist, and Renny dropped his sword. It clattered against the ground. Charles kicked it out of range.

The exertion had barely elevated Charles's breathing.

"Renny, you shouldn't challenge a master at swords," Nick drawled, and picked up Renny's weapon. " 'Twill make you look a fool faster than you think. Charles could easily pierce your rotten heart, making you swallow your insults in a hurry." He stepped on the blade, broke it, and flung the sword into the woods where Renny surely wouldn't find it in the dark.

Charles stared at his opponent for a long moment. "You deserve to die, but fortunately for you I'm not the murdering kind." He pushed Renny hard in the shoulder. Renny tottered back and slid into the water-filled ditch. Slogging through the mud, he swore out loud and cursed all of Charles's relatives and ancestors.

Charles looked at his opponent with disgust. "Let's go," he said to Nick, and sheathed his sword.

"You ought to kill him," Nick said softly.

"Surely you don't kill every rat you encounter, only the truly vicious ones. Renny is more bluster than actual threat," Charles taunted as he looked down upon his floundering enemy.

He had never killed a man, and he had no interest in starting with Renny, but it wouldn't do to show any such weakness to a man who might not hesitate to snuff out another's life.

He walked through the tendrils of fog to the tree where he'd left his cloak and his horse. Nick was already swinging himself into the saddle of his waiting stallion.

Silently, they steered their mounts onto the lane that wound like a pale ribbon among the trees. Weak moonlight illuminated the area, forming writhing ghosts in the fog.

A darker shape rose from the ditch, arms raised. By instinct, Charles turned aside in the saddle, but something hard and uneven crashed into his shoulder—a muddy rock. Shooting pain spread down his arm and into his neck. Furious and oblivious of the pain, he jumped down and sprinted to the filthy figure who had thrown the rock. Cackling, Renny climbed out of the ditch, his fists clenched.

Charles gripped Renny's coat just as a blow hit the side of his face. He reeled back, his ears ringing. With a growl, he threw himself over his enemy and they both went down in the road. Charles grappled with Renny, twisting out of his enemy's grip and rolling to his knees. He bunched his fist and slammed it into his adversary's face, then once more.

Bone cracked against bone, sending excruciating pain up Charles's arm. He looked down at the limp, unconscious figure below him. It would be so easy to snap the idiot's neck, but he couldn't do it.

He stood as Nick came to offer his support. "The devious rascal! Never knows when to stop."

"He does favor an underhanded fight. The damned cur does not play by the rules of a gentleman." Charles nursed his wounded knuckles and gingerly peeled off the tight glove. He swore as Nick pulled the hand toward the moonlight. "You'll have bad bruising tomorrow. The bounder should be drawn and quartered for such behavior.''

"Yes." Charles jabbed a toe into Renny's side. The man did not move. ''Let's go.'' He turned abruptly as pain pounded through his left shoulder and his right hand. ''Damned nuisance!'' He untied Renny's horse and with a slap in the rump sent it galloping off down the lane.

"I don't think the matter has been settled," Charles said, ''but other than killing him, I don't see how we can get rid of Renny.''

"He'll hold a grudge. Forever."

"I think I broke his jaw. That ought to make him think twice before challenging me again.''

"Yes . . . but next time he won't challenge you to your face; he'll shoot you from behind a tree.''

"I can't live in fear of ruffians like Renny. What bothers me is the thought of Marguerite vulnerable to his schemes.''

"We'll have to keep a closer eye on her," Nick said grimly.

Later that night when Charles had soaked and bandaged his hand with the help of his manservant, he pulled out Marguerite's letter. It was smudged and wrinkled after the fight he'd had with Renny. With one hand he broke the seal and read the short message.

Brazen Midnight Bandit, I admit my heart fluttered at your extravagant compliments. I am deeply flattered—thrilled—by your admiration, but under no circumstances would I consent to meet an unknown gentleman in the middle of the night. You have judged me wrongly if you think I will lose my morals by keeping our rendezvous. Any suave persuasion on your part won't overturn my decision.

Marguerite.

Sighing, Charles refolded the letter. Not that he'd truly expected her to run into the night to meet a stranger. He'd be suspicious if she had agreed, but somehow he would have to make her longing for romance topple her better judgment. A challenge, indeed. Thinking of Marguerite's glittering eyes and mischievous smile, he sat down at his desk to compose a response. Then he remembered his injured hand. Damn it all; it would be days before he could hold a goose quill again. . . .

Marguerite found, however, a letter behind the brick two evenings later. Her heartbeat thundering, she closeted herself in her bedchamber and opened the message. At once she noticed the awkward style of the writing—as if a child had formed his first letters.

> *Dearest Marguerite,*
>   *I am devastated; I am distraught. My right hand is wounded, and I despaired that I would not manage to form a love letter to you, but I would let nothing stop me. This is the work of my left hand, since nothing could keep me from conveying my despair that I will not see you, nor hold your lovely form in my arms in the near future. I agree that an underhanded meeting in a summer meadow would not be appropriate, but as you well know, I cannot announce myself at your door. If only! If only you could find it in your heart to meet me once, just so that I can give you a bouquet of wildflowers and explain the feelings in my heart. Nothing more. If it is your wish, I will not touch one hair on your head, even though it beckons me with its copper glow.*

Marguerite chuckled and put the letter in her lap. She pressed her hands to her burning cheeks. The villain had such a wily way with words, a way that insinuated itself into her thoughts and into her heart. Even into her dreams.

If she went to meet him, he would not confine his admiration to flowers and words. And wasn't that what she wanted? To be crushed against his broad chest and forget her station, her nagging problems, if only for one night to be with someone who spent hours writing odes to her beauty. A night of pleasure with someone who wouldn't judge her. It would be and would remain a secret. She continued reading.

I wlll wuit for you at ten precisely, two days hence, when the moon is full in the meadow beyond the spinney. Do not be afraid. I shall wait until the sun rises over the Downs. I shall wait forever for you, my heart.

M.B.

Feeling hot all over, Marguerite tossed the letter onto her bed. Spreading out her arms, she danced around the room, imagining how it would be to feel the arms of a lover around her.

Overcome by a longing so fierce she was surprised, she sat down at the dressing table and brushed her hair. "You're shameless," she said to her own reflection. "But also so very lonely."

Things would change once her possessions were sold and she moved to another house that didn't depress her us this one did. She would start a new life, bring new happiness into her existence, mayhap find a decent gentleman to marry—someone who wouldn't be averse to reading some poetry aloud to her.

Tomorrow all the things, except beds and a table and three chairs, would be gone from the house. Her new life started tomorrow, and she looked forward to the change as she did nothing else—in spite of Renny's threat.

The auctioneer's train of wagons arrived the next day and loaded up everything from the house. Sophie's room was left untouched, since she'd brought her pieces of furniture from

Scotland. When the workers had left, the rooms echoed with emptiness. Even the floorboards were bare.

"I don't see how we'll ever again sit comfortably in front of a fire, sewing," Prunella said gloomily as she eyed the hard chairs around the dining room table.

"We will start over. I shall have new furniture made, and you shall have the most comfortable armchair to call your own, Pru."

"I'm not convinced—"

"Don't say another word. This is our only choice. I cannot afford the upkeep of Lennox House, nor do I wish to live here any longer than necessary."

"Yes . . . I can understand that. You've had enough troubles this last year, and I don't blame you for wanting changes."

"We can only go forward—to a better future."

Two nights later Marguerite went to her denuded bedchamber to get ready for bed—well, rather to decide whether to accept the Midnight Bandit's invitation to the meadow.

Her heart throbbed with longing, but her mind said she was insane even to consider a romantic rendezvous with a stranger in the middle of the night. Sitting in a quandary for an hour, she finally managed to silence her conscience. Before she could change her mind, she brushed out her hair and dressed in a simple blue gown with a row of echelles along the stomacher. It drooped and dragged on the floor without panniers, so she kept them on. Besides, she didn't want the bandit to think she had come to the meeting dressed in her nightgown.

Feeling wild and full of adventure, she sneaked down the back stairs and out onto the terrace. From there it was easy to run past the stables, through the spinney, and . . . and see the meadow spread out in the silvery moonlight. The grass swayed in the gentle breeze, and daisies and bluebells waved as if beckoning her.

Her heart racing, she scanned the meadow, but there was no

sight of a waiting admirer. She walked among the blooms and the grass touched with silver, and wondered if he could see her. She thought she heard a twig break in the spinney behind her and whirled around.

A man walked toward her, his cloak flung back over his shoulders, his hat in his hand. He wore a bagwig powdered white, with two curls over the ears and a face mask that covered most of his face. He was tall, powerful, just as she remembered him from that night in the road.

His smile was alluring as that in her dreams, his hands were in white gloves, as welcoming as the embrace for which she longed. He took both her hands in his and sank to one knee. With his face turned away from the moon, she could not read the expression in his eyes, but his teeth gleamed in a smile.

She felt no fear, no warning bells chimed in her chest, and her body only trembled with longing.

"You came," he whispered. "I worried that you would not care to meet me."

"Curiosity was my downfall," she said with a smile. "Why are you whispering?"

"Shh, listen to the night, my fair. It has its own song, and only he who is quiet can hear it."

She listened to the silence, noting the peace that seemed to stretch out far beyond the limits of the Earth, contained only in the distant dome of transparent darkness that was the sky. "It's lovely," she whispered back. "The stars are looking at us."

"Without condemning us, I'm sure." He stood and squeezed her hand, and she looked into his face, disconcerted by the mask and her inability to see his features clearly. The Midnight Bandit, a shadow figure.

"The world would not be so generous. Am I very scandalous for meeting you like this?"

He nodded, his smile like a beacon "Yes, very wicked."

"Would you mind removing your mask so that I can see

your face?'' She touched the soft leather, but he captured her hand quickly and pulled it away.

"And recognize the identity of the Midnight Bandit? No. If you could identify me, you might be the person to one day send me to the gallows. I'm sorry, but I cannot risk that.''

"I would never denounce you.'' She touched his face again, pulling a fingertip along his jaw.

"You might not, but you may find yourself forced to reveal the secret against your wishes. I'm loath to put you in that position.''

"But not loath to meet me clandestinely,'' she said, and, stung, whirled away from him. ''You are a shameless fellow.''

"A fellow with a shameless heart, mayhap, but I'm not shameless. At the bottom, I'm a dull and upstanding citizen.''

She laughed and ran among the flowers. The breeze caressed her arms, and her hair hung loose, giving her a sense of freedom she hadn't felt for a long time. This was what she'd dreamed of: to be alive, to have the gaze of a desirable—and oh, so romantic—gentleman follow her with longing. He ran after her, his cloak flying behind him. He caught her up in his arms and swung her around until she grew dizzy and her laughter died.

He smelled of wood, of fresh sawdust, as if he'd come from the sawmill, and of crushed violets. It reminded her of a salve her mother had used for all sorts of cuts and bruises.

His hard arms pressed her against him, and she could feel every line of his body through the thin material of her gown. His hands traveled hotly down the curve of her spine, and she moaned at the sensation. A dulcet wave of passion spread through her entire body and weakened her knees.

He gripped her waist right above the jutting panniers and lifted her high above him. She clung to his shoulders and looked into his smiling face, laughing.

"I have no head for heights,'' she said, and he slowly lowered her to the ground, her body raking his as she slipped downward. Her heartbeat pounded, tightened her throat until she could no longer find her breath. His hard thighs and flat belly moved against hers. His unyielding chest seemed to pull her inside him until her softness melded with his strength, and she could breathe again, now uplifted, soaring on a wave of desire.

"You're so lovely I could cry." He groaned against her throat; then his mouth found hers in a kiss that stole her breath again. For one unnerving moment she thought of Charles, almost tasted his passionate kisses that had quite taken her by surprise and ignited her own passion. She pushed aside any thoughts of Charles, and concentrated on this wild, clandestine moment when she didn't have to play a role.

He lifted his head, and she whispered, "Kiss me again."

His tongue moved with hers, and she was filled with the warmth of him, tasting the softness of his mouth, exploring the sensations of shamelessly wallowing in the throes of passion.

He found the laces holding her bodice together in the front and undid the knot with clumsy fingers. He groaned deep in his throat as the lacing gave and he could close his hand over her breasts, now protected only by the thin silk of her shift. He bent down and kissed her straight through the material, sucking on her nipple until it rose and hardened in anticipation.

She gasped with the waves of pleasure surging through her. As he fitted his hand around her breast, she pressed against him, yearning for a more intimate contact that would ignite her longings into a blaze of passion.

"You're so hot," he said, "burning up from inside."

"I've waited so long to throw off the reins. To live, to discover who I am, what could be mine if only—"

He silenced her words with a savage kiss, then bent her neck back and paid homage to the sensitive skin of her throat with his lips. He touched every hollow and teased every hidden spot, giving her such thrills as she never knew existed.

She moaned as he released her. With a quick tug he unclasped the cloak from his throat and spread it among the flowers in the meadow. Impatiently he pulled off his gloves and tossed them aside. He divested himself of his dark coat and waistcoat, leaving only the white shirt to separate her from his skin.

He helped her off with her gown, and she pulled his shirt from his breeches and inserted her hands under the soft white material. His skin felt incredibly supple over the hardness of his muscles, and as her hands traveled the expanse of his chest, a fever rose within her to gather in her loins to a throbbing ache.

He grasped her hands and bore them down over his stomach to the hard swelling in his breeches. She gasped with pleasure, holding in her hand the rigid proof of his longing for her.

"Darling!" The word came as a tortured gasp in her ear. He tore at his shirt and flung it off, only to be hampered by her petticoat and panniers. He fumbled with the ties at her waist, unable to free her from the contraptions of fashion. She felt as if she would explode if he didn't fulfill her yearning, bring her forth into the sensuous woman she'd repressed for so many years, to be newly born.

"Take me," she whispered against his mouth as she pulled him down with her on top of the cloak. She rubbed her thighs together to still the throbbing ache between her legs. She realized she didn't even know his name. "Take me. Make me whole."

He fell heavily against her. With savage twists, he untied his breeches and pulled them off. He struggled with her clothing, and she tried to help, only to discover that the knots could not be unraveled. His jaw rubbed against her breast as he bit her nipple gently through her chemise. They hardened in anticipation, and she pushed herself against his mouth to savor his caress more deeply.

"I need you." She moaned against his neck, tasting his skin with her tongue.

He eased her petticoat up to her waist to better explore her bare legs with his own. His male nakedness pressed against her stomach, and she gripped his buttocks, reveling in the sensation of his hard symmetry. He groaned as her hand enclosed him, and she raised her hips toward him. He caressed the soft insides of her thighs, sending wave upon wave of hypnotic pleasure through her body. He tested her readiness with one eager finger, and she cried out and offered her secrets to him in desperation.

She followed him into the maelstrom of desire, and whimpered in pleasure as he slid into her hot wetness and cradled her close. She gasped with delight.

"God save me," he said hoarsely against her hair.

Tears of pleasure stung her eyes as he moved inside her, rocking her from one side to the other, gathering speed. He was a man full of power, searing her with the depths of his fire as the torment rose within her and tossed her into a wave of rapture so intense she could only cry out her ecstasy.

Charles was aware only of each second filled with the hot scent of her. His fingertips recorded every soft inch of her skin and her silky insides as he bucked against her in a frenzy. *Release,* his body cried, and he arched, climbed onto an incredible peak, teetered, then shattered into bliss. He was vaguely aware of giving a drawn-out groan, and buried his face in her neck until his ragged breath stilled. Hers was a gentle tickle on his skin. He rested within her, spent and deeply content.

"I never want to be lonely and bereft again," she whispered in his ear.

The moment stood still, glowed, glittered; then slowly the world righted itself around them.

"I realize I don't know your real name," Marguerite said against his neck.

Chapter 13

He whispered in her ear, "I'm the infamous bandit, and that is all you need to know, my darling. I do not want to become Ned Knotts to you, or Willy Hopkins. Not very romantic names."

She poked him in the ribs. "You do not speak like a Ned Knotts or a Willy Hopkins; you speak like a lord and a rather poetic fellow. And you know how to write, to melt a woman's heart."

"So do you, Marguerite, though I wish you would have sent me some lines of poetry describing your longing rather than epistles of caution and censure. Admonitions and wagging fingers were all I got for my literary efforts. I thought you ladies liked romance." He gripped a handful of her hair and wound it around his fingers. The grass soughed softly, and dry flowers gave a faint rattle in the cooling breeze.

"Why do you still whisper? No one will hear us."

"Listen to the night, my darling. The wind speaks more eloquently than I. Tell me, why did you not respond with romantic verse?"

Marguerite chuckled. "It wouldn't be ladylike to write love poems to a gentleman, let alone to a roguish stranger."

"Which I am no longer."

"I agree . . . yet I want to know—"

"Do not pry, or the whole magic will collapse like a ruined blancmange. Mayhap you shall know the truth one day, when the time for games has passed." He wound her hair tight until his fist rested against her skull. "You ask altogether too many questions," he said, and kissed her hard.

Something rasped against her skin, and she felt for his hand buried in her hair. "You're wounded!"

He trapped her hand between his stomach and her own before she could explore the extent of his recent injuries.

"Don't," he said in a fierce whisper. "Old wounds. 'Tis nothing."

"Nothing, he says, while he cries himself to sleep with pain," she chided. She arched her hips against him as she felt him stiffen inside her. He moved with singular determination to bring her into the world where nothing but their ecstasy existed. She flared up like fireworks, consumed by her own overwhelming passion.

Afterward, as he whispered endearments in her ear, she drifted off to sleep. When she awakened, her body had cooled, and her arms were empty. She lay wrapped in his cloak, but there was no sign of the bandit, only a posy of flowers tucked into the waistband that so stubbornly had withstood his amorous onslaught. With a shiver she stood, her petticoat falling into place. She hunted for her gown and dragged it over the ruined shift. Satiated and light, she flung his cloak that smelled of horse and damp earth around her and hummed to herself.

She might be alone, but he had left something behind, a warmth around her heart, a piece of himself. She danced through the meadow and vowed she would not think about tomorrow. She would never worry again.

* * *

Charles did not regret his deceit with Marguerite as he sat on the terrace at the Meadow watching the stars pale in the crystal globe above him. A well of bliss had opened in his heart, and he couldn't stop smiling. He sipped a glass of wine, thinking of her, of her lips that tasted better than any wine he'd ever tasted. His only regret was that he'd been unable to stay and watch her wake up to the first rays of the sun If she knew that he'd borrowed the Midnight Bandit's identity, she would reject him forever. Well, perhaps not forever, but she would not easily forgive him.

That single gray thought blew through his mind, but he wouldn't let it return. He relived again and again the feel of her silken skin, her hot, ripe passion, her rounded arms around his neck, and her cries of pleasure as he entered her most guarded secret of all.

After this night, B. C. Rose had fodder for a whole book of poems, but that was secondary to the happiness he'd received from her, a happiness he'd craved since the moment he'd glanced into her amber eyes in the dappled sunlight behind the Ranelagh rotunda. He had caught a fever, and it might have been quenched for the moment, but it would come and ravage him again. He breathed deeply, elation tingling within him like stars popping fire in every direction.

On the following evening, he decided to ride over to Lennox House, as he could not stand the thought of not seeing her that day. He saddled Thunder late, right before midnight, and rode slowly through the moonlit landscape to the spinney behind her stables.

His heartbeat accelerated at the thought that she might be in the meadow, but as he scanned the serene landscape that was so much like last night, he saw nothing but grass and flowers.

She had not come. Not that they had agreed to another rendezvous, but she might have suffered such a restlessness as his.

Disappointed, he waited another half hour, then pulled off his white gloves and mask. He returned to his horse and stuffed the articles of deceit into the saddlebag. It was foolish of him to think that she would sense his longing.

Gripping Thunder's reins, he walked through the spinney and tied the horse to a tree by the stables. Thunder found the grass to his liking, and Charles sneaked across the dark yard.

There was only one light in the house, in Lennox's old study. Like a thief, he crept along the side of the house and peeped through the windows. *What?* There was no furniture, only a hard chair, a tall stack of papers, and ledgers on the floor. Marguerite had one ledger spread on her lap, and she was writing something with a goose quill. Light spread from the candelabra on the floor, and cast a golden glow around her.

Charles heaved a deep sigh as a fierce urge to hold her in his arms came over him. Confused, he stared at her. Why was she working on the estate ledgers so late, and why had all the furniture disappeared? Was she about to move and hadn't said anything about it to him?

He would go around and knock on the door, find out the truth even if he had to shake it out of her. It was clear she had financial difficulties if she had had to sell off all of her furniture. There wasn't a single painting on the wall or rug on the floor. He started toward the front, then realized he didn't want to disturb any of the other occupants.

He knocked softly on the window and called out her name. " 'Tis me, Charles," he said, reminding himself that he could not show his overwhelming love for her, or she might grow suspicious.

Her head snapped up and she glared at the window. "Go away!" she ordered, her eyes blazing with anger. "If that is you, Renny, I refuse to see you. Leave my property immediately."

Renny? Why would he visit her in the middle of the night? Charles pressed his face to the glass and waved. She made a grimace, but her tense posture relaxed as she recognized him. She came to the window and opened it.

"Charles! What in the world are you doing here in the middle of the night? You're supposed to be at home, getting your hours of rejuvenating sleep."

"Seeing you rejuvenates me, Marguerite," he said.

She gave him a chiding smile. "What do you want?"

He threw up his arms. "What a warm welcome! I was at a card party and stopped by to see that everything is in order here. Won't you let me in?"

She crossed her arms over her chest and looked askance at him as he crawled through the window and dusted off his knees. "I don't need a nursemaid, Charles. I'm perfectly safe here."

"Perhaps not a nursemaid, but you don't have any grown males except your old coachman to protect you, and there are villains on the road."

She blushed a deep rose, and he realized she was thinking of the Midnight Bandit. Her eyes glittered with sudden elation, and her lips turned upward at the corners. So lovely, he thought, and could barely restrain himself from sweeping her into his arms.

"You look pleased with yourself, my sweet," he drawled, and twirled his hat on one finger. "At my mentioning of villains. Have you encountered the ruffian we know as the Midnight Bandit? Has he kissed your hand and murmured sweet nonsense in your ear?"

Her gaze burned into him, and her cheeks turned fiery red. "I don't like your scolding tone, Charles."

He put his hands behind his back and circled the one chair in the room with slow steps. Enjoying himself, he gave her a teasing smile. "You didn't answer my question, Marguerite. Did you meet him?"

"I don't have to answer to you." She folded her hands primly in front of her and looked away. He could have sworn she would've pressed her hand against her heart if she'd been alone, but she hid her emotions by holding herself tightly under control. He relented his teasing as he sensed her deep agitation.

No doubt she felt some guilt about making love to a villain when she had perfectly respectable admirers—like himself.

He decided to change the subject. "I'm surprised to find the room denuded of all its 'clothing' and decorations. Are you planning to replace *all* the furniture?" He sauntered the length of the room, and his steps echoed hollowly against the bare wooden floor. "Very Spartan. Is this the new style?"

Her lips had formed a thin line of disapproval. "You are prying into my private affairs."

Charles inhaled deeply as he pondered the implications. Her eyes were hard, and paleness tinted her cheeks as her blush subsided. His happiness dimmed and his heart sank a little. She would not confide in him.

"I thought I was your friend, Marguerite. You're welcome to unburden your problems on me. I'm more than willing to help you—with anything."

"Thank you, and I truly appreciate your friendship, but I don't need your help. Nor do I want you to pry into my private affairs—as I don't pry into yours."

"If the Midnight Bandit—or a complete stranger—were here, you would be more inclined to accept his offer of help than mine. Isn't that true?"

When she didn't respond, only raised her chin with stubborn pride, he longed to shake her. "You trust him more than you trust an old friend?" he asked incredulously.

Granted, she had made love to the "bandit," he thought, but how could a night of lovemaking wipe away a lifelong friendship? The dratted woman would turn to her lover before she turned to a friend. Perhaps ladies acted in that way in general. Confused about her motives, he stared into her accusing eyes.

"I don't think it is your place to claim my undying friendship and demand that I turn to you in my difficulties, Charles. *You* have decided to take the role of my protector; I never once asked you to."

She was right, of course, but the words hurt nevertheless "I suppose the bandit has more material wealth to offer than I, who have lived on the brink of genteel poverty for a long time."

"I don't know anything about the Midnight Bandit!" she cried. "One thing I do know, he doesn't push himself on me as you do."

"So you have met him!" Charles walked around the room and stopped right in front of her. Her sweet scent of roses and feminine flesh wafted toward him, making him slightly dizzy with longing. If he didn't take care, he might lose his reason and crush her in his arms.

She abruptly turned her back on him, and that was answer enough. He slid his hands into his pockets to prevent himself from gripping her shoulders. He was a fool to plead with her. His every visit was a silent plea for her affection.

"I see that whatever he has to offer is more important than my protection and friendship. Mayhap he can deal better with your debts than I am able to. That is, if he doesn't hang before he can deliver the funds into your hands."

"You are abominable," she exclaimed. "Just because you can't have me, you throw venom at all others who hold me dear." She dashed her hand over her wet, glistening eyes. "I *do* like financial security and the small pleasures of life."

"So that's why you chose to marry Lennox, for his fortune." Charles gave the room a contemptuous glance. "I see he frittered it all away."

"I didn't wed Lennox for his fortune! My parents forced me into the marriage. *They* wanted the settlement Lennox brought. Anyhow, you should know how difficult, how tedious it is to live on the brink of bankruptcy. 'Tis not wrong to wish for financial security." She braided her fingers together. "This is beside the point, but the bandit is not going to pay my debts; I shall deal with them myself."

Charles took a step toward her and pulled her into his arms. She didn't struggle against him. "Oh, my dear heart, why do you have to be so strong all the time?"

"I have to be," she said tiredly, "or I'll never find my self-respect again. Lennox's debts are mine now. I am Lady Lennox, and as such, I'll have to bear the burden my husband left behind. When I have solved my problems, I'll be ready to set aside the Lennox name. I'll be myself—Marguerite Langston."

"I understand," he said against her sweet-smelling hair. "You want to retrieve your identity without someone giving it to you."

"No one can give it to me. It was lost during my six years with Lennox, and only I can gather all the pieces together."

"I shudder at the thought of what your marriage was like."

She looked up at him, and he suppressed an urge to cry as he saw the tears of defeat and fear in her eyes. She touched his cheek, and it was all he could do to restrain himself from kissing her.

"I don't deserve your friendship, Charles, or your love. I'm not the young woman you loved in the past, nor am I the saint you want to make out of me. I have a dark past—or rather I was part of a dark past, and only I can struggle against the demons."

"Demons? Really, Marguerite, isn't that a bit strong? Let me—"

"Dark memories, and acts that I became part of by association with Lennox." Her eyelashes fluttered. "More I cannot tell you. If you are my friend, don't burden me. And don't tease me about my flights of fancy. I don't have to answer to you, or to anyone."

He reluctantly let her go, a sense of loss overwhelming him until he felt as hollow as a reed. He, Charles, would never win her love. He, as the Midnight Bandit, might win moments of bliss in her arms, but what about next week, and the next? Next year?

She would never be his. She would not be at the Meadow

waiting for him as he returned from business in London or a ride in the woods. She would not smile at the dinner table as his wife. She might be a guest on someone else's arm, but nothing else.

"I am your friend," he said with a hitch in his voice. "And I shall honor your request for secrecy." He turned away and went to the window. Without looking back, he crawled out the same way he'd arrived.

"Good night, Charles." Marguerite watched and felt curiously torn. One side of her wanted to call him back and beg him to help her; another stared at him with too much pride. She appreciated his friendship, but did not want to encourage his hopes that she would love him.

She could not deny he was a desirable gentleman, more so every day, but he couldn't hold a candle to her secret lover. Or could he? She'd never dreamed she would wonder about making love with good old Charles.

But since that night when he'd caressed her until she blossomed with desire, she had looked upon him as a masculine, erotic creature, who—if she let him—might sweep her off her feet and make love to her until she was drained of herself and filled with him. She blushed at the disturbing image and went back to her ledgers.

The money she had received from the auction of her things would precisely cover her outstanding debts. She had to pay the bills before Renny arrived to demand the money for himself. If it was gone, he couldn't lay his hands on it. She had written a letter to her banker, and tomorrow she would send the packet of bills to him and ask him to pay them. After that, she would have to fight with Renny about the property, and she did not look forward to another confrontation with him.

* * *

Heavy at heart, Charles went to fetch Thunder. In the last hour, so much had changed. All of his soaring hopes had died. Why couldn't he just live in the present and, as the Midnight Bandit, take what she was willing to give? Why did man always want more than he could get? It was the curse of humankind, Charles thought.

He jumped back with surprise as a dark figure stepped out of the stables by one of the back hatches that was used for throwing out horse dung. Charles stopped and stared at the stealthy figure. He dug his pistol from his saddlebag. It was not loaded, but the threat of it would frighten the intruder.

"Who goes there?" he barked.

The figure stopped as if slapped, and slowly turned around. "Charles? Is that you?"

"Nick, what the hell are you doing here, slinking around like a thief?"

"Me, a thief?" Nick laughed and sauntered toward Charles. He was wearing black from head to toe, and Charles noticed the shovel in his hand. He put away the pistol.

"Why are you carrying a shovel? Are you digging your own grave?"

Nick laughed guiltily. "No . . . but I am looking for a grave." He sighed. "I suppose I'll have to explain now. The reason I didn't before is that you're very touchy concerning Marguerite, so I said nothing." He took Charles's arm. "Come, let's get away from any listening ears."

"Listening ears? Who would be here at this time of night?" Perplexed, Charles followed his friend. "I must say I'm surprised to see you here, Nick."

Nick looked over his shoulder and scanned the area around them as if looking for eavesdroppers. Only trees surrounded them, and as far as Charles knew, they did not possess ears, and if they did, they could not speak about the secrets they were about to hear. Nick pulled him behind a huge elm.

"Really, Nick! Is this necessary? Am I about to hear the deepest secrets of government?"

"Listen. Do keep that big mouth shut for a minute—if you can. I'm working with Emerson. You heard about the sergeant who died under mysterious circumstances. Well, Emerson— and others—have reason to believe that the sergeant was last seen at Lennox House."

Charles's chest tightened painfully. "What? Are you implying that Marguerite might be involved in the man's death?"

"She might not have any part of it, but Lennox is a likely culprit. He, or someone else connected to him, could have murdered the sergeant. We're looking for the grave—without asking permission. Marguerite would never give it to us, since the suspicion of Lennox's involvement would ruin the Lennox name."

"She does care about reputation. She wouldn't want another slur attached to her name; being called the Poison Widow is enough."

"She's involved in this whether she wants it or not. If we find the body—"

"Why would Lennox bury a body on his land? That would be stupid."

"Where else was he going to bury it? He couldn't very well sneak over to Admiral Hancock's place and expect to dig a grave for the sergeant."

Charles thought about the implications. "Why would Lennox kill and bury a militiaman in the first place?"

Nick glanced around nervously. He then looked at Charles, and Charles could see his uneasiness. Nick slammed a gloved fist into the tree trunk. "Lennox was a secret Stuart sympathizer. Charles Edward Stuart has his spies, you know. Emerson has discovered that Lennox House was a stop on the way across the Channel. Seems that Lennox helped arrange for safe transportation."

"Ridiculous! You think Marguerite had something to do with it?"

Nick shrugged. "I don't know. I pray she's innocent, but how do we know for sure?"

"First of all, Marguerite is not Scottish, nor is she a Catholic. She does not support Stuart."

"No matter where her loyalties lie, she was married to Lennox and had to obey his orders. As her husband and master, he could have forced her to comply against her wishes."

"Hmm." Charles traced a knot in the bark of the tree. "That's why she's so dead set against marrying again. Perhaps he forced her to conceal spies and . . . help bury the body?"

They stared at each other, Nick swearing in a low voice. "I didn't really want to be involved in the investigation, but when Emerson asked me to look around, I could not say nay."

"You're Marguerite's friend, Nick. She trusts you, and you snoop around her property for dead bodies! When I think about it, you *have* been snooping in all corners. Didn't I see you emerge from the cellar with an ale pitcher not many days ago? Marguerite has servants to fetch and carry."

Nick sighed. "My only reasoning is that I might be able to prove her innocent. That makes it worth creeping about at night with a shovel."

"Even with what happened in the past, I don't think that Marguerite is part of secret Jacobite missions now," Charles said between clenched teeth.

Nick nodded. "I agree. She would not care to do anything illegal, but what about Renny? He hangs about her house rather often, even for an old friend of her husband. Is he offering her money to keep spies in her cellar overnight? I have noticed that Marguerite struggles to make ends meet."

"I don't know why she agrees to see Renny," Charles said, rotating his stiff neck. "She does not seem to like him overly much."

"Mayhap he comes to see Sophie Pierson?" Nick said hopefully.

"Sophie never shows her face when there are guests at the house. I doubt she has any interest in Renny, or he in her. They might have known each other from their time in Scotland, though. Renny still has property in the Lowlands, I believe."

"It is a mystery!" Nick slapped his thigh for emphasis.

"I don't like it."

"I can't help but suspect that Marguerite does have a hand in the Jacobite spy business. It could be very lucrative if she's sponsored by more powerful Jacobite sympathizers in London."

Charles grabbed the front of Nick's coat and tightened his grip. "How dare you even suggest that Marguerite is involved," he spit. "You disappoint me."

Nick's lips quirked in a smile, but Charles could feel the tension swelling in the man. "Your knuckles are still sore, aren't they, Morty?"

"It wouldn't stop me from beating that grin off your face."

"Steady on. You're not thinking logically. You're so befuddled with love for Marguerite that you can't bear the thought that she might be involved in a treasonous cause. Don't forget that she has refused all of our help. Spurned it, in fact."

Charles tried to let out the steam building in the cauldron of anger in his chest. He could not seem to get a grip on his emotions. One part agreed with Nick, but the other loathed his friend for even *thinking* that Marguerite might be involved.

"I should call you out for the malevolent things you've said about Marguerite, for the very thoughts of distrust going through your pea-sized mind."

"So do it!" Nick taunted, trying to pry Charles's hands from his coat. "We can meet at dawn with pistols, and then one of us will have to find a suitable spot to bury the other's body. Just as Lennox did, even though his opponent's death was not caused by a gentlemanly duel."

"Damn you!" Charles snarled and loosened his grip. "You're so deuced coldhearted and coolheaded."

"I'm a realist," Nick said in an icy voice, "and you're a dreamer. With a damned short temper."

"At least I would not choose to think the worst of my friends, especially one whom I've known all my life, as in Marguerite's case."

Nick kicked the tree trunk as if to release his frustration. "You're not the only one who would like to sweep Marguerite into your arms, but I see her imperfections, and I know the frailty of the human conscience. She's not the angel that you see her as."

"You wouldn't be able to see an angel if she stood right in front of you. You're so riddled with anger that you watch the whole world for flaws."

"Is that so damned strange? I wasn't born to an earldom, as you were. Heritage. I was born in the gutter, and my gentlemanly veneer is what it is—a veneer, a learned affectation."

"Damned balderdash! You've lived like a gentleman most of your life."

"You wouldn't know about hunger and hostility, murderers and footpads that would kill you for a farthing."

Charles spread his arms in frustration. "That was your life a long time ago."

"Perhaps. But not something a person easily forgets," Nick said, banging the tree with his fist. His voice was muffled with emotion.

Charles dropped his hand on Nick's shoulder. "Don't. Don't dig through the past like a pile of rubbish. Your father considered you his son as much as he did Ethan Leverton."

Nick snorted. " 'Tis no great pride to be the great Ethan's brother."

"Listen—"

"Let's put a halt to this discussion," Nick interrupted. "It is not going anywhere. I have been a victim of corroding anger for so long I have none left for you, old fellow. Let's forget this and return home. I have put aside a bottle of the finest brandy for a trying evening like this one."

Charles nodded. "Yes, it has been a trying evening, and I'm sure it won't be the last."

Chapter 14

Marguerite found another letter from her secret lover. A melting sensation traveled from the area of her heart all the way to her feet. The longing for his embrace ignited in her a restlessness, and she rapidly scanned the lines. She read the last sentence aloud. " 'Meet me in the meadow at sunset.' "

"Oh, how I'm yearning for you," she said to herself, and rubbed her forehead in frustration. How—and when—exactly had she fallen in love with a highwayman, a criminal? She blushed at her carelessness, her lack of common sense. Yet . . . somehow he had freed her, made her happy again after so many years of quiet despair.

She dared to be daring, to feel alive in every pore of her body. She would go. She had to, no question about that. Soon enough this passion would be spent, and then he would move on to new adventures. She gasped at the pain she felt at the thought of losing him, but at least he'd helped her through this difficult time.

"This *affaire de coeur* does not have a future, and you should have the common sense to see that," she murmured to herself as she went back to the house from the gate. Closeted in her boudoir, she read the letter more closely.

My dearest heart,

I left you—had to leave you lest the bright morning bring ruin to our love—awkwardness, and shame. I left with my heart singing, and my mind filled with golden memories of your beautiful body, of your sweet love. I hope I left memories with you, as I left my heart in your care. I will not be whole without it. Either you leave me your heart to keep, or I shall die, as I can never take mine back. I am already suffering from the tedium of life without you, and can only wish for time to travel faster so that I can behold your golden amber eyes with my own—the window to your soul, the portal to all your secrets, your thoughts. I want to know them all. To burn in the fire of your love is all I ask . . . beloved.

Meet me at the meadow at sunset.

A deep sigh trembled in her chest, and she brushed away a tear from the corner of her eye. He hadn't signed it, she noticed, but what did it matter? No one wrote such touching words, except mayhap B. C. Rose, but he—or she—touched everyone's heart, not only hers.

As evening arrived, Mr. Renny announced his presence. He sported a purplish blue bruise on his jaw, a bruise that spread up the side of his face to disappear into his carefully powdered hair.

"I don't have time to entertain you, Mr. Renny," Marguerite snapped, and turned her back on him as he stepped across the bare floor. The sound of his heavy gait echoed ominously. Betsy stood uncertainly in the background, and Marguerite waved her away. It wouldn't do to let the servant overhear her conversation with her enemy.

"I told you I don't have anything to discuss with you, Mr. Renny."

"But I do," the man said with difficulty, as if his jaw was too sore to move.

She faced him with determination. He glanced around the denuded parlor. Pale squares on the walls were the only signs that art had hung there, and the floor bore scratch marks from furniture now gone.

He pressed his hand to the side of his face, as if to support it. "I see that you've been very busy while I've been gone."

"I have my own schedule to follow, not yours," she said coldly. "Now I must ask you to leave." Marguerite glanced at the timepiece attached to her bodice and suspected that the Midnight Bandit would already be waiting for her. She had to get rid of Renny!

He stood with his hands locked behind his back. A frown had gathered on his rigid brow, and Marguerite felt his anger washing over her in waves. He restrained his temper, but was so much more dangerous for it. Knowing he was capable of murder, she took a step back, closing the distance to the door.

"I want you to hand over the money you earned from the sale of your—Lithgow's—things," he said very softly. His eyes glittered like green chips of ice.

"You're too late, Mr. Renny. I have already instructed my banker to pay all outstanding debts, and I fear there's not a groat left over for you."

"You're lying!"

"Last time we spoke, you didn't mention any restrictions on the sale of the furniture. I acted quickly, just as you suggested, and made sure my banker was involved from the start." She hardened her voice. "This time you have come in vain, Mr. Renny. I won't be bullied by the likes of you any longer." She hurried to the door as the shadows grew darker in the room. "I'll show you out."

He came across the room, wrested the door from her hand and shut it in her face. "I'm not finished with you! This would never have happened if I hadn't been laid up, in excruciating pain."

"If you're seeking sympathy, I have none. Your face does look somewhat livelier than the death mask you usually present."

He smiled, a mere lifting of his lips that offered nothing but a sense of threat. "I've never heard you like this, Marguerite. Where is the graceful hostess I've come to know and love?"

Heat rose in her face. "Don't use the word *love* in my presence, Mr. Renny. I can't abide it on your lips. You have no feeling for anyone but yourself."

A scratch on the door interrupted her condemnation of his character. Sophie slipped in, her face so pale she looked like a ghost. "I heard voices—heard Mr. Renny." She went to stand by his side and looked up at him with hope and admiration.

Fear and loathing crawled over Marguerite's skin. "Sophie, this is a discussion between Mr. Renny and myself. You would be better off not hearing any of it."

Sophie ignored her advice. She gripped Renny's coat of dark red brocade, and he flinched. Evidently his arm was sore. "You must make her listen, Montagu. She's sold everything that Lithgow held dear, and—"

Losing her patience, Marguerite longed to shake the other woman. "None of your things have been auctioned off, Sophie, and the rest Lithgow left to me."

"She has no reverence for our Scottish heritage," Sophie went on, her gaze limpid on Renny's hard face. "You have to make her see reason."

"The deed is already done, Sophie," Renny said, his eyes hard as granite. "Even if I abhor the way she has trampled on the Lennox name, there is nothing I can do about the furniture." He patted Sophie's hand on his sleeve, and a calculating light came into his eyes. "Do you know that Marguerite intends to sell the Lennox property and move to a smaller holding?"

Sophie nodded, shooting a look of venom at her sister-in-law. "Yes . . . we have argued about it, and I am dead set against the proposition."

"Mayhap Mr. Renny has some female relative who would

be happy to offer you a place in her household, Sophie,''
Marguerite said, her legs trembling as a wave of animosity for
her tormentors washed over her.

Sophie's eyes widened with incredulity, and her lips hung
slack. "You're heartless, Marguerite, to suggest such a thing!
I have no intention of living with the humiliation of being a
poor relation.'' She pressed her fingertips to her eyes and rushed
out of the room.

Marguerite sighed with exasperation. Another crisis to con-
tend with later. "Really, Mr. Renny, I think you've caused
enough upheaval for one evening. Could we talk about this
later?''

He moved toward her, his heels clicking ominously against
the wooden planks. "No . . . I will have your promise that
you'll provide me with half of the proceeds from the property.
If you don't give me that promise tonight . . . I shall find ways
to ruin your life and leave Sophie with the whole Lennox
legacy. I think she'll be a great deal easier to handle.''

Marguerite had thought about his warnings before, without
coming up with a suitable solution. She realized he would never
stop harassing her as long as she had anything of value left. A
cold shiver rushed through her as he stood so close she could
smell the wine on his breath. He looked down at her with
freezing green eyes. She raised her chin and straightened her
back to find the courage she needed.

"I've made my decision, Mr. Renny. You shan't have a
penny more from me. I'm quite out of patience with you, and
if you threaten me one more time, I shall take the whole story
to Captain Emerson. He will be a gentleman and listen to
my explanation of how *you* were involved with the sergeant's
murder. He might put me in prison for allowing my home to
be used to harbor spies in the past—against my wishes—but
he will certainly ferret out the truth of your involvement. You
shall hang beside me at Tyburn, Mr. Renny, and I shall have
the last laugh.''

His face froze into a pale mask of loathing. His hand snaked out, and his fingers closed around her chin hard. He could have snapped her neck, and she held her breath for an interminable moment. Pain shot up her jaw, but she didn't cringe once, didn't avert her gaze from his still face.

"Denounce me," she said. "I don't care. You shall not win."

He jerked her chin up, her neck tilting back. She closed her eyes, waiting for the worst, but when she opened them again, only his fingers' imprint burned on her flesh.

"You shall regret this." He shoved her away and went outside, slamming the door behind him. His angry steps echoed along the passage to the front door. Only when it had closed behind him could Marguerite breathe again.

If Renny followed up on his threat to denounce her, there was probably only a little time left before Captain Emerson came to her door to arrest her. She glanced at her watch. Ten o'clock. The sun had set about an hour ago. Oh, dear. The bandit would be gone by now.

She hurried toward the back, momentarily forgetting her predicament. Then she remembered Sophie. Wishing she could do something to soothe their troubled relationship, Marguerite ran upstairs. Even though she yearned with all her heart to meet the bandit, he would have to wait.

She knocked on Sophie's door. There was no answer except muffled sobs. Marguerite found the door unlocked and stepped inside. A candle sent a flickering glow on the figure crumpled on the coverlet of the four-poster bed with its gold damask hangings. As Marguerite moved to the bed, Sophie started and warded Marguerite off as if she were an evil spirit.

"Sophie, I'm not here to argue further. I can see that you're very unhappy." Without an invitation, she sat down on the edge of the mattress. "You must understand that Mr. Renny, for all he's a Scotsman, is not a true friend. He will not help you even if he says he will, and he won't hesitate to rob you of what you have if he's ever in that position."

"You don't know anything about us Scottish people. We stay together; we help each other."

Marguerite went to dip a clean handkerchief in the water ewer on the washstand. She wrung it out and patted Sophie's face despite the other woman's protests. She finally shook Sophie's shoulder to get her attention. "Listen to me: if we don't stand together, support each other, Mr. Renny will ruin us both; he will ruin everything that Lithgow worked for. You don't want that to happen, do you? I *need* your support, Sophie. Don't turn your back on me. I have never done anything to earn your scorn. I admit I'm different, mayhap not as reverent and God-fearing as was Lithgow, and I might be too frivolous for your liking, but I'm not evil. I do not wish anything dire to befall you."

Marguerite frowned as she waited for her sister-in-law to relent. How many times had she tried to make peace with Sophie, only because Sophie was part of her household and would be helpless without her support? "Look at me!"

Sophie reluctantly let the arm that had shielded her eyes fall to her side. She stared at Marguerite from under red, swollen eyelids. The animosity had disappeared; only traces of uncertainty and dislike remained.

"You are my sister. Not by choice, but we have to make the best of the situation," Marguerite pleaded. She inhaled deeply in exasperation, mentally willing Sophie to relent. "We owe that to ourselves, and each other."

Sophie nodded, her lips trembling with a new wave of sobs. "Yes, but I'm frightened."

Marguerite bowed her head, her shoulders slumping with fatigue. It was as if all air had left her body, and a vague sense of relief was taking its place. "So am I. But we have each other, and we have Prunella. I don't see how we can't form an alliance. No one else will do it for us."

"Yes ..." Sophie said more vehemently, and rubbed her eyes frantically.

Marguerite patted Sophie's forehead with the damp handkerchief. "You're going to have a headache tomorrow. Leave this on for an hour." She spread the handkerchief over Sophie's brow.

"I've been beastly," Sophie said with a sob. "But I've felt so lost. I know you mean well, but I miss Lithgow terribly. Only he understood how I've lived in the past. Only he understood the rigid rule of our home."

"Yes, but you must go on, not live in the past. Can we try to be friends?"

Sophie's broken gaze rested on hers, but then slid away—like a memory best forgotten. "Yes," she whispered reluctantly.

With that Marguerite had to be content. She didn't know if she'd managed to wear down Sophie's resistance, but she'd made an effort in the right direction. She only wished Sophie would meet her halfway. Perhaps she would in time.

Running, her heart in her throat, Marguerite arrived at the edge of the meadow. She scanned the dark area, seeing nothing but ominous dark shapes. The elation she'd felt at her previous meeting with the bandit did not fill her this time. She had missed their rendezvous. He'd tired of waiting for her and left.

Her throat constricted with disappointment, and tears burned in her eyes. She'd longed to get away from duty and the tension at Lennox House, even for a short moment, but it wasn't to be this night. Most likely the highwayman had already gone on to other conquests. She would not have another stolen moment of bliss.

The night was unusually hot, almost oppressive, smelling of warm soil and flowers. Strolling through the grass, she waited for half an hour, but there was no sign of her lover. With a heavy heart, she returned home and closeted herself in her bedchamber. She undressed as tears spilled down her cheeks.

"Don't be such a ninny," she admonished her reflection in the mirror. "It's no use feeling sorry for yourself."

She brushed her hair, twisted it into a loose braid, and slipped her nightgown over her head. She blew out the candle on the nightstand and climbed into the bed. A humid breeze stirred the curtains in the open windows. The night had the metallic taste of a thunderstorm brewing in the distance. When she concentrated she could hear a faint rumble. The storm would ease her doldrums, and she would sleep with a lighter heart.

She punched the pillows to make the down conform to her head, then closed her eyes. But there was no drifting off on the waves of sleep, only nagging thoughts about her dealings with Montagu Renny. She had dared to stand up to him, but what would he do in return? He would not hesitate to ruin her life.

If she were hanged, everything would go to Sophie. Renny would find her easier to convince that the funds rightfully belonged to him. "Damn it all!" Marguerite said out loud. "I should flee across the Channel while there's a chance." Still, she knew she couldn't abandon the others. They should not have to suffer the consequences of Lithgow's treasonous acts. The only question was when Captain Emerson would arrive. Tonight, or at dawn? Next week? *If* Renny chose to tell him.

The thunder moved closer, enclosing the world in a cocoon of growing tension. She sat up against the pillows and pulled her knees to her chin. The night had a tinge of purple outside her window, and lightning streaked the sky with bright silver.

She stared. For a moment the window seemed to disappear, only veils of white curtains fluttering weakly. She gasped as the window moved, then righted itself in the usual spot. A dark form had slipped into the room.

"Who are you?" Marguerite croaked, her heartbeat faltering once and her breath clogging her throat like cotton.

"Marguerite?" came the bandit's cautious whisper.

"It's *you!* You're bold to enter my house unbidden," she said tartly as her heartbeat slowed to normal. Feeling weak with fright, she could not move out of the bed. She trembled as she watched him advance toward her.

"I was late to our rendezvous. I waited for you, but when

you didn't come, I realized our paths had met without crossing."
He still whispered, and Marguerite followed suit, as she didn't
want to alert Prunella and Sophie of her lover's daring
maneuver.

"I did go to meet you," she said. With trembling fingers
she reached for the tinderbox, struck a spark to the tinder, and
lighted the candle by the bed. The flame sprang to life, and
she saw him in the shadows at the foot of her bed, all dressed
in black except for the gloves, and a mask concealing the face
she yearned desperately to see. He was smiling.

"I could not stay away from you, Marguerite. I had to come
here when I realized I had failed to meet you in the meadow.
Are you furious at my presumption?"

She could not retain her anger. "No," she whispered as a
thrill coursed along her spine. Warmth filled her, and she flung
aside the cover to get out of bed.

A clap of thunder made the windowpanes vibrate, and lightning flashed across his face. The breath of the night had stilled,
hovering, waiting, for the release of its captor, the storm.

She moved toward him; he moved toward her. Standing close
without touching, Marguerite absorbed his presence, her spirits
lifting miraculously. "I wish you were not a criminal," she
said softly. "I wish you were a gentleman who could court me
properly—not only meet me clandestinely in the middle of the
night."

He said nothing, only touched her face reverently. He slowly
pulled her into his arms, crushing her against his tall body. He
smelled faintly of horse and leather, and the slightly acrid odor
of . . . ink?

"Have you written another love poem for me lately?" she
asked, her face pressed against the hollow of his throat.

"No . . . but I could recite something if you wish."

She lifted her face to be kissed, and a moan erupted deep in
his throat as their lips touched for the first time. Emotion like
thunder echoed outside and within. She untied the cords of his
cloak and flung it aside, unbuttoned a long series of metal

buttons on his waistcoat, opened it, and rested her hands against his warm chest. His heart beat strongly under the white lawn shirt.

He wrenched the coat from his back and discarded his waist-coat. With a soft laugh, he carried her to the bed and laid her down. He struggled with his boots and flung them across the room as thunder rolled across the sky. Lightning lit up his grin as he slid into bed beside her.

She wished she could read his thoughts behind that wicked smile, but his hands soon made her lose her own train of thought.

Charles caressed the softly rounded breasts through the mate-rial of her nightgown, taking one nipple into his mouth until it hardened, then the other. He moved his hands along the remembered paths of her body, the dip of her small waist, the inviting swell of her hips, the erotic curve of her backside, the long line of her thighs. He pulled up the voluminous night-gown to tickle the soft spot behind her knees.

He indulged his urge to kiss it, trailing a wet line with his tongue up the length of her thigh to find the incredibly soft flesh on the inside, the area that guarded her female secrets. He kissed her, moving to the springy nest of her curls, tasting her, filling himself with the heady scent of her. *Marguerite.* The essence of the woman he loved more than life itself.

He licked the sweet folds, rotating his tongue around the hard nub that made her squirm and whimper with pleasure. Charles thought he would explode with his own need for release. His whole body ached for her sweetness, ached to bury himself, to forget, to lose himself in her softness. To touch heaven, if only for a moment. His blood pounded in his ears, the pressure of his need telling him, *Now! But wait. . . .* He had to wait. He pushed the tip of his tongue up her rounded belly to her navel, finding another concentration of her scent there, then went on a journey of discovery along her satiny flesh to encircle her full breasts with both of his hands.

She cried out as he caressed, not so softly any longer, but more roughly, like the thunder vibrating within him and without. She arched against him, her hands moving over his hips, finding the lacing holding up his breeches and tearing them open. When she gripped his buttocks and brought his throbbing member to herself, he thought he was going to burst with need.

She sheathed him within her wetness, wrapping her legs around his hips, pulling him so deeply inside her tight sweetness that he could only groan with pleasure. He kissed her throat, her ears, found her swollen lips—as juicy as plums on a warm day.

"God, you're destroying me," he muttered when he could pull away from her mouth for a moment. He plunged into her yielding softness, feeling the tightness of her contraction around him as she arched and shuddered in a lengthy release. He couldn't hold back; he was drowning—willingly—melting, surging, exploding in a shower of ecstasy.

Marguerite slammed herself against him as wave after wave of fire shuddered through her, finally to slow like a soft tingling in her veins.

"Oooh," she moaned against his strong neck, and felt his heartbeat pound against her cheek. He moved his face toward her.

"I'm . . . speechless," he whispered, and trailed his fingertip along her hairline. "So lovely, so very perfect."

"So wonderful." She kissed his neck, not wanting to relinquish her hold around his muscled back. His body that trapped hers was a welcome burden that she had no intention of relinquishing. Not now, not ever.

"Ours is a union made not by man, but by heaven," he whispered.

She moved her head restlessly. "But the conventions of man would not accept our union."

"We know that our union is beyond convention; do not sully our love with worldly pettiness."

"Unfortunately, most of our time is lived far below these moments of ecstasy. We cannot change that."

"To have truly known love once is better than never to reach it." He caressed her breast, cupping it reverently as if it was worth his whole attention, his admiration.

"How can I love you and know you can never come to me without a mask?" she said, touching his face. "Please take it off."

He leaned on his elbows above her, still resting within her. With a sigh he pulled himself forward and blew out the candle. With one hand he untied the mask and let it fall to the floor.

Marguerite traced his face with her fingertips, feeling his eyelids close, his mouth turn into a taut line. She sensed something . . . a fleeting thought, a warning bell. She felt high cheekbones, a stubborn jaw that would soon need shaving, the hard line remembered by her fingertips.

He hid his face against her neck and started exploring her skin with his hands, inch after inch, as if he were loath to neglect one small part.

Soon she was swimming in the throbbing longing of her senses, and let go of her rational thoughts. He was here; this moment he would pleasure her as only he knew how, and what more could she expect? This gift was freely and generously given, and she returned it, bit by bit.

"I love you," he murmured as he brought her to another crest of bliss. "God help me, but I love you." He moved within her until she forgot every wish, every longing, and dragged her ever deeper into a glorious world that was only theirs. He seemed to be a well of endless longing, as thirsty to explore as she had ever been, and she dared to follow where his longing brought him.

Chapter 15

Marguerite awakened abruptly as a clap of thunder reverberated in the sky outside. Rain pelted against the walls, streaming through the open window. The Midnight Bandit still sprawled over her, his muscled thighs pressing hers to the mattress. She worked herself away from his weight and moved to close the window, muffling the sound of the rain. She found her nightgown on the floor and slipped it over her head, then lighted the candle by the bed.

The flame flickered wildly in the draft, and molten wax formed a waterfall down the side of the candlestick. She stared at the naked, magnificent golden form of her secret lover, admiring his back, his slim hips, and his tight buttocks that always provoked illicit thoughts. He muttered in his sleep, and turned over, flinging out an arm over to her side of the bed.

She gasped and clapped a hand to her mouth. "Charles!"

He opened one eye, staring blindly at her. "Er, ummm," he said, and coughed once.

"Charles, you scoundrel! You dashed liar, you two-faced

villain!'' She grabbed a pillow and started pelting him with it. He warded her off, his arms crossed over his face.

''Marguerite,'' he said between blows. He finally grappled with her for possession of the pillow and flung it across the room. ''What in the world . . . ?''

He finally seemed to realize the reason for her anger. He brushed his face with one hand and stared down at his naked body. The powdered wig and face mask lay abandoned on the floor, as did his clothes. ''I guess you have uncovered my secret,'' he said with a guilty grin.

She thought she would explode with outrage. ''How can you just sit there and laugh as if nothing has happened?''

''Nothing has changed since last night, has it? We made glorious love; you gave yourself to me, and I certainly gave all of myself to you.''

''I thought . . .'' She was going to say she thought she'd been making love to the Midnight Bandit, but it would sound ludicrous—as if only a criminal could gain her love. She threw up her arms and muttered to herself. Pacing the room, she darted angry glances at her old friend who had deceived her most deviously.

''Damn you, Charles! You *stole* my acquiescence. Had I known, I would never have allowed you into my bed.''

''But you would allow a bandit, a stranger, into your bed?'' he asked tersely, and got up. He caught up with her by the window, where the white curtains hung limp with rain. She was well aware of his splendid nakedness, but refused to look at his body. She pinned her gaze to a point on the wall.

''It was easy,'' she said, her lips trembling. She was filled with self-loathing at her show of emotion. ''With the bandit I could be myself, be free. He didn't demand anything from me—only love.''

Silence fluttered like a worried moth between them. Charles inhaled deeply, and she watched his chest rise and fall. ''The bandit was me, Marguerite. *I* made love to you, and *I* wrote the letters to you. *I* helped pull your carriage out of the mud.

The love was still glorious, and free from restraint—whatever restraints you imagine would hamper your lovemaking with me, as Charles.''

"You pretended. You took on another's identity to seduce me. I cannot accept such underhanded behavior." She clenched her fists at her sides, ready to pummel him.

"I realized you wanted—needed—romance, and since you would not accept my courtship, I had to find another way to your heart. It's as simple as that."

"Not simple at all!" She darted a glance at his face, noting the flushed cheeks and darkened eyes. Clearly he suffered a bout of humiliation, but that didn't change the situation. "But why the highwayman? You could have chosen to be anyone."

"You showed your excitement about him—thought of him as a desirable figure. He has the romantic turn of phrase that could touch your heart. It was easy to make that decision. I let the Midnight Bandit clear the path for me."

"Unforgivable! It was the most deceitful, the most underhanded thing to do, Charles, and I loathe you for it." She punched his shoulder. "You crushed my dream."

"But gave you another, a real dream," he snapped, rubbing his shoulder. "Don't fight. We can go on from here now that the secret is out in the open."

"You can go on. *I* don't want anything to do with you. Not after what you did." She glared accusingly at him.

"You admit you liked the letters, and you certainly enjoyed our loving last night. What's the difference who seduced your senses with words and caresses?"

"You! You are the difference," she shouted, and raised her bunched fists. "You deceived me."

He gripped her wrists hard, and slowly pulled her reluctant body toward him. "I write better poems than that flea-bitten bandit of the roads," he murmured. "I can write letters to you that will make you swoon, one a week for the rest of our lives."

"You're so very confident of my surrender," she said, hot tears filming her eyes. A wave of anger and some emotion she

Maria Greene

could not identify went through her body, choking her. "But I will not read your letters, Charles. Not now, when I know what a conniver you are."

He breathed hard through his nose, and she could feel his heart thudding heavily against her. "I can always recite the letters to you."

"I'll close my ears to your voice."

He embraced her before she could pull away. His skin was hot, and smelled faintly of leather and starch, hair powder, and that musky scent of male that made her heart thud harder.

His skin was so soft, softer than kid gloves, she thought, yet so hard underneath. He could crush her. She fought for breath, her senses rapidly filling with him. Dizzy, she listened to his soothing voice wafting through her hair.

"Why is it, Marguerite, that you'd rather take the love of a stranger than the love of a gentleman who knows and adores you? Somewhat strange, don't you think? Have you thought about that?"

"Not your concern," she said to his smooth chest, but he was right. Why was it that her familiar world seemed so much like a prison?

"It is my concern, since I'm involved. I think you never were allowed to find out who you were. You went from father to husband, a piece of baggage that had no label, only holding the required assets: beauty and femininity." He made her take a step back so that he could stare into her face. She looked away, but knew he would see the tears running down her face.

He gently wiped his thumb down one wet cheek. "Is that the truth?"

She nodded, and a new wave of misery rose in her chest to create new tears. She dashed her hand across her face. "Yes . . . perhaps. To Father I was a pawn, but I was still me, Marguerite. When I married, I found that Lithgow had something that mattered more to him than a wife—his religion." Her voice wobbled. "And to him, it was a stern, punishing religion.

Everything was a sin, anything from laughing out loud to wanting to make love in the depth of night.''

She read the compassion in Charles's eyes, his understanding, and, strangely enough, it made her more miserable.

"I suppose Lennox never laughed?" he asked, his eyebrows quirking comically.

She grimaced. "That's neither here nor there, but life with Lithgow was a prison. He lived in a prison of his own making."

"Was he violent? Did he reject you?"

She shook her head. "No, but he gave me a loathing for marriage that I cannot easily dissolve. He also gave me self-loathing, as if my physical desires sullied my character in some way. He said my desire for . . . closeness was indecent."

"I think you're the most lovable and loving creature I've ever held in my arms. Your desires are a gentleman's dream, and should not be suppressed. I like to hear you laugh and to see you dance. I'd like you to be happy again. There's no need for secret rendezvous with masked strangers in the meadow." He took her hands and forced her to look into his face. "You don't have to be ashamed of your appetites, Marguerite."

"Yes . . . you're right, but it is difficult to rub away the brand of sin with which I've lived for a long time. I need to be free."

"You *are* free. What is standing in your way? Or whom?"

She averted her gaze. His blue eyes saw too much, too deeply into the murky secrets of her soul. Charles' concern added guilt to all her other emotions.

It made her angry, since he was the one who had connived his way into her bed. He should experience guilt, not play the role of concerned counselor.

"You don't need to give me permission to admit that I am free. Actually, *you* are standing in my way, your persistence and your certainty that I will fall into your arms, begging you for love. In truth, you have compromised me."

"I'm prepared to do the honorable thing and marry you. I would be more than willing."

She voiced disgust. "But I'm not interested! If you were the last man on Earth, I would not wed you. You have no right to tell me what I should feel." She watched his face darken with hurt and anger.

"And don't feel sorry for me!" she added. "I shall come to terms with my life—without help from the likes of you." Her nightgown swung around her ankles as she stalked to the bed. She gathered up his clothes, including the wig and mask, and tossed them at him. "Get dressed and leave. You can climb out the window, since that's the way you came. I hope the tree outside breaks and crushes you."

"That piece of cruelty was uncalled for," he said under his breath. "If you can't stand to hear the truth about yourself, I do feel sorry for you. What future is there for you if you reject love?" He dragged on his breeches and tied the opening.

"None with you, a penniless dreamer!" she cried, not caring whether Prunella and Sophie could hear her raised voice.

He glared, his gaze piercing her defenses. "Don't drag my penniless state into your argument. Love has nothing to do with funds or fortune."

She already regretted her heated accusations, but the revelations of the night were too heavy and too painful to bear. "Still, I don't want to hear the word *love* on your lips, Charles. If I do, I won't speak to you again. And if you thought that luring me into your arms would be the perfect way to bring me to the altar, you're sorely mistaken."

"To marry a virago would be a big mistake," he said in a flat voice. "You are a person who will destroy everything that is good in your life. Do not cut off your nose to spite your face, Marguerite."

"Oh, damn you! Take your advice with you when you leave. I'm tired of listening to your perfect solutions concerning my life."

He pulled on his dark brown waistcoat, wrenched on his black coat with its brass buttons, and jerked down the wide cuffs. He shrugged to make the shoulders fit and patted his pockets for the white gloves. God, Charles was so handsome, she thought; he'd held her in his arms and brought her to such precipices of love where she'd never visited before. He would never hold her again; she would never taste the drugging sweetness of his mouth. She had thrown out the real man and held the phantom lover to her heart. If only he hadn't cheated her; if only he hadn't filled her with glib advice! He set her teeth on edge.

His lean face twisted into a grimace. There was no trace left of the smiles he'd bestowed upon her earlier. "Good-bye, Marguerite. Your spite will turn you into a sour-faced spinster." He clapped his cocked hat onto his head and swept the cloak around him.

She stared at him breathlessly, unmoving. He went to the window and flung it open. With a last hurt look at her, he swung his leg over the sill and disappeared.

"Charles!" she said, but the night was empty outside.

Charles cursed himself for his belief that Marguerite would be his after the night of wild lovemaking they had shared. He walked through the wet grass toward the spinney, where he'd left Thunder. Dew hung in the trees and in the air, laying a thin film of wetness over his face and clothes. Raindrops rustled in the leaves as they fell, but otherwise heavy silence filled the world after the storm had passed.

If only he hadn't fallen asleep; if only he'd left right after their passion was spent and Marguerite was asleep. He'd been unable to bring himself to leave. To fall asleep beside her had been a dream he'd held for a long time. It had been his downfall.

"Idiot!" he said to himself, and kicked the tall grass at the edge of the spinney. "You handled the situation completely wrong. You should have made love to her, forcing her accusations back down into her throat." *Pride*. He had too much of that at crucial moments. So did she.

Deep in thought, his emotions in turmoil, he walked along

the path. He saw the bulk of Thunder, heard the rhythmic chomp of the stallion's jaws. A darker shadow barred the path, and before he knew what had happened, Charles's skull filled with bolts of pain.

Chapter 16

Captain Emerson had not come to arrest her—yet. Worried beyond reason, Marguerite paced the terrace on the morning after her last quarrel with Charles. He had gone; most likely she would not see him for a long time, and then they would act as strangers.

She tried to analyze her worry, finally admitting that it had its roots in her longing for love. She might not forgive Charles for his duplicity, but the man who had made love to her could not be so easily forgotten. She already longed for his embrace— Charles's embrace, not that of her phantom lover. He'd awakened something in her, a hunger that could not be subdued or denied.

Like the summer around her, she blossomed as if she'd been touched by magic. Even though she dwelt in the house that still bore the bitter aura of Viscount Lennox, she was breaking through the wall that he'd placed around her with his cold silences and recriminations.

The recent rain made everything literally burst with growth around her; every corner of her property was a brilliant green, with columbines, Canterbury bells, and sweet peas dotting the borders with red, pink, white, and pale yellow. The loveliest time of the year, she thought, if only she could handle her life as naturally as Nature handled her garden—without complications.

Lost in her craving for love and her reverie, she was startled as a bell-like female voice chimed, "There you are, Marguerite. There's no one about, so I let myself in."

Marguerite smiled absentmindedly at the tiny, round figure of Emilia Wetherby, and the equally round pug at her feet. Had she come to gossip about Charles? "Emmy, what a surprise! Betsy has gone down to the village with Pru; Sophie is riding. I'm quite alone except for the kitchen staff."

Emmy gave her a thorough scrutiny with her wise eyes. "You look pale and drawn, Marguerite. Is something the matter?"

"No, I was only admiring the garden." Marguerite studied the kind, wrinkled face framed by a voluminous mobcap. Emmy wore a gown with frills at the elbows and on the stomacher. The hooped skirt of pale gray taffeta was almost as wide as Emmy was tall. A blue silk shawl draped her shoulders, and a parasol protected her from the sun. Georgie snuffled and snorted as if disgusted with the effort of walking the length of the terrace. Ill-humored, he nipped at the hem of Marguerite's gown.

"Come inside, Emmy. I shall serve you a glass of sherry, or would you rather have a glass of lemonade?"

Emmy looked around as if to see if someone was watching. Her eyes gleamed with embarrassment. "I know 'tis not seemly in a gentlewoman, but I have a great fondness for ale. Cold ale on a hot summer day."

Marguerite laughed, her doldrums lifting miraculously. "Ale you shall have. I have a barrel stored cold below, and I'll fetch you a glass myself." She settled her guest, who seemed to be in some hurry, in the one chair in the parlor and went in search of refreshment. For herself she chose lemonade, freshly made in a pitcher, with a saucer resting on top to keep out any insects.

"Did you take a drive and decided to stop?" Marguerite asked as she served her guest. "Or did you come to see for yourself if it was true that I've gotten rid of all the furniture? The rumors must have traveled all over the county."

Emmy chuckled. "I'm not above a bit of snooping, but no, I came directly to you." She gave Marguerite a long, searching stare. Her pale blue eyes looked serious in her crinkled face. "I'm concerned—about Charles, and about you."

Marguerite gasped, feeling a flush creeping up her neck. Did the old woman know what had happened last night? No, Charles wouldn't have confessed that he'd spent the night in her arms. She sat abruptly in the chair she'd carried from the study. "What do you mean, Emmy?"

"Charles came home very late last night with a bruised bump on the side of his head, and feverish. He was muttering your name over and over. All I could get out of him before he fainted was that he'd been to your house. I'm here to find out if you saw something, or know something about this?"

Marguerite froze with apprehension, light-headed. "No . . . He was here, yes, but when he left I heard nothing untoward. Has the doctor been to see him?"

"Aye, he told Charles he had to rest one week in bed. Charles is in no shape to move around anyway; he fainted dead away and slept until two hours ago. He said someone attacked him in the Lennox spinney."

"Oh, dear," Marguerite said, as her faintness increased. Her mouth felt dry. She had literally thrown him out. And then this had happened. "I didn't see anything suspicious." She stood abruptly and put her glass on the windowsill. "I shall go with you at once to the Meadow."

"I'm afraid there's nothing you can do. Charles needs rest, not visitors to tire him."

Marguerite averted her gaze from Emmy's knowing eyes. "I understand, but I worry. Mayhap I feel a trace of . . . guilt, as Charles and I did not part on the best of terms. I would like to see him."

"Very well, a short visit will not make him worse." The older woman rose with difficulty. She spilled some ale on the floor, and Georgie lapped it up before Marguerite could fetch a rag. "Sometimes I think I have a pet pig, not a dog. Georgie eats everything."

Feeling limp with agitation, Marguerite managed to drape a shawl over her shoulders and bring her parasol for the drive in the open carriage to the Meadow. She kept up a perfunctory conversation with Emmy as she led the way to the door, but her mind was wholly on Charles and her own guilt.

"Will you order all new furniture for your house?" Emmy asked, and peeked into the bare rooms.

"No . . . yes, perhaps," Marguerite replied, not wanting to discuss her plans. She then remembered that she'd given Renny an ultimatum, and might not have a chance to dispose of her property. If he went to the authorities with the Lennox secrets, she would be arrested for treason, and her property would be confiscated. At least Renny wouldn't get his hands on it, she thought mirthlessly.

They stepped into the coach and set off along the country lane.

"Your mind is elsewhere, my dear. You carry your tension like a cloak."

"I am worried about Charles," Marguerite said defensively. "We have been friends for a very long time."

"I'm aware of that." The old lady fiddled with the knob of her parasol. "I have known for some time that Charles harbors much deeper emotions for you than friendship." She paused, and when Marguerite didn't deny the statement, continued. "He hasn't said anything one way or the other, but I have seen the truth for myself. He has eyes for no one but you. If I may be so bold as to say so, I had hoped that *your* eyes were turned in his direction."

"I don't know. I . . . have great fondness for Charles, but—"

"Say no more! You have the right to look for a more advantageous match, but I had hoped—"

"I don't care about Charles's financial assets," Marguerite said heatedly. "He's a friend, and someone I'm beginning to care very much about."

"In the right way?" Emmy's white eyebrows lifted in inquiry. "I pray for that every day."

"It is too early to say, but I have discovered that Charles has many . . . hidden talents."

"He's a brilliant man. A sharp mind lurks behind that calm, handsome exterior. His passions run deep, and he cares for people. The tenants on the estate look up to him like a minor god. He takes better care of them than he takes of himself."

Marguerite laughed. "You don't have to enumerate his fine qualities. I know—"

"We're here," Emmy interrupted as the coach turned into the gravel drive at the Meadow and curved around a stand of poplars. The old mansion sat as if propped up by the green, puffy eiderdowns around it. The lawns covered small hills and created unexpected valleys. One held a pond where swans glided in silent majesty on its rippling surface. The brick house was surrounded by old trees and flowers—somnolent in the heat. The only busy creatures that Marguerite could see were the bees.

The coachman halted in front of the old oak doors. Three slate steps led to a small portico with painted white columns. No footmen were in evidence. Marguerite assisted first the old lady, then the fat pug, to the ground. Georgie slobbered on her hand. As they stepped up to the door together, Bottomly, the butler, appeared.

"There you are, Bottomly. How's the master?" Emmy asked, and hurried as fast as her short legs could carry her through the hallway with its suits of medieval armor, carved oak paneling, somber portraits, and checkered marble floor.

"Better, Miss Wetherby. He's eating now—a bowl of broth, I believe. Not very pleased with the situation."

Emmy flung out her arms. "He hates broth!"

Marguerite followed Emmy upstairs. Her heart lodged in her

throat at the thought of seeing Charles again. What would he do? Would he be pleased to see her, or would he coolly send her away, just as she had done to him? Perhaps she shouldn't have come. Perhaps it was all a big mistake.

She breathed deeply to calm herself, without much success. She viewed the few pieces of furniture in the corridor: a carved and inlaid table in the ornate style of the previous century, a sofa upholstered in striped silk, a long, worn Oriental carpet. They were austere furnishings, she thought, but tasteful. She could not count the years since she'd last visited Mortimer's Meadow. It was long before her marriage, while Charles was still at Oxford.

Her breath caught in her throat as Emmy halted her waddling progress in front of the double doors at the end. "His rooms. I hear voices," she said, pressing her ear shamelessly to the door. "Sounds like Nick."

She knocked, and Marguerite thought she ought to sink through the floor rather than see Charles again. "Mayhap I should wait. . . ."

"Now that you're here, 'twill do him a world of good to see you," Emmy said briskly, and gripped Marguerite's arm. Marguerite had the sensation that Emmy had planned this moment before arriving at Lennox House.

Nick opened the door and brightened when his gaze fell upon the visitors. "Emmy, Marguerite, and . . . dear Georgie. Charles has been crying for that drooling pug this last hour or longer," he said with a grin. "Can't live without him."

"You don't fool me, Nick. You've already been at the brandy bottle," Emmy said with a snort.

Nick made a face of surprise. "Bottle, madam? That is a bold untruth. I keep a clear head on my shoulders."

"Well, whatever it is, you're not to joke about my dear Georgie. He's the soul of compassion, and he loves Charles deeply."

"*That* I do believe, as I have been the recipient of his adoring tongue on several occasions—Georgie's, that is."

"Really, Nick!" Followed by Georgie, Emmy headed for the bedroom beyond the sitting room into which they had stepped. The pug was the first through the bedroom door. "How is the patient?"

"Better, but in a rotten mood," Nick said with a grimace, hanging back. "Either he's chafing against the pain, or something else happened." He glanced at Marguerite speculatively and touched her arm. "Have you said or done anything to put him in this foul mood?"

"Don't blame me," Marguerite exclaimed. "I did not wield a tree branch or throw a rock at his head."

"Well, someone certainly did. Charles says he saw a dark shape, and then everything went black. An ambush," Nick murmured so that Emmy could not hear him.

Marguerite clutched her throat as if to force her breath to return to normal. "It could have been the smugglers or some other bandits that roam the night."

"In *your* spinney?"

"The bandits go wherever they choose. I don't know their paths." Marguerite saw Montagu Renny's pale, expressionless face before her inner eye. Somehow she had a premonition that Renny had been involved in the ambush. But if he had been, why attack Charles? The answer was clear enough: Renny desired her for himself, as he had informed her on several occasions.

Guilt crawled over her at the thought, and she wished that she could return to yesterday and change everything that had happened. If Charles hadn't come to her house, he would not have been attacked. If he'd left earlier, if she'd asked him to leave . . .

"He was lucky to have been wearing a wig and a hat when the blow fell, or he might have died."

Marguerite cringed as if slapped. If he had died, she would have carried the blame. She still did in a way, but at least she had a chance to make things right with Charles. She had gotten a second chance.

She watched Emmy enter the bedchamber. Wearing a long-suffering expression, Charles's manservant came out carrying a bowl. Marguerite could hear Charles's irate voice, and she walked toward the sound. She was so sure he would be willing to see her that she entered with a smile and a cheerful "Good morning."

He was propped up in bed with pillows, his head bandaged. He was haggard and pale, and his facial expression froze as he laid eyes on her. Emmy was already standing by the bedside, but when she saw his expression, she said, "I'd better make sure Cook is making special arrangements for your dinner." With a vague smile at Marguerite, she hurried out of the room. Marguerite wished Emmy had stayed to lend moral support.

"I hear you were attacked outside my house last night. I'm sorry," she said hesitantly, and moved toward the bed. "If only I hadn't—"

His brows pulled together in a frown. "Don't give me any 'if onlys,' Marguerite. Why are you here? To gloat over my infirmity?"

"No! I was worried when Emmy told me about the accident." She braided her trembling fingers together. "I had to come, you understand, or I would have been unable to eat or sleep."

"I was almost killed, and you can only think of how it would affect your appetite," he said darkly. He moved his head slowly to the side so that he didn't have to look at her. The window was open, letting in the summer breeze and frivolous birdsong.

"No! I didn't mean that. You're twisting my words. What I mean is that I care . . . very much . . . what happens to you." She blushed, feeling as if she were ripping open her chest and baring her soul. She hoped he would accept her explanation and soften toward her.

He moved his head slowly back to stare at her with ice blue eyes. "Care enough about me to marry me?" he asked in a flat voice.

Marguerite could not say yes to that. He evidently noted her hesitation and snorted through his nose in disgust. "If my head wasn't splitting apart, I would personally escort you to the door, Marguerite. You have no reason for being here."

"You're moving much too fast, Charles. I have no intention—"

"I didn't ask you to come here. In fact, I'm tired of facing your constant rejection." His eyes darkened with anger. "You would not be so hesitant to accept my offer if I told you that I'm no longer a destitute man."

"You're wrong!" she said with vehemence. This discussion was going badly, worse than she had visualized. "Your finances have nothing to do with it."

"Despite the denial on your lips you will marry soon enough, marry someone with ample funds. I have no doubt—"

Marguerite stomped to the bed, her hands clenched at her sides with tension. "That's unfair, Charles! I am not a calculating person, nor am I especially difficult."

"You will marry to satisfy your carnal urges, and you won't choose a poor gentleman."

Marguerite glowered. "Why, you are in a foul mood! You're rude and ungentlemanly to say that I would marry only to satisfy my longings."

His lips quirked cynically at the corners. "You'll take a lover soon enough, if not a husband. You'll wait to say your vows until the right *wealthy* idiot comes along."

"Remember, sirrah, that you are the one to blame for my fall from 'purity,' " she said in a low voice. "You schemed for that downfall for weeks, and it should prove that I'm not the light-skirt you have branded me." She clasped her burning cheeks and stared at his lean face, where no tenderness lingered.

"Well, Marguerite. What are you? You rejected my honorable offers all along. Always have." He gripped a folded parchment on the coverlet that she'd not noticed before.

"I had a letter from my solicitor this morning. He tells me I have inherited the title of Marquess of Ransford from a distant relation—and a minor fortune. Therefore, would you consider marrying a marquess with attached funds? The money will be wholly at your disposal.''

"You make me sound like a cold, thoughtless . . . grasping woman. I will not accept a proposal made from cynicism.''

His voice rasped with derision. "Unfortunately my head is swimming too much, otherwise I would go down on one knee and do the honorable gesture.''

"You're laughing at me!'' she said, fighting an urge to run from the room. "That's unfair. I should never have come.''

He nodded slowly. "I think you said everything last night, and my injury has changed nothing between us. You did not have to pretend to care.''

"I do care,'' she whispered, but he had closed her out. She could as easily have been talking to a wall. She reached out to touch his hand, but he jerked it aside.

"Just leave. I think we shall not see each other again,'' he said coldly.

She could only stare at the sharp profile of his face and realize that, in the coldness of his dismissal, most of the happiness had seeped out of her life. "Good-bye, Charles. I'm sorry if I hurt you. I truly am.''

Chapter 17

"Damn you, Charles; what did you say to Marguerite? She was crying as she left. She ran out of the house, and I couldn't get a coherent word out of her." Nick sank down on a chair by the four-poster bed with its green brocade hangings and glared at his friend.

"Tears of stone," Charles said tonelessly. "Tears of self-pity."

"What has happened between you to leave such a bitter residue on your tongue?"

"Rejection—yet again. I think the road is open for you now, but don't be surprised if she chooses to marry someone with a fortune, and *that* you don't have."

"Something deeper than rejection must have happened to give your voice such a tint of vitriol." Nick gave Charles a probing stare, but Charles did not meet his friend's gaze. His head pounded miserably, and nausea churned in his stomach. She had stood there, his goddess, so close he could have touched her. Concern had been on her face, but not love—not what he desired most.

A hollow, raw ache in his chest made his head seem much worse. "Let's not talk about it, not now," Charles said.

"Very well, as you wish." Nick sighed, plucking at the black wool embroidery on his waistcoat. "I take it you know who was responsible for the attack?"

"Didn't see anyone, but the only man I know who holds a grudge against me is Montagu Renny. Besides, he watches Marguerite jealously. Either he hired someone to ambush me, or he lay in wait himself. He wouldn't face me in a fair fight, the blasted cur." Charles closed his eyes, trying to will away the burning pounding behind his eyes.

"I think you should know that I went in search of Renny as soon as I heard of the attack. His house is closed up, and a slovenly servant told me Renny left a week ago. He didn't say where he went. He could be anywhere, especially hanging around Marguerite, or traveling across the Channel on secret business. He is a Scotsman, after all, and most likely loyal to Stuart."

"He'll not stray too far from Marguerite's side," Charles said with a snort. "Be a good fellow and keep an eye on her."

Nick chuckled. "Since you are unable to, you mean?"

"No, not that. I've no desire to hang on her every word like a lovesick youth. I've turned over a new leaf, and my new life does not include Marguerite."

Marguerite walked the five miles to her house, through the woods, up the hills, and across the verdant valleys. The strenuous exercise should have softened the ache in her heart, but it didn't. She reeled at times, as if she'd received a blow, when she remembered Charles's words. So hard, so cold, so precise, proposing to her as if offering her a loan to pay off her wine merchant, or something equally prosaic.

He was hurt, so he said hurtful things. She would have to cling to that thought and not give up the hope that he would one day return to her side. Looking at him with new eyes, she realized she would like to get to know him all over again.

He was no longer the childhood friend who had always been a part, albeit a bit shadowy the last few years, of her life. She wanted to know the virile man who had surprised her with his passion. His secret thoughts, his wishes. She'd never known his talent for writing love poems. The letters had revealed that pleasing and surprising aspect of his personality.

Marguerite shaded her eyes as she came to the ridge behind the Lennox meadow. Tired and bedraggled, she crossed the spot where she'd found such happiness in Charles's arms. It seemed like a dream. Perspiration coursed down her face, and she dabbed at it unsuccessfully with a handkerchief.

The afternoon was still, slumbering in the summer heat. The spinney lent some protection from the sun, and she hurried along the path toward the stables. She would have to throw away her slippers. They were nothing more than rags. At least she had worn away the tempest of her emotions, and felt more at peace.

Just as she came around the corner of the stables, she saw Montagu Renny arguing with Prunella on the terrace. The old woman cringed at something that Renny said as he leaned over the tiny woman, holding a stick.

Anger burned through Marguerite. Would they never be free of the dratted man? At least he had not come with the militia in tow. He had taken her threat seriously; he had as much to lose as she did.

She hastened across the stableyard and along the path to the terrace.

"Mr. Renny!" she cried in anger. "What are you doing here? I told you to stay away from my property." She went to stand next to Pru and put a calming arm around the old woman's shoulders. "He shan't bother you further," she said, and gently pushed Pru through the door. She saw movement inside, and realized that Sophie was watching the interchange.

Renny sat down on the terrace wall as if in no hurry to leave.

Marguerite fumed, but she knew that ranting and raving would not impress Renny with fear. His horse had been tied to an old apple tree, and she noticed that two portmanteaus had been strapped to the saddle. His cloak and hat were covered with a thin film of dust.

"Why don't you continue on your journey, Mr. Renny? It would be best for all of us." She patted her face with her damp handkerchief. Tired and dispirited, she felt her lack of command. His thin face bore a hint of mockery, and he did not move an inch. His green eyes held a hint of ice.

"I've come to see you, Marguerite. All my roads lead to this house."

"I wish they didn't!" she spit, now drained of all patience. "You know 'tis useless to pressure me further. I won't change my mind about the funds or the proposal."

"Your refusal at our last meeting inflamed me with passion," he murmured, and stood. He threw away the stick, which he'd been stripping of bark. He came so close she could smell the sweat and dirty linen he wore. She quelled the urge to run inside and slam the door in his face. "I've been mulling over the implications of your offer. I do realize, more and more, that I don't especially want your money. I want you, Marguerite. I'm obsessed with you."

She gasped in outrage. "I would never consider a union with a murderer. You not only killed Sergeant Rule, but you almost killed Lord Mortimer last night. For that you should hang."

"You're what I want, Marguerite. I'm crazed with longing for you." Dazed, she listened to his outpouring of passion. Would she get another proposal this day, delivered in cynical tones? She almost laughed hysterically.

Marguerite pushed him in the chest. "Stand back! Your stench makes me nauseous. If you don't leave, I shall report you to Captain Emerson for trespassing and harassment."

Renny laughed and gripped her hands so hard she couldn't pull away. "Listen to me! If you marry me, we'll deal with the difficulties together, and you'll never have to pinch pennies again."

Marguerite could not hold back a derisive laugh. "Are you offering me sacks of gold? If you expect me to believe that, you're more foolish than I ever thought. *You* have been pestering *me* for funds, or did that detail slip your mind?"

He stared at her hard, his bony hands crushing her fingers together until she whimpered in pain. "You have nothing to lose, whereas if you refuse me, you have everything to lose."

"I'd rather hang than marry you," she ground out between clenched teeth. "Get that through your thick head once and for all."

He stared at her for an endless moment, his cold green eyes pinning her against the wall. Panic darted around in her chest. "I will kill you for this," he said in a hiss. He dropped her hands and vaulted over the railing. "Watch your back, Marguerite."

She gasped and rubbed her aching hands. Fear coursed through her veins as the fact that he meant every word sank in. She watched him leave as an icy feeling came over her like a draft from a grave.

With a strangled whimper, she ran into the house and almost collided with Sophie. "Did you hear what he said?" Marguerite asked in a voice of grief.

Sophie's face bore a closed expression. She was deathly pale, all the way to her lips. "He asked you to marry him. You should consider yourself a fortunate woman." She whirled around and ran from the room before Marguerite could speak.

Marguerite stared after her in surprise. Shaken, she went in search of a glass of sherry to calm herself.

Death. Renny had threatened to kill her. The walls seemed to close in on her as if conspiring with him. He was capable of turning the threat into reality. There was nothing she could do except try to elude him. Go away. Make him forget her.

The house echoed, empty of everything except bitterness. It was about time she took the final step to sever herself from the memory of Lennox. She would sell the property and write a will—just in case Renny managed to end her life.

Two weeks later, after she'd listed the Lennox estate with the land agents and set her affairs in order, she told Pru, "I've had an invitation from my old friend Louise, Lady Woodvine, to visit her in Surrey. A house party. She claims there are all sorts of entertainments in the area." Marguerite held out a stack of invitations.

Pru's face crinkled in a smile. "A change of scenery will be the right thing. I must admit I can't feel comfortable in this house any longer. Not with everything gone, and the neighbors looking strangely at me as I drive through the village."

"I'm sorry you have to suffer their scorn, but at least I've paid the debts, and we're free to create our own home."

Pru leaned closer and glanced furtively along the hallway. There was no sign of the servants. "And to tell you the truth, Sophie's moping is getting on my nerves. Not that I don't feel sorry for the young lady, so closed in on herself, and so unhappy."

"I've tried to break the walls around her several times, but the progress is excessively slow," Marguerite replied in an undertone. "I'm going to ask her if she wants to join us on the trip to Surrey."

"I can tell you already that she won't leave this house. She's strangely attached to it, as if hoping that Lithgow will return if she only stays long enough."

"Yes, but she has to come to terms with her grief."

Pru patted Marguerite's arm and beamed in approval. "I'm delighted to see that you've made great strides toward putting the past behind you. And you've shown kindness to that awkward woman upstairs. With our support, she'll come about. I'm very proud of you, Marguerite."

"Thank you, Pru. I'll write to Louise and accept the invitation. I would dearly like to see some new faces. It's been ages since I last saw Louise and her numerous offspring. To think that she once was my neighbor, a thin waif in a too-big dress, and now she's a matron with four children.''

''It's about time you had some of your own,'' Pru said with a suggestive lift of his eyebrows.

Marguerite did not respond. She pulled into her shell. Pru went in search of her embroidery, and Marguerite stepped upstairs to speak with her sister-in-law. Sophie flatly refused the offer to spend a week on the Woodvine estate in Surrey. ''Someone has to look after the house while you're gone. I don't trust the servants,'' she said in dismissive tones.

Marguerite looked eagerly up the long, curving drive as the old coach bore her and Prunella to the home of her childhood friend. A piece of fine architecture of redbrick and marble, Indigo House sat in a park planted with oaks, elms, and poplars. The main house was built in three stories from which curved two lower wings on each side. The entrance was built as a long portico over which stretched a balcony the length of the house. Tall windows glistened in the sunlight, and the ancient red-and-green Woodvine pennant flapped gaily on the rooftop. Louise had great fondness for the history of the Middle Ages and collected armor and old tapestries.

Marguerite recalled that the sitting room of Indigo House had been designed to resemble the great hall of a thirteenth-century castle. It housed carved chestnut trusses in the forty-foot ceiling, and boasted a tiled floor and a central octagonal hearth that was never used but reminded the visitors of a time long past. The whitewashed walls had been covered with tapestries and various racks of antlers.

Louise met them on the front steps. She held out her arms and swept Marguerite into a perfumed embrace. Statuesque and motherly, Louise literally smothered Marguerite's smaller form, a hug that gave a comfort that Marguerite hadn't felt for some time.

"It's been so long! Seven years or more," Louise said with wonder in her voice. Her slightly protruding brown eyes looked at Marguerite with kindness, and her round cheeks dimpled in a smile. Brown curls bounced against her round neck, and her plump arms bore a froth of lace at the elbows. That lace was the only adornment on the lady, who liked to think of herself as a woman of simple tastes even though her husband, John, the fifth Earl of Woodvine, had brought her a great fortune and was forever called to attend King George's court.

"I'm so glad you invited us," Marguerite said sincerely. "I needed to breathe different air." She lifted her skirts and followed her hostess's regal form through the door. Prunella was chatting to herself as she joined the small procession, glancing eagerly at the details of the house.

Liveried footmen stood motionless at every door in the long hallway that displayed ancient sculptures, polished suits of armor, and a stuccoed chimneypiece in the Italian style. A staircase soared upward like a lyre to disappear in a passage above. I had quite forgotten the majestic impression, Marguerite thought as Pru chatted in awe beside her.

"The footmen will carry up your trunks. I hope you brought ball gowns; you will of course attend our own ball, then there are others." Louise gestured up the stairs. "Maids will help you unpack, and then I want to hear everything about your life, Marguerite. Come down to the drawing room when you've refreshed yourself."

Marguerite laughed. "You're incorrigibly curious, as usual, Louise."

Louise squeezed Marguerite's arm. "Sometimes I miss the rolling Downs, and the families I know. We're quite constricted in the park here, nothing but trees. No neighbors."

"But you have the river," Marguerite reminded her. "I would like to see it later."

Louise sighed, then smiled in resignation. "You're quite like my other guests. The Thames is the first thing they want to see, even when I have so many recent acquisitions of Flemish tapestries to show. I don't understand the attraction that lazy river holds!''

"The Thames is lovely and the air soothing. You should not forget those are qualities that your guests seek as they leave the bustle of London."

"I suppose you're right. I'm expecting more visitors for dinner: the McLendons, and Lord Bentworth and his wife. They are on their way back to Sussex from London. Lord Ormond."

Marguerite's spirits had lifted as soon as she beheld the great estate, and she looked forward to seeing her friends.

An hour later she had donned a light blue cambric sack gown that hung loosely over hoops and displayed a long row of dark blue velvet bows on her stomacher. Pearls around her throat and white gloves completed her attire, and a parasol of the same material as the gown shielded her from the sun.

She strolled with her hostess along the river path lined with rhododendron shrubs, and divulged the latest news from Sussex. "You should visit more often, Louise."

"I would like to, but 'tis not the same when the family is gone. I never got along with my cousin who inherited the estate." Louise turned a penetrating eye on Marguerite. "You are thinner than I remember, and there are circles around your eyes. I would gladly have received you during your time of mourning, but you always turned down my invitations."

Marguerite twirled the cord of her fan around her wrist. "I didn't want to embarrass you. My reputation as the Poison Widow might rub off on you, and I did not desire to create difficulties for you."

"That is thoughtful, Marguerite, but I would not turn my back on an old friend. You know that. And I'm sure your peers have forgotten that dreadful epithet."

"There weren't many friends left after Lithgow's death. He did not approve of the company I kept before I married him. Nick Thurston has been a great support, and lately Charles Boynton."

"La! So he finally broke his oath not to ever visit you.

Charles has always been mad about you, and he took your marriage to Lithgow hard. I know that."

"I . . . we are not on the greatest terms at the moment, and I doubt we can breach the chasm that opened lately."

"Oh, dear! Charles is here, you know. I invited him up when I heard he'd been attacked."

Marguerite gasped in distress. "Oh, no! I . . . he does not want to see me, I'm sure. I thought he had to rest."

"He's been here three days. As far as I know, he didn't listen to the doctor. He went tearing around Sussex three days after the attack, looking for Montagu Renny."

An uneasy shiver traveled up Marguerite's spine as she remembered Renny's threat. "Did he find the Scotsman?"

Louise shook her head and flapped her fan in agitation. "No. There's no trace of that scoundrel. 'Tis beyond me how Lithgow could consort with such unsavory people. Renny is not religious, and Lithgow had no patience with worldly people. I don't understand the connection."

Marguerite had wondered about that herself in the past, but the Stuart cause had brought them together in conspiracy. "They were friends since childhood. I suppose Lithgow considered Renny almost as part of family."

"Yes . . ." Louise chewed on her bottom lip. "I'm glad Renny has disappeared. I heard he's been pestering you."

"I hear you're current on the latest news," Marguerite drawled wryly. "I've decided to sell Lennox House and the land. Mayhap Renny will stay away from me after that." Marguerite stopped on the sun-dappled path and faced her friend. "Did you purposely invite me here to meet Charles?"

Louise lifted her plump shoulders in a telling shrug. "Mayhap. I think very highly of him, and I can't stand to see him so unhappy." She slanted a cautious glance at Marguerite. "Are you angry with me?"

Marguerite hesitated. "Perhaps a little, but Charles expressed his wishes when we last spoke. He does not want to see me, and I don't want to see him."

"Pish and nonsense! I believe you need to take a close look at Charles. He would be the perfect man for you, if you ever dared to let him close. He's the most thoughtful and interesting character of my acquaintance—including my husband, who can be a dead bore." She smiled. "Charles is never boring, and there are untold depths to his character that he seldom reveals."

Marguerite remembered the love letters he'd written to her. "Yes . . . he has great capability of expressing himself when he chooses to do so."

"That's settled then. You both shall have the opportunity to discover each other's sterling qualities while resting in this bucolic paradise." She looked around herself with a grimace of disgust. "Give me a busy London street any day, not this green idyll."

Marguerite laughed. "You've become a creature of the great city, Louise! Where's the person who longed for the South Downs?"

Louise flapped her fan idly. "Come, let me show you my tapestry collection. Now that you're my houseguest you can't very well say that you have to leave in the middle of the tour."

Marguerite gave another laugh, cheered by her friend's brusque manner. Louise had not really changed behind the stately exterior of a countess. "I've been longing to see it ever since I got the invitation."

Later, as candles glowed in the sconces on the walls and in the candelabras on the many tables downstairs, Marguerite stepped down from her bedchamber dressed in one of her two new gowns, an emerald green silk held back with tapes to show the embroidered flounced petticoat, a scrap of lace scented with rose water tucked into her bodice. A maid had arranged her hair high with rolled curls at the sides, and clustered in the back with a jeweled clasp, then powdered white. Marguerite disliked the stiff arrangement, but she did not want to appear a country yokel among Louise's sophisticated guests. She stepped into the drawing room to greet the others, who chatted in subdued voices.

At first she noticed only the rust and gold tones of the Oriental carpet that had been worn to mellow shades, and the fine furniture covered in rust-colored brocade. Candles, tiny points of light in every corner she looked, gave the room a soft golden sheen.

She stepped over the threshold and beheld Charles, still somewhat pale after his ordeal, but with no outward signs of his weakness. He wore his long, curly hair unpowdered and held back with a satin bow, its chestnut luster warm against the harsh planes of his face. His eyes glowed, blue jewels framed with dark eyebrows and lashes. He noticed her, his smile congealing into a mask of suspicion. His eyes narrowed.

Her heart hammered wildly as she stared at him, unable to remove her gaze from his handsome form. He wore a light gray silk coat trimmed with silver braid along the pocket flaps and the wide cuffs. Silver buttons and a thin band of silver embroidery embellished his waistcoat, and a froth of snowy lace encircled his wrists and edged his cravat. Flawless elegance, and charm to match, Marguerite thought, her throat dry.

After weeks of painful loneliness, she realized she'd fallen in love with the gentleman who had lured her into his passionate embrace. *Charles, my love,* she said silently, vowing she would find a way to appease his ill humor.

Chapter 18

Voices receded, movement ceased around Charles, and he could only stare at Marguerite, a vision in sea green silk and luminous pearls—in her hair, around her neck and wrists, and drops in her ears. She was vibrant femininity, a courageous spirit in flight, her smile aglitter, and her bosom smelling of roses. His sensitive nose picked that sun-drenched scent from the many in the room.

His heart pounded, heating his blood with desire. The bump on his head had receded, but the spot now throbbed with his heightened awareness of her, and reminded him that he'd received that blow because of his hopeless love for her.

He slowly erected the defenses in his heart as she swayed across the carpet, her wide skirts elegantly lifted in one hand. He couldn't let himself be wounded again by her indifference, her lack of love.

"Isn't she lovely?" Louise whispered in his ear.

"Yes, but stubborn and unreasonable," he said coldly, and loudly enough so that Marguerite could hear him. "And greedy."

"That was uncalled for," Marguerite said, her gaze measuring him from head to toe. She idly flapped her ivory fan in front of her face, her golden amber eyes flirting with him over the edge. Heat suffused his body, instantly filling him with the frustration of renewed longing. God, he wanted to crush her to him and watch those teasing eyes grow sultry with passion as he kissed her taunting lips. She seemed different away from gloomy Lennox House.

"I always tell the truth," he murmured, and pulled at the cuff of his coat.

"The truth that you choose to tell," she countered, also sotto voce.

"La!" cried Louise, and waved her fan in delight. "Such biting conversation, such knife-sharp wit. I know this will be a very successful dinner party."

"Only if you feed Lady Lennox poison in the custard," Charles said, his face expressionless, but his eyes challenging Marguerite to battle.

"I'll let you taste every dish first," Marguerite said with a theatrical coo, and Charles could not help but chuckle.

"Only if you force it down my throat."

"Tosh! I would not touch you for anything, Charles, not even under the threat of poison. I'd rather it finish me off first."

"Ah! A fledgling martyr." He flapped his hand in a dismissive gesture. "But I don't believe I could vouch for your pure heart. Martyrdom might be out of your reach. And I shall endeavor not to come near your *poisonous* darts."

Marguerite sniffed and addressed Louise. "If I have to sit beside him, I shall retire with a headache."

"Not to worry," Louise said with a laugh. "You may sit where you choose." She looked regal in a powdered wig, and wore a cream damask gown with gold robings over a yellow quilted petticoat. She took Charles's arm as the butler announced that dinner was served. "Let's find our way to the table."

Only when Charles left, and a portly gentleman came to

claim Marguerite's arm, did she notice her surroundings and the other guests, about twenty, in splendid attire of embroidered silks and satins in all colors of the rainbow.

The dining room walls were covered with tapestries, and above them were long rows of portraits and other paintings. Plaster cartouches and garlands adorned the white ceiling, and a dark red carpet gave muted elegance to the room.

A white tablecloth, napkins, and enormous silver epergnes holding yellow and pink roses completed the setting, and candles glittered in crystal glasses and reflected in the silver.

Marguerite found that her escort had both a wry humor and a fondness for talking most of the time. She listened and made polite conversation as she watched—in impotent fury—as Charles took his seat across the table from her. Francesca McLendon smiled and called out a greeting as she sat down next to Charles.

"I'm glad you're getting out and about, Marguerite. I've missed you at the various events in London," she said.

Marguerite was not about to tell her friend about her lack of funds and therefore her lack of the elegant clothing necessary for the social gatherings that Francesca frequented. "I've been very busy at home," Marguerite said evasively, "so much to put in order."

"Yes, she has been busy—alienating all the people who are eager to help her," Charles said lightly, but his voice held a sharp edge.

Francesca gave Charles a look of surprise, and Marguerite blushed. "There is no call for insults," she said, and Charles inclined his head as if offering a humble apology. She knew he did not mean it; there was not one ounce of remorse in his bearing.

"I hear there's a new volume of B. C. Rose's poetry about to be published," said Marguerite's partner on her left, the thin, asthmatic Lord Wiltern. "My wife is mad about Rose's work."

"I find the poetry very touching," Marguerite said. "I've

been stringing some music on my lute to the lyrics—mostly for my own pleasure, as I'm not blessed with a good singing voice.''

"But blessed with other virtues," Charles said, and raised his wineglass toward her. His eyes glittered with an emotion she could not define.

Her cheeks burned with mortification at the double meaning of his words. Marguerite's portly partner on her right coughed, and demanded to know what Charles meant.

Charles smiled, his eyes taking on a wicked gleam. "She sews a neat stitch, reads, writes, and knows her arithmetic like a gentleman."

"That is praise," Lord Wiltern said with a wheezing chuckle. "Most females of my acquaintance cannot count to one hundred."

"Surely that is a gross exaggeration," Marguerite said stiffly. "The ladies of my acquaintance can count much higher than that."

"Ah, enlightenment has reached the fair half of humankind," Charles said in his most supercilious voice. His eyes still held that teasing glitter, and Marguerite wished the table were narrow enough for a swift kick to his shin. She could always throw her wine in his face, she thought as she glowered. But she was not one to provoke scenes. She abhorred scenes. Besides, she had no desire to embarrass Louise, who stared at her from the end of the table. She smiled at Marguerite and chatted with a duke on her right.

Marguerite said, "Enlightenment came to the ladies a long time ago, before the Garden of Eden, I'd say. The gentlemen have never understood the truth. I daresay it's due to a lack of vision. In my opinion, gentlemen sadly lack perception."

Lord Wiltern gasped beside her and stared goggle-eyed. The gentleman on her other side grew quite still, fork lifted halfway to his mouth.

Charles only patted his mouth with his napkin while idly

studying Marguerite. She wished she could show as cool a face as he did.

He said, "The snake in the apple tree shared its poison and its character traits with Eve. The ladies shall forever speak with a forked tongue."

"Rather speak with a forked tongue than walk with a cloven foot like yours," Marguerite said bitingly, and the whole table laughed. She had not realized that their conversation had garnered the guests' attention. Blushing, she lowered her gaze and glanced at the napkin in her lap.

Louise cleared her throat, and shifted the conversation to other subjects. Marguerite froze at Louise's next words.

"I hear the militia is still chasing a spy all over Sussex. He evidently managed to get through Surrey without getting caught. I say, these Jacobites are desperate! It makes me shiver to think that he might have crossed our property at some point."

"They'll get him in the end. Captain Emerson and his men have worked to form a net along the coast for the fugitive. He shan't leave English soil; you may depend on it!" said the duke seated beside Louise.

Before her inner eye, Marguerite viewed the succession of spies that Lithgow had shielded ever since the failed Stuart rebellion in 1746. Would this desperate spy seek shelter at Lennox House? The thought made her almost choke on the piece of roast trout she'd put into her mouth. She gulped down some wine to clear her throat.

"Sussex is rather a boiling pot of illegal activities," said Lord Wiltern.

The duke said, "Emerson has help from the excise men on the coast. The smugglers will be forced to talk."

Marguerite looked up and noticed Charles's eyes on her. His eyebrows were lifted as if in question. The knowledge struck her that he somehow knew her secret.

She glanced away quickly, her heartbeat pounding in her ears, muting all other sounds. To her relief, the footman behind her chair removed her plate and offered platters of salmon smothered in lemon sauce, souse of pike and shrimp, and roasted lobster. She accepted a small portion of each and helped herself to walnut pickle and melted butter from the dishes on the table.

Could everyone read her guilt like a black cross painted on her forehead?

"If they catch them—the smugglers, that is," Charles said, and lifted a forkful of fish to his mouth. "I doubt it. The villagers are a closemouthed lot."

"I have all confidence that Emerson will solve the problem. When the secret coves and estuaries have been cleared of smuggling vessels, Emerson will put all his energy into catching the Midnight Bandit who has fooled the law long enough, in my opinion," the duke said, and others chimed, "Hear, hear."

The duke continued, "I've heard Emerson's found certain clues, and that 'tis only a matter of time before the matter is cleared up. The bandit will hang from the highest oak along the highway as a deterrent to other miscreants."

God, let me have sold Lennox House by the time Emerson catches up with the smugglers, Marguerite prayed in desperation. If Emerson found out about the cellars that had hidden many a Jacobite refugee, she would be clapped in chains. If the smugglers told him the truth, she would be finished. She prayed he would never catch them.

"Mayhap we should not speak so loudly about Emerson's plans," Charles said. "Do you know who is a Stuart sympathizer and who is not? Your neighbor might live a normal life outwardly, while illegal activities take place on another level."

"Hmm," the duke said, his pale blue gaze roaming, as if wishing to penetrate everyone's mind. The guests stared at each other uneasily.

"Does anyone know the identity of the alleged spy?" Charles asked, and looked around the table, pointedly ignoring Marguerite.

The duke cleared his throat pompously. "The authorities don't know for sure, but think his name is Tiernan—"

"Irish!" Charles blurted out. "Why would an Irishman be involved with the Stuarts?"

Marguerite stared at Charles in surprise. He'd stiffened noticeably and his lips had paled. God, did he know the identity of this fellow?

"Irish? Hmm. You have a point there, Mortimer."

"Mortimer!" Louise cried, tapping the table with her hand. "Your Grace, haven't you heard that he is now the Marquess of Ransford?"

Charles made a grimace but bowed graciously to acknowledge the spontaneous applause. "I never thought this title would come to me. That branch of the family had two cousins in line for the Ransford title. Seems they perished in France, and I can't say I'm overly pleased to gain from their loss."

"Kindly spoken, Charles," Louise said, "but you have done nothing wrong. The war took your relatives. Do not scorn yourself. Blame the Crown for going to war."

Charles chuckled and raised his glass to his hostess. Louise's husband, Lord Woodvine, said, "You'll bring order to that rambling Ransford estate in Berkshire."

"Are you going to move from Mortimer's Meadow?" Marguerite asked, trying to convince herself that she cared not where Charles lived.

His eyes glittered mischievously. "Would you mind terribly, Marguerite?" His voice held a wealth of suggestion.

"Not at all! Call it base female curiosity." She wished she could cover her burning cheeks with her hands. Why did he always gain the upper hand in their arguments?

"Another trick you learned in Eden, no doubt," he drawled so low that only the people in their immediate surroundings could hear him.

"I say, Mort— Ransford! There's no call for subtle insults," Wiltern said, straightening his cavernous chest. He patted Marguerite protectively on her fingertips. "Shall I demand satisfaction with swords?"

Marguerite laughed. "That would serve him right, but there's no need to create a scandal, surely. I give as good as I get."

Charles's lips curved in a sarcastic smile, and Marguerite watched his face breathlessly as she longed to trace her fingers along the hard contours. She had not lain in the arms of a phantom lover; she had lain in *his* arms. And she remembered the ecstasy of it. She remembered every moment.

"I have arranged for a treasure hunt tomorrow," Louise said, changing the subject. She gave a grand smile. "I pray the weather will hold. There's nothing like a rain shower to ruin the plans of a hostess."

The platters of fish and seafood were replaced by dishes of lamb, mutton, and roast beef, along with meat pies, chicken, and duck.

Marguerite ate with good appetite and especially liked the pistachio-flavored almond paste, the candied fruit, and the apple pie that were served at the end.

She didn't speak to Charles until later that night, as she strolled on the terrace to get some fresh air before going to bed. She had no desire to speak with him, but he sought her out. Without asking her permission, he walked beside her.

Darkness held the night in a cocoon of black velvet. The stars did not light up the blackness, but Marguerite's eyes had adjusted to the gray hues of nighttime. Tension heightened, like the beginnings of a storm, as Charles mingled his presence with hers.

"Did you eat too many sweetmeats, Marguerite?" he asked.

She listened more to the softness of his voice than to the teasing words. "No more than you indulged in the wine bottle, Charles. Too much, perhaps, but who is to say? Is your head spinning?"

"Is your stomach queasy?"

"Oh, Charles! Have you come to spar, or will you stroll in peace? If not, you might as well leave."

He gripped her arms and shoved her up against the brick wall. His eyes glittered in the faint light seeping from the library windows. He looked dangerous, yet so desirable. The bricks dug into her back, but she was barely aware of any discomfort as the excitement of his proximity overcame her.

"I thought you had completely dismissed me from your mind, Charles. But your actions speak differently."

"You sat across from me at the table, taunting me until a helpless rage filled me. A rage that urged me to wring your lovely neck, and muffle those sweet insults you threw my way." He groaned. "I could only stare at your mouth as you ate lobster as if it were *me* you had taken into your mouth. Don't you see? Don't you understand how you drive me to distraction? To insanity?"

Marguerite could only stare mutely. As far as she knew, she had done nothing to arouse his ardor. She breathed hard, her heartbeat pounding in her throat, her belly filling with a sweet, hypnotic feeling that wanted to draw her in, and him with her— a longing so fierce she felt faint with weakness.

With a growl deep in his throat, he took her mouth, mauling it with a suppressed rage she could not understand, only give herself to, and be captivated by, until she forgot everything. Hard and smooth, hot and moist, their tongues fought, their mouths desperate for more. Charles's breathing had turned ragged when he lifted his face from hers.

"Damn it all to hell!" he muttered savagely, and crushed her to him. He sobbed with rage as he pressed his face to her throat.

"What's the matter?" Her lips felt tender and swollen after his onslaught.

"You've poisoned me, a slow poison that is spreading under my skin until I can't think of anything but you. I'm dying, the hours—days—when I'm away from your embrace. I can't live without you, Marguerite. It's a damned weakness; I might do something I'll regret."

"Charles," she said softly, an overwhelming tenderness cupping her heart. "I . . . what we did in the meadow and later in my bedchamber was beautiful, but don't tell me the feeling is like poison. The words make me cringe.''

He stilled, his hands holding her face. His warm breath gusted over her, his gaze so intent her knees weakened. ''Darling Marguerite, you got that epithet, Poison Widow, for one reason—that you killed your husband. I know it is not true, but what? What is the secret you hold so close to yourself?''

She squirmed as she thought about the Stuart spy somewhere in Sussex. Was he even now trying to approach Lennox House in the dark to seek shelter? ''I don't know what you're talking about,'' she whispered.

''Tiernan . . .'' He let the name drag. ''You are involved, aren't you? A Jacobite sympathizer. You know Tiernan.'' His grip hardened on her face. ''Tell me the truth!''

Marguerite said truthfully, ''I don't know anyone by that name. Seems somewhat familiar, but I can't recall anyone. . . .'' She stared at Charles, noticing the pain crossing his face like a spasm.

''Nick's young cousin Tiernan Leverton. Not his real cousin, but nevertheless. Nick and Tiernan have been friends since childhood, and Tiernan always was a hothead and an adventurer.''

''He sounds like any number of gentlemen that I know. Why would he be Tiernan, the sought-after spy?''

Charles dropped his hands with a sigh. ''I just know he is.'' He stared up at the black sky and rubbed his jaw in thought. ''Oh, Marguerite. What is going on?'' He took her arm firmly and led her along the terrace. She protested, but he would not let go of his grip.

''Charles, you can't force me to talk about the past—or the present,'' she said breathlessly as he finally faced her again. They stood at the very end of the terrace, the park spreading out before them, immaculate lawns, trimmed box hedges, and symmetrical flower borders. The river was a dark, moving ribbon among the shrubs. Marguerite stared at the night landscape as if hoping to gain strength from it. "I can't talk about the past, not to anyone."

"Listen," he said in a growl close to her ear. "Emerson will force you to talk if he finds that you're hiding something."

Marguerite shrugged recklessly even though the terrace seemed to be tilting under her. "Emerson is not here, and why would he want to talk to me? I have nothing to tell."

Charles closed his eyes and leaned against the balustrade. He sighed in exasperation. "Marguerite, are you a Jacobite spy?"

Silence hung over her like a specter ready to pounce and take her life. She gulped in masses of air, but none of it seemed to reach her lungs.

"Well, are you?"

"I'm not!" she croaked. Without another word, she turned on her heel and rushed into the house.

Chapter 19

Charles watched Marguerite leave, wondering just how many secrets she carried inside. A chill flowed through his blood as he pondered the implications of her evasive answers. She couldn't be involved with the Jacobites, she just couldn't! It was a sure ticket to Tyburn Tree. She could be hanged, or drawn and quartered.

He punched the stone balustrade with his fist and flinched with pain. He stared into the night. A fog had moved up from the river, shrouding the trees and shrubs in a mantle of smoky gray. His body heavy with fatigue, he forced himself upright.

His eyes felt gritty from the lack of sleep, and a melancholia that he could not quite understand enveloped him in a cold inner mist. As he headed toward the open door, he noticed a sudden movement on the grounds.

The candles in the lanterns along the terrace had died, as had the harpsichord music, leaving behind only the emptiness that always came after a merry gathering. He stared hard into the darkness and saw the dark flutter of a cloak as its wearer rounded a tree.

Someone had been spying on him. Charles forgot his exhaustion and sprinted the length of the terrace to vault over the balustrade. He cut across the lawn to the tree, and saw the cloak dance among the shrubs as if someone was running fast.

Charles took a deep breath and pursued the stranger. A cocked hat, boots, and a scabbard were other parts he recognized in the gloom. The man ran fast, straight across the park and into a thicket. Charles lost him there, but he heard the whinny of a horse, then a crunch as the animal crashed through the undergrowth at a gallop.

Hanging his arms at his sides and breathing rapidly, Charles knew he'd lost his prey. Who had spied upon him and Marguerite? The hoofbeats pounded close by, but he couldn't see the horse. The chill deepened in Charles's veins, and his scalp tingled.

Gray fog wound around his legs, rising as if trying to enclose him in an icy embrace. The horse burst through the thicket farther away, and at the same time a shot rang out.

Charles threw himself on the ground just as a ball whined past his head and mangled the leaves in the shrubs behind him. "By thunder!" he said softly, his nose pressed to the damp grass. Now he praised the concealing fog, which he'd cursed earlier.

Hoofbeats halted, hesitated, moved closer, trampled the ground. Charles heard twigs breaking, clumps of sod flying. Snorts, and the sound of hooves came ever closer.

There was a creak of leather, a jerking of reins that set the harness ajingle. If the villain had another loaded pistol and the fog dissolved . . . Charles did not want to finish the thought.

He felt eyes of death scanning the ground for him, but heard only silence, heavy with foreboding. Charles held his breath as the seconds ticked by. Nothing, the night listening.

A flurry of muffled moves brought the horse trotting in the other direction. For a long time Charles remained still on the ground until no sounds of pursuit remained. Only silence filled the night.

Charles brushed the dampness from his coat knowing the fabric would be ruined. But did it matter? He'd rather live than protect his coat from water stains. He sought the tracks of the horse, but the shape of the iron shoes told him nothing, nor did the broken twigs.

With a heavy heart, he returned to the mansion. Someone who wanted him dead had followed him to the Woodvine estate. A bullet might find him when he least expected it. He debated whether to leave the area quickly so as not to endanger any of the other guests, or to stay. He would be damned if he let some unknown enemy dictate his movements! Worried guests had gathered in the hallway, probably due to the shot, Charles thought as he hurried up the stairs. He had no desire to enlighten them.

At midday, after a sumptuous breakfast, the guests gathered outside on the terrace. Charles arrived late. In a foul mood, he thought of returning to bed, where he'd gained very little sleep last night. But there was Marguerite, lovely in a light blue cambric gown and a wide-brimmed straw hat with silk ribbons. He might endanger her life if he—

Louise pulled him out of his reverie rather forcefully. "Come along, Charles; don't dawdle! You shall accompany Marguerite, since she has no escort for the treasure hunt."

Marguerite's gaze locked with his accusingly, and he realized she thought he'd machinated the arrangement. He shook his head, but she abruptly turned her face aside. She was still prickly, still angry with him for voicing his suspicion last night—still as elusive as the mist.

In his mind, he pictured a gloved hand holding a flintlock pistol, a puff of smoke, a burst of fire, the ball finding Marguerite, and she would just evaporate as if she'd never existed. No, she would crumple, lifeless. God, what should he do? He couldn't bear the thought of leaving her to God knew what dangers, yet if the villain wanted him, it would be best to say good-bye to his hostess and somehow flush out the scoundrel. He decided to stay, to keep an eye on Marguerite and the other guests.

"What is the first clue, Louise?" he asked, his jaw aching with tension.

Laughing and chatting, the guests gathered around the hostess. Louise handed out folded billets. "You read this and figure it out. 'Twill lead you to the next clue, and so forth until you find the treasure."

"And what is the treasure?" asked Lord Wiltern, and coughed.

"If I told you that, the surprise would be ruined." Louise smiled and wound her arm around Prunella's. "Anyone with more sedate tastes may join us in the green salon for a hand of cards or a chat."

Charles faced Marguerite. "What do you say? Would you rather withdraw with the ladies to the green salon?" One part of him wanted to goad her into accepting the challenge of the hunt; another part wanted to see her safely within the house.

She twirled her parasol. "I love a treasure hunt, my only complaint being that Louise paired me with you."

He nodded stiffly, all the while noticing the pearly sheen of her skin, the flush in her cheeks, her plump red mouth. "I don't mind withdrawing. You could always ask Ormond or Lord Woodvine to escort you."

"Oh, Charles! Where's your sense of play?" she asked, her sudden smile dazzling him with its brilliance. She took his arm and pulled him toward the river. Standing apart from the others, she unfolded the paper. She read, " 'Something round, a wedding cake for romance, something Moorish. Where lovers tread softly, second from the top.' "

Charles could not take his gaze from Marguerite's graceful throat and the throbbing pulse at its base. Porcelain and velvet, he thought, feeling dizzy from lack of sleep and the warm scent of her flesh wafting toward him.

"Marguerite, the greenhouses have Moorish tile." He leaned closer to better inhale her feminine scent.

"There are two round white tables there. Come, let's go before the others figure out the spot." She took his arm and literally dragged him along the path winding past the maze and the flower borders.

The greenhouses were located behind a tall hedge at the east side of the property. Filtered through hundreds of windows, the sunlight seemed more concentrated inside than in the open. Within, the sun splashed the plants liberally with gold, and Marguerite exclaimed at the beauty of the orange trees, their blossoms sending out a sweet aroma.

"There are the tables," Charles said, pointing at a seating arrangement of wrought-iron benches and two round tables laden with potted green plants.

Marguerite's face was agog with curiosity. "But where do lovers tread? I don't understand, do you?" She turned her amber gaze on Charles, and he was acutely aware of the barrier of all the unspoken words between them, the silent secrets.

Suddenly very tired, he said, "I don't give a damn. This is a silly game."

"Charles! You cannot bow out of the competition now. I'm certain Louise's treasure is something splendid, well worth the effort of finding it."

He leaned closer to her. "The others will be in hot pursuit. May the most eager couple win." He gently nuzzled her nose with his own. She took a startled step back.

"Charles! Do not flirt with me. The gardeners will gossip," she whispered.

"I don't care." He folded his arms around her and drank in her scent. She wrestled out of his embrace, leaving him bereft, igniting a smoldering longing in his loins. He hardened as he viewed her bosom rise and fall with her rapid breathing. God, he wanted only to touch her, to hold her.

"Quickly, where is some other Moorish detail?" she said

as the sounds of laughter came to their ears. "The others are coming."

"You are taking this too seriously," he drawled as he battled an urge to carry her off to a meadow or, preferably, his bed-chamber.

He kept his hands to himself nevertheless, and studied the palm trees in the thick, humid air. "Hmmm, Moorish? There are more tiles around a fountain in the garden."

"Is the fountain round?"

"Yes, but I don't recall any wedding cake, or lovers' soft tread. We can of course step softly around the fountain," he said, laughing.

"No need to be sarcastic." Marguerite bustled past the other guests. "Come along! Louise might have put something there for the occasion."

They circumvented the hedge, Charles admiring her deter-mined back, straight as a rod, her head held high, her skirts over panniers swaying provocatively. She went through a gate shaped by climbing roses, and disappeared behind a lilac hedge. He caught up with her, halting her progress by gripping her arm.

She stared at him in question, her tongue moistening her lips. "What is the matter with you, Charles? You don't have to touch me at every corner."

"But I do. I can't keep my hands to myself, and I don't think you're averse to my touch."

"It is the middle of the day; we're in a park, and I like to show some decorum—"

"We have unfinished business from last night. Eventually you'll have to confide your secrets to me." He kept a firm hold on her arms even though she struggled to get away.

"I don't have an obligation to confide in you or anyone else. Let's go." Her voice brooked no nonsense, but he kept her prisoner, a struggling kitten that he did not want to let go. And she was as soft and as comforting as a kitten in his arms.

He buried his nose in the curve where her neck met her

shoulder and inhaled. Overcome with longing, he stood there for a long time, her struggles meaning nothing to him, as he could easily control her movements. He let go only when she clouted him over the head, jarring the sore area where the lump had throbbed.

"Charles!"

He set her free, meeting her gaze, a blaze of anger in her face. "Come to think of it," he said as if nothing had happened, "there are Moorish carvings on the belvedere."

Marguerite shaded her eyes with one hand. The billet hanging loosely between her fingers flapped in the summer breeze. "Let's try the fountain first."

Charles offered his arm gallantly. "Marguerite," he murmured, "say that you long to make love with me as much as I want to love you. Say it. I need to hear the words."

She blushed to the roots of her hair, then tilted her head so that all he could see was the flat crown of her straw hat.

"No need to feel ashamed. I know you're a sensuous woman, and that will not change because you changed your mind about me. If I'd remained the Midnight Bandit, you would have gladly taken me into your arms."

"But you aren't the bandit, are you? You're my tormentor, my bane. My nemesis. My destroyer."

"The one who destroys your defenses, perhaps. Nothing but good will come of it, if only you care to trust me."

She walked faster, almost running toward the rushing fountain. He lengthened his stride to keep up with her. "Trust makes you vulnerable, Charles. As soon as you lay your trust at someone's feet, it is in jeopardy of being trampled. I trust only in myself."

"Ah! The bitter truth will out. That is where your difficulty lies, Marguerite. You have to learn to trust gentlemen again before you can give your heart wholly."

She stopped abruptly, her eyes like dark wounds in her face. He knew he'd touched a raw place in her heart. "I've seen friends who trusted each other. Friendship became a battle of wills that finally ended in death—the death of an innocent person." She took a deep breath. "You and I have a battle, Charles, and where it will lead, I fear to speculate."

"You lack faith as well, fairest Marguerite."

"Whereas you possess both of those qualities," she chided. "Really, Charles, you're an incurable romantic."

"You make it sound like an insult."

"Mayhap I meant it to be," she cried in frustration as she arrived at the fountain's edge.

Charles's spirits fell. She would not let him into her heart. "I don't see a single clue," he said to move away from the dangerous ground of romance. "It has to be the belvedere."

Leaving him behind, she ran up the slope, on top of which the white-painted belvedere sat in carved and turreted splendor. She stepped onto the circular floor and lifted cushions off the benches. "Belvederes are for lovers, even for wedding ceremonies sometimes," she said thoughtfully.

"Treads," he said, and folded his arms across his chest as he watched her movements. "I see only six of them."

She looked at him in suspicion. "Six treads? Where?"

He pointed at the six wooden steps leading to the interior, and she cried out in delight. She felt around under the edge of the protruding second plank from the bottom and found a pouch of folded pieces of paper. "The second clue!"

I wish I had a clue to your heart, he thought as he dragged the palm of his hand over her raised buttock. She moved as if stung.

"What are you doing?" She gave him an aggravated stare. "You're taking annoying liberties, and I will abandon this treasure hunt if you don't behave properly."

"I'm sorry," he said, and smiled.

"You're nothing of the kind," she said between clenched teeth. She unfolded the note while the other hunters scrambled up the slope. Pulling him with her, she ran down the other side of the mound.

"What does it say?" Charles asked.

" 'Five hundred steps to T. Fifty to the east, where the sun shines.' " She furrowed her brow and chewed on her bottom lip. Charles could barely contain his longing to kiss her.

"The T stands for Thames," she said. She glanced toward the folly, where the others had found the plank. "Dash it all! We have to go back up and count the steps from the stairs where we found the clue."

He hung back, suffering from suppressed desire as he watched her lithe body running back up the slope. The others were already counting, passing him with triumphant waves. He didn't give a damn about the hunt. He rushed after Marguerite, realizing they were alone by the belvedere. As she started counting steps, he pulled her into his arms and smothered her face with kisses.

"Don't!" she complained hoarsely, but he trailed the line of her lips with the tip of his tongue, making her shut up. She whimpered and closed her startled eyes, then wound her arms around his neck.

"Darling." Charles grew dizzy as hot desire tightened his loins, making him throb. With a groan, he lifted her into his arms and carried her into the belvedere.

"No . . . Charles, I can't. . . ." She pushed against his chest.

"You can and you will," he said, setting her down.

"No! Don't push me." She tore away from him and ran back out, counting the blasted steps down the hill. His heart pounding hard with carnal hunger, his body aching for her, he wished he could turn off the symptoms of his yearning.

With a heavy sigh, he followed her down the hill. They caught up with some of the others. Laughter and suggestions for possible routes to the treasure filled the air. Charles watched as Marguerite concentrated, pacing the fifty steps to the east. She ended up in a spot on the lawn. No visible clues there.

He strolled up to her even as his mind told him to abandon the search, to abandon her and the influence she had on him.

"Where the sun shines?" she said, and turned helpless eyes in his direction.

"How can you behave as if nothing is happening here except for a silly parlor game?" he snapped. "The tension jumps like lightning between us."

"Don't exaggerate," she replied coolly with a sideways glance. "Put your mind to better use."

He flung out his arms in frustration, then pointed toward the extensive formal gardens, where glimpses of a sundial shone golden through the clipped hedges. "Does Louise mean that sun?"

Marguerite's eyes lit up with renewed fire. "Yes! It must be. Come, we're late. Others have already gone on to the next clue. I can hear them by the maze."

They went around the sundial, Marguerite searching the low shrubs below.

"You have to trust me, Marguerite," Charles said, not caring if they ever found the third note that would lead them on.

She glanced up from her search. "Why should I trust you now? With your love letters and your impersonation of the Midnight Bandit, you showed that you're not beyond cheating."

Charles glanced around. "Speaking of which, the others have cut across the lawn directly to the maze." He scanned the nearby woods, seeing nothing suspicious move about the undergrowth. Nevertheless, the villain from last night might by lying in wait. Worry flowed up his spine and through his body. He didn't like to stand around in the open with Marguerite so close to the forest. Anything could happen.

"Come. Let's get on with it. The others will show the way and we shall beat them at the last leg."

"Charles! How can you even suggest it? The others might have figured the next step wrong." With a triumphant smile, Marguerite found the note tucked under the base of the sundial. "See? It says, 'Go to the place where the water giggles. Walk across, statue smiling. The gnome will give you the answer you seek.' "

"It has to be the fountain in the middle of the maze," Charles said. "There're several statues there, and one has to be a gnome. Let's go."

Tapping the corner of the paper against her teeth, Marguerite did not move. "Does the water giggle in the fountain?"

"No, it laughs," he said sarcastically. "Practically howls."

She twisted her mouth in a grimace. "No need to be cynical. I know the right place. Louise means the spot in the river where it parts and tumbles—giggles—over stones. There's a small island on the property, a bridge, and statues. Not many guests know about this spot, but Louise showed me once."

God, her eyes shone like jewels under the brim of her hat, and her lips looked sweeter than strawberries and just as red. Worry gave way to a new wave of desire. He took her by the hand. "Let's find the damned treasure. Hurry."

Marguerite laughed as they ran away from the garden and down toward the river.

"I can tell you're enjoying this simple game."

She sighed with pleasure and righted her hat. "I enjoy everything that is a puzzle or an enigma."

"Like the Midnight Bandit? You were drawn to him because he's a mystery person?"

"He let me forget myself and my difficult situation. He let me *live*—until I discovered the lie, your damned lie!"

The islet lay in a curve of the river where the banks had eroded and created three small diversions to the main body of water. Charles said, "I don't think the river giggles over the stones; it mumbles."

"Have some imagination!" she said with a snort. "I'm going out to the island."

She crossed the narrow bridge, holding on to its one wooden railing. Charles followed and sat down on a bench while she searched the various bronze statues of Pan, a faun, a deer, an elf, an owl, and a laughing Cupid. He started inventing a story.

"Marguerite giggled like water over stones at the ludicrous

idea of love. Derision poisoned the water green—or was it envy?—at the idea of love. She had no one, nothing, only a dream of what was love. A dream as insubstantial as mist. She cried for that mist while true love lay at her feet crying in frustration due to her blindness.''

"Stop it!'' Marguerite stomped past the statues and stood before him, a blazing goddess of anger. "How dare you give me such a belittling story?''

"I like to see your eyes turn dark with anger.'' He gave her a lazy grin "I like to stir the emotions under your aloof facade, touch the raw spots. I like to—''

"I don't want to hear another word from you, Charles, if you can't be civilized.''

"Then you have to silence me.'' He pulled her resisting body down onto his lap. He sensed her surrender in the slumping of her body before she wound her arms seductively around his neck.

"I see there's no other way to make you stop harassing me.'' She moaned softly as she kissed his lips, first lightly, then harder, as if a hunger had awakened in her blood.

Marguerite had fought their attraction all morning hoping that it would disappear, hoping it would return to her the old friend Charles of the past. But he was insistent, always crowding her with his male presence, a prickly burr burrowing in under her defenses. And, truth to tell, she loved him.

"You're beautiful,'' he whispered against her throat, and she felt beautiful—desirable. Desire, hot as fire, tore through her body. God, she'd longed for this since he'd left through her window so many nights ago.

"Someone will come and find us,'' she said as he carried her behind a dense shrub of holly at the other end of the islet.

"Shh, don't worry. Let that threat add spice to our adventure.'' He laid her on the ground and unlaced her bodice rapidly. Through the shift underneath, he caressed her breasts until the nipples swelled to hard pebbles of desire.

"Dearest, I've waited, mooned like a schoolboy for this," he murmured as he pulled apart the drawstring and found the naked flesh beneath. He kissed her breasts hungrily, tracing lazy patterns with his tongue. She whimpered with pleasure.

Excited voices and laughter sounded in the distance.

Chapter 20

"They're coming!"

Charles silenced her protests with his mouth and caught her flailing hands against him, pushing her to discover a way under his shirt and caress his skin. "Please," he begged. "Touch me."

Her eyes were heavy-lidded with desire, and her hands obeyed his plea. She unlaced the front of his breeches and pulled his shirt up. Her hand caressed his swollen manhood, and he muffled a cry against her throat. With an impatient hand he lifted up her skirts to her waist, wishing the panniers and every other fabric obstacle to hell.

"Charles," she whispered as his hot member touched her secret place—insistent velvet probing her.

He fumbled, feeling stupid and clumsy, but desire rode him like a devil. She was hot and smooth and wet, he registered in a daze, driving his way into her sweetness as jolts of pleasure shot through his body. He tasted the soft, full mounds of her breasts, unable to slake his thirst for her with mere caresses. He assaulted her lips, tasting, savoring her silken mouth, her seductive tongue, squashing her protests as the voices neared rapidly. She whimpered against him, growing rigid in mounting pleasure.

He drove into her in desperation, wanting every inch of her for himself, and wanting to give her everything. He felt her contract around him, her face flushed and soft with pleasure, a silent cry of ecstasy forming on her lips. She looked at him, not seeing, as she convulsed in his arms. He let go of his rigid control. Instantly an intense wave of hot release flooded his being. Panting, he held her hard against him as steps clumped across the bridge.

Marguerite stiffened, breathing heavily against his throat. "God," she whispered. "What if they find us? I'll be ruined."

"Lie absolutely still," he whispered back, holding her hard as echoes of his ecstasy rocked through him. With any luck, no one would think to look behind the large shrub.

This was where he wanted to be every night: in her arms with nothing between them except surging desire. He wanted her in his bed, cradled up against him like a spoon; he wanted to see her sleepy eyes widen in the morning as they fastened on him. Her smile! He craved her smile like a starving man craved food, damn her. She grinned now, a secret, wicked smile.

Marguerite looked into Charles's eyes, reading the tenderness. He was the most impudent, daring, outrageous, desirable . . . well, she couldn't think of all the words that would fully describe his character. Elusive, unpredictable, exasperating, stubborn. Kind, caring. Erotic. A lover who took her breath away with his touch.

Her blood still sang from the elation of his lovemaking, but she needed more, craved the deep satisfaction that she'd tasted only a few times in his arms.

"Where's the next clue?" she heard Lord Wiltern ask in a

peevish voice. "Lady Woodvine has made it singularly difficult for us to find this treasure."

"I found it," Charles whispered in Marguerite's ear.

"It had better be worth the trouble," Wiltern's lady said ominously.

Marguerite stifled a giggle even though she was frightened to death that they would find her in this compromising position. She held her breath as the other guests tramped around the statues fifty yards away.

"Which one is the gnome?" someone asked.

"That evil-looking fellow, I believe," a light female voice said. "Yes! Here it is." She read aloud. " 'Many steps and turns to the middle, under the diamond-bright surface, a hand of great value. The treasure is yours.' " The voice rose at the end. "What in the world does Louise mean with these cryptic remarks?"

Charles looked down at Marguerite, his dear face alight with mischief. She could read his thought, the suggestion in his eyes that he hadn't had to search very hard to find the treasure. Heat rushed into her cheeks. He had power over her, power to touch her soul, and she felt naked, afraid, that if she joined her life to his she would ultimately be closed in a prison like the one Lithgow had made for her. Charles was nothing like Lithgow— yet he was a male. Gentlemen craved power, craved control over their dominion, including wives and children.

"What the devil is this—many steps and turns?" Lord Wiltern thought aloud. "Mayhap she means the circumference of this island."

Marguerite stiffened, and Charles tightened his grip around her. He slowly eased away from her, pulling down her skirts and rolling over on his side so that he could tie up his breeches. Marguerite laced up the bodice with trembling fingers, and made sure it was straight. She patted her hair and tied the ribbons of her hat as she listened tensely to the next comment.

"No," someone said, "there aren't any turns here; the island is mainly circular. I think we have to go back. Louise is sending us all over her park.''

''Good for the constitution,'' someone chimed. ''I vote we return to the garden. Many turns there.''

''The maze,'' Marguerite whispered.

Charles's eyes gleamed. ''Of course. Louise will laugh as we get helplessly lost in the labyrinth. She's a devil at heart.''

The rest of the treasure hunters marched across the bridge, and Marguerite could draw a sigh of relief. ''I don't believe we had the nerve to behave in such a wanton fashion,'' she said, and looked away as his gaze took on that hot look that said he desired her anew.

'' 'Twasn't nearly enough, my sweet. I need a whole night in your arms to slake my thirst, and then that might not be enough. The thirst returns quickly. You must have thrown a spell on me.''

''Not at all!'' Marguerite said firmly as longing for more slowly crept through her body. ''Do you think they'll come back?''

''No . . .'' he drawled. ''What devious plan is going through your mind? I thought you first and foremost wanted the treasure.''

''You just gave it to me, and I want it again,'' she said, and pushed him down on the grass. He laughed and threw himself into the tantalizing game with gusto.

It was the maze, and the diamond brilliance was the water, Marguerite surmised as they joined the rest of the search party in the center of the maze half an hour later. Everyone was clamoring for the solution to the last riddle, and Marguerite was the first to look down into the fountain and detect the barely visible marble hand on the bottom at the center of the spray.

''Charles?'' she called.

''Yes?'' He bent over the side of the fountain to study her

find. "I shall have to take my boots off for this part of the game," he muttered.

"It won't be the first time today," Marguerite said under her breath.

He gave her an enigmatic smile. She studied those bold lips that so recently had kissed her breathless, mindless, and felt she could kiss him again. And again.

He tore off his boots and his coat and climbed into the fountain. "Argh, icy cold! Why did I let you talk me into this?"

"Because you had no other choice," she said sweetly.

Charles rolled up his shirtsleeve as the others gathered around to watch. They bore disappointed expressions. "You were late here, Lady Lennox," Wiltern's wife said with a pout. "The treasure should rightfully be someone else's, since you entered the center of the maze last."

"She figured out the location of the treasure first," Wiltern said.

Marguerite thought she didn't care about the treasure, but she had enjoyed the puzzle.

Charles brought up the marble hand in which rested a small gold statue of a cherub, the wings made in delicate filigree. Charles handed it to Marguerite with a bow. "Yours, Lady Lennox. You have earned your guardian angel."

Marguerite sensed the double meaning of his words and wondered why she would need a guardian angel. Charles certainly was no angel in her arms.

He smiled and climbed out of the water. Water dripped from the statuette, and Marguerite stared at the treasure that had been given to her. It would always remind her of this carefree day when she'd lost more of the bitterness she wore like armor around her. Every day was a piece of her new life.

"Well, let's get ready for the ball," someone said, and the group headed for the first wrong turn in the maze. Laughter soon echoed, and Marguerite was amazed how difficult it was to find the right way out.

She lost Charles at some turn, but she thought she saw the flash of his black coat at some corners. But . . . he hadn't been wearing black. None of the gentlemen did. There it was again, whisking away as if the owner was eager not to show himself.

She hurried forward, but only an empty lane awaited her. A cold sensation prickled on her neck, and the sunlight seemed to dim around her. She whirled around, but there was no one behind her. Alone, and shivering with sudden premonition, she rubbed her arms, where gooseflesh had risen.

Whimpering, she ran back the way she'd come, running straight up against Charles's firm chest.

"Dearest," he said, laughing. "Eyes of doe, looking hither, looking tither, startled, body tensed as willow bow, poised for flight."

Relieved, she pressed her hand to her heart. "Bosh, Charles, you can't use the word *tither* in a poem. It means taxes."

He shrugged. "I used what came to mind, anything that rhymed."

She breathed rapidly, her knees shaking. "Rhyme your way out of this maze then, or I'll squeeze through the hedge."

"Why in such a hurry, my dear?" He took her shoulders and looked deeply into her eyes. "You look like you've seen a ghost."

"A malevolent one, mayhap. I had the strangest premonition of disaster."

Charles's smile left his face, leaving room for determination. "We should go back to Sussex, Marguerite."

"We have to attend the duke's ball."

"We will leave directly after the ball then." Charles hastened her through many turns and alleys, and she looked everywhere for the black coat.

"Why the sudden speed, Charles?"

Charles looked at her long and hard as if deliberating whether to tell her the truth. He decided to be honest. "I think someone is trying to kill me."

Chapter 21

Someone wants to kill Charles. The words kept revolving in Marguerite's mind. *Who?* she had asked, but he'd evaded her question.

She couldn't tell him that Montagu Renny might have murder in mind for her. Charles would charge off in search of the Scotsman and demand satisfaction. Marguerite could not take the risk. The ghost of Renny's threat had followed her here; there would be no reprieve for her until Renny was gone. Dead.

She could not shake the dark premonition as she ascended the stairs at the neighboring estate, the residence of His Grace, the Duke of Netterton. She had dressed with great care in a silver tissue gown, had had her hair pomaded and powdered, and had forced her feet into silver slippers that really were too small for her. She suffered their tight hold on her toes as she entered on Charles's arm.

A headache had begun at her temples as the maid had arranged her hair, and it had only increased during the drive from the Woodvine estate. Charles was tense beside her, his gaze darting over every detail along the road as if looking for something.

Marguerite glanced at him, and when she noticed his set expression, she wished she had told him about Renny. She just couldn't.

Most likely he would see her as someone soiled with the blood of an innocent man even if she hadn't killed Sergeant Rule. She couldn't bear the thought of Charles's love turning into loathing. What to do?

She smiled mechanically at her host and hostess, and glided over the polished floor, exchanging inanities with the other guests. There were hundreds, it seemed: ladies in embroidered silks, satins, and glittering gems, gentlemen in colorful brocades and velvets, gold buttons, a fall of lace at their throats, and wearing powdered wigs. They all wore smiles, some with inviting velvet patches attached to rouged cheeks. Marguerite suddenly thought of a theater, a play performed by amateur players who laughed too much and spoke too loudly, with the occasional lisp, or in the overwrought tones of a dowager.

Her headache increasing, she sought the cool evening air by the balcony windows. Francesca McLendon, who had arrived earlier, joined her. She wore a rose damask dress with silver robings that set off her dark hair and the silver gleam in her eye. "You look preoccupied, Marguerite. Is anything the matter?"

"No ... well, I don't know. I am confused about certain things. My life is changing very rapidly." She fanned her hot face, wondering if she dared to confide in her friend. What to confide, though? There were secrets she could not share with anyone.

"I noticed how you looked at Charles earlier. As if you were seeing him for the first time."

Marguerite blushed and glanced away. "Mayhap I am. I have been so blind concerning him."

"You will find happiness with him if you dare to give him your all. Love is no other way. There are no compromises if the bond will grow strong, and remain strong."

"You sound as if you think love should be tested." Marguerite felt uneasy as she studied the pastoral scene painted on her fan.

"My love for Carey was tested when he discovered some unsavory facts about my past, but he showed that he still loved me."

Marguerite stared at her friend through narrowed eyes. "What do you know about me? Is there gossip besides the general suspicion that I killed Lithgow?"

Francesca shook her head. "I don't know anything except what you've told me. I . . . I sense that you're hiding something, playing Charles false, mayhap. He deserves the truth from you, no matter how difficult."

Marguerite cringed at the blunt words and stared at her earnest friend. Francesca was right, of course. "God, 'tis so difficult. I don't know what I feel for Charles."

"Friendship at the least, and as your friend, he has the right to know your secrets. Do you know you have the power to destroy him?"

Marguerite gasped in surprise. "That's ridiculous. He does not need me in the sense—"

"He needs your trust. Tell him everything, or you'll destroy his love." Francesca gave Marguerite a long stare, and Marguerite knew she had to do something before she burst with the tension of all her secrets.

"You're right, Francie. I do need to talk with Charles tonight, or something terrible will happen." Marguerite touched her burning cheeks and gave her friend a tremulous smile. "Thank you for pushing this to a head. I've been avoiding the truth, hoping I would not have to pay for my actions in the end; I've been such a coward—still am. But the time for reckoning is here."

Francesca gave her a quick smile and a hug. "Don't be afraid. It cannot be that bad. Find Charles before you change your mind."

Without another word, Marguerite sought Charles among the

guests in the ballroom. He was part of an elegant minuet figure along with his elderly hostess, whom he treated with wicked gallantry, if the lady's delighted expression was any indication.

Marguerite trembled. The fragile violin music grated on her nerves. She would have to speak with Charles. Somehow now that she'd decided—with the push from Francesca—there didn't seem to be any time left.

When he looked up, she waved at him to indicate that she needed to see him. He gave her a smile that blazed through her body, leaving only longing in its wake.

She walked toward him, waiting impatiently for the dance to end. If she didn't speak with him now, she would lose her nerve. Feeling as if she were balancing on the edge of a precipice, she dared not think of the result her revelations would bring. If Charles turned away from her in disgust, she could not bear it. Not now, not when she'd finally started to feel alive—to truly love.

The violin music came to a trembling halt, and the couples moved off the floor, silk gowns brushing against the floor and fans creating a cooling draft on heated faces.

Charles was moving through the throng, a handsome panther among the cats. Marguerite wet her dry lips and took deep breaths to steady her pounding heart. Her fingertips tingled with nervousness.

He surged toward her, filling her vision, smiling, stumbling momentarily on a lady's lace-edged train.

Hurry, Marguerite said silently.

Something cracked behind her. She registered a sudden explosion that deafened her. It all went so fast, a buzzing draft along her head, a cry.

It wasn't hers. Dazed, she stared at Charles. He had frozen in place. Someone wailed behind him, and a figure crumpled— a man in a blue embroidered coat. Gentlemen guests pushed the screaming throng aside, then scrambled outside in pursuit of the killer.

Marguerite watched Charles's face, seeing confusion, then

anger as he whirled around and saw the blood seeping through the front of the man's waistcoat.

Marguerite moaned in fear. "Lord Ormond," she whispered. "Stephen."

Charles knelt by the dying man, who feebly flapped his hands. Charles held them still, speaking softly in Ormond's ear. A lady cradled Ormond's head to her bosom, crying copiously. He gave a faint smile, a grimace. Ormond's head tilted sideways; then his hands went limp. Charles folded them gently on the bloody chest, then rushed out through the open doors. His eyes had been burning with fury, with the desire for revenge.

Marguerite could not think. She stood as if turned into stone, dread filling every corner of her being with ice. Somehow she felt responsible for Ormond's death. She didn't know why, but she suspected that Montagu Renny had been at the other end of the pistol. The ball had whistled close to her head, close to Charles's. If he hadn't stumbled . . . Marguerite dared not think the thought to the end.

Renny was out there in the dark. He had to be—waiting, perhaps with another loaded pistol. The thought made Marguerite gasp with fright. Charles had thrown himself into danger to search for the murderer.

Marguerite clasped her icy hands and tried to think of a plan. Nothing but a welter of confused thoughts raced through her mind.

Shouts and curses came from the extensive gardens, running men crashing through shrubs, searching, seeking to avenge the outrage of the sudden death. The impudence alone made everyone grit their teeth.

Pale and trembling, Francesca pulled Marguerite aside. "Do you know what is happening?"

"They are trying to capture the murderer. I don't think they'll succeed," Marguerite said. She sighed in defeat. "I never talked to Charles."

"You shall speak with him when he returns."

Marguerite shivered. *Unless Renny reaches him first.* She

could not voice her fears, only told Francesca she would await Charles's return in the hallway. Most guests had gathered there to file out to their coaches. The ball had been ruined; the house was in shock. A dead man lay on the dance floor, his blood-soaked body covered with a tablecloth.

Lord Woodvine, the local justice of the peace, had already assembled the militia when Marguerite and Charles returned to the Woodvine mansion with Prunella and Louise.

A grim set of young men in red uniforms stood outside as Woodvine issued orders to the head officer. Marguerite looked at the group with misgivings. If Renny had managed to escape from the hot pursuit at the ball, he would easily evade these men if he rode a horse, which was most likely. But the questioning would begin, the ferreting out of details until they found a description of Renny. Then the net would close.

When the others had gone to their bedchambers and Marguerite watched Charles pour himself a glass of brandy in Lord Woodvine's study, she decided to throw herself over the precipice of confession.

If she ended up crushed at the bottom, it did not matter anymore. "I'm sure the murderer is Montagu Renny. He was possibly trying to kill me," she said. "He said last time I saw him that he would kill me. Ormond is dead because of the secrets I've kept with Renny."

Charles's hand halted in midair, and his face paled as if he'd received a vicious blow to his stomach. His eyes darkened with suspicion, and he set the glass down with exaggerated care. "My ears are playing tricks on me, Marguerite. Would you please repeat your statement?"

"Renny killed Ormond," she said tonelessly. Her legs were giving way, and she slumped onto the armchair by the desk. The room smelled of leather and mildew, and she felt as if she couldn't breathe in the closed atmosphere of the many books lining the walls.

He strode to her side and took her shoulders in a hard grip. "What are you telling me?"

"Renny threatened to kill me if I didn't promise to marry him. I said I'd rather be dead than marry him." Marguerite fumbled for a handkerchief in the pocket of her gown, but found none. Her eyes overflowed and she dragged the back of her hand over her face.

Charles thrust his folded square into her hand. "Here. Now tell me everything from the beginning." He went to sit in Woodvine's chair on the other side of the desk, a judge, mayhap an executioner, Marguerite thought. Well, she had reached the end.

"My husband and Montagu Renny killed Sergeant Rule. I knew this; I've known it all along. I saw them, saw the body, but where they buried him I have no idea." Her voice trembled so much she could barely speak. She sensed Charles's tension, and she did not dare to look at him. His accusation washed over her even before he spoke.

"Why didn't you tell me . . . tell *anyone* of this? Captain Emerson has been searching for his friend for a year. He has never given up hope of solving the mystery of Rule's disappearance."

"I . . . I was afraid. Afraid for my own skin." She threw a cautious glance at Charles. "I should have the word *coward* blazed across my forehead. I thought that the secret would go away, the whispers of the past fade away."

"The truth will out," he said grimly. "Always."

She could see he was holding his anger tightly in check. Now that she'd opened her soul, some of the terror left. There was no other choice but to forge ahead.

"Rule is buried somewhere in Sussex, but I truly don't know where. He lost his life because he discovered Lennox and Renny's clandestine missions to deliver Jacobite spies back and forth across the Channel." She swallowed hard to clear the lump in her throat. "Lennox House has been a refuge for the spies ever since the failed Stuart rebellion in Scotland.'' Her voice lost its momentum and she collapsed in a sob.

Charles sat completely still, and she sensed the displeasure, the accusing thoughts going through his mind. She might as well hang herself. She continued.

"I knew about the treasonous dealings and did nothing. Renny has since blackmailed me. I paid him money to keep quiet about Lennox's Jacobite leanings. But finally I told Renny to stop harassing me, that I would not pay him another penny. Then he tried to coerce me into marriage, but I said no. He is a sore loser. Ormond would have been alive now if I'd said yes to Renny.'' A burden had lifted from her shoulders as she confessed the whole, and her future now lay in Charles's hands.

"Did you take part in the actual transporting of the spies, or feeding them meals, or giving them clothing?'' he asked in a toneless voice.

She shook her head. At least this was the truth. "Lennox and Renny saw to everything themselves, but I was well aware of what was going on. For a whole year, ever since Rule died, there have been no more spies at Lennox House.''

She finally looked fully at his face, flinching at the hardness of his jaw, at his expression of suspicion.

"How do I know you're speaking the truth this time? You have not been truthful in the past. In fact, you have lied with ease, Marguerite.''

"Only to protect myself,'' she said. "Wouldn't you do the same in similar circumstances?'' She watched him anxiously as he heaved a deep sigh. His hands played aimlessly with a quill on the desk.

"I would never find myself in the same situation. For one, I would never harbor spies—enemies of England—and I could never bury a dead body to conceal a crime.'' His anger cut like a blade through her. "I don't understand how you could hide the truth from Emerson! How could you, in good conscience, Marguerite?''

She did not know what to answer. She latched on to the spy

issue. "I do not sympathize with Charles Edward Stuart, but I regret what the English did to the Scots after the revolt. Whole clans were killed and their privileges revoked. They can't even wear their tartans any longer. The spies were hunted men— still are—and even if they believed in the wrong politics, they had a firm conviction they were right. Even the French king supported Stuart."

"Not anymore. After the peace treaty, Stuart is not welcome in France. The Prussians might sell arms, but I don't believe any country will seriously back another Stuart rebellion."

"Be that as it may—"

"Nick has believed for some time that you're involved with the Jacobites. I almost called him out for that accusation. I thought it was utter nonsense."

"Nick? What does he know?"

"He's helping Emerson search for Rule's body. Nick is thorough and single-minded. He never gives up until he discovers the truth."

His words hit her like whiplashes. Marguerite trembled with exhaustion. She stood on wobbly legs. "You might as well get it over with. Woodvine will know what to do with me, to which prison to take me, once you explain the situation."

Pale with fury, he stood, his movements stiff and jerky. "I don't condemn you for the treachery of your husband, Marguerite, but I deeply resent your total disregard for my feelings. How do you think it makes me feel to know you kept such grave secrets from me? You toyed with me, used me, while underneath you were a different woman from the Marguerite I courted with my love letters."

He leaned across the desk, his words stinging her. "You thought you could succeed with the deception."

"I'm not eager to be drawn and quartered, or to hang." Marguerite felt naked, flayed by his anger. Defenseless. She had been wrong to mistrust him. "Can you ever forgive me? I did not plan to deceive you."

"Why didn't you trust me? Why didn't you confide your difficulties to me?"

A flare of anger tightened her chest. "I did not want you to meddle! I've had enough of gentlemen meddling in my life and never listening to my opinions. If Lennox had listened to me, there would have been no Jacobites hiding in the cellar. Sergeant Rule would still be alive."

"If you'd listened to me when I begged you to divulge your problems," he spit, "Ormond would not have died tonight."

Guilt squeezed her in its bitter embrace. "I know. But what would you have done to Renny? Killed him? That would not have solved anything."

"I would have seen to it that Renny confessed his crimes. Sergeant Rule should have a decent burial." He slapped the gleaming surface of the desk. "You are corrupted, egotistical, and false. You have ruined the only thing I believed in—true love."

His voice rose in fury. "You kicked me out of your house; you chided me, then, ultimately, let me into your arms so that I could slake my desire. You had an ulterior motive, of course. Keep Charles besotted, get control of his newly acquired fortune. Sail on top of the dirty secrets to new horizons, new areas to corrupt."

"You're distorting the truth!" she said, her own voice rising.

"As you did. You're the conjurer of false dreams and promises, a schemer who will stop at nothing to forward herself."

Marguerite went around the desk and pushed him hard in the chest. "I knew it! You will not understand my view, my reasons for acting the way I did; you won't even try. You're blind, Charles, blind to anything but your own stupid dreams."

He shook her so that her teeth rattled. "In my dreams, I always wanted the best for you. I was willing to listen to your wishes, and protect you. I lived to fulfill your wishes, Marguerite! But now—"

"I'm not a perfect person, nor are you. If you can't accept that truth, then we don't have anything to build a life on. I will not live in a dream castle of your making. As you can see, it has already collapsed.''

They glared at each other, Charles's eyes dark and thunderous. Silence, taut as the string of a harp, hummed between them.

''What are you going to do?'' she asked, her lips so stiff she could barely form the words.

He shook his head as if unable to follow a coherent thought. ''I don't know.''

Marguerite turned abruptly and marched to the door. She could not stay to watch him denounce her to Lord Woodvine. She could not hear his condemnation.

Chapter 22

Marguerite waited all night for Woodvine to arrest her for treason. She paced the guest room until she could not carry herself upright any longer. As dawn's gray fingers crept over the world, nothing had happened. No one came. She finally fell into bed without bothering to remove any of her clothes. She didn't care that the ball gown of silver tissue would be forever ruined. There would be no opportunity in prison to wear it while she awaited her trial.

Charles rode all night down to Sussex and Nick's estate. His eyes ached with unshed tears as he stared into the charcoal darkness, seeing nothing but the bleak road, a pale shade of gray. A poem came to him as his heart wept with the futility of his emotions.

> *I met you at dawn,*
> *Worshiped you in joy,*
> *In awe before thy splendor*
> *Of golden valley and shady mound.*

Then one day you turned away,
Gave me shadowed face,
Maze of lies.

Cries of sorrow
Tore my heart asunder.
Love, love, lie in life,
Lie in death.
Breath, yours and mine,
Mingled for one perfect moment.

Sparks of ecstasy
Shot exuberant aloft,
Then drizzled into dust.

Charles wiped the moisture from his face as he rode up to the slumbering estate. A gray dawn permeated the night, and light shone in the kitchen window. He'd spent a lifetime hoping, waiting for the love that would transform his life.

It had, for a brief moment, until Marguerite revealed her total lack of faith. What had made her so secretive and untrusting? What had poisoned her mind against love and trust? He really didn't care, Charles thought as he slid from the saddle and led the horse to the stables. It was over.

After rousing a stable boy and seeing that the horse was being rubbed down thoroughly, he went in search of his friend.

Nick was a light sleeper, but Charles had to shake him several times before he stirred.

"By thunder, your house could be on fire and you wouldn't know it," Charles said in disgust.

Nick yawned and looked as if he'd just fallen asleep.

"Late night, eh?" Charles asked, and flung open the windows to let in the cool, moist morning air.

"Are you intent on giving me pneumonia?" Nick mumbled between yawns. He reluctantly eased his legs over the side, and Charles noticed that Nick was still wearing his breeches and shirt.

"Begad, sleeping in your own dirt now, Nick? I thought a fop like you would not wrinkle your best shirt."

Nick's eyes widened. "Fop? That's an unfamiliar slur. What maggot of ill will has gotten into you, Morty?"

Hatred, Charles thought. "You were right, Nick. Marguerite knew about Rule's death and the Jacobite activities. She swore she was not personally involved, but by her silence, she was an accomplice."

"Damn!" Nick cursed and dragged his hands through his unruly hair. He got up and removed his coat, cloak, and white gloves from the coverlet, then tossed them on top of a chest. "What are you going to do? Report her to the law?"

"She could be tried for treason."

"Hmm, can't have that. I don't think Marguerite harbors a treasonous heart."

"Our opinions might differ on that score," Charles said grimly. He felt as if he didn't have enough strength to continue. "Ormond is dead. If Marguerite had trusted me and told me the truth, we would have had a chance to catch Montagu Renny before he used his pistol. Evidently he and Lennox killed the sergeant. They also transported the spies across the Channel." He studied Nick's pale, exhausted face. "She deceived me, Nick, as she deceived everyone. A superb actress."

"Yes . . . I understand your anger, Morty. Personal hurt, however, must be set aside for the higher cause."

Charles gripped the windowsill hard and looked across the old knot garden. Stocks and jasmine scented the fresh morning air. "Part of me wants to throw her to the wolves."

"You could never do that!" Nick stepped across the room and slung an arm around Charles's shoulders. "I take it your courtship of Marguerite has gone beyond mere friendship?"

Charles nodded, his jaw aching with tension. "I was a fool to believe she was my true love, my only love. She always called me a romantic fool. She deceived me as easily as she would steal a sweet from a child. Probably reveling in it, too."

Nick laughed. "No! There's where you are wrong, old fel-

low. Marguerite is not malicious or shifty. She was afraid of
the hangman's noose, and I don't blame her. I would have kept
silent in the same circumstances.'' He sighed. '' 'Twill be our
responsibility to help her now—if we want to clear her name.
If we find Renny, we'll make him confess the truth and keep
Marguerite out of the sordid business. If only we could lay our
hands on Rule's corpse, the problem would be easier to solve.''

"I can't see our next step clearly—perhaps chase Renny
until he collapses.''

Nick removed his arm from Charles's shoulder. "You ought
to make peace with Marguerite and protect her while I contact
Emerson and report some facts to him—not all of them. He
and I shall scour the countryside for Renny. When we catch
him, we shall force him to confess.''

"He'll implicate Marguerite, I'm sure of it,'' Charles said.

"I'd better find Renny before Emerson does,'' Nick said
with a grim smile. "We're balancing on a thin rope over an
abyss, old fellow.''

Charles had to agree that someone had to watch over Marguerite. Renny might try to fulfill his threat to kill her, and Charles
realized that he'd let his anger rule him. He should not have
left Marguerite to find her way home alone from Surrey.

As soon as he'd shared breakfast with Nick, he started back
toward London, only to meet Marguerite's traveling chaise on
the road south of Hayward's Heath. Prunella stared at him with
bright, knowing eyes, and Marguerite gave him a stiff smile.

"There you are, Charles,'' Prunella said in a confiding voice.
"I wondered what became of you after the upheaval at the
duke's ball. A most unfortunate ending to a delightful trip.
Poor Ormond. I feel for his parents.''

Marguerite said nothing, only held her chin high and stared
at Charles with stony eyes. His bitterness stirred, but he had
to push it aside for the greater purpose of catching Rule's
murderer and protecting Marguerite from losing her life. He

could not let his anger get the better of him. He crushed the reins of his horse with both hands.

"Come along; I'll escort you home."

Marguerite did not protest.

She seemed reluctant to let him inside the echoing Lennox House when they arrived. "We are grateful for your escort, Charles, but now that we've reached home, I'm sure we'll be safe."

"I doubt that you will, what with Renny still roaming free. He will return here at some point, and well you know it." Without listening to further protests, he made his way into the study, the brightest room at the back, with a view of the spinney and the stables.

He placed one of the two chairs at an angle to the window, sat down, and lay his hat on the floor beside him. He'd brought his saddlebag, which held two loaded pistols, rags tucked into the barrels to hold balls and powder in place. He leaned the bag slowly against the wall, within reaching distance.

Marguerite stood in the doorway, her face closed and pale. "I see that you're making yourself comfortable."

"I don't exactly call this hard-backed chair comfortable. Far from it." He crossed his arms over his chest, a protective gesture against her hostility. A leaden fatigue had come over him now that part of the danger had been circumvented: Marguerite had arrived home alive.

"I see no reason why you should wear out its seat by sitting on it," she said in dismissing tones.

"Mayhap you see no reason, but I certainly do. While I keep watch, I would truly appreciate a hot cup of tea and some food."

Leaving a hollow space in his chest, she moved away without another word. He could hear her argue with Sophie Pierson at the other end of the house. Sophie had not come down to greet the homecoming party. Odd, Charles thought. The Scotswoman was as sour as a lemon.

A prickle of compassion for Marguerite went through his

stomach, but he clenched his jaw and squelched it, just as he'd pushed aside the disturbing memories of their lovemaking. The recollections arrived to tantalize him constantly if he didn't stay on guard.

Prunella carried in a cup of tea, along with slices of bread with ham and mustard on a plate. "You must be exhausted if you've traveled the roads ever since that unfortunate ball. Such a scandal!" Spreading her skirts of pale green taffeta, she sat down on the other chair as if settling in for a cozy chat. She tilted her head toward him conspiratorially. "Marguerite is taking it rather badly, I'm afraid. Her nerves have been tied into knots since the incident."

Charles didn't know how much Prunella knew, so he said nothing, only nodded. Bored, he stared out the window, seeing only the peaceful stableyard and the unmoving trees beyond.

"Some say she murdered her husband, but I know she would not be capable of such a heinous crime. Someone else might, though," she said, and looked toward the ceiling.

Sophie, he thought, but could not go further with that thought as Marguerite stepped into the room, her scent of roses seeming to fill it—and his mind as well. He wished he could block his nose. No matter what, he had no choice but to focus on her, suffering in his sudden burst of longing.

"Pru, some of the servants have abandoned us. I wish you would speak to the others and soothe their ruffled feathers."

"She's telling me to leave," Prunella said in an undertone. "Jealous, I believe."

Charles snorted at the unlikely possibility. He suspected that his actions did not matter one way or the other to Marguerite. He stood as Prunella left, then drank his tea and ate the food, all the time trying to forget Marguerite's presence behind him.

"Renny won't come back here, not now," she said. "He thinks I'm still in Surrey."

"We don't know what he thinks, or are you a mind-reader, Marguerite?"

She heaved a loud sigh. "What I mean is, I'd prefer it if

you leave me alone. After our last conversation, I'd say we are no longer on speaking terms."

"What do you call this then?" he drawled, and drank the last of his tea. "Talking to a wall?"

"About as enlightening," she said dryly. When she noticed that he wouldn't take up the gauntlet, she left the room.

Afternoon dragged into evening. Shadows lengthened in the slow summer twilight. Nothing more interesting than a handful of sparrows moved in the stableyard. The stable boys slept at their posts in the empty stables. They had led the beasts to one of the meadows, swept out the boxes, and let boredom carry them to the land of sleep.

Charles had great difficulty keeping his own eyes open. Just as twilight turned into darkness, his head jerked up and his sleepy eyes widened. A shadow moved across the yard, a darting figure of a man, cloak hanging loosely, hat pulled low over his eyes.

Renny? Charles wondered, fumbling for the saddlebag. In the span of a breath, he'd pulled out one of the pistols. He sank to his knees on the floor and took aim, his hand against the windowsill.

The figure hesitated, flitted another few yards, then hid behind a tree. After long, breathless seconds, he emerged and ran out of Charles's vision.

"Damn it," Charles swore, then got up and rushed to the other side of the room and looked out the window. All sleepiness had disappeared as apprehension shot through his body. Renny had arrived, perhaps with the intention to kill again.

A knock came on the front door, a series of knocks like a signal. Charles cursed and moved cautiously down the hallway. *The bastard.* He thought he could come in here and demand to see the mistress of the house. Well, he would look a pistol in the eye.

Marguerite rushed down the stairs, her face a pale oval in the darkness.

"Don't open the door," Charles whispered. "Let Renny break in. All to our advantage."

The knock sounded once again, a ghostly series of sounds that made unease crawl along his scalp.

Marguerite hesitated, then stepped to the door.

"Don't!" Charles said in a hiss, but she'd already pulled aside the bolt and turned the key. "Damn you, Marguerite," he added, and pushed her aside. As the door creaked open, Charles shielded her with his body.

"I have a pistol aimed at your head, Renny," he said in a snarl. "Don't try anything, or I'll shoot."

The tall, slender figure hesitated on the threshold. "Lady Lennox?"

"It's not him," Marguerite said to Charles's back.

"Who are you?" Charles barked.

"Gentleman of loch and thistle," said the stranger in a subdued voice.

Marguerite gasped and sprang forward. "A spy! I don't believe this." She groaned. "You can't come here. There is no safe harbor here for you now."

"This is Lennox House, I believe. I was told—"

" 'Tis no longer a haven for the likes of you," she said, but pulled him inside and slammed the door shut.

Charles lowered the pistol. "You're that damned Jacobite spy. I should have known."

"Not at all," Marguerite said impatiently. She busied herself with a tinderbox and had soon lit a branch of candles. She held it up to shine on the stranger's face.

Charles reeled as the truth sank in. "Tiernan Leverton!"

"Are you sure?" Marguerite asked, her voice full of uncertainty.

Chapter 23

"You have to help me," Tiernan said, slumping against the wall. He seemed to shrink within his cloak, and slowly started sliding down to the floor. He fumbled feebly for support, but failed.

Charles looked outside. He saw no one in pursuit and closed the door, bolting it. This was an unexpected twist that had his mind tumbling. "I suspected you were involved in the Stuart cause, Tiernan." He knelt beside the man and untied the grimy cravat.

"He's wounded," Marguerite said. "Look at the blood on his sleeve." She knelt on the other side of the still body and opened the cloak. The coat sleeve hung in tatters, as did the shirt underneath. Dark, sticky blood oozed from a hole in the upper arm.

"He's been shot." Charles looked at the man's deathly pale face. "Idiot," he said under his breath. "Damned idiot!"

"We can't turn him away," Marguerite said, her eyes enormous in her white face. "I'll give him shelter here. He'll die if we send him away without cleaning and tying up his wound."

Charles swore silently. "Very well. I suppose there's no other choice. Find bandages and water while I carry him upstairs to your room." There were sounds of doors closing in other parts of the house, and Charles turned to Marguerite sharply. "Do Prunella and Sophie know about Lennox's activities?"

"Sophie does, and I will have to put Pru into the picture. She won't say a word, but I daresay the news will come as a great shock to her."

Charles hoisted the lifeless man over his shoulder and carried him to Marguerite's bedchamber. Tiernan moaned as Charles carefully lowered him to the bed and cut away the ruined fabric around the wound with a dagger he'd stuck into his belt. Blood kept seeping out of the wound, but Charles could not see any evidence of a musket ball.

"It exited on the other side, tore the flesh badly," he said to Marguerite as she entered carrying a ewer with steaming water and a pile of clean rags.

Tiernan muttered and groaned, and Charles gave Marguerite a long glance, wondering if she was afraid—this was another secret to add to her previous ones.

Marguerite did not think about herself. She suffered with the delirious young man and registered his face in her memory, a lean face that ladies might find attractive if it were not so haggard and pale. The nose was a bit too long and too thin, but he had boldly curved lips, and dark eyelashes shaded the hollows under his eyes. The long, tousled black hair needed washing. She wondered when he'd last eaten. She helped Charles to undress the lean torso. It gleamed with the sweat of fever.

"You know him well?" she asked Charles.

"He's been at university, as far as I know. I met him at Nick's often enough, but I didn't know he had any political interests. A hothead, though, always entering dangerous races, or betting on the least favorite contender, gambling at all hours, and partaking in duels at dawn.''

Marguerite clucked her tongue. ''Sounds like the description of any gentleman in my acquaintance.''

''This is not the time to rake me and my friends over the coals for gambling and betting,'' was Charles's clipped reply. ''I know Nick has worried about Tiernan since Tiernan's father died three years ago. His mother is a Scotswoman with Irish connections. I suspect the Scottish blood running in his veins is the reason why Tiernan chose to side with Stuart.''

He muttered a curse about divided politics as he raised Tiernan's arm so that Marguerite could spread a folded linen towel underneath the wound.

''We'll pour some brandy on the injury to cleanse it.'' Squeamish, Marguerite pulled a small bottle from her apron pocket and pulled out the cork. ''We'd better finish bandaging the wound before he wakes up.''

''He isn't likely to wake up. He's exhausted and weak. Who knows how long he's been evading the militia. He may have crossed Sussex many times over.''

Charles held Tiernan's arm as Marguerite poured the liquor onto the wound. Tiernan twitched and moaned, but he did not open his eyes.

''It looks like the bleeding has slowed down,'' she said, and tore clean towels into strips. She quickly bandaged the arm tightly and fashioned a sling to tie around Tiernan's neck.

Charles sponged off Tiernan's torso and wiped the dirt from the young man's face. ''Looks like he's been eating poorly.''

''If he's been chased across Sussex these last few weeks, he would be worn out. He could not make contact with the smugglers, as the coastline is patrolled by excise men, and the militia is searching every house and hamlet for him.''

She rummaged in a chest in one corner of the room and returned with an old, yellowed shirt that smelled of crushed lavender.

"This was once Lithgow's. He wasn't a tall man, but this will fit Tiernan tolerably."

"You show much concern for a fugitive," Charles said dryly.

"And so do you! Mayhap you understand now that I couldn't very well throw out needy persons in the past. No matter this young man's political leanings; he would die if we didn't take him in."

Their eyes clashed over the prostrate body. "Admittedly we didn't have a choice," he said at last. "But what we're doing is illegal."

Marguerite trembled with tension and fatigue. "Do you understand now why I did not dare to shout my secrets to the world? I was not only protecting myself, but the fugitives."

"I am not the world," Charles said quietly, but she saw that some of the rigid tension had left his face. "I do understand, but I'm still disappointed, nay, deeply hurt that you would not confide in me."

A melancholy silence filled the room, punctuated only by Tiernan's feverish moans. Marguerite put a cold, wet cloth on his forehead, and Charles plumped the pillows behind the fugitive's head.

"If the militia comes to investigate . . ." she said, letting the words hang for a moment before continuing, "we will have to hide him in the cellar. There is a secret room behind a sham wall, and a tunnel underground that leads to a dry well behind the stables."

She'd revealed every secret detail and expected a sharp comment for her effort, but Charles only looked at her, an unreadable expression on his face. Mayhap he felt shame for shielding a spy.

"Do as you think best. I'd better go downstairs and watch for any suspicious activities outside," he said, rising heavily as if very tired. "You'd better stay with Tiernan and assure him he will be safe here if he awakens."

Charles walked so close to her his legs touched her wide skirts. She could not bear to see the disillusionment in his eyes, and longed to throw her arms around him, to hold him until all animosity melted away, and she had her laughing lover back. Another side of her refused to show any kind of weakness toward him, any emotion.

"I shall look after him," Marguerite said, her heart filling with dread.

One hour later, Charles saw movement on the road outside the gate. He stood close to the window, trying to get a better glimpse in the moonless night. More than one man, he thought grimly, on foot, running. One man on horseback, riding up the short drive.

"Damn and blast! It's Emerson," Charles muttered. He recognized the blaze and the four white stockings on Emerson's horse. He ran up the stairs two steps at a time and tore into Marguerite's bedchamber.

"The militia is here," he said roughly, and pushed Marguerite aside so that he could haul Tiernan over his shoulder. The young man came to and slurred a series of questions. "Downstairs," Charles said to Marguerite, staggering under his burden.

Marguerite said nothing, only ran downstairs to the kitchen to open the door to the cellar. Thumps already sounded on the door. Pru and Sophie, carrying lit candles, stood in the corridor staring wildly as Charles staggered by them with his burden. "Go downstairs and detain the visitors," he barked to Sophie. "Not a word about what you've seen!" He ran through the house and followed Marguerite down the steps to the dank cellars. She carried a candle, and shadows leaped over crates and ale barrels.

"In here," she said grimly as she pushed one part of a wall aside. It looked like the cellars ended here, but behind the wall was a narrow room with several cots.

"I meant to burn these, but I didn't have the nerve to come down here after Lithgow died," she said as she watched Charles lower the delirious man onto one of the cots. "You'd better stay with him."

"Yes . . . I don't want Emerson to see me here in the middle of the night. Highly scandalous," he said with a faint quirk of his lips.

She gave him the candle and hurriedly pushed the wall back in place. To conceal the minuscule crack from the sharp eye of the law, she pushed a stack of empty crates in front of it.

After righting her gown, now wrinkled from much use, she tore off her apron, bundled it under the stairs, and ran up to the kitchen, closing the door behind her softly. Her heart raced as if ready to jump out of her chest.

Emerson's voice boomed in the hallway, and Sophie raised hers in an evident argument. Marguerite straightened her hair under the cap and took a deep breath. She joined the group in the hallway.

"Captain Emerson. What is amiss?" she asked, and yawned as if she'd awakened suddenly. She rubbed her eyes indelicately.

"Lady Lennox," he said with a stiff bow. No smile for her this time, she thought, nervousness keening in her blood. "I have a warrant to search this house. We've had suspicions that illegal activities took place here in the past. Not that we can prove anything now that Lord Lennox is dead, but—"

"I know nothing about that," Marguerite said in a stern voice. "I would not allow the smugglers to use these premises for their nefarious schemes."

"We're not talking about smugglers, Lady Lennox. We're talking about Jacobite spies. One particular spy, in this case." His sharp gaze traveled over Sophie's and Pru's dressing wraps and nightcaps, then over her fully clad body. "I am surprised to find you up so late, Lady Lennox."

Marguerite shrugged as if completely unconcerned. "I could not sleep, so I warmed some milk. Then I started reading poetry and fell asleep by the kitchen hearth. I only just awakened as I heard the commotion out here." She gestured to him to enter, and at the same moment remembered the bloody rags in her bedchamber.

"Surely you're not going to go through our . . . er, private chambers, Captain." She tried to smile at him, but her face felt rather stiff.

"The whole house, milady." He went to the far end of the hallway and gestured for the other militiamen to enter. They filed in, about ten men with grim faces and muddy boots.

"They will ruin the floors," Pru wailed.

"Betsy will see to the floors in the morning," Marguerite said, and glanced at the landing above the stairs. The servants were clustered in a knot, their faces creased with worry.

"You'd better start with the servants' quarters in the attic so that those poor souls can get some rest."

"Very well." Emerson and his men headed up the narrow stairs, and Marguerite held her breath as the captain questioned the servants one after the other. She had hoped she could rush to her room and hide the offending rags. She went upstairs, listening tensely as the servants replied that they hadn't seen or heard anything unusual. *Thank God for that!*

"Milady 'ad a visitor, Lord Mortimer, or what's 'is name now that 'e's got a new title?"

"Lord Ransford, Betsy," Marguerite filled in. "He's long since gone," she added, while wondering where Charles had hidden his horse. If Montagu Renny happened to arrive now, would he denounce her secrets? She didn't dare to finish that thought.

Emerson did not move, but it was clear the servants' replies had satisfied him. Marguerite held on to the railing hard, as she feared her legs would crumble under her.

She glanced down at Sophie in the hallway below, for once seeing worry instead of hostility in the other women's face. Sophie would not denounce a Stuart spy. She came upstairs as if sensing Marguerite's near collapse and offered a steadying arm.

"I find it ungentlemanly of you to barge into the house and disturb our rest, Captain," Sophie said.

"Believe me, miss, I am distressed at this grim intrusion, but the spy was seen heading in this direction last evening, and we have to search every house along the road. The Duke of Atwood's orders, ladies."

Atwood was the justice of the peace in the area, and a zealous one. "I thought you were looking for the Midnight Bandit," Marguerite said.

"Yes, we are, but there have been no more reports of robberies these last two weeks. The knave may have moved to another area where he's not so well known."

"Excuse me, but I have to take a headache powder," Marguerite said, clutching her temples with her fingertips. She hastened to her bedchamber as she heard the militiamen coming down from the attic. To her chagrin, Emerson entered the room right behind her. On the floor by the bed sat a stack of blood-soiled rags and a basin of pink water. *Dear God,* she thought. *Emerson will see this and draw his own conclusions.*

Prunella entered hot on Emerson's heels, and Marguerite exchanged frightened glances with the older woman. Pru's gaze swept the room, widening with a flare of understanding as she saw the rags.

"How dare you storm in here, Captain Emerson, and embarrass Lady Lennox in this fashion? She has been ill, and is just recovering from two days of continual pain."

Captain Emerson's gaze landed on the bloody rags, and Marguerite lowered her gaze. She sank down onto the bed expecting the worst. Concealing her blushing face behind her hands, she waited for his condemning words.

Silence hung heavily in the room.

"Shame on you, Captain," Pru continued in her most disapproving voice.

"Ill?" Emerson asked in a strangled voice.

Pru said scathingly, "If you must pry, it was a female complaint—the usual curse—much pain and suffering."

"I understand," Emerson said in a croak, then turned on his heel and fled from the room with a mumbled excuse.

Marguerite lowered her hands and gazed at Pru in appreciation. The older woman had propped her hands on her hips in a militant stance, and glowered as hard as a plump, sparrowlike person could glower. "Such untidiness is a disgrace, Marguerite," she admonished in a loud voice for all to hear.

Thank you, Marguerite mouthed. "It can wait until tomorrow." She pulled Pru with her out of the room and closed the door behind them. The soldiers made a cursory investigation of Sophie's and Pru's rooms. Captain Emerson swept by in the corridor, his face still a deep, mortified red. "We will continue downstairs."

"I handled him!" Pru whispered as the soldiers tramped downstairs and searched all the rooms.

"It isn't over yet. I pray the captain won't find the secret room, but we might have left footprints in the dust."

Prunella took her arm. "Come, let's distract them with an offer of tea in the kitchen."

Marguerite glanced at Sophie, who nodded. She looked pale as a sheet, but evidently determined to do her part to save the household.

The soldiers politely refused the offer, but Pru handed around a plate of currant cake that she'd cut into generous wedges. Two men, one of them the captain, went down into the cellar carrying lanterns.

Marguerite's hands trembled as she listened to their progress. She hid her hands in the folds of her gown, and propped her boneless body against the doorjamb.

She could breathe properly again when she heard the soldiers return upstairs. A deep sigh filled her chest with relief. Emerson shot her a penetrating look as he stepped into the kitchen, but she could not see any trace of accusation.

"Come along, men," he barked. "No time to dawdle here and empty the ladies' larder." He bowed formally to Marguerite and the others. "I apologize for the inconvenience."

Marguerite forced a smile to her stiff lips. " 'Tis your duty. I wish you luck in finding the spy. Must be difficult on a dark night like this."

"Aye," one of the men said. "Cold as a grave outside, and coming on to rain, no doubt. But we clipped the scoundrel's wing; he shouldn't get very far—"

"That's enough," Emerson shouted, and the men scurried outside to search the stables. Her heart filled with relief, Marguerite closed the door behind them.

"What cheek!" Prunella grumbled. "Rousing us at this late hour I shan't get another minute of sleep tonight. Might as well brew up a pot of tea for us all."

"Yes, a good idea." Marguerite watched the men from the study window, and did not move until they were well away from the house and heading north to the next estate a mile away. A leaden fatigue burdened her as she returned to the kitchen. She gratefully accepted a cup of hot tea and a buttered slice of brown bread.

"You'll have to move the man away from here," Sophie whispered, and glanced toward the dark hallway to see if any servants were lurking. " 'Tis not safe. Emerson might come back."

"She's right. If I hadn't managed to embarrass him so deeply, he would have demanded to know about the bloody rags upstairs. We'd better burn them before sunlight."

Marguerite nodded. "Yes. I'm going to deliver two cups of tea to the secret room. I'll see if the fugitive has come to, or if he's still raging with fever."

The three women stared at each other in fear. "What if he dies?" Sophie said nervously, putting everyone's thought into words.

"We'll have to bury him, or leave him somewhere where the militia will find him," Marguerite said.

"Sounds very callous," Prunella said.

"We cannot let our emotions rule in this case. Pru, I'll explain all this later."

"I think I know the whole," the older woman muttered. "Don't worry; I won't say a word to anyone."

Marguerite heaved a sigh of relief. "I know I can always count on you, Pru." She gathered the two cups of tea, and as Sophie lighted the stairs ahead of her, Marguerite said, "Thank you, Sophie. You showed a great sense of control when the men were here."

" 'Tis not the first time we've had fugitives—"

"But the last!" Marguerite interrupted her. "I will not stand for any more illegal activities, but we couldn't throw out a wounded man."

Tiernan Leverton had come to. Pale and sweaty, he sat propped against the wall, a lumpy pillow his only support. Braced on one elbow, Charles lounged on another cot. He rolled to his feet as Marguerite entered the narrow opening in the wall.

"They left," she said tonelessly. "I've never been more afraid in my life."

"We heard them, only a few feet away on the other side of the wall. I'm glad Tiernan didn't moan." Charles threw a dark glance at the other man.

"I don't moan," Tiernan said with a haggard grin. "That's for old women and small children."

"I heard you distinctly when we bandaged your arm," Marguerite said dryly. "How long have you been fleeing from the lawmen?"

"Three weeks. I've tried on several occasions to rendezvous with my contact on the beach, but without success. The smugglers are wary, as there are excise officers every two hundred yards along the coast."

"You are exaggerating," Charles said with a snort.

Tiernan shook his head.

"How long have you had that wound?" Marguerite asked.

"Since yesterday. Lost some blood, but I'm feeling better now, much better. Thanks to you."

Marguerite hauled the flask of brandy from her pocket and

splashed some in the men's tea. "You'd better rest. As soon as you're strong enough, you must leave. I'm not a Jacobite sympathizer, as my husband was," she said tersely. "I will not accept illegal activities in my home."

The young man looked crestfallen. "I understand. If you could give me an escort to the Kent border, close to the sea, I'll find my way across the Channel. I have contacts in Kent."

"Why are you involved with the Jacobites?" Marguerite asked. "Nick won't be happy if he finds out the truth."

"No need to enlighten him then," Tiernan said lightly, but she could see the tension on his face. His feverish eyes moved mercurially from Marguerite to Charles. "You might not understand my position, but my Scottish relatives gave me happiness to remember in my old age, more than my father did. They deserved something in return." His shoulders slumped. "I suspect I'm involved in a lost cause now that France and England are at peace. Who knows when this will end, and how? It depends on Stuart."

"You'll lose your life if you come back to England, Tiernan," Charles said darkly. "If I decide to help you, it's because Nick is my friend, and I would not want him to hear of this."

Tension hung heavy between them. Tiernan finally eased himself down onto the mattress. "Thank you."

Marguerite spread a moth-eaten blanket over him. "We haven't promised to help you."

"Yes ... I know, but you've already helped me a great deal," Tiernan said, drifting into sleep.

Charles pulled Marguerite with him out of the room and carefully pushed the wall closed. "I'll ride with him. No need to worry your head further. Tomorrow night I'll come back with a horse for Tiernan. He should be rested by then."

They stared at each other for a long moment in the weak light of the lantern. Charles touched her chin, lingering. "You were brave," he said, and placed a light kiss on her mouth.

"So you don't disapprove of my clandestine activities any longer, my secrets?" she asked, doubt lacing her voice.

"I can see your predicament, but I never approved of your secrecy. I still don't."

Marguerite drew a sharp breath, but he added before she could speak, "However, I admire your fortitude and your compassion. A lesser lady would have closed the door in Tiernan's face and prayed that he would leave her alone."

"I try to find solutions to my problems, not pretend they don't exist."

"I know there are many reasons to love you, but right now I can't find that warm feeling." Charles's eyes glittered with some emotion she could not read, and as he ran up the stairs, she felt as if part of her had been ripped out, leaving a gaping wound behind. She gasped for air and steadied herself against the damp wall. She loved him, but he might be forever lost.

Chapter 24

Marguerite fell into exhausted sleep but awakened with a start three hours later. A pale dawn had arrived. Even though her eyelids felt gritty with sleep, she could not return to the blessed kingdom of oblivion. So instead of tossing and turning she got up and dressed, putting on a serviceable serge dress with a kerchief crossed over the front. She plaited her hair and tucked it into a cap with a frilled edge. Dark rings circled her eyes, and her cheeks were unnaturally pale.

She got up from the edge of the mattress as if poked with a sharp tool as she heard the servants talk on the way down from the attic. Thank God she had remembered to burn the bloody rags in the hearth last night. She had no desire to explain about the rags to the servants. As she already had a dubious reputation, she wanted no whispering, no new talk around the village about Lennox House.

The day crawled by at snail's pace. The fugitive slept for most of the day, only to awaken for a drink of water and a bite of the bread Marguerite had brought down after burning the rags. She rebandaged his arm. The wound showed no sign of inflammation. She reassured him that she would return soon, and left a candle and a tinderbox with him.

To pretend that nothing was amiss, she set the servants to cleaning the house from top to bottom. A fresh house and sparkling windows would impress interested buyers.

She prayed that Montagu Renny would not turn up and demand her surrender in considering his proposal. If she scorned him one more time, he would not hesitate to kill her. Of that she was sure, as a chill of premonition traveled up her spine.

When night came, Renny had not shown himself, nor had the militia. With any luck, the soldiers were at the other end of the parish, but she couldn't know for sure, as they moved about constantly.

She waited eagerly for Charles to return. If only she could set things straight with him. At least he had not abandoned her when she needed his help, and he had not denounced her to the militia. She realized her confession about Renny and Sergeant Rule would go no farther—a great relief. She could trust him.

Tired and nervous, she was staring into the night when Charles arrived, knocking softly on the window. She shone a light on his face, sudden happiness surging through her. If only the circumstances had been different. She opened the window.

"Hurry, Marguerite!" he said hoarsely. "The militiamen are at the other end of the village, scouring the woods. They have witnesses that swore the fugitive never left the village. They are bound to return here and search more closely."

Marguerite inhaled sharply in fear. She put her hand to her racing heart. "We'll have to bring the spy to the Kent border. There is no other way. He's too weak to flee on his own."

"Yes ... there's no other choice," he said, and heaved himself over the windowsill. He looked grim. "I don't like this, especially since Emerson is a friend of mine. But I can't see Tiernan apprehended either. I brought an extra horse."

"Come. Let's see if Tiernan is strong enough to ride."

"He has to be," Charles said stonily.

"If the militia catches us on the way . . ." Marguerite did not finish her statement as she hurried down into the cellar.

Charles pushed aside the wall. A lit candle beside him, Tiernan was sitting up against the pillow, his face still flushed with fever, but it had lessened, Marguerite noted as she placed her hand on his forehead.

"I was getting bored staring at these dark walls," he said. He heaved himself unsteadily to his feet.

"Come along, old fellow. Time to leave," Charles said, and flung Tiernan's cloak over the young man's shoulders. "Hope you're strong enough for a quick ride to the coast."

Tiernan gave a lopsided grin. "I have to be, don't I?"

Marguerite heard the faint jingling of harnesses, and the clumping of boots on the brick path outside the house. She clapped a hand to her mouth. "Listen! I think the soldiers have returned. We must flee through the tunnel."

Charles grimaced and pushed the false wall closed. Marguerite turned aside and untied her panniers at the waist and let them fall to the floor. She blushed and glanced away lest the gentlemen would laugh at her. But she had no choice; the tunnel was too narrow for the panniers. She kicked the undergarment beneath a cot in the darkest corner.

Charles blew out the candle. The small room seemed airless as she made her way in the dark to a trapdoor at the back. With Charles's help she lifted it. It creaked, and she feared the whole house would be alerted to the screech belowstairs.

Tiernan breathed heavily with the effort of stepping down the rusty ladder to the musty tunnel below. Earth and stones impeded their progress, and Tiernan kept stumbling. He's too weak, Marguerite thought, touching the damp walls on each side as she walked bent double toward the old well. She could see nothing, and cobwebs touched her face, a silken horror that would normally make her recoil.

She clenched her jaws together and stumbled on, feeling her way. Dust and mustiness clogged her nose, but she breathed easier when the sweet night air finally pierced the underground stillness. *Almost there.*

Charles swore farther back as he brought up the rear. At least the soldiers hadn't followed ... not yet, anyway. She prayed they would be gone from the property soon so that the men could ride clear.

"Better wait until the militia has retreated," she whispered. "They can't find us here."

"They will wonder why you're not at home."

"I'm not under house arrest, Charles," she said with a wry smile. "I have the right to participate in the local entertainment, or refuse to see callers."

"Yes ... but if I know Emerson, he'll sniff out any under-handed dealings. Has a nose like a bloodhound; he'll poke around every corner of the house."

"He hasn't been very successful so far," Marguerite scoffed.

"Not enough men, but he will never give up."

"Just my luck," Tiernan said with disgust.

"Serves you right," Marguerite said. "You've put yourself in this situation, and for what purpose? Whatever message you're bringing to Charles Edward, it won't help him regain the throne of England and Scotland."

"You carry too pessimistic an outlook," Tiernan said, slumping against the brick wall of the well. Overhead, stars blinked among the brambles as a heavy bank of clouds moved aside. At least there would be enough light to ride through the forest, Marguerite thought.

She looked at Charles, wanting to thank him for helping her during this desperate time. By that generous act, he'd put his own neck in danger, and she could not help but admire him for his courage. Charles was loyal to his friends. He had many endearing qualities besides his ardor in bed, she thought.

"The soldiers are on the grounds. I can hear them," he said tersely. "Better keep silent."

The minutes dragged on as if stuck in syrup. Marguerite felt fidgety and shattered. If she came through this night intact, she would try to mend the fences with Charles, pray that he could forget all that bitterness.

"I think they have left. Emerson's horse is trotting down the road toward Hancock's place."

Without another word, Marguerite climbed up the rusty rungs to the surface, which was hidden by two planks and a snarl of brambles. She pushed aside the planks, leaving the opening just big enough for her to step through.

"Hurry! Some militiamen could still be around," she whispered, and helped Tiernan over the edge as Charles pushed behind. Tiernan's hands were clammy with sweat, and he trembled uncontrollably. Evidently the fever had risen with his exertion. At least the bandage was dry. The wound was healing.

They listened tensely behind the stables, but there was no sound of movement. Charles lifted his face and sent a piercing whistle into the night. "I left Thunder in the meadow, the other horse tied behind."

The crashing of undergrowth and snorting of horses came on the wind, and seconds later Thunder ambled through the brambles with his attendant, a roan with three white stockings.

"Marguerite, you should return home. You've done your part in this adventure," Charles said, his face grim.

"No, you might need help with Tiernan," Marguerite said, and even as she spoke, Tiernan slumped against Charles, who had to take a step back to keep his balance.

"The devil! He's fainted." Charles carried the younger man to Thunder and heaved him like a sack of grain over the withers. "I'll have to hold on to him." Charles heaved himself into the saddle and glanced down to Marguerite. "You've done enough. I'll come back later."

Marguerite wanted to argue, but that would make them lose precious time. She followed on foot some way along the path. Charles set Thunder on a course through the spinney, the roan still ambling behind. Just as they reached the fringe of the trees, there was a shout and the sound of running feet through the tall grass. A shot rang out.

"They're still here," Marguerite whispered frantically. "They have seen us."

Charles swore under his breath and untied the other horse from the pommel of Thunder's saddle. He threw the reins at Marguerite. "Let's go!"

He waited until Marguerite, out of sheer terror, had managed to climb astride the horse without help. Her breath in her throat, she found the stirrups and steered the mount onto the path after Charles. Galloping in the darkness, lying low over the horse's neck, she prayed the roan would not make a false step into a hole or stumble over a root.

Moments later they had left the foot soldiers far behind.

Charles reined in. "That was a close call," he said, breathing hard. He eyed Marguerite's indecent straddling of the horse and smiled. "You had great presence of mind. Another female might have fainted dead away."

Marguerite blushed and tried to smooth down her skirts, which were not fashioned for a man's saddle. "I'd rather flee indecently astride a horse than to fall into the hands of the militia." She glanced around the forest, where the moon splashed a ghostly light on the trees. "There might be others searching the woods tonight."

"Yes . . . we'd better hurry east. We have to reach the Kent border as soon as possible." He set off, Marguerite following closely.

The moon played hide-and-seek with the clouds, finally losing out. A storm front shrouded the world in darkness. Thunder slowed down to a trot, and Marguerite's horse fell into step.

"As black as the devil's heart," Charles said, his voice laced with frustration. "We'll be delayed. I can't see my hand in front of me."

Half an hour later, Thunder broke through the thicket and ended up on the Lewes road. Marguerite recognized the twisting limbs of two dead oaks she always admired when she drove to town.

"This is dangerous," she whispered as she rode at Charles's

side, so close their legs touched occasionally. "The soldiers are bound to have set up a barrier to search all travelers."

"You're right, I'm sure. We'll continue, however. At the smallest sign of movement on the road, we'll return to the forest."

Tension hung dense as fog in the night. Lightning embroidered the sky in the distance, and Marguerite wiped her hand over her sticky forehead. Warm, humid, and tasting slightly metallic, the air promised a giant storm. It moved closer at great speed

"We should seek cover," Charles said, his gaze sweeping the forest on both sides. "If Tiernan gets wet, he might die."

"Is he still unconscious?" she asked, already knowing the answer as she glanced at Tiernan's limp form.

"Yes, he needs rest," Charles said grimly. "I don't know what we'll do if he dies. Deuced difficult to explain to Nick, who dotes on the boy."

"He isn't exactly a boy, Charles."

"Old enough to be a spy, damn it all! I should flay the skin off his back."

They rode on in silence as bright flashes streaked across the sky, nearer every minute. Marguerite flinched every time a flash lit the clouds. Rain started falling; fat, warm drops that soon turned into a deluge that drummed and lashed the trees and turned the road into mud.

"Come!" Charles shouted over the din. "We'd better find a thicket to protect us, but stay well away from high trees." He rode through a stand of poplars, down into a shallow gully through which ran a brook. It swirled and gurgled, rain hissing against the surface. Marguerite's mount followed Thunder along the spongy riverbed. She tried to conceal her face from the rain, but in minutes her dress had turned soggy, and tendrils of water ran from her head down her neck. *Misery.* There was no other word to describe the discomfort.

Charles finally found a wide cliff overhang completely covered with green moss. He jumped down and led the horses under the rocky roof. A shallow cave lay beyond, but not large enough to conceal both horses and humans.

At least it was protection against the rain. Thunder rumbled and crashed overhead, sometimes a drawn-out muttering sound—like rocks rolling down a ravine. Marguerite slid off her horse and wiped her face. She wrung out her skirts and hair, and thought she would pay a fortune for a towel and dry clothes.

"We'll stay here until the storm passes." He lifted Tiernan from the stallion and gently straightened the limp body out on the ground.

Tiernan moaned and opened his eyes. "Where am I?"

"You're still a free man, thanks to us," Charles said.

Marguerite wiped Tiernan's sodden face with a corner of her petticoat, and Charles found a pewter mug in his saddlebag. He filled the mug with water in the stream and held it to Tiernan's lips. "Drink."

Tiernan's teeth chattered, and most of the water ran down the sides of his chin. Marguerite's heart ached for the brave young man. The fever might take him if the militia didn't, she thought.

Charles wrapped his heavy cloak around Tiernan. It was damp but still good protection from the weather. Thank God it was a warm night, Marguerite thought, but the storm might force the temperature to drop.

Tiernan drank some more water, then slumped back against the ground. He fell into fitful sleep as Marguerite caressed his forehead.

"Come," Charles said, "I have something to say." He held out his hands and pulled Marguerite away from the wounded man. They stood at the edge of the overhang and watched the storm, a blowing gray curtain of rain and flashes of light. "If something happens to me, I want you to take Tiernan to Nick's house. Nick'll take responsibility," Charles said. "You've done all you can for Tiernan."

Marguerite shivered with apprehension. A foreboding of danger came over her—hardships that had to be overcome before this ordeal was over. The outcome was uncertain.

"Nothing will happen to you, not when we've come this far," she said with forced lightness. She tried to arrange her sodden hair into a bun at the nape of her neck. There were not enough pins left to hold the heavy tresses. Dispirited, she let the hair fall down her back as she looked at Charles's stern profile.

He slowly turned to her, and she could see his serious expression in the white glare of lightning. "Anything is possible. What we think is important right now might not be important tomorrow. It's an ever-changing world. I know we have our differences, and I'm sorry about that." He paused as if weighing his words. "I don't want to leave this cave until we've found an understanding between us. I would not want to go to my death with our quarrel still unsolved."

Marguerite shivered with the intensity of his gaze. "Yes, I would like us to make peace. Please forgive me for not trusting you with my secrets," she said in a small voice.

"And forgive me for lashing out at you," he said flatly. They stared at each other for a long moment, and even though she ought to feel at peace with his apology, she felt nothing but a nagging emptiness. He might say the words, but his heart had not forgiven her. She sensed his reluctance.

" 'Tis easy to state that you forgive me," she said, and looked away, "but your heart is closed to me. I don't believe you will forgive and forget. But remember that I hurt as much as you do."

"If I didn't have such high expectations of you, I wouldn't have been so hurt by your lack of trust," he said tonelessly, and flexed his hands as if they were stiff.

She slanted a glance at his face. "I told you I'm only human. I've made many mistakes in my life."

"All of us have."

"Charles, I sense that you cannot reconcile your romantic idea of me with what I really am."

He didn't reply, so she continued, "Underhanded, distrustful—"

"And harboring total disregard for my feelings. You know how much I love you, always have, yet you could not share the smallest problem with me. I would have given you the moon, had you but asked, Marguerite. But what you shared with me were the most shallow commonplaces, things you would share with anyone. You never told me anything that mattered."

She touched his arm, but he pulled away. "You wished that I would treat you differently—like a lover, Charles—but you knew my feelings, or lack of them then. I did not plan to hurt you in any way."

His body grew rigid beside her. "Damn you, Marguerite," he said savagely. "You still talk to me as if I'm a stranger."

I love you, she wanted to say, but choked on the words. She was tired of his bitterness and his refusal to see her point of view. "You can't wring my love out of me as if I were a wet rag. I'll give it to you freely when I'm ready."

"Thank you! I can't wait," he said scathingly.

"Don't expect miracles," she replied just as cuttingly. She turned her back on him and shivered as a gust of wind blew in under the rock ledge, moaning in the crevices. Rain rustled in the leaves, adding to the dismal atmosphere.

"Listen, Marguerite, I said I was sorry."

"Don't apologize to me!" she spit. "You don't mean it." She closed her ears to his subdued curses and groans of pain as he kicked a rock, then hobbled off to see to the horses.

"Hope that hurt," she muttered to herself as she leaned over Tiernan and tucked the cloak closer around him. He had fallen asleep again, this time peacefully. When he awakened he would have regained some of his strength. She sat next to him and pulled her knees to her chin. When the storm was over, this would be a different world.

Chapter 25

Someone nudged Marguerite's side, urging her to wake up. A bad dream only, she thought, wondering why she was bathing with her clothes on.

"Marguerite! Rouse yourself; it's time to continue."

Befuddled, she stared at the man beside her, instantly recognizing Charles. She smiled happily until she recalled their argument. The chasm . . . it was there between them, so tangible she thought she could see it if she looked down.

"Tiernan?" she asked sleepily, and glanced at the man prostrate at her feet.

"He's better. Just woke and is eager to go on."

Tiernan gave her a smile, and Marguerite realized she could see more than just dark shapes around them. A pale moon hung over the trees, the sky as clear as black crystal and as deep. Stars sparkled, and as far as she could see not a single cloud marred the horizon.

"The storm is over." She got up and shook out her wet clothes. The night was still warm, but damp. It would take time to dry her garments, and she wished to end this adventure so that she could have a hot bath and crawl into her bed. One never appreciated one's bed as much as when it was not available, she thought wryly.

She watched Charles lift Tiernan into the saddle on Thunder's back. The young man sat stoop-shouldered, but remained upright.

She found a boulder to use as a stepping block. "I can assist you," Charles said.

"I can take care of myself," she replied stiffly. The memory of their argument sat like bile in her throat.

"Damn you, Marguerite," was all he said, and swung himself up in front of Tiernan.

Tiernan clung to Charles's waist, and Marguerite noticed his struggle to remain on the horse.

"Let's go," Charles ordered, and set off up the slope and through a stand of beeches. Marguerite's horse followed, eager not to lose sight of the stallion.

"It's unladylike to show such eagerness," Marguerite whispered in the mare's ear. "Thunder will feel only contempt for you if you bow and scrape to him."

The horse snorted, unheeding of the free advice. Charles paused at the ditch bordering the lane and scanned the area. Stillness reigned. The air smelled sweetly of honeysuckle, and Marguerite breathed deeply. This ride could almost be pleasurable if it weren't for the—

A shout went up just as Charles came to a curve in the lane, and from a barrier consisting of a traveling coach and a hay wagon streamed militiamen. Marguerite gasped with fear as the mare reared and almost flung her out of the saddle. They bellowed and barked, quickly surrounding the horses.

Tiernan swayed, clinging desperately to Charles's back. Thunder trampled the ground in a circle and tossed his head nervously. The militiamen raised their muskets or drew their swords. "Surrender, or we'll shoot! In the name of King George, stand and state your name and purpose."

"Let peaceful travelers through!" Charles barked, at his most authoritative.

"Your name, sir?" the leader asked, and stepped forward, his pistol aimed at Charles's chest.

"I will not give my name to a man who points a pistol at my heart," Charles replied haughtily.

"We are looking for a fugitive, a spy, and it's likely he's not alone. He's wounded."

"I am not a spy. This is my wife, and my brother, who is three sheets to the wind. We were caught in a storm as we rode from a gathering in Hayward's Heath."

"Then you won't mind if we take a closer look at you and your family. I'm Sergeant Bent, and these are men from Cuckfield."

Marguerite gasped and swallowed hard. Her heart raced. The sergeant looked burly and powerful, a man used to getting results. She thought of possible solutions, her mind jumping from tussock to tussock of possibility, but she could not form a plan.

The men circled closer, and the roan took exception to the invasion. She trampled the ground, lunging this way and that so that the men had to pull back. Marguerite had difficulty controlling the nervous animal. If only she could scatter the men so that Charles and Tiernan could get away.

"I demand to see your captain, Sergeant Bent," Charles ordered to stall for time. Marguerite glanced at him and at the others, wondering if they recognized him or the beautiful horse. Thunder had a reputation in the area as the finest stallion around.

The sergeant gripped Thunder's halter, but the great stallion jerked his big head up, almost toppling the soldier. Bent swore, and fought to get a grip on the horse. Thunder sidestepped and whinnied.

Marguerite could see that Charles had difficulty keeping the horse under control while supporting Tiernan, who was drooping more and more. She judged he was within seconds of falling off.

She had to do something. She pulled the mare's head around and urged the horse straight toward the sergeant. He shouted and fought with the crowding animals. One of the soldiers let off a musket blast, and the shot made fear ripple thorough the horses. They pawed the air, creating total confusion.

A rider thundered down the road in their direction, pulled in before he trampled anyone, and halted right among the men. Marguerite saw a dark cloak, a mask, white gloves.

"The Midnight Bandit!" she cried, overcome with surprise. And fear. And embarrassment, as she remembered her own secret dreams.

"Do not tarry here," the bandit shouted over the din of the soldiers. He hauled the collapsing spy into his arms, and his horse bounded off down the lane. The great horse jumped the ditch, circumvented the barrier, and galloped down the road toward Lewes.

Charles and Marguerite followed, using the confusion to move their mounts away from the soldiers and across the ditch. During a minute of breathless fear, Marguerite realized she was clear of the barrier, and her horse was galloping side by side with Thunder.

"Damned close call," Charles shouted over the blasts of the muskets. He reached out and jerked her head down to the neck of the mare. "Don't present a target!"

He pulled the mare's reins, and both horses jumped off the road. In a clearing, Charles stopped to let the mounts calm their heaving chests. The bushes swayed, and the sounds of another horse came farther down, at the other side of the clearing.

"Must be the blasted bandit," Charles said under his breath. "Don't say anything; I shall deal with him."

The bandit approached, Tiernan slumped against his shoulder. The large black horse pawed the ground and snorted.

"You could have lost your precious cargo there," the bandit drawled.

"I didn't know you cared for spies, bandit. Only heavy purses."

"I don't like spies, but there are times when I have to dabble in things that don't catch my deepest interest. Right a wrong, take charge."

"Ah! You see yourself as a gallant savior, no doubt," Charles said, his voice laced with derision.

The bandit did not respond to that sally. "I think we'd better leave the area at the greatest speed."

"We're taking him to Kent, to a contact on the coast."

"You need my help," the bandit said, taking the lead.

Marguerite stared at the criminal, and thought she'd met him before, many times. *How strange.*

They rode in silence through the woods for about an hour, and Marguerite drooped. The tension had drained from her, leaving a feeling of utter exhaustion behind. The militia could not come after them on foot, and as far as she knew, only Emerson rode a horse. He was far away.

Their progress was slow through the forest. Two hours later she could, however, smell the salty brine of the sea, the invigorating freshness of a vast stretch of water.

"Almost there," Charles said into her ear. "The bandit seems to know where he's going. And he won't let me take Tiernan even though the young man must weigh as much as a barrel of lead."

Marguerite jerked herself upright at the sound of his voice. It was a miracle that she'd not fallen off the mare as she faded in and out of sleep.

"A strange fellow," Charles said.

"You pretended to be him," she reminded him tartly.

"That's because you had foolish notions in your head about him. The height of romantic gallantry, I seem to remember you said about him."

"This is a story many would like to hear—"

"But one we will not mention under any circumstances."

"I agree," she said, yawning.

"Strange that we would be in accord about some issues," he muttered under his breath. He covered the distance to the

bandit, who had kept the lead all the way. The coast was hilly
and bare of anything but gorse and grass, steep chalk cliffs
leading down to the water. The bandit skirted the coast, heading
down into a valley, where a small village was situated on an
estuary. A sandy beach stretched between steeply rising hills.

In the cover of darkness they rode to an abandoned farm in
the outskirts of the village. The bandit got down, pulling the
wounded man with him. Tiernan had come to again and could
walk the few steps to the gaping hole in the barn that once had
been a doorway. Wind moaned through the rafters above, and
Marguerite looked into the dark cavern. Old hay was scattered
in a corner, and the bandit assisted Tiernan to the musty straw.
With a groan, the spy sat down in the hay.

Marguerite touched Tiernan's forehead, finding it cool and
clammy. At least he had no fever. She turned as the bandit lit
a candle and stuck it into an old bottle. Shadows leaped across
his masked face, and a shiver traveled up her spine. Not that
she was afraid, but the anonymity of his mask reminded her
vaguely of nightmares.

He held the light toward her. "Please look at his wound to
see if it needs rebandaging."

Charles's breath hissed in shock, and Marguerite glanced at
his face. A smile of surprise lit his features, and his eyes were
narrowed as he stared at the highwayman. "Nick, by God! You
devil, you've been playing a wicked game all this time, and
no one knew about it!"

"I knew it was only a matter of time before you would
recognize me," Nick said with a rueful laugh, "but I had no
choice but to save my cousin from certain death. The idiot!"
He untied the strings of the mask and let it drop from his face.
He pulled off his hat and pushed back his long hair, which had
fallen in disarray during the escape.

"Nick," Marguerite said feebly. "To think how many times
we've spoken of the highwayman, you speaking in earnest
about his punishment." She busied herself with Tiernan's arm,
which trembled with fatigue. The wound was healing nicely.

"How in the world did you know about Tiernan and us?" Charles asked.

"I went to see how Marguerite was handling the fervid search of the militia. The soldiers might bother her, I thought, and I wanted to protect her."

Charles nodded, but he did not look pleased, Marguerite thought. "You should have known I would see to her welfare," he said.

"That didn't stop me from worrying," Nick said, and rubbed his face vigorously. "I found out the truth from Prunella Trent. She was very reluctant to tell me anything, but when she heard that I was worried about Tiernan—he'd written he would arrive for a visit last week—she told me the truth. I rode after you, thinking you were heading for the coast. Sheer luck that I found you, but the militia was searching the property and said they thought the fugitive had found the aid of accomplices and ridden through the spinney toward the Lewes road."

"I'm eternally grateful that you found us in time," Marguerite said, shaking with the memory of the encounter with the soldiers.

"Why, Nick? Why are you the Midnight Bandit?" Charles asked, and flung himself onto the hay next to Tiernan. "Surely not for the thrill?"

Nick shook his head. "No . . . not for the excitement, but I cannot tell you the truth. 'Twould only hurt the cause."

"Robbing travelers is illegal," Charles said, his voice sharp with anger. "I never expected that you, my best friend, would be a lawbreaker."

Nick got down on his haunches, his face serious. "If I could, I would tell you the truth of why I am a highwayman. All I can say for now is that the money goes to a worthy cause that helps many people. I am not a spy, nor a traitor to England. What I have created brings happiness to young hearts." He gave Charles a pleading look, but his mouth held a slant of defiance, as if he expected Charles to condemn him. "If you are my friends, you'll both have to trust me. When 'tis all over, I shall explain the whole.''

Marguerite and Charles exchanged glances, and she realized that Nick had hurt his friend by keeping secrets—just as she had done. A tense silence hovered.

Charles looked away. He tossed up a handful of hay in a gesture of resignation. ''We have been friends for a long time, Nick,'' he said at last. ''I choose to trust you in this, but that doesn't mean I approve of your work.''

''Thank you, Morty.'' Nick turned to Marguerite. ''And you? Are you going to denounce me?''

Marguerite immediately shook her head. ''No. I don't throw stones into glass houses. Besides, I trust you, Nick. You are a good man.''

Nick grinned. ''Thank you, my fairest.'' He looked at Tiernan askance. ''This young fellow has destroyed his life. He will never be able to live peacefully in England. I thought he devoted himself to his studies at Oxford.''

Tiernan's head came up, and he stared with bloodshot eyes at his cousin. ''I have a cause, too, and if you don't approve, there's nothing I can do to change you. I made the choice during the rebellion, and I have not once changed my mind. And I will stand by my beliefs.''

Silence hovered. Nick heaved a deep sigh. ''Each man follows his own path,'' he said.

''Yes . . . he does. I've been through Sussex many times this last year, but I've avoided visiting you, Nick, as I knew you would not approve—had you discovered about my Stuart sympathies.''

No one spoke, and Marguerite finished rebandaging Tiernan's arm with strips of a clean old shirt that Charles had packed in his saddlebag.

''I'm grateful to you all. I owe you my life,'' Tiernan said with a sigh. ''If not for you, the soldiers would have caught me.''

''You're right on that score,'' Charles said sharply.

"Did you not know my husband was dead?" Marguerite asked.

"Yes, but I did not know your personal leanings. I had to try to reach Lennox House and ask for shelter. As I was wounded, I had not much strength left to evade the militia."

He took Marguerite's hand and kissed it. "You are strong, and gracious, too. Thank you."

"I did not approve of Lennox's political leanings, and I will not continue to harbor spies in the cellar. I don't hold with the fanaticism my husband displayed. It led to murder in the end."

"Murder . . . yes, I know," Tiernan said with a deep sigh. "At the time, I stayed overnight at Mr. Renny's house. As I left I saw them—Renny and Lennox—carry a body from a coach and into the garden. I left before they noticed my presence. I would have questioned them, but I had to reach my rendezvous point on time."

Charles sat up, tensely listening. "At Renny's house? We thought the sergeant would be buried on the Lennox property."

"No. He's buried in Renny's garden. Who is the dead man?"

"Sergeant Rule, of the Hayward's Heath militia," Charles said.

"I've been helping Captain Emerson with the investigation into Rule's death," Nick said.

"The Midnight Bandit helping the militia with the investigation?" Charles commented scornfully. "You are a most amazing fellow. They have been searching for the bandit for months."

"Where better to hide than right under their noses?" Nick said with a devilish grin. He got to his feet. "I'll have to get in touch with your contact, Tiernan, and send you away to your future across the Channel." He turned to Charles. "You'd better return home, or there might be questions. I'll see to it that Tiernan is taken care of properly."

"Very well. I can't deny that the adventure has tired me." Charles rose and pulled Marguerite to her feet. She thought she would faint with fatigue.

"I'll take you to the Meadow," he said. "Emmy will care for you, and I don't want to go back to Lennox House. Who knows if Emerson has given up his search there, and he might ask you difficult questions."

Marguerite nodded. "Thank you. Besides, your house is closer."

"I'll return in the morning and we'll discuss how to go about finding Rule's body," Nick said, and stuffed his mask and gloves into the pocket of his black coat.

Chapter 26

Lingering over a late breakfast of kippers and eggs at the Meadow, Marguerite tried to stop herself from yawning every two minutes. She'd slept four hours in one of Charles's guest rooms, her visit made respectable by the presence of Emilia Wetherby. Still, a lady did not spend the night in a bachelor's establishment, not even a widow with the nickname Poison Widow.

Georgie growled and swiveled on his fat hind legs to get a tidbit from the table. Marguerite tried to ignore him, but he had the bad habit of nipping the toes of her slippers if she did not obey his command. She unobtrusively slipped a piece of fish under the table. Georgie slobbered on her foot as he devoured the kipper. *Beast!*

Charles did not seem to suffer from lack of sleep. His eyes were bright and his gestures full of vigor. Not with as much as a word or tone of voice did he hint of their disagreement. He cut into a slice of ham as Nick arrived, elegant in a green camlet coat and looking as relaxed as if he hadn't been part of last night's adventure.

"Good morning, Emmy," Nick said, and pecked the old lady's cheek. "You're fresh as a rosebud."

"And you're an inveterate liar, Nick," Emmy replied with one of her bell-like laughs. "If a charming one."

"I fetched Miss Trent on my way here, Marguerite."

Marguerite brightened as she saw her dear companion in the doorway. Pru waved and sat down next to Emmy. "I couldn't say no to the opportunity for a chat," she said. She glanced at Marguerite, and pointed with her fan. "And I worried about this young lady." An uneasy silence fell. "We didn't get much sleep at Lennox House. The militiamen looked everywhere for spies, even into the wood bin in the kitchen!" She snorted. "As if we were harboring spies within. I was furious."

"As far as I know, they did not come here," Emmy said. "Thank goodness for that."

Marguerite sipped her coffee and toyed with the eggs on her plate. "Delighted I wasn't there. I would have argued with Emerson and his boorish soldiers."

"I'm so glad Marguerite stayed the night after getting caught riding in the rain. I miss my friends," Emmy said between bites of toast.

Marguerite and Pru exchanged tense glances. Emmy did not know the whole story. "I worried," Pru said, "and I'm grateful that we have friends to help us in an emergency."

"Yes, 'tis good to have helpful neighbors. I adore this spot of bucolic paradise, but it gets lonely at times without female company," Emmy went on. "The Meadow should be filled with children."

"You don't have to be alone, Emmy. I've asked you to invite your cronies," Charles said, and passed a cup of coffee to Pru since the butler had gone to the kitchen.

"Yes, but—"

"No buts, Emmy. I insist that you write to them. I look forward to a gathering of gossiping ladies."

"Bosh! You're as much a liar as is Nick," the old lady said, touching the ribbons on her cap. She stood, however, as did the gentlemen. "Come, Pru, bring the coffee to my boudoir. We shall enjoy a long chat." She gave Charles a stern glance. "If I write those invitations, I hope we shall have something important to announce to all our friends." She gave Marguerite a wink. Marguerite blushed and looked away. She listened to the tapping of the ladies' heels as they left the room. She thought Georgie would waddle after his mistress, but he remained at her side, one of his gimlet eyes visible at the edge of the tablecloth.

Nick and Charles continued their breakfasts, and Marguerite was surprised at their appetites. "How can you eat after what happened last night?" she whispered as the butler returned.

"A solved problem is a problem less," Nick said cryptically. "I'm always famished after a successful mission. Tiernan has the luck of the Irish," he said under his breath. "Got away just in time."

Bottomly brought in a platter of steaks, and Nick set to work with knife and fork. He waited until the butler had left, then said, "Any plans on how to find the, er"—he looked around as if suspecting minions of hiding behind the curtains—"sergeant's body?"

"We could always search Renny's property for moved or agitated soil," Charles said.

"We'll be shot for trespassing," Nick said. "We don't know when Renny comes and goes. He might not stay much at his house, but there are bound to be servants."

"We will have to force Renny to confess," Charles said, but he sounded unconvinced.

"No, Renny will never confess. We'll have to trick him," Marguerite said. "But we don't know where to find him."

"We could always spend some time at his house; he's bound to return at some point," Nick said, and drank deeply from his coffee cup.

"He's more likely to visit me," Marguerite said with a sigh of exasperation. "He's hoping that I've decided to marry him now that he has shown what he can do to me if I refuse. Mayhap he thinks I might relent and give him money—as I was foolish enough to do a few times after Lennox's death.'' She threw up her arms in disgust. ''I wish this debacle were over. I know 'tis only a matter of time before Renny confronts me. He is like an avenging angel following me.''

''A very dark one at that,'' Charles said, his lips set in a grim line.

''I have an idea,'' Marguerite said. ''I believe Renny is extremely frightened of anything supernatural. Remember how he reacted to the ghost at Lennox House?''

''What is your devious mind plotting, Marguerite?'' Nick asked with a smile.

''One of you could dress up as Rule's ghost and frighten Renny into removing the body. If he thinks Rule will continue to haunt him, he'll try to get rid of the corpse.''

''Hmm.'' Charles laughed. ''That's the slyest idea I've heard in a long time. There's a small chance it will work. Renny is horrified of ghosts.''

''Who will impersonate Rule, then?'' Nick asked.

Charles spoke. ''What did he look like, Marguerite?''

''He was tall, about as tall as any of you, slender, wavy brown hair.''

'' 'Twill have to be you, Charles,'' Nick said. ''My hair is too dark.''

''But you're used to playing a role,'' Charles said dryly.

''So are you,'' Marguerite said, then averted her gaze when she realized that the statement might inspire Nick to start questioning her. She would never confess her short-lived infatuation with the Midnight Bandit, or rather her dream of him and romantic love.

Nick chewed his last piece of bread. His gaze moved from Charles to Marguerite. ''What have I missed?''

''Nothing but a series of mistakes,'' Charles said with a heavy sigh. He slanted a glance at Marguerite and she gulped down a wave of unhappiness.

Georgie nipped her toes, and she was forced to relinquish her last piece of buttered toast to his superior will. "Bad dog!"

She laid her napkin next to her coffee cup. "You should ask your housekeeper for some old sheets, Charles. I'll see to fashioning a suitable ghostly shroud for one of you."

The two men exchanged glances.

"Very well! I'll be the ghost," Charles said, and flung down his fork. "To make a good ghost dressed in a *sheet,* I'll have to be three sheets to the wind. It might help me to see the humorous side of the ordeal."

Marguerite glared at him. "I don't see any humor in this. It could be dangerous if Mr. Renny recognizes you."

"I won't let that happen," Charles said.

Nick gave a groan of frustration. "The question is, how do we find Renny? If we are to frighten him out of his wits, we'll have to lure him to his house."

"I'll send him a message at his club in London," Marguerite said. "He used to stay there with Lennox at times. I'll ask him to meet me at his house."

"I don't like the idea of you putting yourself in danger, Marguerite," Nick said, leaning back in his chair.

"He won't come if *you* send him a note," Marguerite said.

Charles grimaced. "You have a point. Anyhow, Nick will protect you. He can remain hidden close by while I deal with Renny."

"After all, I don't really have to meet Renny," Marguerite said. "The main idea is to lure him to his house and make him reveal the grave."

"Yes . . . this plan will have to work. I know Renny cannot be forced to speak. He'll continue denying the accusation of murder, and without the body, we can't prove that he killed Rule. We have only one chance," Charles said.

Nick snorted. "Unless we dig up the entire garden ourselves."

Charles pulled his hand around his chin. "Possibly they buried the sergeant in some other spot on the property."

They pondered that grim fact in silence.

"The garden seems convenient," Nick said.

"Garden, you say? Acres of weed, I call it. The estate is sadly dilapidated," said Marguerite.

Charles spoke. "Renny is lazy. He would bury the body where the ground is easy to dig."

"He probably made Lennox do all the digging," Nick said with a sarcastic curl of his lip. "But you're right."

Feeling uneasy with the morbid turn of the conversation, Marguerite stood. "Let's set the plan in motion."

That same morning, Marguerite sent the note to Renny's club in London asking him to meet her in four days at Dentley Court, Renny's estate. She spent one day at home sewing a billowing robe for Charles, and he visited on the morning of the day when Renny was expected to come south. It had to be dark for the ghostly "apparition" to take place, and the rendezvous was set for nine in the evening.

"Renny thinks I will surrender in the end. He thinks I'm going to marry him," Marguerite said to herself in disgust as she sat by the window in her bedchamber at Lennox House. She bit off a thread and studied her handiwork. She'd seen much better needlework in her day, but this would have to do, uneven stitches included. After pricking her fingers ten times, she finally laid aside her sewing. Renny wasn't worth the wounds on her fingertips!

She picked up her lute and tuned it. How stiff and clumsy her fingers had grown these last six years, and how rusty her voice. Sadly, she picked at the strings, and sought the words of the ballads she used to sing before her marriage.

Charles watched her from the open doorway. A ray of sunshine streamed through the open window, framing her in gold. A halo of light surrounded her red-gold hair, and the hesitant tunes of the lute went outside and rose toward the bright summer sky. He listened, his heart touched by her evident struggles to create music. He thought of his ideas, and how little Marguerite resembled his idealistic pictures of her. Yet her vulnerability, her cracking voice and jarring tones, made her infinitely more human, more attractive to him.

He needed her, and listening to her inept music he realized that she needed him, too. He wasn't perfect, and neither was she. They would fight and reconcile, but who cared as long as they could be together?

He couldn't bear the thought of being separated from her again. Just as that realization came to him, he forgave her for keeping her secrets from him. She had done what she thought best. She hadn't kept the secrets to hurt him.

If he'd faced such problems as hers, he might not have been inclined to share them with anyone, at least not with someone whose opinion about him mattered.

Light steps sounded behind him. Betsy. She gave him a searching glance and knocked on Marguerite's door.

"There's a gent t'see ye, milady. Lord Ransford."

Marguerite could not get used to Charles's new title, and she felt a stab of uneasiness that he'd believed she wanted to renew their relationship only because of his recently acquired wealth.

"The relationship has gone awry, so why worry now?" she murmured under her breath.

"What, milady?"

"Please show him in."

Betsy made round eyes at Charles as he stepped over the threshold. He looked handsome and desirable in a dove gray coat of flawless linen, moleskin breeches, and top boots. His chestnut hair had been brushed back and was held together with a riband. The curly hair glinted with red lights as he stepped through a patch of sunshine. She put aside the lute.

"Good morning," he greeted her, and kissed her hand formally. A smile hovered on his lips.

So impersonal, she thought, yet a jolt of attraction leaped between them at his touch. She wished those strong fingers would travel intimately over her skin. A spurt of longing so fierce that she had to gasp rushed through her, and a flush warmed her cheeks. She looked into his eyes and wondered if he could sense her desire. Something bright glittered in his eyes, and she lost her breath momentarily. The air shimmered and crackled until she forced her gaze away. She focused on the distant horizon.

"It is a good morning, Charles. Peter is cutting up the fallen branch for firewood, and there is nary a puddle to muddy the hooves of the horses in the stableyard."

"I thought we had more important matters to discuss than the condition of the horses' hooves," he drawled, and leaned against the window frame. He looked at the white bundle on the window seat.

"Yes. I'd like you to try this on; then we're going downstairs to give the appearance of respectability. So far no one but Betsy knows that you're in my bedchamber, but they soon will."

"Not that we would behave in any way unrespectably," he said with a suggestive curl of his lip.

"I trust that we won't," she replied in a firm voice. She stood, shaking out the shroud. "Here, slip this over your head. I'll have to make sure it won't impede your progress if you have to escape in a hurry."

He snorted. "I'd rather fight him than run away. 'Twouldn't be the first time we've had an altercation."

"He would not hesitate to kill you," Marguerite said with a frown. She thrust the garment at him, and he crushed it between his hands while giving her a long, searching stare.

"Sounds like you care very much what happens to me," he said with that annoying drawl in his voice.

"If you want me to confess my worries, you will wait in

vain.'' She plunged her hands into the pockets of her apron.
''Please try it on.''

Charles slipped the shroud over his head, and it fell in voluminous folds around his body, dragging on the floor at the back.
She went down on her knees and measured how much she
would have to shorten the material.

''I never dreamed that one day I would see you kneel in
front of me,'' he said lightly. ''The very picture of humility.''

''Don't you dare tease me!''

He gripped her arms and made her stand, so close her breasts
rubbed against his chest and her legs pressed against his. He
smelled of coffee and leather, a strange combination, but attractive nevertheless. Her heart started pounding in that reckless
way his touch always provoked, and she sighed with longing.

''We're not supposed to stand like this,'' she said breathlessly.

''How are we supposed to stand? On all fours?'' With a
wicked glint in his eyes, he pulled her even closer. His hot
breath wafted over her face. ''As far as I know, you don't have
to stand anywhere as long as I hold you. Besides, I like you
better prostrate and silent. Naked and with stars of happiness
in your eyes,'' he added in a hoarse voice. His eyes had darkened
with desire.

''I can stand on my own two feet very well,'' she said, but
the temptation to give in to the pressure of his arms was great.
Oh, to lean against him, to let him lead her once more into
the realm of bliss where she didn't have to think about their
differences, only *feel*.

''I know that, dearest Marguerite, but I offer you an alternative.''

She smiled cynically. ''You have forgiven me for my rotten
heart and false tongue?''

He stood silent, a thoughtful look on his face. He gently
pushed an errant curl of hers behind her ear, and kissed her
forehead.

''Lets just say I've had some time to digest everything, and

I realize I've been an utter fool. I let my anger cloud my judgment. I lacked vision—understanding—and it should be me asking for your forgiveness."

She wound her arms around his neck happily. "No, I should have trusted you. So do you accept that I am a flawed lady, not the perfect goddess you envisioned?"

He nodded, his head bending until their lips touched, light as butterfly wings at first, then harder until their teeth ground together in a furious wave of desire. His tongue penetrated past that barrier to plunge and plunder her mouth.

She gasped for breath under the sweet onslaught, her head spinning. She forgot everything except the pressure of his seductive mouth and the feel of his hard body squeezed against hers.

"Oh, God," he murmured as he finally lifted his face. His heart hammered so hard she felt it as keenly as if it were her own. "I have missed you more than I can say, Marguerite."

"Only your stubbornness kept you away from my arms," she said, her senses still dazed with the storm his kiss had created within her.

"Not as simple as that," he muttered, "but I am a stubborn man, sometimes making things difficult for myself."

She helped him pull off the shroud and folded it on the window seat. "There. No longer a ghost."

"No, a man of fleshly desires," he said in a growl, and pulled her once again into his arms.

"Charles . . . we can't . . . what if Pru or Sophie enter? They would be very shocked."

He lifted her unceremoniously into his arms and carried her to the bed. "I know the remedy for that." He set her down on the mattress, oblivious of her protests. Two long strides took him to the door. He slid the old iron bolt home and gave her a predatory smile. "We will not be disturbed, my sweet."

Heat pounded through Marguerite's body, and she couldn't stop what was happening. She did not want to, no matter what the rest of the household would whisper in the aftermath. She watched him strip off his coat, waistcoat, and untie his cravat. With a laugh, he pulled off his shirt and flung it across the room, untied his breeches, and kicked off his boots. Naked and glorious, he began the slow seduction of her senses.

"Oh, Charles." She moaned as his hands moved up her legs and pulled down the garters securing her silk stockings. He tossed them to the floor and rolled down the stockings, kissing every inch of skin that was revealed. He caressed the arch of her foot, one long finger gently massaging the skin around the protruding bone of her ankle. Warm rivulets of desire curled up her legs to pool in her womb. A dulcet ache started at the apex of her thighs, and she strove to soothe that ache by pulling him toward her. Hard muscles played in his arms and over his chest, taut buttocks invited her caresses, but he resisted her urgent tugs on his arms.

"Darling," he murmured, his hands moving up to play in circles over the tender skin on the inside of her thighs, and she gasped with pleasure.

"Charles, come to me," she begged as he accidentally brushed the curls that concealed the center of her hunger.

"A slow seduction will ignite your senses beyond your dreams. Be quiet and enjoy." He held himself away, his aroused manhood mocking her with its blatant desire. He continued the slow exploration of her body, untying every string and lace, and removing her garments one by one until she lay naked before him. His hands moved up the sides of her hips, to her waist, and finally circled her full breasts, which had been begging for his touch ever since he took her into his arms.

She pulled his head down, and his hair, which had come untied, swept in a caress over her breasts. He took one swollen peak into his mouth and suckled until she forgot to breathe. His silken tongue played maddeningly over her skin, down to her belly. She gasped with pleasure as it made slow circles around her navel. His tongue moved down in a hot trail of exploration, and she arched up as if begging silently for the fulfillment of her longing.

His tongue did not assuage her desire, but increased it with its suave seduction. She dug her fingertips into his hard shoulders and cried his name as a wave of intense pleasure rose through her body.

With a groan he pressed her into the mattress and rose over her, falling into her arms, hard flesh, soft golden skin against hers, soothing her urge for contact. She wound her legs around his hips, pushing him to enter her body. He plundered her mouth, held himself just out of reach as she struggled to pull him inside.

He kneaded her breasts, slid a soft palm over her stomach, and inserted a long finger into the wet crevice of her desire. He teased and played, and she rose on a crest so wild she was thrown into a mindless sea of pleasure where nothing else mattered but his loving. Then, just as she rode on the sweetest wave, he plunged into her, ravishing her with his ardor, pulling her to another pinnacle, and throwing her into another velvet abyss of pure delight.

Charles moaned, fearing he would die if he didn't find release from his aching need *now*. He bit her shoulder, not hard, but hard enough to feel the life throbbing through her, to feel *her*, to become part of her racing pulse and of her ecstasy. He rode her hard, holding on to her hips, finally falling, toppling into a devastating release that led to a sea of stillness. As if in a faint, he collapsed on top of her, and held on to her as though she would disappear at the slightest movement.

Chapter 27

Warmly tingling, Charles looked down at Marguerite's flushed face framed with wildly tousled hair. He laughed as a great wave of happiness surged through him. It was as if a part of her had entered him, bringing him brightness that lingered. *Renewed,* that was the proper expression, he thought. Alive. He was in awe of the beauty he'd shared with her.

A verse came to him unbidden, and he recited it as he held her dear face trapped between his hands. "A love beyond reason / Came to me one season / A beggar had been I / Living once a lonely lie. Yet I found / Two hearts a-bound / In a love beyond reason."

Marguerite chuckled. "A merry poem. I'm surprised you're such a fountain of verse. Have you been taking lessons from Nick, the Midnight Bandit?"

He pinched her ears lightly and rubbed his nose against hers. "Mayhap 'tis the other way around."

He tickled her mercilessly, and Marguerite squirmed, her hot velvet skin moving against him, alluring curves that would inspire poetry in the most barren heart, he thought—and told her so. She blushed prettily.

"Pink roses on your face / I saw them through a haze of desire / A dangerous mire / Epilogue of suffering / If we don't walk apace."

"You're talking such nonsense," she said with a laugh, and pushed against his chest. Her squirming movements ignited his desire anew, and he lost himself in the pleasure of the moment, fully in accord with her responsive body.

In the aftermath of shimmering happiness, he said with mock regret, "You are doubly compromised now, my dearest. I suppose I'll have to make an honest woman out of you at last."

She punched him lightly in the shoulder. "I'm only marrying you to get my hands on your fortune. You know that, don't you, Charles?"

"My cynicism has been playing havoc with my better judgment," he said, and slapped her backside lightly. He heaved himself to his knees beside her on the soft mattress and took one of her hands in his. "This is a formal proposal, Marguerite, my darling. Will you make me happy; will you be my wife?"

Marguerite bubbled with laughter. "I daresay not every lady has had a naked god propose to her." She held his hand against her cheek and pulled it up and down over her peach-soft skin. Her eyes glittered brightly with unshed tears. "Yes, I would like to be your wife, Charles, despite your suspicious and deceitful nature Who would ever have thought a gentleman would dress up as a notorious bandit just to seduce a lady?"

He lay down next to her and cradled her against him. "Poverty breeds inventive minds, be it emotional or physical. I was desperate as I realized I would not win you by conventional means. Besides, that damned Nick made a pest of himself at your door."

"Ah, to be so much desired," she said sarcastically.

He jumped out of the bed and stretched his tired but content body. "We shall announce the good news to the world."

"We'd better dress first," she said, "or Pru will have apoplexy."

He grinned. "Yes. But I won't dress in that ghostly shroud. Prunella will definitely succumb to apoplexy, and Miss Pierson will surely kill me with one of her withering stares."

"Yes . . ." Marguerite said with a laugh. "But she'll be glad when she hears that I'll settle half of the funds I receive for this house on her. She can live the life of her choice, and Pru and I shall live at Mortimer's Meadow, or at the Ransford estate with you."

"I like the idea," Charles said, and pulled her into his arms, her scent of roses, heat, and lovemaking surrounding him. "With you installed, the Meadow will be a happy home."

"Charles, I have gotten a generous offer from a London businessman for Lennox House."

He gave her a long, loving glance. "Please accept it. The sooner you can move in with me, the better."

When they arrived downstairs, they discovered that Pru and Sophie had traveled into the village. Marguerite had braced herself against recriminations for entertaining a gentleman in her room, but since none was forthcoming, she spent the day with Charles, getting to know him all over again.

Charles practiced lamenting noises and moans he would use to frighten Renny. He didn't sound convincing in the warm sunlight of summer, Marguerite thought. It was difficult to be afraid in the midst of so much happiness.

Evening came with high winds and a clear sky. Around eight, Nick arrived on his horse. Charles collected his disguise and saddled two horses, one for himself and one for Marguerite, even though he protested that she would be safer at home.

"I would die of suspense not knowing what is happening," she said as he helped her into the sidesaddle.

"You stay well hidden with Nick. There's no other way I can accept your participation."

Marguerite promised, and they rode slowly over to Dentley Court, three miles to the west. Darkness deepened among the scrubby trees and shrubs that surrounded the dilapidated mansion. The flower beds had not been weeded in the last five years. It was only from the old brick edging that Marguerite recognized the borders.

The moon covered the landscape with a silver sheen.

"A good night for ghosts to be abroad," Nick said with a rueful chuckle as they slid from their horses in the shelter of the trees crowding the house at the back.

"Yes, I'd better get ready. I shall lament my lost life until the hairs stand up on your heads," Charles said, and unfolded the white shroud. "If only I could rig up some green light to illuminate my face, or perhaps red, I would easily frighten Renny out of his wits."

"I'm afraid ghosts don't carry lanterns," Marguerite said softly. "Promise me you will be careful. Renny might be armed—"

"And he won't hesitate to make use of his weapons," Nick inserted.

Charles slipped on the disguise and pulled the hood low over his face. Marguerite pushed it back and, on his face and hands, applied a great amount of white powder laced with silver, which she had once used in a charade.

"If you can, you might let the moonlight shine on your face for a moment in Renny's presence," she said. "Your skin will have a ghostly sheen."

Nick pulled a pouch from his saddlebags, and Marguerite shuddered with revulsion when she saw the congealed blood he rubbed onto the front of the shroud. "From a chicken," he explained. "Cook saved it for me, and gave me a strange look as I collected the pouch."

"Well, we all know you're slightly strange in the head, Nick," Charles said. "Especially when you take to the roads as the Midnight Bandit. You're playing hide-and-seek with death."

"There is no other way," Nick said with finality.

Marguerite sensed his suppressed agitation, but she did not dare to pry. There were layers of his character that she knew nothing about. Mayhap it was for the best. "We don't know how Renny and Lennox killed the soldier. Mayhap they strangled him. Then the blood would—"

"Easier with a knife or a sword. I'm sure they ran him through. Renny always carries a sword as if ready to fight."

"You're right," Charles said. "The blood looks grisly."

"But how do we make Renny believe he's seeing Rule's ghost?" Marguerite said, pleating the edge of her cloak.

"Someone will have to convince him afterward that the ghost he saw was Rule's," Charles said. "He'll come looking for you at Lennox House when you're not here as promised. You'll have to convince him."

Marguerite was filled with icy premonition. They waited in silence, and Charles practiced gliding across the ground in a ghostlike manner. "Ridiculous!" he said under his breath.

"He'll arrive any minute now," Marguerite said, worry nagging at her mind.

"I don't know how this will work." Charles heaved a deep breath, and Nick put a friendly hand on his shoulder. "If he recognizes you, I'll step in and we'll force the truth out of him."

Marguerite thought that Renny would rather die than give away his secret. Either way he would die. Treason and murder were serious matters.

Her thoughts were interrupted as the sounds of a horse filled the night. The wind battered the trees, but the distinct clip-crop of hooves came through.

"Renny is here. He'll wait for me, but not for very long," Marguerite whispered, tensing as she saw the black outline of the rider coming up the drive.

"He'll find the surprise of his life," Charles said grimly, and pulled the hood forward over his face as he walked to the side of the house where Renny couldn't see him.

They waited, Marguerite's throat dry with suspense. There was not a sign of Renny until a flickering light lit the inside of the house. "He's in the study," she said. "I wonder if there are any servants present."

"There was no smoke coming from the chimney and no light on in the kitchen region. I doubt anyone is here besides our victim."

The flickering light came to the window, glowing right above Charles's downbent head.

"Perhaps I'd better call him outside," Marguerite said, and folded her trembling hands. "Otherwise 'twill be difficult for Charles to play the ghost."

"Hmm, you might be right. What if he just leaves the house and rides off?" Nick slanted a glance at her in the gloom. "Would you mind coaxing him outside?"

"No! I want to reach the end of this mystery. Renny has plagued me long enough." She stepped out from the trees, closer to the house but still concealed by shrubs. Cupping her hands to her mouth, she shouted, "Mr. Renny, where are you?"

Startled by the sound of her voice, Charles jerked his head around, but he could not leave his spot. He had to wait for the perfect moment to frighten Renny.

"Mr. Renny?" Marguerite called from farther away.

The light in the window dwindled and disappeared. There came the sound of a slamming door. "Marguerite?" Renny called, his voice laced with suspicion. "Where are you? Are you playing a game of hide-and-seek?"

"Mr. Renny, help!" Marguerite cried, her voice softer now, so as to give the impression that she was moving away.

He came around the corner of the house, his stance questioning, his movements spasmodic. Marguerite called once more, "Mr. Renny?"

He moved forward on the path, his head slewing from one side to the other. Marguerite watched Charles, who had not moved away from the shrubs. He waited as Renny stepped gingerly along the garden path. It was clear that the man was uneasy. The wind moaned in the trees, and branches rasped against the windows at the back of the house.

A night for ghosts.

When Renny had walked far enough away from the house, Charles stepped into the path Renny would have to take to retrace his steps. Marguerite admired Charles's self-control. He had waited until he was sure to cross Renny's path to try to make a frightening impression.

Marguerite crouched, hidden behind spreading currant bushes as Renny came closer. She held her breath, her palms sweaty with nervousness.

"Marguerite?" he asked. "I could have sworn I heard your voice."

Nothing. Marguerite barely dared to breathe at all. Everything was quiet except for the wind and a faint, unearthly moaning coming from the area of the house. *Charles.*

He glided along the path, his shroud billowing around him in the wind. He slowly lifted his arms, looking like some great swooping bird of prey. Would Renny be fooled? Marguerite's legs trembled with tension, and she tried to prevent herself from collapsing into a heap of nerves.

Renny stood uncertainly on the path, looking in every direction, but evidently doubting her presence. "Marguerite?"

She waited.

Everyone waited. Renny finally turned abruptly and headed back toward the house. Charles had halted in a streak of moonlight on the path. The silver light had given him an unearthly glow. He raised and lowered his arms in a circle, his shroud flapping madly.

He keened, a blood-chilling sound that filled the night.

Marguerite's hair rose on her scalp. She shook her head, surprised at her reaction.

Renny halted and stood motionless on the path. Marguerite sensed his confusion, then his rising fear as his shoulders went up, and his arms rose, palms out, as if warding something off.

He remained standing in the spot as Charles slowly moved toward him.

Charles lifted his arms, the wide sleeves flowing as he clutched the front of his shroud where the bloodstain had been applied. He made gurgling sounds and staggered on the path as if in the throes of death.

Renny clutched his head and sank to his knees on the path. "What do you want? Who are you?" he said in a tortured voice.

Charles stopped, his hand over his heart. He slowly lifted his face toward the moon. At first the only thing visible was the black hole of the opening of the hood; then came a hint of Charles's ghostly pale face, black hollows, silver cheeks.

Renny moaned as he knelt on the path. Marguerite could see him trembling so hard he could barely remain upright.

Charles progressed slowly, and Marguerite knew he could not move all the way to Renny's side, or Renny would know the apparition was a man.

Charles made frightening—inspired—noises, keening with the wind. Renny gave a great gasp, then fell flat to the ground in a faint.

Marguerite ran to Nick's side and Charles soon joined them. They would have to wait and watch what Renny would do next. He came to five minutes later, staggering to his feet and clawing at his head. By then, Charles had folded his disguise and hidden it in the saddlebag.

They watched in silence as Renny furtively turned his head in all directions. Fear was evident in every tense line of his body. Leaning forward, doubling at the waist, he ran erratically toward the house. As Renny turned the corner, Charles let out a chilling howl that made Marguerite jump with fear.

"Oh, dear, you almost made my heart stop," she said, pressing her hand to her chest.

"He's leaving," Nick said.

Marguerite listened to the hoofbeats. "Unless he's heading

for London, 'tis likely he's heading for Lennox House. We'd better get there before he does.''

"That's where he's going—the closest house for a glass of brandy,'' Nick said. ''He wouldn't dare to be on the dark road all night.''

Without another word they gathered their horses and chose a shortcut through the woods. Panting with the exertion of staying atop her galloping horse, Marguerite slid off the saddle behind the stables at Lennox House. It wouldn't do to announce their approach if Renny had arrived ahead of them.

''He will ask for me,'' Marguerite said, and righted her lace-trimmed cap under the hood of her cloak. ''I'll open the window in the study and you can listen to our conversation.''

The two men nodded. She ran into the house through the terrace door, just in time to hear the banging of the door knocker at the front.

Breathless, she rushed down the hallway, her bodice clinging to her back with perspiration. She hung her cloak on a peg, and righted her dress. She looked a sight! Her dress bore wrinkled and muddy smudges, and she pulled a currant leaf from the lacings of her bodice. Hopefully he wouldn't notice her disarray in the gloom. Only one candle glowed in lonely splendor in a sconce on the wall.

Pru and Sophie hastened down the stairs when another series of knocks sounded on the door. Marguerite put her fingers to her lips and motioned with her other hand that they return upstairs. With frightened expressions on their faces, they obeyed.

Marguerite opened the front door a crack. It flew out of her grip as Renny pushed it inward and stomped inside. She staggered but managed to keep her balance.

''Mr. Renny! You are late,'' she admonished.

He stared at her, his face thunderous. ''You were supposed to meet me at my home,'' he said in a snarl.

She shook her head and donned a confused expression, hoping her deceit would strike him as true. ''*Your* home? I specifically wrote *my* house." With any luck he had not brought the letter she'd sent him.

He grumbled something under his breath, and Marguerite closed the door and led the way into the study. She pointed to a hard-backed chair. "Please have a seat."

He obeyed, never taking his eyes off her. She shivered with unease, and hurried to open the two windows in the room. "Awfully close tonight. A storm brewing, no doubt."

"I don't know about that," he said suspiciously. He trembled visibly, his face a pasty gray. "Why did you want to see me? You told me to leave your property and never come back last time I was here."

She evaded his question. "Why, Mr. Renny, you look so pale and sick. Is there something the matter?" She poured a glass of brandy from the decanter on the tray resting on the wide windowsill.

He dragged his hand slowly over his face. Perspiration ran from his forehead and hung in drops under his nose. He wiped away the moisture with a handkerchief. "I had a harrowing experience not an hour ago." His voice shook and ended in a gasp. His shoulders slumped, and he had to set the brandy glass on the floor.

"Really?" Marguerite sat on the other chair and pulled it closer to him. "Tell me about it."

His narrowed gaze swept over her, and her skin crawled with disgust. "First tell me why you wanted to see me."

"I changed my mind about the money," she said in a louder tone, hoping that Nick and Charles could follow her conversation with Renny. "You shall have two-thirds of the proceeds from the sale of the property. I've had a generous offer."

"Why the change of heart?" He leaned forward, his face almost touching hers. His eyes glowed with a cold light. "I sense something rotten under the surface."

"I had hoped you would agree to an exchange," she said. "You get the funds, and in return you shall tell me where Sergeant Rule is buried. I want to make a clean start, not have his death hanging over my head. I'll tell the authorities that Lennox killed Rule and buried him alone. That way you'll go free from any blame. You can start afresh.''

''Hmm, a very generous offer. What about my proposal? If you marry me, you shall have all the funds from this property— through me, of course.''

Marguerite cringed, but she forced a bright smile to her face. ''That is generous of you, but I cannot accept. I long to move away and start over, without any bad memories.'' She stared at him hard. ''Sergeant Rule's burial place, please.''

He thought for a long, tedious moment. Marguerite could barely breathe for the tension in the room.

''You'll have to give me a written promise that you won't reveal the truth to the authorities,'' he said, looking paler than ever.

''You're positively green in the face, Mr. Renny. Are you going to be sick?''

He flapped his hand in dismissal. ''Don't worry that I'll soil your floor, Marguerite,'' he said with a cynical twist to his thin lips.

''Then . . . what is it? What's wrong?'' A dog with a bone would not gnaw more persistently at one spot than she was doing, she thought. ''Tell me. Mayhap I can help.''

''Oh, Marguerite,'' he wailed, slumping against her. ''I saw a ghost at my house, all shrouded in white, with the palest, emptiest face. A silver face.''

''A ghost! Dentley Court is haunted, Mr. Renny?''

''I have never seen anything like it before,'' he said defensively. ''Never heard any stories of sightings in the past.''

''It's the sergeant who wants peace,'' she said in a gloomy voice. ''He rests in unholy ground.''

He jerked upright and stared at her hard. ''Who says he's buried on my land?''

Marguerite inhaled deeply to steady her thumping heart. ''If he's not buried here, there's only one other alternative I can think of: your property.''

Silence hung heavy as he studied her face. She feared he might understand the part she'd played in this evening's game. A twig broke outside and the grass rustled. Nick and Charles, she thought. Thank God they were here!

"You have an uncanny knack of ferreting out the truth, Marguerite," Renny said with an explosive sigh.

"You'll have to move Rule to sacred ground. In fact, if you put him in the churchyard, no one will know who brought him. On the other hand, if he's found on your property, who knows what conclusions Captain Emerson and the Duke of Atwood might draw? You would have to stand before Atwood's bench and answer probing questions."

Renny rubbed his jaw. "However much I'm loath to admit it, you're right, Marguerite." He gave her that cold, bloodless smile she had always despised. "If I didn't know better, I'd say you're eager for my friendship. I do know better, so what is it?" He rose and stood over her, a dark menace, a man who was capable of killing.

She said nothing. If she repeated her desire for a new start, all bad memories scrubbed away, he might not believe her. "I think you should go, Mr. Renny. Ponder my words, my offer to you, then come back here."

At least she had sown the seed of removing the body in his mind, and that was all she could do. Filled with a buzzing tension, she stared up at his cold face. "Please, think about it."

He hesitated, then shrugged his shoulders. "Very well. I'll return tomorrow morning."

Marguerite let her breath trickle from her nose. Relief washed through her. She smiled stiffly. "You are a wise man, Mr. Renny."

"Or a singularly foolish one," he said in a growl, and tore the door open. Marguerite caught a glimpse of Sophie's pale face in the gloomy hallway. Sophie had been eavesdropping; that much was clear. She said something in an undertone to Renny, who pushed her aside.

Marguerite went after him, but he slammed out of the house, and Sophie ran upstairs. Marguerite contemplated going after her, but resisted the urge. She had no time for Sophie's tantrums at this point.

As she returned to the study, Charles was squirming his way through the window.

"That slimy rat," he said between his teeth, as he pulled his long legs over the sill.

"We'd better follow him," Marguerite said as she flung herself into his arms. He held her tightly. "With any luck, he'll remove the body tonight."

"You were splendid, my darling," Charles said. "He dangled like a fish on a hook."

"Where's Nick?"

"He decided to search the countryside for Captain Emerson. We need the soldiers on hand to apprehend the villain. The more witnesses, the better." He looked at her face, and the familiar breathless feeling of wonder crept through her. Even now, in this worst of circumstances, he had the power to stir her senses.

"Let's go," he said, and released her reluctantly. Just as he was about to open the door, a knock sounded. Prunella stepped inside, clutching a book in her hand.

"Oh, Marguerite, I have had such a surprise!" she cried. She noticed Charles, and her face lit up in a glorious smile. "Good evening, Charles, or should I say B. C. Rose?" she asked slyly. "I visited your aunt this morning and she had another visitor, Mr. Joel Berber, of Berber and Sons, your publisher. He gave me a copy of your latest volume, and Emmy said he'd come to pick up your new work, which you had failed to deliver on time." Pru beamed. "Emmy is ever so excited, so proud of you. We managed to wangle the truth out of Mr. Berber, even though he was very reluctant to reveal your secret identity."

Marguerite could not believe her ears. She gripped the slender volume of gilt and brown leather. *"Journey of Love, Volume*

Three, by B. C. Rose,'' she read. Charles had kept the truth from her. She glared at him, noting his high color and embarrassed grin.

"You wrote this? You are B. C. Rose?''

He nodded sheepishly.

"Why didn't you tell me?'' she asked, disappointment rising in her dark as bile.

"To tell you the truth, I'm not very proud of my poetry,'' he said after some deliberation. "If my cronies get wind of this, I'll never hear the end of it.''

Prunella stood uncertainly in the middle of the room. "I love B. C. Rose's poetry,'' she said in a quavering voice. "You have given me many hours of pleasure through your work, Charles. If I were you, I would take the praise given and hoard it like pearls.''

"Kindly said, Miss Trent. Thank you.'' Charles looked away, clearly mortified. He shot a quick glance at Marguerite. "If you must know, dearest, I wrote the poems for you, when my longing became too heavy to bear. It filled my sleepless nights and eased my heart.''

Prunella wiped her eyes with a lace-edged handkerchief. "Oh, Marguerite, isn't that the most romantic compliment you've ever had?'' Prunella went to the door. "I shall leave you two alone.''

"I am deeply flattered, but why did you keep this from me, Charles?'' Marguerite asked tensely as the door closed. "You're not proud of your poetry? How can anyone be so arrogant as not to acknowledge a God-given gift? You should have your head examined!'' She flung the book at him, and he caught it against his chest.

"It was a way to raise funds when I had nothing else,'' he said. "Poetry just comes to me. 'Tis no grand effort, and—''

"Don't belittle your accomplishments!'' Marguerite snapped. "And how you lectured me about keeping secrets! All this time you harbored your own. I am shattered.''

Silence fell, and no one moved. Finally Marguerite broke

the frozen tableau as she hurried toward the door. "I'm going to follow Renny."

Charles caught up with her at the stables. "I'm sorry for keeping my pseudonym a secret. I just didn't want anyone to know. I might have told you later, but for now—well, I could not reveal it."

"How can you be ashamed of your work?" Marguerite asked indignantly as she received the reins of her horse from Peter. "Your poetry is lovely. It has sometimes moved me to tears."

"We'll talk about it later," Charles replied in a dismissive voice, then hoisted her up into the saddle.

She applied her heels to her horse, and it galloped down the drive. Still filled with disappointment at his subterfuge, she did not wait for Charles.

Chapter 28

Charles swore as Thunder stumbled in a hole at the gate and almost went down. Charles slid out of the saddle as the stallion limped to a stop. He examined the fetlock, but it was too early to notice any effects from the misstep. A sprain, he thought, hoping that it wasn't a more serious injury. He led the lame horse back to the stables.

"Peter," he said, "put a fomentation on Thunder's front leg and wrap it tightly, then saddle up Lady Lennox's carriage horse."

"That ol' nag will put ye to sleep," Peter scoffed, and examined Thunder's leg. "Cor lumme, 'tis already swellin'."

Charles swore and led the horse into a box. He didn't have time to oversee Peter's work, and Thunder's predicament worried him, but there was no time to linger. Good God, he'd already lost precious minutes. He had to catch up with Marguerite. She should not face Renny alone. "Peter, just concentrate on Thunder. I'll be back as soon as I can."

Anxiety making his movements clumsy, Charles hurriedly saddled the carriage horse. Peter was right; the nag could not be urged to go faster than a feeble trot. The wind moaned in the trees along the road. Dropping twigs startled the mount.

Fear and guilt rushed through Charles as the minutes ticked away much too rapidly. He should have told Marguerite about his secret. Now she might never forgive him. He had scolded her for keeping secrets, and he wasn't much better himself. One secret was as bad as the next, even if his did not involve crimes like murder and treason. *Idiot!* he told himself, and coaxed the nag to move a bit faster.

Marguerite reached the dark garden at Dentley Court. She waited in the spot where she'd kept an eye on the house with Charles and Nick earlier. What if Renny decided to wait? What if he decided not to dig up the body at all? She rubbed her cold arms under the thin silk cloak. If only Nick would return. And where was Charles? Surely he should be here by now, unless he'd decided he would rather go home and write poetry. Why had he blamed her for deceit while being dishonest himself? Hot tears clouded her eyes. He had not seen fit to tell her his most guarded secret. But, dash it all, she still loved him!

She stiffened as the sounds of a horse came from the lane in front of the house. She had deduced that Renny was already here, as light glowed in one of the windows. Probably drinking brandy in the study, she thought, and strained her eyes to see who the visitor was. All she saw was a black cloak flying around a slender figure.

A knock on the door. Hinges creaking, hushed voices. Marguerite wished she could overhear the conversation.

The door slammed. The sound of steps, one heavy pair and one lighter, hurried around the corner. Marguerite saw Renny walk among the shadows thrown by the shrubs toward the woodshed at the end of the dilapidated stables. He carried a candle in a lantern. A thinner and smaller figure followed him, and she heard a pleading female voice.

"Don't do this, Montagu. It's a trap. You'll be caught and hanged."

Sophie! Marguerite thought, dazed. She followed the two by sneaking from one shrub to another. Her hands felt numb with fear, and her legs trembled. She wished she'd thought of bringing a weapon, but she'd left home in the heat of anger. Anyway, Nick and Charles would be here in a minute to protect her if Renny found her.

"I love you," Sophie wailed. "I don't want to lose you."

Marguerite tensed. That was why Sophie had been so secretive. She had always acted strangely around Montagu Renny. *Love!* What could she find to love in that totally selfish, devious, deceitful man? A murderer.

"Nonsense! Why should you lose me?" he chided. "You've never had me." He set the lantern on the ground of the empty woodshed, and put the spade against the wall.

"You promised me marriage if I kept silent about the sergeant," Sophie said hoarsely. "You promised—"

Renny rounded on her. "Damn and blast! I have no intention of burdening myself with you. You mope about, and your hatchet face would give any gentleman nightmares."

Marguerite flinched at the harsh words. Even though she'd had many differences with Sophie in the past, the woman was slowly changing into a softer, more approachable person. She did not deserve such treatment. Marguerite was on the verge of stepping forward to defend Sophie if need be, but she realized that would imperil the whole mission. Even so, she had a rather good idea where the sergeant was buried. Right there, under the dirt floor.

"You betrayed me," Sophie said in a snarl, her fists curled in anger. Renny only shrugged his shoulders.

He started flinging aside the few pieces of firewood strewn across the floor. Then he hefted the spade and started digging.

Sophie walked back and forth outside, wringing her hands. Marguerite's attention wandered from Sophie to Renny. She prayed that Charles and Nick would arrive soon to lend their support. If Nick came with the militia in tow, they could catch the murderer red-handed. But Marguerite battled an uneasy feeling in her stomach. She sensed trouble for herself rather than the imminent arrest of Montagu Renny, but she couldn't leave now.

She stared in horror as Renny heaved aside the soil in a fury, then dragged out a mummylike figure wrapped in an oilcloth tarpaulin. A skeletal hand fell out of a rip in the shroud, and Marguerite felt faint with revulsion. Darkened flesh clung to the bones.

Sophie gasped and stared at the sagging brown bundle. "What are you going to do with it—him?" she asked, her hand clasped to her throat.

"Bury him at sea. The tide will take the remains deep into the Channel and carry them away." He tilted the corpse over the mound of soil and got out of the hole. "He'll never be found. The man caused nothing but trouble in these parts."

"He was only doing his duty and discovered your treasonous dealings with my brother," Sophie said. She darted looks into the surrounding shrubs. "What if someone sees you?"

Renny gave her a hard glance. "Nobody will, unless you were followed. I expect you to keep silent about this."

Sophie sobbed into a handkerchief. She rushed toward him. "Don't break your promise, Montagu! We can live happily on the proceeds from the sale of Lennox House. You said that was our goal, a life together once Marguerite had given up what should be rightfully mine."

Marguerite froze. Every one of Sophie's words stabbed her, leaving pain behind. She had tried so hard to make things right with Sophie, who had been ready all along to claim the Lennox legacy.

"I loathe you, Sophie," Renny said with a sneer. "I will not share my life with you, nor the inheritance. Marguerite has promised to share the proceeds with me. Once she is mine, I will control everything. She will surrender to my superior will in the end."

Sophie pummeled his head and shoulders. "You rotten liar! Marguerite hates you. She would never consider sharing another groat with you."

He fended off her feeble attack. "Your jealousy is speaking, Sophie. Get away from me!"

"Marguerite has helped me." Sophie's voice rose to a wail. "That is more than you ever did! I used to hate her because she did not love my dear brother, but she has always tried to improve our lives."

Renny's face darkened with fury, and the flickering light in the lantern formed leaping shadows over his face. Evil shadows, Marguerite thought, pressing her lips together. Renny clenched his fist and slammed it against the side of Sophie's head.

Sophie crumpled with a moan. As he was about to kick her head with his boot, Marguerite rushed forward. "Don't!"

Too late did she realize she'd exposed herself to danger. She had no weapon, she had no support, but she could not stand by and watch Renny kick her sister-in-law to death, no matter what Sophie had done in the past to make Marguerite's life difficult.

Montagu halted and looked up. His glance darted to the brown bundle, then to Sophie. "Marguerite! What a surprise," he said with sugary sweetness. "Have you come to fetch Sophie home? 'Twas thoughtless of her to wander about at night without a chaperon."

"I've been watching you dig up the sergeant—or what pitiful remains there are. You will not get away with this, or another murder. It will be murder if you kick Sophie to death."

He crossed his arms over his chest and spread his legs in a stance of arrogance. "Murder? The haughty Lady Lennox has spoken, and everyone has to stand up and take notice."

"I did not know that Sophie was involved in your nefarious schemes," Marguerite said. If she made Renny talk, mayhap help would arrive in time.

"She wasn't. She threw herself at me when Lennox died and begged that I take control of the family fortune." He jabbed his toes into the side of the fainted woman. "A pathetic spinster, totally deluded. No one ever wanted her." He laughed. "Neither did I."

"Precious little left of that fortune when Lennox died," Marguerite said.

Renny took two menacing steps toward Marguerite. "Well, she will inherit all of it when you're dead. She'll be a lot more malleable than you have been. You heard her begging me to marry her." He smiled coldly. "I might."

Marguerite started running as the meaning of his words sank in, but she did not advance far along the path before he pounced upon her, slamming her to the ground. She lost her breath momentarily, her life seemingly suspended by a gossamer strand until she could find another breath. Her head flashed with stars.

"You're coming with me," Renny said hoarsely, and gripped her hair. Her cap had disappeared, and as he twisted her hair, pins fell out. She kicked and swore, but his iron strength had soon subdued her bid for rebellion. He untied his cravat and twisted it quickly around her wrists behind her.

She screamed at the top of her lungs, but her voice melted in the wind. Nothing. No one had arrived to rescue her. Where were they? *Damn Charles. Damn Nick.*

Renny jerked her upright and shoved a handkerchief into her mouth as soon as she gathered herself for another scream. It was locked into her throat by the cloth, and Marguerite thought she would choke. She fought an urge to throw up. If she did, she would certainly choke on her own vomit.

She breathed hard through her nose as he jerked her along the path toward the shed. He pushed her to the ground next to Sophie. He might kill them both. Marguerite was filled with icy fear, her senses sharpened by the danger.

Soil . . . the smell of decaying flesh . . . rotten leaves . . . male sweat. The glow of light reflected in steel as he raised the spade. It winked; the metal flashed. She rolled aside, but the tool caught her shoulder hard. Pain exploded in all directions, and she fell into a cold darkness. Anguish sizzled along her nerves all the way into oblivion.

Charles arrived at Renny's house and drew a sigh of relief as he found Marguerite's horse in the place where they had hidden their mounts earlier.

She was not at the spot where they had observed Renny's terror. There was no sign of her.

He did not dare to call her name. He hurried around the front of the house, but there was no sign of Renny's mount.

He scanned the dark surroundings. The moon had surrendered to a bank of clouds, the lightless world filled with diffuse humps and darker shadows.

Charles did not see any clues to Marguerite's whereabouts. She ought to have seen him if she was hiding somewhere nearby. Muffled hoofbeats sounded along the path behind the house, and Charles ran to the rendezvous point. Nick and Captain Emerson arrived and slid from their mounts.

"I can't find Marguerite," Charles said. "Her nag is here, but she's nowhere to be found."

Nick frowned as the captain lighted a lantern. "I thought you two were together. Don't say you left her to fend for herself."

Guilt washed through Charles. "I didn't leave her, but she left me in a huff after a minor altercation earlier."

"You quarreled? On this most important of nights?"

Charles stared at Nick's incredulous face and nodded. "Yes, we had a fight, and she stormed off here alone. I followed on Thunder. He sprained a fetlock as he stepped into a hole." Charles swore under his breath. "Damned bad luck! I was right behind her. I had no intention of letting her come here alone."

Captain Emerson raised the lantern. The light illuminated Nick's worried face. "We'd better find her," Emerson said. "She can't be far away."

"There's no sign of Renny either."

"Mayhap our performance earlier did not frighten him enough," Nick said.

They searched the grounds, and finally came upon Sophie's prostrate body by the old woodshed. Charles found her when he almost stumbled over her legs. Captain Emerson shone his light on her as Charles rolled her over.

"Miss Pierson, what in the world . . . ?" Charles snapped.

Sophie moaned and flung her arm over her eyes. "He hit me," she said in a small voice.

"Who?" Captain Emerson asked, and helped her to sit up.

She rubbed her head and grimaced. "He took the body and Marguerite. I saw them, but was too weak to get up. Marguerite is either dead or in a deep faint. She did not move when he slung her over the horse."

"Body?" Nick said, supporting Sophie as she rose on unsteady feet.

"The sergeant. Buried in the woodshed." She gripped Captain Emerson's arm. "My brother did not want to kill the sergeant, but Mr. Renny made him take part. They stabbed Sergeant Rule to death." Her voice trembled, and a floodgate of tears opened. "I saw the horrendous deed from the window. My brother was never the same after that. He grew thin and racked with guilt." She looked imploringly at the captain's face. "He had decided to tell the authorities the truth, but Renny poisoned him before he had a chance to clear his conscience. I found that out only days ago." She buried her face in her hands. "I've been such a fool! Such a complete imbecile! I thought Renny loved me. He said he did, and promised me a new life—as his wife."

"That's why you kept silent about the truth," Nick filled in. He gave Charles a grim glance as Sophie nodded her head.

"Yes, I can't bear the thought of spending the rest of my life alone." She covered her face with her hands and wept.

Charles could barely remain still as worry gnawed at his reason. "Where did Renny take Marguerite?" he asked. "Think, Sophie, think! You can't protect Renny any longer."

"I don't want to protect him," she said defiantly, and mopped her face with her sleeve. She raised her swollen eyes to look at Charles. "He took her to the coast. He'll throw her into the sea with the soldier, I'll warrant."

"Can you prove that Renny poisoned your brother?" Emerson asked.

"Yes," she said feebly. "One of the servants we used to employ bought the poison for Mr. Renny, and I shall see that he testifies at the trial, as will I. Mr. Renny shall pay for all the misery he has caused the Lennox family. I shall also bear witness that he killed the sergeant with my brother."

"I'll escort her home," Nick said with a grimace. "You two ride after Renny, and I'll join you shortly."

The captain quickly examined the grave in the woodshed as Nick carried Sophie to his horse. Charles fetched Marguerite's and the captain's mounts, and tied the carriage horse to one of the trees. Emerson hoisted himself in the saddle. "Let's gallop up a lather. Not a minute to lose."

"Damn it, I wish Thunder were here," Charles said with a snarl, and dug his heels into Marguerite's mare.

Marguerite awakened as she slid to the ground. She noticed vaguely that her hands smelled of sweaty horse hide. Her middle ached, and nausea swam through her in waves. She retched, only to find her mouth blocked with a rag. Breathing hard through her nose, she tried to stem the great wave of nausea that threatened in her stomach.

She lay on the ground, hard pebbles biting her cheek and wetness lapping at her feet. Every inch of her ached, but the center of her misery was the throbbing heat of her shoulder. Pain pulsed with every heartbeat. She blinked away the tears, but could not wipe the wetness from her face.

The gravel crunched with heavy steps. Her consciousness came and went, but she was increasingly aware of the tangy scent of seawater. Waves whooshed over the shale, then retreated in a sizzle of froth. The sea. He meant to drown her.

Anything was better than this excruciating pain radiating from her shoulder. He gripped her hair and jerked her head up. Her injury screamed, fingers of agony moving up her throat and down her chest.

"Awake, are you?" Renny laughed, and disgust crawled down her spine. "That's good. I like that you'll be aware of your own death. You'll sink like a stone with your hands tied behind your back."

Marguerite wanted to protest, but she slipped into merciful darkness as he dropped her back to the ground. She was vaguely aware of his movements. She heard a horse trampling the ground close to her head, the bottom of a boat scraping over shale. She had heard that before . . . but the memory eluded her. The creak of leather. Iron against stone.

Nothing.

Icy wind slapping her face. A dull ache in her stomach. Light waves lifting her, lolling her back to sleep.

A warning bell chimed frantically in her tired mind. She forced her eyes open. Above the stars glinted. There was only blackness everywhere around her, a heaving mass of sound and movement.

She struggled up, the restraints digging into her wrists. There was a strong smell of earth and decay right beside her, and she shuddered as she viewed the bony whiteness of the skeletal hand, with its black flaps of dead skin. The bundle of remains lay right next to her.

She moaned and tried to move aside, but there was no room in the small rowboat. The black, narrow back of Montagu Renny worked as he rowed through the swell of waves in the bay.

Panic rose in her, and she struggled to tear apart the cravat tied around her wrists. If she didn't free herself, Renny could just throw her into the water without so much as a struggle.

She would sink like a stone even though she knew how to swim. Her clothes would pull her down.

Gritting her teeth, she worked her wrists along the sharp edge of the molding that topped the sides of the boat. Her skin burned, and warm stickiness slid down her hands, but she could not stop. Not if she was to maintain hope of survival. She watched Renny's back as she worked. Intense hatred flowed through her. If she could find something heavy, she would attack him. But first she had to free her arms.

Charles could smell the sea before he saw it. He and Emerson had chosen the straightest line to the coast, to a small harbor two miles from the Meadow where fishermen stored their boats and dinghies. He prayed the whole time that they would be in time to save Marguerite. Renny would receive his just rewards. . . .

The shale crunched under the horses' hooves. Charles pulled in the reins and jumped down. Emerson stood by the water's edge staring out into the bay.

"There!" he said, and pointed. "A small boat and a man rowing. Must be Renny. No one is out at this time of night."

"I'm a strong swimmer," Charles said, and started pulling off his boots. Panicking, he could think only of Marguerite and the terror she must be going through.

"Better take one of the dinghies. The undercurrent is much too strong, Charles. You'll be pulled out to sea."

"You're right." Charles helped the captain pull one of the rowboats into the water. They each gripped an oar, and, sharing a seat even though it was narrow, they rowed furiously to catch up with Renny, who had almost reached the mouth of the bay and the open Channel beyond.

Marguerite drew a sigh of relief as the cravat finally split. Her arms ached and were so stiff she had difficulty pulling them around to her front. Her wrists screamed with pain, but she ignored it. She pulled the wad from her mouth and searched the bottom for something heavy to slam against Renny's skull.

She could not find a weapon. Nothing at all. The wood was damp to her touch, and when she accidentally brushed against the grisly bundle, she flinched back in revulsion.

She did not want to share a watery grave with the remains of Sergeant Rule.

She gasped in fear as Renny set down the oars and slowly turned around,

"You've come to, I see. Better to meet your maker awake than asleep," he said with a mirthless chuckle. "You can beg for salvation."

Marguerite could think only of getting away from him. She acted instantly, throwing herself at him, taking him by surprise. He swore as he tilted back on the middle seat and fell into the boat, Marguerite on top of him. She tore at his hair and slammed his head against the floor of the boat. He gripped her upper arms with such strength she thought her bones would snap.

The pain made her weak. She sobbed, punching her fist into his face. He forced her back, slowly overpowering her as he gained a foothold. She tumbled back over the seat, her shoulder screaming.

"Damn you to hell," she cried, sobbing as he took her aching wrists and twisted them until she moaned. He dragged her up, lifted her into his arms. For one wild moment, she stared into his cold face, then . . .

She was whirling, spinning through the air, her skirts hampering her, flapping in the wind. Cold water closed around her; a wave washed over her head, dragging her down. She fought, held her breath until she could hold it no longer. Her dress pulled her downward, a leaden weight around her legs. She could swim; she had to save herself. She kicked upward, ever up through the liquid crystal that burned her skin with cold and salt. *Up!*

She jarred her head against the bottom of the boat, and,

swimming frantically, she gained the side, gulping in precious air as salt stung her eyes. She groped for a hold on the railing, found one, but the boat jolted viciously, tilted precariously, then jolted back. She almost lost her grip. If she did, she would be dead. Exhausted, she clung even though the waves tried to rob her of her hold every time they slammed over her.

"You bastard! Where is she?"

Charles? She thought she had turned delirious.

"Damn you to hell, Mortimer," Renny said with a snarl.

"Here. I'm here," Marguerite croaked, but no sound came past her lips.

The men grappled, tilted the boat this way, that way. The wooden side kept ramming into Marguerite's chest, and she sobbed with pain. She lost the feeling in one arm, her shoulder throbbing so much she could concentrate on only one thing: *Don't faint . . . don't faint . . . don't faint.* She did not know if she still clung to the boat, or if her hands had given way. She was sinking into darkness again.

"You threw her in, damn your eyes!" Charles shouted.

Bone crunched, feet scrabbled. A jolt, a thud. A moan. Then silence. Only the waves crashing.

Charles was shouting her name. Marguerite struggled to come awake. She swallowed a mouthful of water. It choked her. She coughed. She could not move.

"Here," she said in a moan when she could find her voice. She tried to wave, lost her grip with one hand. Then the other.

Two warm hands caught hers as she was slipping away.

"Hold on, Marguerite!" Charles ordered. He groaned as he pulled her from the water. Her shoulder screamed with pain, and she sobbed. Another pair of hands assisted, and she was hoisted into a second boat that bobbed side by side with Renny's vessel. She vaguely recognized Captain Emerson. He bent over Renny's limp form. Marguerite thought the villain was dead.

Charles was settling her on the uncomfortable bottom of the boat, but she did not care. Any hard surface was better than the watery depths of the Channel.

"Thank God you're alive," he said, smoothing her wet hair away from her face. "If your life had ended, mine would have ended, too."

Marguerite coughed and gasped for breath. "He threw me in . . . but I fought . . . to stay alive. I . . . managed to swim . . . to the boat and cling."

"Thank God for your astute mind and your courage. Thank God," Charles repeated over and over. He pulled off his coat and placed it around her shivering body.

She snuggled under it gratefully and inhaled the scent of him trapped in the material.

Charles turned to the captain. "I'll row ashore. Do you need help with the prisoner?"

"No, I'll manage. He's in a dead faint. Luckily he didn't have time to throw Rule's remains overboard. We can give the fellow a decent burial."

"Yes," Charles said grimly. "Damn Montagu Renny for causing so much havoc in our lives."

He rowed in silence for a while, and Marguerite studied his dear face. She could forgive him anything, she thought, *anything,* as long as they could be together. She fought a powerful urge to sleep. Not yet, not until she was safely ashore and Renny was led away in irons.

Shouts came from the beach, and Marguerite recognized Nick's voice. "The soldiers are marching here. I found them in the lane outside your house, Charles, and told them about the development at Renny's place."

Marguerite felt a great wave of relief wash over her. "Sophie? Is she all right?" she asked.

"Nick took her home. She had a nasty bump on her head; otherwise she was quite recovered. Marguerite, I think she worked against you at first, then decided to denounce Renny."

"I know," Marguerite said with a sigh. "She plotted to marry Renny and somehow contrive to get the Lennox money— except there was none left."

"Renny poisoned your husband," Charles said cautiously.

"Sophie said she would testify against him, and she knew where to find the servant who procured the poison."

Marguerite pondered his words. "Somewhere deep inside, I understood that Lennox did not die a natural death, but I could not accept it. I can't think why anyone would want to kill him." She sighed. "Renny could have poisoned me, too."

Charles nodded, his mouth pulled into a grim line. "Yes, but I think Renny hoped you would marry him. He didn't want to ruin his chances for marital bliss."

"He's an idiot," Marguerite spit.

"He was afraid that Lennox would collapse with guilt and reveal their secret to the authorities. Renny is cold and calculating to the end."

The dinghy reached the shore with a thud, and Nick pulled it deeper onto the shale to secure it. He lifted Marguerite into his arms and kissed her on the cheek. "Thank God you survived."

Marguerite moaned in pain as he jostled her shoulder. "You're wounded," he said.

He spread his cloak on the shale and laid her down. Charles knelt beside her and tucked his coat over her. "Where does it hurt?"

"My shoulder and my wrists," she said with a sob as her injuries throbbed more than ever. "I suspect a bad sprain or a cracked collarbone. I can move my arm, but barely."

"I will carry you home," Charles said, and wrapped Nick's cloak tightly around her.

Captain Emerson's dinghy arrived, and as Nick pulled it up onto the shale, a dark form twisted to a sitting position and aimed a pistol at Emerson's chest.

"Watch out!" Nick shouted, and at the same time threw himself at Renny, chopping down on the arm that held the deadly weapon. Renny's shot shattered the night air, but went wide. Renny swore, and the pistol clattered to the bottom of the boat. Nick punched his jaw, and all strength left the villain's body.

"Thank God, Nick! You saved my life," Emerson said

breathlessly, and squeezed Nick's arm. "I owe you my life." He forced the stunned prisoner out of the boat.

"Don't mention it," Nick said as he helped the captain to fasten iron manacles around Renny's wrists. Renny swore viciously.

"Save that vocabulary for the devil. You'll meet him soon enough," Nick said, and shoved the prisoner away from the shore and Marguerite.

Captain Emerson gathered up the grisly bundle from the bow of the dinghy, and Marguerite said a silent prayer for the luckless sergeant who had met such an undignified end.

Charles lifted her into his arms. She flinched as a savage pain rolled through her. Gritting her teeth, she did not complain.

"I thought I had lost you," he said, nuzzling her cheek with his nose. "I thought I'd lost my chance to apologize, to set matters right with you. I will never again keep anything a secret from you. It's just that I was embarrassed."

"I don't think Shakespeare was ever embarrassed about his work. I bet he was proud of his accomplishments."

Charles laughed ruefully. He stood her gently on the ground by his horse. "You're probably right. I will have to take a close look at myself and accept my romantic streak. No gentleman possessing his full mind would ever accept such a weakness."

"It makes you all the more manly, in my opinion," Marguerite said softly, and lifted her face to his for a kiss.

He obeyed. "Oh, darling, I was so afraid I wouldn't reach you in time. Thunder sprained a fetlock, and your horse" — he nudged the mare with his thumb—"has four left feet."

" 'Tis a wonder she can run at all," Marguerite said, her voice gently chiding. "But somehow the old horse can still show mettle."

Charles thumped his chest. "Once you're well, I shall show you that this old horse has some mettle."

"You'd better." She cuddled close to him. "I love you, Charles, with all your flights of fancy."

"And I love you, Marguerite. More than life itself. Emmy and Pru will be busy planning a grand wedding for us."

"Pru will live with us at the Meadow, and Sophie shall have her own establishment when I've sold Lennox House."

Charles nodded, and concentrated on kissing her. His kiss definitely had the power to lessen her aches, Marguerite thought in a daze as his mouth roved silkily over hers, but it did rouse other aches that would have to be soothed in the near future.

Holding the reins of his horse, Nick watched them from a distance. The sea crashed in waves of loneliness against the shore, echoing in his heart. The froth sizzling over the shale reminded him of the pain burning in every part of his being.

He would like to cry over losing Marguerite, but he could not. He'd known for a long time that he would never have Marguerite's love. It hurt, but it also gave him great pleasure to watch Charles so happy at last.

He had watched their love slowly unfold, sensing the depths of their passion.

Yes, Charles's happiness will have to be enough until I can forget Marguerite's sweet smile, Nick thought, his hands clenching around the reins. Work would help to deaden his loneliness. He swung himself into the saddle, and the horse neighed and pranced around in excitement. When Renny's trial was over and the man had been executed, Nick would continue his important mission. The Midnight Bandit would ride again.

If you liked **A BANDIT'S KISS,** be sure to look for Maria Greene's next release in the Midnight Mask series, **A LOVER'S KISS,** available wherever books are sold in September 2000.

Nick Thurston harbors a dangerous secret. Known as the Midnight Bandit, a devilish rogue who charms the ladies even as he lifts their purses, his life of crime must remain hidden at all costs—even if it *is* for the noblest of purposes. Thus, when Serena Hilliard pulls off his mask, he has no choice but to take her hostage. Now the Bandit's most reckless quest is to claim the woman who has robbed him of his senses . . . and stolen his heart.

BOOK YOUR PLACE ON OUR WEBSITE AND MAKE THE READING CONNECTION!

We've created a customized website just for our very special readers, where you can get the inside scoop on everything that's going on with Zebra, Pinnacle and Kensington books.

When you come online, you'll have the exciting opportunity to:

- View covers of upcoming books
- Read sample chapters
- Learn about our future publishing schedule (listed by publication month *and author*)
- Find out when your favorite authors will be visiting a city near you
- Search for and order backlist books from our online catalog
- Check out author bios and background information
- Send e-mail to your favorite authors
- Meet the Kensington staff online
- Join us in weekly chats with authors, readers and other guests
- Get writing guidelines
- AND MUCH MORE!

Visit our website at
http://www.zebrabooks.com

Put a Little Romance in Your Life With
Betina Krahn

__Hidden Fire	$5.99US/$7.50CAN
0-8217-5793-8	
__Love's Brazen Fire	$5.99US/$7.50CAN
0-8217-5691-5	
__Midnight Magic	$4.99US/$5.99CAN
0-8217-4994-3	
__Passion's Ransom	$5.99US/$6.99CAN
0-8217-5130-1	
__Passion's Treasure	$5.99US/$7.50CAN
0-8217-6039-4	
__Rebel Passion	$5.99US/$7.50CAN
0-8217-5526-9	

Call toll free **1-888-345-BOOK** to order by phone or use
this coupon to order by mail.
Name _____
Address _____
City _____ State _____ Zip _____
Please send me the books I have checked above.
I am enclosing $_____
Plus postage and handling* $_____
Sales tax (in New York and Tennessee) $_____
Total amount enclosed $_____
*Add $2.50 for the first book and $.50 for each additional book.
Send check or money order (no cash or CODs) to:
Kensington Publishing Corp., 850 Third Avenue, New York, NY 10022
Prices and Numbers subject to change without notice.
All orders subject to availability.
Check out our website at **www.kensingtonbooks.com**

COMING IN SEPTEMBER FROM
ZEBRA BALLAD ROMANCES

__A KNIGHT'S VOW, The Kinsmen
by Candace Kohl   0-8217-6681-3 $5.50US/$7.50CAN
When Sir Lucien engages in a passionate tryst with a peasant, he is shocked
to discover she is the granddaughter of the man he has sworn vengeance upon.
But though Lucien has strength and courage beyond measure, he has no defense
against his growing desire to sacrifice his anger for her instead . . .

__A MATTER OF CONVENIENCE, The Destiny Coin
by Gabriella Anderson   0-8217-6682-1 $5.50US/$7.50CAN
Corinna Towers can't believe her luck when enigmatic Stuart Grant offers her
money to pose as his betrothed. Deciding it would be foolish to cling to notions
about her mother's lucky coin bringing true love, she accepts his offer . . .
only to discover that an unlikely romance can surpass dreams.

__GAME OF HEARTS, Happily Ever After Co.
by Kate Donovan   0-8217-6683-X $5.50US/$7.50CAN
Suzannah Hennessey is stunned when she realizes her best friend Megan is
marrying Aengus Yates, Suzannah's ex-lover. But when a twist of fate sends
her to the altar in Megan's place, it won't take long for sparks to fly, passion
to flare, and Suzannah to realize that Aengus just might be the one for her
after all . . .

__A LOVER'S KISS, Midnight Mask
by Maria Greene   0-8217-6869-7 $5.50US/$7.50CAN
Known as the Midnight Bandit, Nick Thurston is a devilish rogue who charms
the ladies with poetry even as he lifts their purses. His life of crime must
remain hidden at all costs, so when a bold beauty pulls of his mask, he has
no choice but to take her hostage. Now the Bandit's most reckless quest is to
claim the woman who has stolen his heart . . .

Call toll free **1-888-345-BOOK** to order by phone or use this
coupon to order by mail. *ALL BOOKS AVAILABLE SEPTEMBER 1, 2000.*
Name _____
Address _____
City _____ State _____ Zip _____
Please send me the books I have checked above.
I am enclosing $ _____
Plus postage and handling* $ _____
Sales tax (in NY and TN) $ _____
Total amount enclosed $ _____
*Add $2.50 for the first book and $.50 for each additional book.
Send check or money order (no cash or CODs) to:
**Kensington Publishing Corp., Dept. C.O., 850 Third Avenue,
New York, NY 10022**
Prices and numbers subject to change without notice. Valid only in the U.S.
All orders subject to availabilty. *NO ADVANCE ORDERS.*
Visit our website at **www.kensingtonbooks.com.**

ZEBRA BOOKS are published by

Kensington Publishing Corp.
850 Third Avenue
New York, NY 10022

Copyright © 2000 by Maria Greene

All rights reserved. No part of this book may be reproduced
in any form or by any means without the prior written consent
of the Publisher, excepting brief quotes used in reviews.

If you purchased this book without a cover you should be aware
that this book is stolen property. It was reported as "unsold
and destroyed" to the Publisher and neither the Author nor the
Publisher has received any payment for this "stripped book."

Zebra and the Z logo Reg. U.S. Pat. & TM Off.

First Printing: August, 2000
10 9 8 7 6 5 4 3 2 1

Printed in the United States of America

Midnight Mask:
A BANDIT'S KISS

0040935906

Maria Greene

Zebra Books
Kensington Publishing Corp.

http://www.zebrabooks.com